THE BIG FROG THEORY

Other Books by Ian Gouge

Novels and Novellas

The Red Tie
17 Alma Road
Tilt
Once Significant Others
On Parliament Hill
A Pattern of Sorts
The Opposite of Remembering
At Maunston Quay
An Infinity of Mirrors
The Big Frog Theory
Losing Moby Dick and Other Stories

Short Stories

Dust, dancing
An Irregular Piece of Sky
Degrees of Separation
Secrets & Wisdom

Poetry

Less
Bound
Grimsby Docks
Crash
not the Sonnets
Selected Poems: 1976-2022
The Homelessness of a Child
The Myths of Native Trees
First-time Visions of Earth from Space
After the Rehearsals
Punctuations from History
Human Archaeology
Collected Poems (1979-2016)

Non-Fiction

So, you think you're a Writer
Shrapnel from a Writing Life

Ian Gouge

The Big Frog Theory

First published in paperback format, 2012; this edition
also published by Coverstory books, 2025

paperback ISBN 978-1-0684498-8-8
ebook ISBN 978-1-0684498-9-5

www.iangouge.substack.com

www.aingouge.com

www.coverstorybooks.com

ONE

He sat in a Malvern tea-shop watching the steam from his coffee rise unevenly above the rim of a faded white cup. Through the porous surface of its filter, he could imagine the liquid dripping slowly — drip, drip, drip — and adding to the volume of the dark fluid beneath. Despite his present preoccupation (or perhaps because of it) he welcomed this diversion, and he sniffed, searching for the coffee's distinctive aroma. One of the two women on the next table — a large, well-coiffured, Conservative kind of individual — looked coldly across at him, eyes betraying her reaction to his nasal interruption. Perhaps he had sniffed a little too loudly — though given the nature of the offence, it was not something he permitted himself to dwell upon. He returned her stare without emotion and, seeming to have failed in her challenge of him, she resumed her conversation.

The tea shop — a tired establishment which, he imagined, owed more to the past than the present — was mostly empty. Apart from the Conservative lady and her companion, there were only two other patrons present; a younger couple in muddied walking boots sitting against the back wall, their bright waterproofs a marked contrast to the plain and drab decor. When they had entered, Neville, drawn to their arrival by the weary "ping" of the door's bell, had watched as the Proprietress — a well-built lady who looked as if she might have personally sampled every meal ever served there — had stared warningly at their boots, almost as if the intensity of her gaze might physically clean them. To the credit of the boots' owners, they had, in consequence, been zealous in the vigorous attention they bestowed upon the doormat, which seemed momentarily to groan under the pressure of their scrapings and rubbings.

Neville, having relived that recent incident, glanced back down at his coffee. The filter appeared to now contain more water than it had a few moments before, as if the drip, drip, drip had ceased and the cup, in some kind of rebellion, had started to force the liquid back from whence it had come. He felt too tired to respond to the evidence of his own eyes and, ignoring the impossibility of what was happening on the table in front of him, looked out of the window by which he sat as if, in doing so, he might remind himself of his situation, of his relation to the outside world, and of the reason he was there.

'So why *are* you here?'

The voice had come suddenly to him from nearby; it was a quick, shrill, impatient voice, carrying with it a not insignificant air of menace. He hesitated a fraction then turned, expecting to find himself confronted by either the Conservative lady or the establishment's owner; but the former was still in conversation and the latter nowhere to be seen. The smell rising from his cup — and that which he had been seeking just a few moments earlier — forced him to look down at his coffee again. The filter was empty. Lifting it away, he revealed a cup full of dark coffee. Outside an old bus rumbled slowly past the window, coughing from its exhaust like an old man about to expire.

Was it an accident that he now found himself here, sitting alone in this quiet and somehow forgotten tea-shop? And of all places, that it should be in Malvern! Unable to give up the past, he recalled how he had left his office quietly and without fuss, collecting his briefcase on the way to the lift. His Boss had been as sensitive as the situation and his own humanity allowed; which meant precious little considering his not undeserved reputation for being a complete bastard.

'Neville, my boy' — he had tried his most wheedling, ingratiating, and "I hate doing this to you, Old Son, please believe me" type voice — 'Neville, this company's going down the toilet, and something's got to be done about it. Something, indeed. No doubt you'll have heard the chatter and seen the stories in the local press — and the national press, come to that. The place is rife with rumours, I know. Scaremongering, I call it! Nothing but scaremongering. Of course, given our present difficulties we *do* have to look at costs. The shareholders are concerned: poor dividends, poor exports, poor forecasts. So we need to make one or two' — he hesitated over the next word — 'economies. You understand?'

Had he understood? Did he understand now? He wondered if he had said anything, but could not recall.

'So — as part of a whole raft of measures — we've decided to restructure your department; we're going for a leaner, fitter approach. Fighting fit for the future! That's it! We're giving Brian a broader brief, Colin the challenging clients, and David the difficult decisions. So, I'm afraid that makes you redundant. Sorry. Lovely working with you. See Celia on your way out, she's got your cheque.'

And that had been that; with a sudden rush of words his career was in ruins.

'You should have punched him on the nose!'

Again the disembodied voice. Neville, struggling with knowing how he should respond — and, if he was honest with himself, whether he had actually heard anything at all — sat and looked out of the window, trying to ignore the unwanted intrusion. Returning to his recollection, he vaguely remembered standing up — probably without saying anything, though he couldn't be sure — and leaving. Briefcase, coat, door, lift, car, motorway. It had been as simple as that. From the centre of Birmingham he had been on some form of automatic pilot which, without any conscious design on his part, had brought him here.

It was probably two years since he had last been in Malvern; since he and Mirelle had walked the hills together. With a stab, he remembered happiness.

He picked up his coffee and, in doing so, noticed the Conservative lady was now alone, the walkers had gone, and there were two waitresses tending the vacant tables. He checked his watch — the watch that one year had been a reward for "exceptional service and loyalty to the company" — and wondered if, despite all appearances, at 3:21 in the afternoon they might be expecting some kind of rush.

Two years seemed a long way away. Two weeks even further. He had propelled his most recent scenes with Mirelle toward ancient history with such force that they had overtaken more distant events in their headlong rush for oblivion. The sharp tang of the coffee on his palette brought them back. Mirelle's coffee always tasted like that; sharp and bitter. Perhaps because she was half-French. Perhaps because she made awful coffee.

Luckily the last cup he had seen in her hand had been empty — or at least it was empty by the time it flew past his head and crashed into the dining room wall. He had seen it late, and, without time to calculate trajectory, simply ducked. Instinctive self-preservation. When he looked up again she was gone; the door open, the room empty.

'She was a bitch anyway! What did she ever do for you?'

There was no-one near him. The Conservative lady was now talking to the owner by the counter — about him, perhaps? — and the waitresses were busy re-laying the walkers' table. He had put his coffee down. As he did so, it seemed as if the discarded filter gave him a muddy grin. He rubbed his eyes. He was suddenly tired.

Outside, the old bus he had seen a few moments before had now reappeared, this time going slowly and noisily the other way. He watched it as it stopped.

The driver, having switched off the engine and re-established the ambient quiet, got up from his seat and opened the coach door. He looked as old as the bus, and Neville wondered if he and the bus had been inexorably linked since the former's birth or the latter's construction. The driver's uniform — a serge jacket — finished abruptly at his waist, at which point vaguely shabby corduroy trousers took over to look after his legs. Without concern, the man stepped into the road, evidently heading for the tea-shop.

Mirelle had hated his own cords. In fact, she had hated his entire wardrobe. She used to moan —

'Constantly!

— about how she herself had so little to wear, and that everything she did have was either old or cheap. How Theresa from number seventeen — the one with the silicone implants and the stock-broking husband — went to Paris every year to buy her underwear. Marks & Spencer just wasn't the same! And if it wasn't clothes or underwear, then it was the car they didn't have, or the holidays they never took, the dinner parties they never gave, or the cannabis they never smoked. She was obsessed with the things they didn't do or didn't have. And all because *they* could never afford anything as a result of *him* choosing to work in a "shabby office" for a pittance, rather than better himself in the world.

He had tried. If he could say anything in his defence it was that. He feigned ambition to see where that would get him (it got him the watch) but ran out of steam. In a brief excursion to the opposite pole, he had even tried gambling for a while, such was his desire to satisfy her. But, after losing three hundred pounds on six consecutive Epsom favourites — something unheard of the Bookmaker had told him as he relieved him of his last fifty quid — he gave that up too. The beginning of the end came when Mirelle, in her quest for fortune, started charging him for sex.

'She was a tramp; forget her! You're well rid of the bitch!'

Despite attempts to ignore its unwanted intrusions — which were becoming strangely comforting — Neville knew the voice was unquestionably right. He had been well and truly shafted — even before he started paying for it. And where was he now? What did he have? He had been completely usurped on all fronts, and was now sitting alone in a Malvern tea-shop cradling an empty coffee cup.

The bell above the door rang as the bus driver entered. He gave a slight "old boy" kind of nod to Neville (the sort one might expect to receive from a stranger one vaguely recognised) then made his way over to the counter. Neville put his cup down on the yellow tablecloth, noticing as he did so a large slice of Black Forest Gateau on a blue and white plate before him. He couldn't remember ordering it; and, if he had, it would certainly have been to accompany — rather than follow — the coffee which he had so recently finished. Replacing the old filter on top of the cup, he made to pick up the cake.

'Forget it, brother!'

That shrill, angry voice again. From the top of the cake, two eyes of cream and glacé cherry stared back at him.

'Eat me and I'll give you gut rot so bad, you won't be able to stand up for a week!'

Neville, with an acute sense of embarrassment, glanced up. No-one was looking his way, and his sudden discomfort seemed to have gone unnoticed. Indeed, despite the presence of the Conservative Lady, the Waitresses, and now the Bus Driver, he felt strangely alone. He looked down at the cake again.

'I mean, do you have any idea how old I am?!'

He fought the desire to respond, fought an instinct which was tempting him to give in and to enter into conversation with this rather tired slice of Black Forest gateau — tired, despite its attempts to appear alluring. He didn't even like Black Forest gateau; not really.

'OK Neville, I know what you're thinking: you're thinking "what the hell's going on?" Right? "What am I doing talking to a slice of cake?" Right? Shit, forget it, man! I understand! Just relax, OK? I know what you're going through.'

'You know...?'

It was involuntary but he had opened the door — and the cake slid a crumb right in there to keep it open.

'See, that was easy wasn't it? My name's Hans. Black Forest. Germany. Get it? Mind you, this is a piss awful place to end up after that — those are *real* mountains, man! But there you have it. Don't really get too much say in the matter, not when you're like me.'

'Like you? What's going on?'

Neville, suddenly feeling very warm, heard the sound of geese. He looked out of the window, expecting to see a small flock flying low-level along the street outside.

'Forget them, that's nothing. Hey, Nev. Hey!'

Hans was insistent. Neville looked back at the cake, which proceeded to roll its cream and cherry eyes upwards.

'On the wall, there.'

Between the counter and the door, about six feet from the floor, three china geese hung on the wall, line abreast, largest at the front, smallest bringing up the rear. Now animated, their beaks worked angrily as they cried, flying as hard as they could but getting nowhere.

'They're pissed too. They feel hard done by. They don't want to be stuck in here; they want to be somewhere else; *out there*.'

He loaded the last two words with such meaning, that Neville forgot the geese and looked back at Hans.

'Where?'

'Out there. In the Real World, Nev. Where you've just come from. Or from where you've just been thrown. That shitty little experience you call existence. Those dummies on the wall think it's all pond weed and stale bread out there; know what I mean? So they're bitter about being stuck in here. *I* know the Real World's not so hot; I mean, look at you.'

Neville tried to understand what Hans was getting at. From his coffee cup he saw steam rising again, the filter half full of water, and the drip, drip, drip beginning again. The Real World? In the last two weeks, the "Real World" had dumped on him in a major way; it had ripped the guts out of his life, and trampled them into the mud.

'But you're not alone.'

'Sorry?'

'You. You're not alone, even though you think you are. Shit, you're sitting here talking to me aren't you?'

'But...'

'I know what you're going to say. People always say the same thing; "But you're just a cake", they say. I've heard it all before, so just don't, okay? Don't, and we'll get along just fine. I'm just trying to help, that's all.'

Neville struggled vaguely with the notion of being aided by a stale slice of chocolate gateau.

'Help?'

'Just drink your coffee, Nev, and shut up for a minute.'

The filter was empty again, and when he lifted it away, there was another brew of coffee. He sipped it gently, almost cautiously. It tasted better this time.

On the wall, the geese had stopped their cawing and seemed a little more contented. The sun had broken through the clouds outside and a shaft of light — reflecting off one of the windows of the bus — bathed them in a small patch of warmth. The Bus Driver was sitting down talking to the Conservative lady at the table next to Neville's, and the Proprietress — who seemed to be growing ever larger — had taken a stool by the counter. The two waitresses were still re-laying the walkers' table.

'Nev, you're in the pits, OK? There's no easy way for me to break this to you — not that you don't know it anyway — but really, you've fucked up in a major way. Your life's going down the toilet and, quite frankly, the whole thing's a great big sodding mess. Sorry, but there it is.'

Neville, who had the very real sense that he was being lectured, kept dutifully quiet, sipping his coffee and looking at Hans — who, in spite of his physical limitations, had taken on a kind of professorial aspect.

'So, what do you do? You're stuffed — and you're sitting in a tea shop talking to a slice of cake. Can't go any lower really. I mean, I've been there myself. I used to be a fresh young thing, full of life and 'get up and go'. But if you miss your chance the bastards somehow manage to just beat all of that out of you. Know what I mean? So, when it happened to me I took a long look at myself and decided to try and do something about it; to salvage something.'

'And?'

'And, now I do this. It's my job. Sitting here, talking to guys like you. Mostly guys, anyway. I can't understand women, you know? I always try and leave the women to Maurice, he's better at it.'

'Maurice?'

'Yeah, the croissant.'

Slowly, Neville replaced the cup on the table and, with an involuntary sob, dropped his head into his hands. The room was silent.

TWO

He was unsure how long he remained there, motionless. Eventually — his eyes still closed — he raised his head until he was confident that, on opening them, he would be looking high above the table. After a pause, he let the world in. On the far wall, the three geese were rigid. The patch of sunlight that had illuminated them was no more, and in their lack of motion they seemed reassuringly dull. Perhaps he had been dreaming; perhaps it was all some kind of mistake, or an elaborate joke.

He began to lower his head, gradually, as slowly as he could. So slowly in fact, that for a moment he doubted if he were moving it at all. Then the first glow of the yellow table cloth; the definite edge of the table; the tired flowers; the faded menu. And then the top of his coffee cup, the discarded filter. So far, so good.

'Feeling better?'

Hans. He dropped his eyes. There was the blue and white plate, and on it the Black Forest gateau. He stared at it without comprehension, without feeling. Trampled and beaten, at that moment he would have given in to anything. And then, from his right, a new voice.

'Are you all right, dear?'

It was the Conservative lady, now sitting close by. Except that she was a different person. That hard, blue-rinse bossiness had gone, its superiority replaced by something softer. And in her face he caught the warmth and familiarity of his old grandmother.

'You had quite a turn there. We were worried.'

'We?' he echoed. Glancing up, he saw the driver and the Proprietress silently looking his way. The bus driver gave him another of his nods (perhaps he had legion), and in the corner the waitresses continued noiselessly relaying the walkers' table.

'You'll be fine; you're in good hands.'

'Hans?'

'One of the best.' With that she rose, and then — as if on a cushion of air — slid across the tea shop and out through the door. The bell failed to ring.

'It gets people like that, the suddenness of it: anger, self-pity, confusion. The works. I should know. I've seen them all. The way they take it.'

'It?'

'It, yeah. The "situation". Shitsville. Where you are. See what I'm saying?'

Neville said nothing. He knew, somehow, that his coffee cup would be filling itself again, and when he checked, sure enough the steam had begun to rise once more.

'Hey! You're getting the hang of this!'

'But I don't know what "this" is. I don't know who you are. *What* you are.'

'You're pissed, right? Confused too. I understand, Nev. Hey, when I first came here I was so fucking angry no one could talk to me for a week! Really! But it's okay for you; at least you can get out.'

'Out? Out from what?'

'From here; this tea shop. Back out into the Real World. Back into the sodding rat race that you laughingly call your life. Back to your petty...'

'Okay, okay', Neville cut him short. He didn't need a semi-arbitrary mixture of butter, eggs, flour and cocoa powder telling him how depressing his existence had become.

Something had changed however. For the first time he began to understand that there might be something to get "out" of — or back to. He looked round. The bus driver was reading a paper (from a picture on the front page, a politician winked at him) and the ever-larger Proprietress behind the counter seemed in danger of becoming permanently wedged there.

He expected Hans to say something again. Expected more words of wisdom; but nothing came. He took the filter from the cup and tasted the coffee. Was this his third or fourth cup? He couldn't remember, but did it matter anyway? Back at the office Brian, Colin and David would have already forgotten about him; in fact, they were probably taking a trip to the pub to celebrate their good fortune. Brian would be coming up with a new scheme to organise his files; Colin would be talking about the latest pub quiz he had entered; and David would be contemplating his next political coup. "Poor old Neville" someone might say as they stood at the bar, and then everyone would laugh. And somewhere else, Mirelle would be arching that French back of hers to allow her latest beau entrance to the Tunnel of Love; "Ride of a lifetime! £100 round-trip!"

'So?' He couldn't take the silence from Hans; it seemed unnatural. Then, as he waited, he caught himself having the somewhat absurd thought that an *inanimate* Black Forest gateau might actually be considered "unnatural". From somewhere inside him the beginnings of a smile stirred.

'So?' responded Hans after a pause.

'Oh, there you are. I thought you might be asleep — or whatever cakes do.'

'Right, Nev. Very funny. And don't forget I'm not just "a cake", OK?'

Neville said nothing. Suddenly a little more buoyant, he thought about lifting his hand and flicking one of Hans' eyes from his "head" — if he could call it that — to see if he could hit the geese on the far wall.

'Forget it, buster!'

'But if this is a game...'

'Game? Who the hell said anything about a game? Don't you get it, what's going on here? We're talking about your *life* and you want to start playing stupid juvenile games!'

'Sorry. Really.'

Neville could tell that Hans was experienced at this. He'd been on interviewing courses at work and knew bits of theory about Subject Manipulation; but that was all it was to him, theory. Here was a master at work.

'Thanks. It's nice to be appreciated.'

'You read minds too, of course.'

'Of course.'

To their right, the bus driver put down his paper and looked across. Another nod.

'OK, let's get moving!'

Hans' sudden urgency — implying the need for action — took Neville by surprise.

'Sorry?'

'Time, Nev; time! You can't sit here all day. We've got to get you sorted.'

'To get me "out"?'

'Exactly! To get you out, yes! Which means, of course, that there is a need for something to happen.' Hans waited for a moment. 'So, any idea what are you going to do?'

'Do?'

'Shit, yes; "*Do*"! You have to *do* something don't you? Can't hang around on your butt forever. What are your options?'

Despite the turn the conversation was taking, Neville could still feel the smile brewing. It was buried a long way beneath the surface, but it was there, somewhere. It gave him a hint that some of his humanity remained.

'Why don't you tell me. It'll save time.'

'Good idea! Okay, let's go!' Hans paused for a moment, apparently organising his thoughts. 'There are choices, okay? One. There's a nice deep river not far from here. Plenty cold enough. And enough big stones handy, so you could easily fill your pockets. Wouldn't take long, you know.'

'You mean...'

'Yeah, I know. Not my favourite option either, but some guys like it. Strange how it's always the angry ones who choose the quick exit. I don't reckon that's for you though. You're not really the type.'

'Thanks.'

'Option Two — another easy one. Just go back. Get a new job with another company that's destined for the toilet; the "Armitage Shanks" principle we call it. Which means, of course, that one day they too will sack you. And you could get yourself another woman who may look a bit different and be called something else, but will just be Mirelle all over again. Go back to that, and when you've lost your job and your woman again I'll see you here in a couple of years — if you're lucky.'

'If I'm lucky?'

'Sure. Most people just slide off the rails, go completely nuts, or kill themselves. Or kill someone else, come to that. Ever thought of topping the old bitch? Yeah, I bet you have! Well, you didn't, so be grateful. Anyway, number Two's just more of the same, more of what you've already got — because it's just more of the same old you.'

'And Three?'

'Did I say there was a Three?'

'No. But, I got the impression...'

Neville's words failed him. Hans let the plea hang unanswered for a second.

'Well, lucky for you there is, see? Number Three; it's a bit tougher than the other two, 'cos the other two are just running away, right? Yellowville City, Arizona. You may be a bit thin, Nev — guts-wise — but you're not completely lily-livered; know what I mean?'

'Thanks.'

'You're welcome. So, Three.' Across the room, the bus driver stood up. Alarm crept into Hans' sense of urgency. 'Shit, is that the time! Okay, okay!' He shouted to some unseen voice. 'Three is where you face it head-on, go for the balls. Try and sort out the "big problem", hear what I'm saying? It ain't easy, and there are no guarantees.'

'Okay.'

'And there's a big risk too. See, there's Three "A", and there's Three "B"; and you don't get control over the ending.'

'The ending?'

'"A"; everyone lives happily ever after — just like in James Stewart's movies. What a guy! "B"; well, you don't. That's it. The risk.'

'And I don't get any choice, even though one ending is…?'

'Sorry, pal. I don't make the rules.'

A grunt from the far corner distracted them. The bus driver was trying to pull the owner from behind the counter where she now seemed firmly fixed. Both were red with struggling. Neville was amazed at the woman's increasing girth.

'She must be…'

'Forget her, Nev! Decide! What's it to be?'

He stared back at Hans, trying to focus on the question before him.

'Not Number One; I don't have the guts.'

'Debatable, but okay.'

'And Two doesn't sound so great, either.'

'Terrific; so it's Three then?'

'I guess so.'

Hans whistled.

'More commission for me.'

'Commission?'

'Don't you worry about that, you've got other things to sort out; like deciding what you're running from. What is it that you need to face up to, that causes you the greatest problems?'

'Don't you know?'

'Sure, *I* know! But if this is going to work then you need to see it too. That's the first big step. So come on, pal; tell me!'

Neville, drawn in by Hans' sense of urgency, thought hard. The goings-on behind the counter now seemed more threatening than comical, and there was an embryonic air of danger in the room. The waitresses had stopped laying the walkers' table and were watching as the Proprietress grew still larger. On the wall, the geese seemed restless again.

'Come on, Nev! Why are you here? What brought you here?'

'The job. Today it was the job.'

'Okay. And? Is there more?'

'More? Mirelle, I guess. That's why I came here too. Malvern and Mirelle. And...'

'And? Shit, that's enough! Okay, pal; now what's the connection? What's one thing joins them together? What one thing has dominated the last ten years of your miserable little life, ruled you, and made you subservient? Think!'

Neville looked to the counter, the geese. He glanced out of the window, searching. There was the old bus. "Don't miss the bus" — Hans had said something like that. From inside the café there came a the crash as the bus driver flew backwards having finally released the Proprietress who was now floating in the air by the baked potato machine. Neville, making an obscure connection somewhere in the depths of his mind, had an idea.

'Money?'

'Money!' Hans was triumphant.

'Mirelle wanted money. Always! I worked for it. Gambled to try and get it. I kept up a job I hated because if it. Because of her.' Animated, he remembered his watch. 'And this.'

He pulled the watch from his wrist and threw it across the room. One of the waitresses caught it between her teeth and swallowed it whole.

'Great Nev, great! So what are you going to do? How can you free yourself from it? How are you going to get out?'

'Get it all, every last penny I have; then use it to do the things *I* always wanted to do, but never did. Because of the job; because of her.'

'Use your money to free yourself; the very stuff that's held you back! Fuck, that's poetic! I'm proud of you pal!'

'I'll sell everything I have; change it all into money. Then *I'll* do things! And if it's Three "B" in the end, then I've nothing to lose anyway. Right?'

'Right!'

Neville had now warmed to the task, feeling as if he were about to embark on some great Crusade.

'I need to make a list.'

'Hey Sister, give this guy something to write with!'

From the far side of the room, one of the waitresses — her prim black and white uniform billowing — rose into the air and flew towards them. In her hand she carried an oblong piece of card. As she gathered pace, she began to imitate the roar of a Lancaster bomber before dropping the card on the table in front of Neville. It was white, with the word

MENU

printed at the top. Immediately she had had flown her first sortie, the other waitress took off. From her pocket she pulled a cheese straw and from six yards away, launched it towards him like a torpedo. It bounced once on the table then landed straight in his hand.

'What..?'

'A list, Nev. Make your list!'

The bus driver, who had now risen from the floor and dusted himself down (though with little external effect) coughed meaningfully in their general direction.

'Shit! Look, at least start the list! A list of your money, of the things you are going to sell; you know? You need to get your enemy out into the open; flush him out. What have you got on you now?'

Neville pulled out his wallet and emptied the contents on the table.

'Trash the plastic, Nev. What's left?'

Neville counted.

'Three pounds forty seven.'

'OK. Write it down.'

And Neville, using the cheese straw, wrote

CASH: THREE POUNDS FORTY SEVEN PENCE

on his Menu. Then there was the cheque.

REDUNDANCY: TWO THOUSAND FIVE HUNDRED POUNDS

'Now, what else?'

'My car. The house. I've got some shares.'

To his right he was aware the Proprietress had grown so large that she now filled half the shop. There was a ring from the doorbell. The driver was standing on the threshold and looking his way.

'Okay, okay! Nev, get the idea? Nev! Finish the list. Later, but do it! Turn your life into money, then burn it. It's the only way! Okay? Okay?!'

'Yes, but...'

'Now, GET OUT!'

Neville rose and, with the huge bulk of the owner towering above him, made a dash beneath her apron to the door. He felt the swoop of her arm and a draft of air rush past him, then suddenly he was out into the street clutching his list and the cheese straw he had used as a pen.

The driver, now at the door of the vehicle, waited for him to step onto the bus. It was not until he was on board that he looked back to the tea shop.

Through the window he could see nothing but the pattern of the owner's apron pressed hard against the glass. His table, the coffee cup — all was hidden from view. From beneath his feet he felt the rumble of the engine as the driver started the old bus. The gears groaned as they were forced into action once more; then, slowly, they pulled away.

Neville twisted in his seat to look behind, back towards the shop; and, just as they were turning the corner, he witnessed the entire front of the building explode into the street, the road instantly covered in a shower of apron fragments, table cloth, and Black Forest gateau.

THREE

'Where to, Sir?'

The driver's voice roused Neville from his general state of paralysis which had been induced by the fleeting sight of the tea shop exploding into the road. He looked along the aisle of the bus (he was sitting about half-way down) and saw the driver wrestling with the ancient controls.

'Sorry, what did you say?'

'Where to, Sir?'

There was some attempt at cheerfulness in the literal repeat, but Neville wondered whether — despite this — he detected a fading note of enthusiasm in the voice of the speaker. He wondered how long the Old Boy had been ferrying people around like this. In his pocket he could feel the firm edge of the now-folded menu, and — lifting his fingers to his nose — was reacquainted with the smell of the cheese straw. Those last few moments came back to him.

'Where do you usually go? I mean, what's your route?'

Conveniently, the traffic lights ahead turned red with a sly wink. The bus stopped, and the driver shifted in his seat to face his solitary passenger.

'Route, Sir? I don't "usually go" anywhere. I mean it's entirely up to you; begging your pardon.'

Neville marked the contrast with Hans; the subservient tone, the deferential air. Despite his still unresolved situation, now that he was out of the tea shop he felt a little more in control.

'Well, I need to go back to my car.'

'Your car, Sir?'

'My car, yes. I parked it in that pay and display place down by the station. Take me there. That'll be fine.'

The driver hesitated.

'Sorry, Sir; but I don't think you quite understand...'

'Lights.'

In front of them the green now shone and Neville's observation forced the driver to return to his duty and press on. The bus swung unsteadily left, then gradually downhill (a little right all the time) until it came to the car park. As they pulled in, Neville notice two things: the first was that someone appeared to be examining his car, and the second that his was the only car there. This latter fact seemed strange as he distinctly recalled there had been just a few spaces left when he had originally parked. Indeed, he now realised that, apart from the old bus in which he was now riding, he had not seen any other vehicle since he had left the tea shop.

'How much to do I owe you?'

The driver looked quizzically at him as he prepared to disembark.

'Owe me? Nothing, Sir. Really.'

Neville, a little exasperated at the seemingly constant repetition of every question he posed, shrugged his shoulders and stepped down onto the tarmac.

'I'll wait,' the driver called after him.

'There's no need; I've got my car.'

'I'll wait anyway, Sir; if you don't mind.'

As he walked towards his car, Neville realised that he was beginning to feel a little better; a little more "normal". Perhaps it was the fresh air, or the accumulation of coffee he had drunk in the café. He remembered the menu in his pocket and the cheese straw; and he remembered his conversation with Hans, and the three options. But here, out in the open, he now felt much less inclined to believe what had happened. The notion that he might have been hallucinating came back to him, but this was only partially satisfactory as an explanation; there were too many unanswered questions — such as where were all the other cars?

Ahead of him, the figure — cloaked in a long fawn raincoat — was bent over the bonnet of his car; he appeared to be rubbing the headlights. As Neville approached, he straightened and turned towards him.

'Your car?'

Neville was confronted by a well-built man who, he guessed, was in his early fifties. From what Neville could see, he was smartly dressed beneath the raincoat and carried himself with a remarkably upright stance. He boasted a stunning handlebar moustache which was so long, it seemed to leave his cheeks and disappear behind his ears. Neville guessed he might once have been a military man.

'My car? Yes, it is.'

'Um.' The man paused. 'Fine machine.'

'Not really. I mean, it's only a bulk standard Ford. There's nothing spectacular about it.'

'Nothing spectacular?' The man stared at Neville as if he was verging on insanity. 'Nothing spectacular?! I'll have you know that this is one of the finest vehicles ever made.'

'Really?' Neville felt he could only humour the other man.

'A superb example of British craftsmanship. Magnificent! And such a wonderful colour!'

Neville looked at his maroon Sierra (which he suspected had been manufactured in Spain) and wondered exactly how long the old soldier had been drinking. As he moved towards the driver's door, the man tried to block his way.

Neville, whose perceptiveness seemed heightened, shouted 'ATTENTION!' as loud as he could — and while the other drew himself to his full height, clamped his feet firmly to the tarmac and straightened his back even more, Neville slid round him and opened the door.

'I say,' a large hand landed on the open door frame, 'that was rather cunning, you know. Still, I admire a man with a little guile.'

'Thank you. Just a hunch, you know. Now, do you mind?'

'Look. How would it be if I offered to buy the car off you?'

'Buy it?' Neville felt a stab from the cheese straw which was suddenly awfully firm. 'But it's only an old Sierra. It's not worth very much.'

'Perhaps not; but all the same...'

Neville hesitated.

'I need to get back to Birmingham.'

'To where?'

'Birmingham. I've got things to do.'

'Yes; of course.'

Slowly, the old Soldier unbuttoned his raincoat. For a moment, Neville expected to see a sawn-off shotgun or some semi-automatic weapon of Eastern European extraction hanging from an inside belt loop. Instead, the coat revealed eight internal pockets — four on either side — with bundles of cash peeping out from the top of each.

'I can pay.'

'Yes, evidently.'

'What would you want for it?'

Now it was Neville's turn to straighten. He faced the man, eye to eye.

'What's it worth to you?'

'Five thousand?'

The car was, at best, worth no more than fifteen hundred pounds. He would never expect to get two thousand for it, let alone five. Was there a catch? He eyed the soldier cautiously; the offer seemed genuine enough. He remembered his deal with Hans. If it wasn't true, if he had imagined the whole affair and there was no such thing as "3A" or "3B", then selling the car would still net him a cool three-and-a-half grand profit. He couldn't lose.

'Very well, I can see you drive a hard bargain,' — Neville had said nothing — 'I'll make it six thousand, and throw in two thousand for the lights.'

The man extended his hand. Neville paused but a moment, then shook it. Seconds later, the Soldier was divesting himself of the cash from his pockets — a thousand pounds from each — and depositing the money into Neville's hands.

'Any idea how I might get back to Birmingham?'

'To where?'

'Home?'

The Soldier turned and glanced at the bus. The driver was standing by the door, watching the conclusion of the transaction. Neville nodded. The driver nodded back.

'Yes; of course.'

A few minutes later, Neville was once again back on the bus. He had removed the Menu and the cheese straw from his pockets and wrote

CAR: EIGHT THOUSAND POUNDS

under the previous entry. As the bus jolted into life again, he could see the old Soldier standing by the car, stroking its lights.

'You know' — this time Neville had chosen to sit at the front of the bus, almost alongside the driver — 'that guy gave me about five times what the car was worth.'

'To you, Sir.'

'What do you mean, to me?'

'Five times what it was worth to you, Sir; or what you might have paid for it yourself. He simply paid you what it was worth to him.'

'But it was only an old Sierra.' Neville was inclined to debate, but sensed that might be futile. He changed tack. 'Did you see the way he stroked the headlights?'

'Always does, Sir.'

'Always does?'

'The Colonel; that's what we call him. Loves cars. Always buying them — though he can't drive of course.'

'Of course!'

'He had a son who used to work in the Rover factory just down the road. He died when a two litre Vitesse fell from the over-head conveyor. Squashed him flat. It was his job to put the lights in you see; but he never quite managed it on that Vitesse.'

'But that was a Rover, not a Ford.'

'Ah well, Sir, the poor old Colonel can't tell the difference. He just loves cars because they remind him of his Son. That's all. So you see, your car was really worth much more to him than it was to you.'

Neville looked away from the driver and out of the front window of the bus. They were, to his surprise, already out in the countryside, rattling along an open and empty road. The speedometer showed twenty seven miles an hour.

'Oh Sir, almost forgot. You had a phone call.'

'A what?'

'A phone call, Sir.' The Driver pulled a mobile phone from a recess in the dashboard and offered it to Neville. 'Someone calling himself "Your Broker". Could you call him back, please.'

'Richie? How did he know where I was? I mean...'

Neville took the handset. It was incredibly light, and appeared not to possess all the usual buttons. Undaunted, he rang Richard Robinson Associates (Stock Brokers) on their office number. The purr of the phone, then loudly — 'Nev!'

'Richie. How did you know it was me?'

'Expecting your call, Old Boy. Chap said you'd phone back.'

Neville glanced at the driver who seemed intent on the road ahead.

'How did you get hold of me?'

'Got a message. Look, can't explain; we're in a flap here! Bloody shit's hitting the proverbial, and I've got a tip that the whole bleedin' market's just about to collapse. Nev, you've got to sell everything! Get out!'

'Get out? What do you mean? I thought things were pretty stable at the minute?'

'Didn't we all, Chum! My source — bloody reliable chap — says there's a major disaster on the stocks' — pause — 'in about seventeen minutes actually. So you've got to sell. And fast!'

Richie sounded a little different; perhaps it was the pressure. Perhaps he too was going bananas. But, despite the odd eccentricity or two, Neville had never known him to be wrong. He may not have invested much over the years nor had much at stake, but Richie had never let him down. All this — along with the vague sense that he was riding some unstoppable roller-coaster — meant that his hesitation was minimal.

'OK, do it.' There was silence at the other end. 'Richie?'

'Yep?'

'Do it, Richie.'

'In the pipeline, Chum!'

'What's it worth — all of it?'

'Hang on.' Another pause. 'After tax?'

'Forget the tax; what's it worth?'

'Well, couldn't get top dollar for the Utilities, but we've cleared three two seven five. OK?'

It was a little less than Neville had expected which — given his recent experience with the car — came as something of a surprise to him. Richie sensed his disappointment.

'OK, I know it's less than four — but in about ten minutes you wouldn't even get two. Trust me!'

'Thanks Richie.'

'OK. Must dash; more Suckers to save! Money's on its way to the bank. Ciao!'

The phone seemed to go limp in Neville's hand as Richie rang off. He handed it back to the driver.

'Everything all right, Sir?'

'Yes, I guess so.'

'You sound a little disappointed, Sir.'

Neville said nothing.

'Funny how things can change their worth isn't it, Sir? Depending on how you look at them, I mean.'

Neville had withdrawn his Menu and was already writing

SHARES: THREE THOUSAND TWO HUNDRED AND SEVENTY FIVE POUNDS

For a short while there was nothing but the sound of the tired old engine breaking the silence. Outside, the hedges rolled by (at twenty seven miles per hour) and occasionally Neville thought he could see Birmingham skyscrapers in the distance. But then a hill would rise and the image would be lost.

'What's your name?'

'My name, Sir?'

The driver seemed slightly thrown by such a personal question. He glanced at Neville, then back to the road.

'Samuel, Sir. That's my name.' It sounded more like an impromptu decision than a fact.

'And how long have you been doing this — whatever "this" is?'

Slowly the bus decelerated from its standard speed. Ahead there was a lay-by, and it was evident that Samuel was making for this.

'We're stopping?'

Neville's question remained unanswered as Samuel concentrated on grinding down through the gears and slowing the complaining bus to a halt. The rumble changed in tone once they were stationery, then, as the engine was turned off, it spluttered and coughed like a dying man as it faded to silence.

'Now then Sir, what was it you said?'

'How long have you been doing this?'

'And what do you mean by "this", Sir, if I might be so bold?'

'Driving this bus. Looking after people like me; people in my "situation". I don't know. Any of it.'

'Ah, I see Sir.' Samuel paused. 'Not sure I could rightly say to be honest. A long time, I suppose. It must be.'

'And all of this — Hans, the car, Richie. What exactly is happening Samuel?'

Samuel coughed, and was then silent. Having stopped the bus, he seemed intent on giving the impression that he was reluctant to say anything.

'Would you like to go on, Sir?'

It was a feeble attempt, and Neville resisted it. Samuel had obviously chosen to stop in order to allow them to talk, and Neville was determined to get some sort of answer from him.

'Not yet; not until you tell me — something, anything.'

'I see.'

'Please?'

And then, in an instant, Neville got the distinct impression that all this had been rehearsed; that Samuel went through these same motions every time; and that there was nothing unique about this situation whatsoever. But before he could interject, to protest — maybe about the vague sense that he was little more than a specimen in a vast and sophisticated laboratory experiment — Samuel started speaking.

FOUR

'Of course, at this precise moment in time — where we are, here and now — you aren't really sure what's going on, are you? So far you have had a rather bizarre experience in a tea shop, a man has bought your car for a vastly inflated sum of money, and you suddenly get a phone call telling you to sell all your shares — which, had you kept them, would now be worth two thousand pounds, if that.

'In addition to all of this, you find yourself sitting in a rather old bus (but a faithful old bus, I must say) talking to the driver — myself — who is probably at least old enough to be your grandfather.'

He paused to offer a slight smile. Since Samuel had begun to speak, Neville had perceived something of a change in him. The smile was the same as the first he had given Neville in the shop, but the man who delivered it now seemed so much more than a shuffling old bus driver.

'I am here to help you, Sir. That's my job; that's all I do. You are actually a very lucky man. You have been given a rare opportunity. Hans helped of course; but even Hans — despite his wonderful qualities and that abrasive style of his! — isn't able to help everyone. Do you realise Sir, that some people never actually make it out of the Tea Shop? I say Tea Shop in this instance, but it needn't be of course.'

Neville marked the "of course" again, as if what was happening was so self-evident as to make explanation redundant.

'In any event, you have been given a chance to see your life. Do you mark my words, Sir? To "*see*" your life. Most people simply live their lives, don't they? They have a pattern, a plan if they're lucky — most often drawn out for them by some force or other — and they try to live to that plan, that formula. They rarely see their lives, see what they are living. Do you understand, Sir?

'You have been given a special chance; the chance to see your life for what it is. Perhaps it is too late, perhaps not. I cannot tell you. Hans certainly could not either. At least you have begun to see something of it yourself, and that is a good beginning.'

'Money?' It was Neville's first offering in the conversation. Samuel smiled. It was an old smile; lips parting with the tired wisdom of many journeys.

'Indeed, Sir. That was a very good start, but it is not enough, not on its own. You must realise — in both senses — the goal you have set for yourself.'

'The third option?'

'And make no mistake Sir, there is nothing unreal about that. All of this may seem very strange, but there is nothing light-hearted about what awaits you. You have — unwittingly or not — set out on your quest, and you must endeavour to succeed. You must, Sir, you must.'

There was, in Samuel's delivery of those words, a quiet insistence that Neville found absolutely unnerving. For a moment he seemed unable to control his voice.

'Or else?' he said, in a whisper that was not his own.

Samuel raised his right arm, and slowly extended it to point out of the windows on Neville's side of the bus. There, beyond the hedge and as far as the eye could see, were row upon row of white tombstones.

'Hundreds and thousands of fading monuments to anonymous people; millions of forgotten and unfulfilled lives.'

And as Neville looked, from amongst the gravestones a sudden wind raised a moan that encompassed all that could be said and felt about loss in a single note. It lingered but a moment, and then was gone.

Neville looked back at Samuel who was lost in his own private reverie. He waited. Eventually Samuel turned to him again.

'There.'

Neville did not know what to say, or even if he was expected to say anything. He was struggling with the sense that he might be lucky; that he might be on borrowed time; that he might, in some unusual way, have a purpose to fulfil or a chance to take. His eyes, he suddenly realised, had filled with tears.

'Please look at your menu, Sir.'

Neville pulled the menu from his pocket and looked at it. There was a new entry at the bottom of the page:

HOUSE: FIVE THOUSAND THREE HUNDRED AND SEVEN POUNDS 53 PENCE

and beneath it the final line

TOTAL: NINETEEN THOUSAND AND EIGHTY SIX POUNDS

Although he had written neither, both were in his hand.

'I'm afraid we couldn't get as much as you might have liked for the house; they charge so much for fees and legal expenses these days, and by the time we paid off the mortgage... But at least it has been sold and so you don't have to worry.'

'Yes, of course.' Neville, unconsciously adopting the literal acceptance of the obvious, wondered again who Samuel might be referring to when he said "we".

'So you see, Sir, you now know that your life is worth just a little under twenty thousand pounds. That's what it translates to; the bottom line, if I might be so bold.'

Neville found himself focusing on that single line — the bottom line indeed — and the words began to slowly blur into a single scrawl that was nothing more than a meaningless smudge.

After a short while, Samuel cleared his throat. Neville had been given enough time for reflection. He looked up and sensed — now, as in the tea-shop — the need to get on; that, even in this strange new world, time was passing and waiting for no-one, least of all a temporary visitor like himself.

'Yes. Yes, I see. So, what happens now?'

'Well Sir, it is really up to you. Perhaps you should consider what you have.'

'Apart from the money, you mean?'

Samuel nodded, and from within his pocket Neville felt the cheese straw dig him in the leg. He had never considered cheese straws to be sharp, either physically or intellectually, but this one appeared to be the exception.

'My Menu, I guess. I can't think of anything else.'

'Indeed, but perhaps it is only half a menu; only half of the equation. The first half. The means, perhaps.'

'To the end?' Neville offered, having been led towards that inevitable conclusion.

Samuel seemed pleased, and his face broke into another reassuring, grandfatherly kind of smile. Neville reflected for a moment how he had been seeing echoes of ancient relatives: the Conservative Lady in the tea-shop; now Samuel...

'So I need to decide what the end might be?'

'Indeed.'

'To write down what I want to do with the money?'

'You need to think about how you might like to "see" your life; what you would like to experience in order to put it into context.'

Neville was beginning to get a picture of how the game might be played.

'A frame of reference?' It had been an expression he had first heard on a late-night Channel Four talk show, and since then had kept it in the wardrobe of his business vocabulary where it hung, nicely ironed and ready for use.

'Ah.'

'Another list.' Neville imagined how, at the end of all of this — and how soon that might be, he could not tell — the two sides of his menu would probably need to either balance or cancel each other out. He suspected that he may have little or no control over what he would be left with. Indeed, he failed to conceive how there could possibly *be* a judgement or on what his future might be decided.

'I'm sorry, Sir. I'm afraid I can't help you; I don't know.'

Neville smiled. Of course Samuel could read minds too.

'Thanks Samuel. I'll just try my best.'

He looked out of the window. In the fields, crops now swayed gently in the breeze where the solid tombstones had been, and across a hedge, four Friesian cows, dressed as a Barber Shop Quartet, began to gently harmonise a cappella accompaniment to the rhythm of the wind.

The reverse side of the menu was completely blank. Neville hesitated, thinking for a moment of scrawling his own heading "Menu" at the top. The cheese straw was shorter than it had been originally. The writing had evidently worn some of it away. The numbers from his "bottom line" danced on the paper, rearranging themselves into ever less meaningful combinations, distracting him from the task in hand.

'Samuel?'

'Sir.'

'How do I know how much things cost? For my list.'

'For example?'

'Paris. I've always wanted to visit Paris — despite Mirelle being French. Or perhaps because of it. How do I know how much it will cost me, or how much I will have left afterwards?'

'How much would you expect it to cost you?'

'I don't know. Maybe five hundred pounds.'

Samuel smiled.

'Yes, I would guess you might not be far off there. It does, of course, depend on what you decide to do while you are there. And what the visit might be worth to you.' Samuel paused for a moment. 'But for the moment, don't worry about that. We'll look after the costs for you. That's the way it is, and I'm afraid you'll just have to trust us, Sir.'

Neville was tempted to ask about the reference to the "we" again, but decided to let it pass. He turned to the menu and entered

VISIT PARIS

at the top of the blank side. He paused.

Samuel sensed the hesitation.

'If it's any consolation Sir, this bit is often the most difficult. You should try and think of the things you have always wanted to do but never have because money held you back; because you couldn't afford to do them.'

'And nothing else?'

'For example?'

'To be honest…' He paused, uncertain whether honesty was prudent — never mind avoidable — in his new circumstance. 'Well, to be honest I'd quite like to fall in love again. After Mirelle, you know. Just once more.'

Samuel shook his head. The lilt from the cows had a distinctly Parisian air, and from somewhere Neville could hear an accordion playing.

'If you can't buy it, Sir…'

Neville nodded. He knew Samuel would read his resigned, but unspoken "okay".

The task seemed immeasurably difficult. Perhaps he didn't have that much money to play with after all; perhaps — and this was something of a shock — an historical lack of money was not the issue he had imagined it to be. He tried not to analyse. What had he always wanted to do? He wrote:

EAT A REALLY EXPENSIVE MEAL

FLY AN AEROPLANE

and then stopped. He could certainly buy all of those, but it did not seem to be much of a list. And how much of his twenty thousand had he allocated so far? He wondered about a cruise. It might be too expensive; it might denude his reserves too much.

Neville told himself that there must be other things; there certainly would have been with Mirelle around. Indeed, he would have needed pages and pages to include all of her ideas! Thinking of Mirelle led him again to thoughts about holidays away from Birmingham, and in consequence

GO ON A CRUISE

was added to the list.

'How am I doing, Samuel?'

Samuel had been watching him all this time, saying nothing. Neville had the sensation that the old boy had been mentally calculating as each item was added to the list.

'Fine, Sir. Presumably you were only thinking of a short cruise; nothing too elaborate?'

Neville smiled, pointing to the last entry with the ever-shortening cheese straw.

'I guess am now!'

'Indeed. And I should warn you that, just because you put something on your list, there is no guarantee that you will be able to have that wish fulfilled.' Samuel paused. 'Might I suggest, Sir; is there anything you would like to possess? Some little extravagance, perhaps?'

'I had assumed that having something material was out of the question.'

'Not necessarily. For example, have you ever wanted to buy yourself an expensive hat, or a half-hunter watch? I'm sure such things might be acceptable. And you could take them with you on your trips if you wished.'

'And after?'

His question found no response.

Neville thought about a hat and discarded the idea. Yet he had always fancied owning his own tuxedo; something that might be appropriate for the expensive meal. With his scope thus broadened, he continued

TUXEDO

then stopped again.

Neville looked at the remains of the cheese straw which was now so short he was having difficulty holding it. He might have only one choice left.

He thought again of Mirelle and how she had nagged him constantly to do things, to take her places. "Nagged". She had wanted him to take her horse riding, and had once pestered him for weeks on end. He did not like horses; indeed, he did not trust them. But having thought of the idea, he remembered how he had occasionally talked about going to the Derby. Despite his failed flutters on the ponies, was this to be it? Determined, he gripped the cheese straw for one final time and wrote

GO TO THE DERBY

finishing the last word just as it vanished from his hand. He sniffed his fingers; only its smell was left.

There was almost instantly a rumble from beneath his feet. Samuel had started up the bus.

'Is that it?' Neville asked.

'It?'

'The end of my list? Can I add nothing else? Is all my money gone?'

Samuel smiled.

'I think you have enough on your list to cater for most of the money you have. Perhaps you will get the opportunity to add something else later, Sir. Who can say?'

Neville caught a glint of playfulness in Samuel's eyes as he said this, as if he knew all too well who could say; as if he could already see the future and was keeping its secrets hidden.

For the first time in a long while Neville suddenly laughed. Perhaps it was the same laugh that had begun to brew back in the tea shop. It was enough, however, to signal the movement of the bus which Samuel now swung back onto the road. Sedately — at twenty seven miles per hour — they began their journey forwards. Neville, preparing to sit back and enjoy the ride, was amazed when, after only a few moments, Samuel pulled the bus round a corner and revealed Paris stretching out below them in the distance.

FIVE

In spite of the impossibility of its sudden appearance, there could be no mistaking that the city beneath them was indeed Paris — but a Paris almost devoid of suburbs. Neville recognised the snaking shape of the island-bearing Seine, and then — as if any further confirmation were necessary — the unique frame of the Eiffel Tower standing proudly against the skyline.

Even from this distance, he could make out some of the more prominent landmarks as the old bus made its slow way down the hill and closer to the city. Occasionally the sun — which had now broken through the clouds — reflected on fragments of ornate, gilt-encrusted roofing, sending Morse-like greetings towards him.

For those first few seconds Neville was spellbound, not owing to the fact that he was suddenly here (he was beginning to feel as if nothing could surprise him now) but simply because of the bewitching beauty of the place.

Samuel had said nothing since he had re-started the engine.

'Paris,' Neville observed with a kind of naïve certainty.

'Indeed, Sir.'

'Because it's first on my list? Is that why we're here?'

'Not necessarily. Perhaps it is simply the best place to start.'

This was immediately a little too cryptic for Neville to pursue. Indeed, he had already decided that Samuel's inclination to stray into obscurity — like his open-ended references to "we" — would be left unchallenged, partly due to the fact that he sensed a futility in embarking on *any* literal challenge, but also because he hoped that such an approach might tempt Samuel to gradually lower his guard.

'Where would you like to stay, Sir?'

'I have a choice?' It was a possibility which not been expected.

'Of course.'

'But it will be a question of money?'

'Partly, yes — although at this point I am unable to say exactly how much things might cost.'

Neville smiled. He had begun to get a sense of the game Samuel was playing; a test almost, revolving around the notion of "worth" that the Colonel had so ably demonstrated.

'Nothing too grand then. Comfortable perhaps, and certainly where I will fit in.'

'As a visitor?'

'An English visitor, yes.'

They were nearing the bottom of the hill and had arrived at the outskirts of the geographically-shrunk city. Four-storey apartment blocks lined the road on either side. Not particularly attractive, they somehow still seemed to possess an air of the Parisian about them. Perhaps it was the cream coloured concrete or the preponderance of shutters.

'I know a nice place just south of the river, not far from the military academy. It should suit you fine, Sir.'

Through the window, Neville could see Parisians going about their daily business. It seemed he might soon be amongst ordinary people again; about to return to a world which shared his model of reality. Since the tea-shop, Neville had lost a grip on that reality and what he expected of it — one which had been loosened further thanks to their unruly temporal travel to Paris.

Cars whistled past them, often tooting as they did so, and Neville realised that Samuel, now sitting immediately in front of him, was driving — quite correctly — on the right side of the road. More than that however, the steering wheel, dashboard, and all other controls had moved with him. Above the dash, Neville noticed the logo of the Citroen motor vehicle company, and wondered if — again without his being aware — the whole bus might have changed too. The only thing that seemed to remain constant was their modest rate of progress, though even that had been translated into kilometres per hour.

'Perhaps you would like to check your wallet, Sir.'

Neville pulled his wallet from his back trouser pocket and opened it. Inside was a collection of French bank notes.

'A few hundred euros, I believe. The hotel has been paid for in advance, so you should really only need spending money.'

'Can I keep track of the money I spend, Samuel, just in case?'

'Check your watch, Sir.'

'My watch?'

Neville looked at his wrist. The watch — that recognition of loyalty from his former employer and which had been swallowed by the tea shop waitress — was strapped to him once again, yet now it boasted a small crystal display tastefully inset into the face. The numbers 18558 stared back at him.

'My balance?'

'Not counting what you have in your wallet. We have booked you into the hotel for three nights. Is that enough? If you want to stay longer, there will be no problem.'

'No; three nights should be fine.' He allowed himself a moment of mental arithmetic. 'But isn't a little over five hundred pounds a bit much for such a short stay?'

With the somewhat arbitrary relationship between monetary value and worth already established, when Samuel declined to say anything Neville gave up the enquiry.

Despite the fact that he was on the verge of a mission of self-discovery, Neville could not help but feel that there might be little true exploration to be undertaken. How much, for example, had been laid out for him already? He already had confidence in Samuel's decision that three days at the hotel was the precise amount of time he needed to spend there, in spite of anything he might suggest himself.

'Thank you for your faith, Sir,' Samuel had been mind-reading again, 'but I do assure you that our skills are merely organisational; I think in the modern world of business, you might call us "facilitators".'

'Yes, perhaps we might.'

By now they were in the heart of the city. Occasionally Neville caught glimpses of the Eiffel Tower between buildings, across open spaces, or at the end of long tree-lined avenues. Although it had represented little more than a landmark up to this point — a geographical stake in the ground as it were — he now began to feel as if it might hold some greater significance within his overall visit.

Samuel pulled the bus round a corner and — accompanied by the obligatory tooting of other road users — came to an almost immediate halt outside a large and impressive hotel. It looked expensive.

'Not too pricey, Sir. We have found it very reasonable in the past for the services it offers.'

'Of course.'

Samuel turned and smiled.

'Your bags are on the seat behind you. Just a few things for your visit: toiletries, changes of clothes, that sort of thing.' The door opened with a moan that was, quite noticeably, Gallic. 'I'll be here in three days to pick you up.'

'But if I need you before then?'

'Don't worry about that, Sir. You just make the most of it.'

The journey was evidently at an end. Samuel had made his final statement, and smiling but tight-lipped, waited for his passenger to disembark. Neville rose. Two bags — taupe canvass ones he had owned for some years now — awaited his attention. He lifted them up and made for the steps.

'Thank you, Samuel.'

Samuel nodded, and Neville climbed down from the bus.

With a complaining hiss, the door of the vehicle — now a rather dirty yellow Citroen which had also seen better and brighter days — closed behind him; then, accompanied by a chorus of car horns, Samuel swung the bus out into the speeding throng. Neville stood and watched as it became submerged in the stream of traffic and then veer suddenly out of sight.

When he turned his attention to it, the hotel facade proved even more impressive than he had first thought. Either side of the large revolving entrance doors, two majestic stone lions stood guard, growling menacingly at passers-by who strayed too close. The doorman, surprisingly rugged despite the elegance of his uniform, looked more like a lion-tamer than a member of a noble service industry. Indeed, the rather gruff "Good day" he bestowed on Neville — with one eye firmly fixed on his stone charges — did little to dispel the notion.

Inside, the foyer offered both warmth and intimacy. Its decor, once presumably the height of fashion, had lost a degree of its lustre, and its plushness seemed slightly warn. It was a hotel on the way out but still tenaciously clinging to the traditions of a more glorious past.

Neville rested his bags at his feet when he reached the unattended desk. He raised his palm to press the bell provided for those seeking attention, but before he could complete the action, the bell rang itself.

'Pardon monsieur, but I am — how you say — "pissed off" with being banged all the time.'

Neville, now feeling quite unfazed by such animated interruptions, nodded and lowered his hand. When he looked up, he was faced by a middle-aged woman dressed in a neat, if somewhat prim, suit.

'Monsieur?'

He was uncertain whether or not to try out his rather rusty schoolboy French at this point, but then he realised that both the Doorman and the bell had already addressed him in their own interpretation of English. He decided to stick with his native tongue.

'Good day. I believe you have a room booked for me.'

The woman smiled professionally, and nodded.

'Of course — and may I say, Monsieur's French is most excellent.'

Neville had spoken in English — yet apparently this had been instantly translated into fluent conversational French. He decided to try something a little more elaborate.

'I must say I am impressed by your welcoming vestibule. It retains the character of a bygone era and expresses all that is quintessential in elegance and style.'

Again, perfect French.

'Monsieur is too kind.' Again the smile and the nod.

A young man had appeared at Neville's side, and was already holding a taupe bag in each hand.

'Room 206, Sir.' She looked at the boy. 'Chambrés deux cent six, Albert. Allez, vite!'

Neville followed the boy to the far end of the hall. Stairs swung upwards in a wide sweeping spiral enveloping as they did so the wrought iron lift that rose in their centre. The boy pulled back the lift's trellis door and Neville stepped in. As they rose to the second floor, Neville watched the hotel foyer disappear beneath his feet and the first floor pass before his eyes. The lift — which reminded him of one he had ridden as a child in Foyle's London bookshop — seemed typically French. He would have expected nothing less.

Room 206 was a few yards along the corridor. The boy opened the door and led Neville into a large room. That feeling he had sensed in the entrance hall of a more luxurious past was echoed here too: the slightly fading wallpaper; the slightly tired curtains; the slightly worn fabric of the arm chairs. There was comfort too, but mingled with that a sense of sorrow and regret.

Neville turned to tip the boy, but he had already left; the door was closed and his two bags were resting on the large double bed. Neville walked to the window, drew back the curtains, then opened the shutters onto the street below. There was a table near the chairs, and on the table some hotel stationery. He thought of the Eiffel Tower again and wondered if, in order to make the most of his visit, he ought to plan an itinerary.

He pulled off his jacket, laid it across the back of one of the chairs, then sat in the other. The stationery, not surprisingly off-white (though this time presumably by design), bore the name of the hotel beneath its rather elaborate leonine crest, as did the ball-point pen that had been placed nearby.

Neville picked up the pen — no cheese straw this time! — and reflected how he seemed to be doing nothing but making lists. From outside the tooting of car horns was joined by the shouts of street vendors who had stalls across the road, and the combination of the two began to take on something of a rhythmical quality. In the corner of the room a water dispenser bubbled in time, and from the vase on the dresser Neville noticed the aroma of the fresh flowers.

'Ambiance.'

He looked behind him to where an antique grand-mother clock tick-tocked quietly with the rhythm.

'Ambiance, we call it. A very French word, you do not think, Monsieur?'

'Indeed. And thank you. I am quite relaxed.'

The clock tick-tocked on. Neville turned his attention to the paper again.

'Not everyone appreciates it you know; the ambiance,' the clock interrupted again, 'especially — if I might be so bold — the English.'

'Ah.' Neville resisted the temptation to turn round; he wanted to work on his list. On the dresser, the flowers appeared to be leaning in his direction, listening to the conversation. He wondered where he should start.

'A list; that is good, Monsieur. And La Tour Eiffel; of course you must go there.'

Neville turned to the clock. A small moon-like hand, swung from side to side beyond a glass aperture in the face, keeping time with the pendulum that swung out of sight within the clock's mahogany case.

'Should I go there first, do you think?'

'Monsieur?'

'After all, you're a local; an expert in these matters.'

'Oh, you are too kind.' The clock tick-tocked slightly louder, as if with pride. 'But you are correct; I have helped people in the past. It is not my job of course, but then if one can be of assistance...'

There was now the faint sound of dripping behind him, and Neville turned to find a fresh filter coffee brewing on the table in front of him.

'Déjà vu?' The clock asked, and then chimed the quarter hour with such relish that it was almost a laugh.

'Déjà vu, indeed.'

'Now, La Tour. I would suggest that you leave her to last. She will give you a view of all you have seen here; it will be a memory to take away with you. Do you not agree?'

'Sounds very sensible. So, apart from the tower, what else should I see?'

'Monsieur, in Paris where does one start?!'

Neville picked up the pen and divided the page into three, one part for each day. At the very bottom he made a note of his final destination.

'I would start with the city. Just to drink her in, to feel her. That is how to start your visit, Monsieur.'

'And you would suggest?'

'A walk down Le Champs Elysées; a cognac on the terrace, watching the city pass you by. Magnifique! Then perhaps to simple stroll through the streets; perhaps a little shopping. That is the way to start your visit.'

Neville wrote almost as if he were taking dictation.

'And then?'

'Then you must do two things: see our history, and see our art. I would suggest Sacré-Cœur, Montmartre, Notre Dame. And for our art you should see the Louvre, and the Musée d'Orsay.'

The visitor continued to write.

'Monsieur?'

'Yes?' Neville looked up. This time the interruption was a little more hesitant.

'The evenings; les nuits. Do you wish to see Paris — at night?'

This question seemed a little loaded, as if it carried with it some special challenge.

'If I have come to see Paris, then should I not see as much of her as I can?'

'Bravo! Bien sûr! So, to your list you must add a visit to La Pigalle — you may take in a show if you choose — and, perhaps, la Rue St Denis.'

'Rue St Denis?'

'I offer it to you, Monsieur, simplement. I say nothing further.' And with that the clock stopped.

From the dresser, Neville thought he could make out the sound of whispering, but when he looked round, the flowers were still and silent. On the table in front of him the paper revealed

DAY ONE: THE CHAMPS ELYSÉES — SHOPPING

DAY TWO: MONTMARTRE — NOTRE DAME

DAY THREE: LOUVRE — MUSÉE D'ORSAY

THE EIFFEL TOWER

As he re-read his list and pondered its appropriateness, there came a knock at the door.

SIX

He opened the door to find the Doorman facing him. Instinctively, Neville looked down half-expecting to see his visitor accompanied by one of the two stone lions from the hotel's entrance.

'Monsieur,' the doorman was alone, 'your taxi is 'ere.'

'My taxi? I wasn't aware that I had ordered a taxi.'

The Doorman said nothing, standing motionless and with the air of a man who was determined to take his charge — however unwilling — down through the hotel and to the waiting cab. Neville recalled the earlier image of the man complete with whip, and decided not to argue the point.

'Just a minute.'

He left the man at the door and walked into the en suite bathroom. Again the air of faded glory: the fixtures were a little worn and ornate, attractive in their own way yet now seeming somewhat over-elaborate.

Sitting on the porcelain toilet, Neville heard a hiss from his right. At the head of the bath, the taps boasted a hand-shower attachment and it was this that was now moving slowly snake-like in the bottom of the bath. A small amount of water dribbled from the steel head.

The attachment stopped moving and looked hard at him, its spray holes combining to form a curious one-eyed stare.

'Off out?'

'Apparently so.'

'You pay good money for facilities like this, yet no sooner do you arrive than you go out! And when will we see you next, eh? Tonight, when you come back — drunk, probably. You'll come in here for a quick piss and then go straight to bed. Have you any idea how neglected that makes us feel? Have you?'

Neville stood and pulled up his trousers. He took objection to being nagged — especially as he might have expected his status as "visitor" to demand a little respect to be shown towards him — but couldn't deny that the shower head might have had a point.

'I'll make full use of you tomorrow. Really.'

'They all say that!'

'Promise. OK?'

The shower head hissed again and turned away from him. Neville expected to find the Doorman still waiting for him, but although the door to the room was still open, there was no-one there. Picking his coat from the chair, he left the room. There was no-one in the hallway outside either, so — ignoring the lift — he made his way down the stairs.

The lobby was also deserted, except for a small figure standing by the entrance, looking through the window onto the street outside. Neville looked behind the desk to see if he could locate the Concierge, but failing to do so decided to take his key with him.

As he walked towards the exit, he could see a bright yellow taxi outside. It had been badly parked, with its two near side wheels up onto the pavement.

Neville had one hand on the revolving door when a voice to his side said, 'Taxi?' It was strange guttural voice, almost as if it had become encrusted with years of prolonged coughing or chest infections. He turned. The voice had come from the figure at the window, and the figure belonged to a toad.

'Sorry?'

'Taxi? You wanted a taxi?'

Again the strange voice. Neville expected the last question to be followed by a kind of croak but it was not; he sensed that might have been suppressed, the only trace a vague and almost inaudible "hic".

'Yes. Thanks.'

He let the toad leave first. He was wearing a bomber jacket with the collar turned up, and a faded baseball cap with the letters "N" and "Y" stitched in white. His legs were adorned with silky track suit bottoms, the legend "St. Etienne" embossed in green down the sides. From a distance, there could be no telling that the owner of the clothes was an amphibian; not from behind at any rate.

Neville followed the toad's odd gait to the car, where a green, three-fingered hand fumbled with the door.

'Great. Thanks.'

The cab had a strange, distinctly saline odour to it. And on the back shelf behind Neville, was a model of a plastic newt with a nodding head. It bobbed caustically at him as he got in.

'Bonjour.'

'Morning.'

By now the driver had managed to get himself into the car and was fiddling with the controls. His apparent lack of dexterity gave Neville little confidence; a concern that was redoubled as the taxi suddenly lurched off the pavement with a bang, and sped out into the traffic. They did not appear to be following too straight a line.

'Champs Elysées, oui?'

'Yes, please.'

The driver looked at Neville in his rear view mirror.

'You OK?'

'Fine, yes.'

They were racing along the street with the driver still looking at Neville rather than at the road. He gave a slight toad-like grin.

'Surprised?'

'At what? Sorry.'

'Me.' And with that the car suddenly lurched around to the left and began to career down another avenue. 'I am a toad, yes?'

'It would appear so, yes.'

'And you are a little surprised, no?'

'A little' — though not as much as he might once have been.

'Special treat for the English. Toad taxi drivers. Get it? Sophisticated French joke, non?'

And with that the toad gave a sudden laugh that sounded like all the plumbing in the entire city had suddenly ceased to function and was belching water and sewage everywhere. Neville smiled politely, but was, by now, too nervous to laugh. From behind him he heard the newt whimper "Oh, shit" and when he turned he found its head had been withdrawn into its hollow body and was nowhere to be seen.

It now appeared that they were travelling at least twice as fast as any other vehicle on the road, and the toad seemed determined not to change his driving style — if it might be called that — in order to accommodate anyone. Neville thought about saying something, complaining even, but felt that to distract the toad now might actually end up being his last ever action: "3B" a little prematurely perhaps.

Within a short while — though to Neville it felt like a period of torture — the Arc de Triomphe was in sight and the toad spun the taxi out onto its mesmerising roundabout without a moment's hesitation. Suddenly the Champs Elysées stretched before them. The taxi bounded on for a hundred yards or so then suddenly dived to the right and came to a screeching halt on the pavement. Neville could smell the burnt rubber. He handed over some cash, uncertain of its value or the amount actually required. The toad checked it and seemed satisfied.

'OK. Get out.'

'Thanks.'

'I should have a cognac if I were you,' and with those words of advice hardly uttered, the toad rammed the taxi into gear and speed out into the traffic again, the door from which Neville had exited flapping and banging against the side of the cab where he had not even had time to close it.

Conveniently, the taxi had dropped him immediately outside a café. Even though its pavement tables were very busy, it appeared that the rather alarming manner of his arrival had gone unnoticed. There was a table free near the front of the terrace area and, as Neville made his way to it and sat down, he decided that if the toad's driving might not be much to write home about, then his advice could well prove worth taking.

The waiter — a stiff individual who gave every impression of having an ironing board shoved down the back of his jacket — was at his side in an instant, offering him a napkin and some cutlery. Neville raised his hand and smiled politely.

'No thank you. Just a coffee — and a cognac, please.'

'Au lait?'

'Thank you, yes.'

Leaving the napkin, the waiter removed the cutlery and disappeared into the café.

Relaxing a little in anticipation of the cognac, Neville eased himself a little further back in his chair and began to take in the scene. As he did so, he realised that the occupants of the table to this left — two suited businessmen

— had indeed taken an interest in his arrival and were evidently talking about him.

'Poor English Bastard! That old toad-driver stunt gets them every time!'

'Bet his pissed his little white panties, don't you?'

Both men laughed.

'Now watch the waiter sting him for his drinks. Here he comes!'

Neville was considering speaking to the men (though what he might have said was uncertain, especially as doubts about his command of the language were returning) when the waiter reappeared with his coffee and brandy. He pulled a note from his wallet and handed it to the waiter, who nodded, then disappeared.

'Told you! That's the last he'll see of that!'

The two men laughed heartily again then rose. They exchanged pleasantries with another couple nearby and then moved away. As they did so, one of them brushed Neville's shoulder.

'Excuse me. Terribly sorry.'

The accent was impeccably English.

'That's quite all right, really.'

Once the two men had gone — they lingered on the pavement for a moment, shook hands, then went their separate ways — Neville took up his coffee and scanned the boulevard.

The avenue was, of course, busy and bustling. Six lanes of traffic pulsated in that stop-go way major arteries do, punctuated all the while by the tell-tale repetition of yellow taxis. For a few moments Neville concentrated on these, to see if he could count the number of toad drivers there were; or indeed, if there were any other members of the animal kingdom who had taken up the hackney carriage as an occupation. He gave up after a while, a little disappointed to find his search inconclusive.

People moved about the pavement in seemingly ever greater numbers; a pavement which might well have benefited from the kind of markings which attempted to impose some modest discipline upon the traffic. In just in a few seconds, he witnessed numerous bumps and near misses, and soon picked out the many phrases of "Excuse me" or "Pardon" which accompanied them.

It was obviously a wealthy street in a wealthy city. Many of the women were wearing fur coats, and such a large proportion of the men were adorned in sharp and fashionable casual clothes that he might have been forgiven for mistaking half the population as members of the modelling profession.

The coffee tasted wonderful — "really French", Neville thought — and half way through this he took his first sip of the cognac, which warmed him even more than the coffee. He felt himself sigh internally. Yes, he had imagined Paris to be like this.

After a few minutes, a pony and trap pulled to a temporary halt outside the café. It was a ride for tourists, taking them for a one-way trip along the Champs Elysées. The driver had dismounted from the trap and was now collecting his fare from two middle-aged American ladies who were struggling with their French and, in consequence, offering the man less than half the standard tariff. The driver simply spoke slower and louder. Neville had thought it was only the English who did that.

The horse, which had for a brief moment shown some interest in the negotiations, now turned his attention to Neville.

'Having a nice time?'

'Yes, thanks. You?'

'Oh, so so.' The horse attempted to shrug his harnessed shoulders — presumably much in the manner of his master — but simply succeeded in rattling his hooves on the tarmac. 'You know; up and down, up and down. Still, I suppose it's better than being sliced up and served to voracious Italians.'

'So I would imagine.'

The horse looked back at the driver. Negotiations were coming to a conclusion.

'Fancy a ride? Down to the Louvre, perhaps?'

'Not today. But thanks anyway.'

'Sure. It's nothing.' And with that, the horse and trap moved sedately off, the driver looking for their next customers.

Neville finished the last of his coffee and chased it down with the remainder of the cognac. Remembering the bill, he looked around for the waiter who had served him. He could not see him. He waited for a few moments then, with casual resignation, gave up on getting any change, rose, and walked onto the pavement proper.

To his left, the Arc de Triomphe stood large and proud against the skyline, with the heads of visitors who had climbed the monument just visible at the very top. To his right was the long stretch of the tree-lined avenue, and it was in this direction he decided to go.

SEVEN

He had not gone very far when he decided to cross the road. There appeared to be a greater variety of things to see on the other side of the avenue, and so with this in mind he walked to the edge of the pavement and came to a halt.

The traffic roared past him at ever increasing speeds such that crossing on foot began to look nothing short of suicidal. He waited for a few seconds, trying to catch a break in the onrushing wave of cars, but still they came like an unstoppable tide.

'Monsieur! Monsieur!'

From somewhere above his head a voice called down to him, and Neville looked up to discover a man in the cage-like bucket of a small mobile crane suspended some twenty feet off the ground.

'Yes?'

'You wish to cross the road, no?'

'Actually I do, yes. But it's very busy.'

'Eh! It is always busy. People have died trying to cross here. Morte, n'est-ce pas? Perhaps I can help you.'

With this the man signalled to his partner sitting in the cab parked in the centre of the road. Immediately the basket began to descend. Once at pavement level, the man opened the gate and beckoned Neville on-board.

'We are checking the street lights, and this little machine' — he tapped the cage — 'means that we don't have to climb ladders all day long!'

'Very useful.'

By this time they were already off the ground and swinging out over the speeding traffic.

'They drive very fast,' Neville offered to his host, keeping a special eye on the taxis.

'Fast? Bien sûr; they are French, monsieur!'

Within a few moments they were out across the centre of the road (Neville remembering a wave of gratitude to the man in the cab) and on their way to the other side. As they began their descent, Neville noticed that the pavement he had just left now seemed the more bustling and attractive. However, it was too late to go back.

With a bump they hit ground.

'That was very kind of you,' Neville said, as he stepped from the cradle.

'My pleasure. Always happy to help an American.' And with that the workman was up again, once more aloft and brushing the branches of the trees.

Neville continued his walk away from the Arc de Triomphe. He strolled slowly, relaxing as the cognac took effect, not a little hopeful that the drama of this extraordinary day might be over.

The shops promised a variety of delights: clothes shops with immaculately turned out mannequins displaying chic beyond most people's wildest dreams; music shops pumping out popular songs by renowned international singers; jewellery shops, glittering in the mid-afternoon sun. And punctuated between these, the terrace cafés where occasionally all three — chic, jewellery, and fame — would come together as the rich and famous paraded themselves as if they too were part of one gigantic shopping experience.

Neville only browsed in the windows. He had no desire to go into any of the clothes shops — he had not forgotten his tuxedo, but Paris he had decided, was not the place to buy it — and music shops held little fascination for him.

After a short while, he came to the entrance of an arcade which seemed to offer something a little different. Inside was a plaza populated by small shops of myriad variety, and a number of mobile stalls selling everything from perfume to parasols. He thought of Covent Garden. Perhaps every capital city had its own version.

He had been looking at some silk handkerchiefs on one of the stalls, when a voice called to him from the barrow alongside.

'Psst! Over here!'

Following the call, he found himself looking at a display of earrings, brooches, and general ornamental trinkets. He smiled noncommittally at the stall holder, who smiled back. The voice had not been hers.

'Hey! Here!'

Neville was beginning to gain some experience in locating disembodied voices by now, and his semi-trained gaze turned to a small tray of brooches and badges. Apart from the standard jewelled offerings, there were a number of slightly more unusual objects on offer; one of these was a small brooch boasting the white painted face of a Pierrot.

'Monsieur; how are you?'

'Very well, thank you.'

Neville looked up at the stall holder and smiled again, just to affirm that she would not be concerned over his conversing with an item of her stock. She nodded back with a little more conviction than before, perhaps entertaining the idea that she might soon have a sale.

'How has your day been so far?'

'My day? Pretty eventful, I guess.'

'You like Paris?'

'It's my first visit, and this is my first day, so it's a bit early to say — but yes, I think I do.'

'Sure you do! That is good.'

Neville began to glance at some of the other items when the Pierrot called him back.

'Hey! Need a guide?'

'A guide?'

'To Paris, while you are here. Can't do worse than ask a native!'

There was something about the Pierrot's accent which suggested that its birthplace could be called into question; the lilt, if it could be called that, was more American than French.

'Are you offering?'

'I'm your man! I know this city inside out; you just tell me what you want to see and I'll show it to you. I'll even show you some of the things you don't know you want to see!'

'May I?' Neville extended his hand in order to pick the brooch from the tray.

'Sure.' And the badge winked at him as he lifted him in his palm. 'Not so heavy am I? And you could wear me on your lapel; that way I'd be nice and close to give you a commentary whenever you wanted.'

The lady behind the stall had now risen and was smiling hopefully at Neville.

'Deal?' The Pierrot asked hopefully.

'Deal,' Neville said, and asked the woman the price. He pulled some notes from his wallet and handed them over. She smiled again.

'Thank you, Monsieur.'

Neville eased the pin from the Pierrot's fastening and attached it to his jacket collar.

'Hey! Thanks man, that's great!'

Neville thanked the stall holder again, and continued to wander around the stalls in the arcade, all the while the pierrot chattering excitedly and full of generally useless information. Neville stopped walking.

'Look...'

'Pierre. Can you believe it?! Pierre the Pierrot. Some people have no imagination!'

'OK Pierre, do me a favour; I know you're pretty excited, but can you keep the chatter down — maybe restrict yourself to giving me advice when it's obvious I need it, or if I ask you something. Is that OK?'

'Sure, that's fine. But...' Pierre paused.

'My name's Neville.'

'Neville, we will just chat sometimes, yeah?'

'Of course.'

'Good,' Pierre paused again. 'Neville; that's not a French name is it?'

'Pierre.'

'Yes, Neville?'

'Shut up.'

'Oops!' And in the reflection of a shop window full of cheap imported Chinese T-shirts, Neville saw Pierre smile a little.

Within a few minutes Neville completed his tour of the arcade and made his way back to the street. To his surprise it was now dark, and the Champs Elysées was already brightly lit by cafés, cars, and street lamps. The suddenness of the vision took Neville aback a little and he came to a halt on the pavement.

'Pretty, n'est-ce pas?' Pierre offered.

'Yes, very.'

There was something magical about the place. People still thronged the pavements, cars still raced up and down the avenue; yet the myriad of lights against the darkness gave the whole experience a different tone.

'Where too, Monsieur?'

'Any thoughts, Pierre?'

'A little night life perhaps?'

'Why not?'

A bright yellow cab pulled up in response to Neville's raised arm. Once bitten, he bent low to get a good look at the driver before opening the rear passenger door. This time all seemed normal.

When seated, the driver looked at him in the mirror and uttered a low guttural grunt rather than anything as intelligible as an enquiry about his destination.

'Rue St. Dennis', Pierre whispered, and Neville echoed this back to the driver.

Again there was nothing more than a murmur in response. Neville wondered if he might now be receiving the treatment normally reserved for Parisian natives; he could certainly equate the attitude with a number of Birmingham taxi drivers he had encountered.

Briefly they headed up the Champs Elysées towards the Triomphe, then pulled right and headed into the city. Pierre — as good as his word — was dutifully silent, except when his role as guide demanded he make a little professional interjection to point out some feature or other to his client. Thus, as they drove past the brightly lit Opera, Pierre offered a potted guide to the building that took all of seven seconds, yet seemed to Neville as if he had been told all he would ever need to know about the place.

'Boulevard Haussmann', Pierre offered as they entered a broad street, lined on both sides by more shops and more cafés, each providing their own particular illumination of the scene. Neville tried to recollect an image of Paris that he had locked away somewhere in his memory.

'I know the painting you mean, but that is of another avenue on the south of the river.' Evidently, Pierre could read minds too.

After a few more minutes the taxi pulled to a halt and Neville handed his fare to the less than monosyllabic driver. As he stood and watched the taxi pull away, he felt disappointed by the ride, as if it had offered him little and added nothing to his experience. Perhaps he was simply beginning to expect too much.

'So, what now? What is this "Rue St Dennis"?'

'What or where?' Pierre teased. 'Where? It is just there, fifty metres ahead on the right. What? It is Paris!'

Neville walked on, allowing Pierre his cryptic indulgence because he was so boastfully a Parisian, and because he professed to love his city so much. They passed a small shop which was in darkness, and a café that was less lustrous than those he had seen earlier. Indeed, he began to realise that they were now in a markedly less fashionable area.

On the corner of Rue St Dennis, Neville stopped. Their destination appeared to be nothing more than a side street; indeed, it was sufficiently narrow for it to be one-way only to traffic, though this did not deny it a steady, if somewhat subdued, flow of vehicles. There were also a fair number of people strolling along its pavements. The whole picture was of a darker and slower Paris that he had seen thus far.

Without waiting for the prompt he sensed was on the verge of Pierre's lips, Neville began to walk down the street, adjusting his pace in accordance with his fellow pedestrians. After a few yards, he had seen nothing at all inspiring.

'Pierre.'

'Monsieur?'

'What am I supposed to be doing here?'

Pierre laughed quietly.

'For now Monsieur, just looking.'

'Looking? At what?'

'Across the street, now; what do you see?'

'People walking. A couple of girls talking in a doorway. That's about it.'

'And the girls?' Pierre's whispered glee betrayed him as almost revelling in some kind of private game. 'What do you notice about the girls?'

Neville glanced across again.

'They are quite young, I suppose. Attractive, too. What of that?'

'And their clothes?'

Both were wearing short skirts and skimpy blouses that seemed a little risqué.

'A little provocative perhaps.'

'Now Monsieur; watch!'

And as Neville slowed his gait a little, he saw a man approach the two girls. After a few seconds talking, the man and one of the girls disappeared through the door outside of which she had been standing.

'Perhaps in a few minutes he will be out — and with a smile on his face too!' And with that, Pierre gave a low whistle.

Neville's recognition of the situation came as suddenly to him as the night had come to the Champs Elysées. The girls were of course prostitutes, and the street was full of them. He looked back over his shoulder: he had already walked past at least four doorways with two or three girls standing in each. Ahead — no more than ten yards ahead — there was another.

'Ah,' Pierre exclaimed with hushed enthusiasm, 'the centime has dropped, n'est-ce pas? Now, do not appear interested Monsieur; a casual glance, no more. Remember you are a tourist, not a customer!'

With that advice — and he *had* asked Pierre for advice — they approached the next group. Neville glanced, for the briefest of seconds, to see three girls again dressed in very little (hot pants appeared to vie with miniskirts for favouritism) and all dissembled being disinterested in the passers-by. Without exception they were young and attractive.

'Amazing,' Neville confessed as soon as they were past.

'Magnifique, yes?'

'Compared to England; the girls here appear so beautiful, and so aloof.'

'That is their skill, Monsieur; because they are Parisienne. They can all make themselves attractive, it is their magic. And aloof? Non! They have a kind of radar, yes? They can sense a customer, always. And when they fish, they never fail to catch. You understand?'

'I think so, Pierre.'

There was a brief pause. Neville noticed a policeman controlling traffic a little further down the street.

'Ah yes. The government is also Parisienne. It knows that she cannot stop this, so she looks after it, takes care of the girls; there is no trouble here. It is very safe. And for the customer too.'

Had Pierre been able to, Neville felt certain that at this point he would have felt an elbow dig into his ribs. Pierre had made a distinction between tourist and customer, yet perhaps if Neville had decided to "trade up" then the Pierrot's poorly disguised secret project might have been a complete success. But Pierre had no arms, and in any event, at this precise moment, Neville would not have felt the prod at all.

He had come to a complete halt on the pavement and was staring, quite blatantly, across to the other side of the road. Heading in the opposite direction to him — but separated by some twelve feet of tarmac — was the most stunning woman Neville had ever seen in his life. She was tall and slim, with long dark hair. Her face was not classically beautiful, but simply captivating, and she walked with a confidence and pride that added to her aura. As she was wearing a long flowing coat, he could see little else of her — apart from exquisite ankles above small leather boots. Indeed, in the half-light of this particular street, even the colour of the coat was denied him.

'Monsieur. Neville!'

Neville was roused by Pierre's voice and a bump delivered by a passing pedestrian. He was in the way. He apologised automatically. When he looked across again, the woman was nowhere to be seen.

'Monsieur!'

'Did you see her, Pierre?'

'Who?'

'You know who I mean! You can read my mind can't you?'

'Unfortunately at this time, yes I can.'

'Who is she?'

'Who is she?' Pierre paused for a split second. 'Do you mean, do I know her? Or does she "work" here?' He paused again. 'Perhaps. But we should go, yes?'

Neville did not want to go, but he could see no sign of her and he sensed that his dithering might be rousing a degree of interest in the other girls.

'If you would like a little more night life, we could try La Pigalle. More wonderful Paris!'

'Not tonight. Perhaps tomorrow. I think I would just like to go back to the hotel.'

And accompanying those words, another yellow taxi pulled to Neville's side and he got in.

EIGHT

Neville awoke to the sound of the telephone at the side of his bed. It rang three times and was then silent. On his return to the hotel the previous evening he had arranged an alarm call and that triple chime was, he assumed, the result.

The room was still dark, the heavy curtains keeping out most of the early morning light. It seemed quiet too, so perhaps they kept noise at bay as well. For a few moments he lay still, allowing his mind to retrace the events of the previous day. He recalled the Champs Elysées and Pierre — his jacket hung on a hook at the back of the door — and remembered the Rue St Dennis and the raven-haired woman he had briefly glimpsed there.

He smiled to himself. Appropriate, was it not? After all, wasn't Paris supposed to be a romantic city, full of chance encounters? Not that the woman had really been any kind of 'encounter' at all; an encounter assumes some kind of contact, rather than a one-way stare across a one-way street. Still it was a memory for Neville to lock away for the future, whatever that might be — and however long it might last.

Getting out of bed, he went into the bathroom and began to run a bath.

From his room came a knock at the door. He grabbed a complementary bath robe, donned it, and answered the door. A young maid stood there with a small tray: his breakfast. He had not ordered breakfast in bed, but perhaps the service was standard here.

'Good morning, Monsieur.'

'Morning. Could you put it on the bed please?'

He watched the girl as she walked in, placed the tray on the bed, then left. He wondered, as he took a bite out of a warm chocolate-filled croissant, how often the maid — a pretty if slight young thing — had been propositioned in the line of duty; her job could take her into dangerous territory. Then — more abstractly — he wondered if he might not be chewing on a chunk of one of Maurice's "relatives".

The coffee — which was piping hot — brought back a memory of the café he had visited the previous day, and also — for a fleeting moment — an image of Mirelle. From the sublime to the ridiculous.

Neville carried the coffee and the remains of his first croissant into the bathroom. The bath was nearly full. He checked the temperature of the water, stuffed the last of the croissant into his mouth, slipped out of the bath robe and into the bath. The shower head, which had been motionless a few moments before, began to unwind as soon as Neville turned off the water.

'Made it then?' the shower head said as it joined Neville in the bath, lying along one side, fixing him with its one-eyed stare.

'Apparently.'

'Good time last night? Didn't hear you come in.'

Neville choose to ignore this rather grumpy line of enquiry and looked around for the soap and shampoo.

'Behind you; small green bottle.'

'Thanks.'

'Not as good as the stuff they used to give guests here, but then I suppose it's a sign of the times.'

Neville cupped some water in his hands and doused his hair. The shower head wriggled uncomfortably.

'Hey, what's wrong with me? That's my job.'

'Really?' And again Neville poured water on his hair from his cupped hands. He couldn't be certain why, but he was in no mood to be nagged at; he wanted to be in control.

He unscrewed the cap from the small green bottle and poured some of the shampoo into his hair. As the cold gel began to run against his scalp he started to massage it in, creating a reasonable rather than luxurious lather. By this time the shower head was beginning to get excited, and its originally rather relaxed movements had begun to get more and more exaggerated.

'Okay, okay!' it hissed, 'Now you have to use me!'

'"Have to"?' And Neville made to fill his cupped hands with water again.

'I'll give your scalp a really healthy massage too. Pulsating jets; no extra cost. Come on!'

Neville pulled the shower head from the water, then turned the knob on the tap unit. After a slight splutter, water gushed out of the shower head with a satisfied hiss.

True to its word, the shower head delivered pulsating jets of water firmly into Neville's scalp as he rubbed. The soap suds flew away, and Neville could feel his head tingle under the refreshing barrage. After a few seconds the rinsing was over, and Neville was able to turn the water off and return the shower head to its resting position.

'Hey, wasn't that good?' It dripped enthusiastically. 'Best shower head this side of the river.'

Neville slipped down in the bath — which was actually very long — so that only his head remained above the surface of the water.

'So what's on the agenda today, Monsieur?'

'Today?' Neville remembered his itinerary. 'Montmartre and Notre Dame I believe; but I'll have to check with my guide.'

'Your guide?'

'Yes. A little badge; called Pierre. Picked him up yesterday.'

'No a pierrot by any chance?'

Neville was a little surprised.

'Yes. Why?'

'You know what a pierrot is, Monsieur?'

'A clown, of sorts.'

'Of sorts, yes. But from a pantomime. And sometimes these pierrot are not what they seem.'

'Meaning?'

'Just be careful, Monsieur. In French pantomime the clown often makes others look the fool, rather than himself. You understand? I don't know about your Pierre, but I have heard stories; that is all.' And with a final dribble, the shower head uttered its last hiss and was suddenly motionless.

Neville remained in the bath a little while longer, and then pulled the plug and rose. Within a few minutes he had demolished the remains of his breakfast and dressed. It was only on this second morning, as he prepared for another day in Paris, that he noticed how well packed his suitcases had been and the appropriateness of the clothes they contained.

Having consulted some of the tourist pamphlets provided with the room, Neville pulled his jacket from the door. The badge still in place, the movement woke Pierre. The pierrot gave a long yawn.

'Bonjour, Monsieur. Did you sleep well?'

'The sleep of the just.'

'Pardon?'

'Sorry; English saying.'

'That's OK.'

'Tell me,' the shower head's words were fresh in his mind, 'I've been wondering; what kind of role does the pierrot have in French theatre?'

'Role, Monsieur?'

'What do you actually do?'

'Do?' Pierre paused. 'We are clowns — I think that is your English word. We make people laugh, enjoy themselves; that is the point of pantomime.'

'And who do they laugh at, you?'

Pierre paused slightly.

'I understand in your English theatre the clown is something of an idiot, non? Ridiculous, comical. In French we are a little more subtle, with a little — excuse moi — "savoir faire".'

Neville said nothing further, but walked to his bedside table to pick up his wallet.

'Why do you ask, Monsieur?'

'Oh, just interested.'

Five minutes later they were walking through the foyer of the hotel. A bell boy came over.

'Can I get you a taxi, Monsieur?'

'No thank you. I'll walk a little first.'

The boy nodded, and disappeared behind the Concierge's desk.

'Walk?' Pierre seemed a little surprised.

'For some fresh air,' Neville explained, as they left the building, 'It's good for me. Now, which way?'

'Left, Monsieur. But where are we going?'

'I thought history was on the list today; Montmartre, Notre Dame...'

'And later?'

'Pierre; one thing at a time. Now, are we going in the right direction?'

'Bien sûr.'

Neville walked on. It was relatively early and the city was, to a large extent, still waking up. Shutters rolled up on shop windows as he passed them, and buses rumbled by full of people on their way to work. Always there was the sound of car horns, and the flash of speeding taxis. Neville suddenly thought of Samuel, and wondered what he would be doing during his three days here.

At the next junction Neville waited for the traffic lights to change so that he might cross safely. He noticed a MacDonald's restaurant on the far corner, and heard the rattle of the metro as it passed nearby. He closed his eyes for a moment and remembered his six years in London. He had met Mirelle at a party in Hammersmith.

'Monsieur, the lights.'

Neville crossed on command, then paused.

'OK Pierre; Notre Dame or Montmartre first?'

'That depends Monsieur on a number of things, but given the general time of day and the weather etcetera, I would suggest Notre Dame.'

'Taxi?'

'Bien sûr.'

Within minutes he was once again ensconced in a yellow cab heading across town.

When they reached Notre Dame, large and looming against the skyline, Neville was surprised to find only a few tourists loitering in its precincts.

'It is early, Monsieur. In Paris we are a little more enthusiastic for the late nights rather than the early mornings.'

He had read a little about the cathedral from one of the guides in his hotel room and expected much from the rose windows, the vaulting architecture, and the view from the top of the tower — especially after the five hundred steps it took to get there. Each of these expectations was met with a little disappointment. He had visited Chartres once with Mirelle and remembered the glory of the windows. Here he found nothing awesome in the architecture, and the view could in no way match that initial sighting of the city from the rickety old bus when they rounded the road on the hill.

When he left the cathedral and found himself in bright sunlight again, he wondered if the day was due to be one of disappointment and anti-climax.

'That is up to you, Monsieur,' Pierre offered. The pierrot had been a dutiful if somewhat subdued guide during their tour of Notre Dame, and Neville had sensed his boredom. Where Pierre's passion lay was all too evident.

'So.' Neville said, open-endedly.

'Monsieur?'

'And now? What shall we do now?'

'You are a little bored, non?'

'A little.'

'And Montmartre? She is still on your list?'

Neville nodded.

'But perhaps a coffee first.'

Pierre directed him to a small café nearby where Neville — sitting inside rather than on the pavement this time — ordered a coffee and a small pastry described by his guide as "one of the best in all Paris". In the event, that proved an exaggeration too, but at least the coffee did not let him down.

He was preparing to leave — the coffee was finished and he had begun to address himself mentally to the prospect of Montmartre — when he saw a woman across the far side of the café who looked vaguely familiar. She had just risen from her table (where she had been sitting alone) and was chatting to the waiter who had served her.

'Pierre?'

'Monsieur?'

'That woman; over there, walking to the door.'

'Oui?'

'Do I know her?'

It seemed a ridiculous question, and he had no time to retrieve it.

'Do you know anyone in Paris, Monsieur?'

Neville ignored the rhetorical nature of Pierre's reply. There seemed something about the woman as she moved, in her attitude. For a moment, although she appeared very different — almost blonde hair, for instance — he was certain it was the same woman from the Rue St. Dennis.

'Pierre, is it her again? The woman from last night?'

'How can I say, Monsieur?' And Neville felt the word "perhaps" form on Pierre's lips but then fall silently away, unspoken.

He rose sharply from the table, pulling a note from his wallet as he did so, and walked to the door. Once outside he looked around, knowing his search would be in vain.

And so it proved. The crowds had thickened all the while he had been in the café, and finding someone amidst this new, animated throng was impossible. Neville thought briefly about Pierre's attitude to the woman, his lack of assistance, the warning he had received in his bathroom just a couple of hours ago... He was suddenly not happy.

'Taxi,' he said, almost as a command, and turned his back on the cathedral and the crowd in the square.

NINE

By the time he reached Montmartre, Neville had calmed down and was in possession of a more even temper. The journey across the city had not been particularly quick, which, under the circumstances, had probably been a good thing. Pierre had been noticeably silent throughout, not even offering the briefest of guide-book commentary.

The taxi dropped Neville off at the foot of a long hill which led up to the white church that dominated the summit. Ahead were two parallel chains of steps that zigzagged in a mirror image to the top. He was struck by the whiteness of the whole scene, and — as he placed his foot upon the first of the steps — the strangely solid nature of the stone.

At various stages, the steps were broken by large plateaux. These were populated with bench seats, boys playing impromptu games of football, and North Africans selling trinkets from brightly coloured blankets. Neville paused at one selling necklaces made from various materials; coral, ivory, wood. As their owner chattered away, the necklaces writhed in time with the music from a nearby ghetto blaster whose owner was busy showing off his break-dancing skills.

As they left the necklaces to move on, Neville detected a sound from Pierre that appeared less than approving.

'Something wrong, Pierre?'

'Monsieur?'

'You don't approve of these people selling things here?'

'The selling? Mais oui. The people, perhaps non.'

'Why? Because they are not French?'

Pierre said nothing. Neville assumed an affirmative answer.

'But I thought Paris was proud of her multi-cultural background; of the variety it brought to the city.'

'But these people are scum — pardonnez moi, but I have to say it. They turn areas of our city into slums. They do not know how to live like Parisians!' Pierre paused. 'But is it not the same in England?'

'The same?'

'Do you not have ethnics too? Are there not problems?'

'Yes. And there are problems. But we must try to overcome them.'

Neville realised that he was in danger of sounding like a politician, and almost forgave Pierre the Gallic sigh that closed the conversation. A thump in the back from a football just at that moment also helped to terminate the debate. He turned to seek out the offending footballer, only to find the area deserted — except for the football which was trying to slink away unnoticed. From somewhere in the bushes Neville heard someone say "Gazza", and then muffled laughter.

Suddenly taken by a desire for boyish revenge, he set his sights on the football, took one stride forward, then aimed at the bushes. With a strange "crack!" he sent the ball flying towards the undergrowth where it arrived with such velocity that there immediately came the sounds of breaking branches and the faint smell of singed wood.

'Very good, Monsieur!' Pierre was impressed.

Neville — resisting the temptation to relate the story of his schoolboy soccer prowess (which was average at best) — resumed his climb to the top of the hill. As he neared Sacré-Cœur, it seemed to grow ever larger before his eyes, its whiteness becoming brighter all the while.

Pierre had obviously relaxed a little thanks to the incident with the football, and was once again offering stories about Saints and Martyrs — and how, after each of whom, there was at least one avenue in the city named to commemorate them.

The cathedral was quiet and peaceful. Neville noticed the difference between his first impression here, and that from Note Dame just an hour or so earlier.

'We are lucky, Monsieur,' Pierre offered, 'there is a service.'

In the body of the church, a few dozen people sat listening to a priest talking to them quietly. Neville remarked the lack of microphones which seemed to dominate modern English churches.

He made his way round to one side, glancing alternately between the service — to which he was getting closer — and the statues and figures set within the fabric of the walls. By a large pillar he paused.

'What kind of service is it, Pierre; a wedding?'

'Non, Monsieur. I believe it is the taking of vows by some novices from a Monastery in the country. Sometimes they come here, just for this purpose.'

'So they're tourists too?' Neville suggested a little facetiously.

'Non. They are more than that, n'est-ce pas?'

'Yes; sorry.'

Neville resumed his walk which had now taken him a little ahead of the front row of pews. As he glanced back he saw seven young men, each dressed in brown, intently listening to the words of the Priest. He tried to interpret, but could understand little of the ecclesiastic litany. Strangely, however, he felt a sense of peace in the voice of the older man, as if he were imparting years of experience upon his young charges.

Then, as he finished speaking, the young men rose as one and began to hum a Gregorian chant. The melody was taken up by those sitting behind them, with strange harmonies being added from all around the church. Even the statues seemed to be contributing their voices. Standing silently, Neville became enveloped in a wave of emotion transmitted through the echoes and harmonics of the building.

This lasted for a few minutes, and then the young men sat down — their habits now changed to a radiant and peaceful blue — and the priest began speaking again.

'Magnifique, n'est-ce pas?' said Pierre, who had obviously been affected by the spectacle too.

'Marvellous, yes.'

'And only in Paris, Monsieur; only in Paris.'

Neville wandered for a little longer, his visit punctuated by the occasional deep bass of the organ. By the time he regained the sunlight outside, he found himself in a much more relaxed mood.

'And now?'

'Maintenant, la Place du Tertre!'

'Where the painters are?'

'Oui, Monsieur. Another famous Parisian institution.'

'But,' Neville paused, leaning against a balustrade and looking down the steps to the base of the hill and the city below, 'there is Art tomorrow, isn't there? The Louvre...'

'The Musée d'Orsay,' Pierre prompted.

'Yes. Of course. So more paintings today?'

'But Monsieur, one does not go to the Place du Tertre for the paintings; one goes for the atmosphere, for the spectacle. And I know a small café...'

'Where they do a fantastic pastry, n'est-ce pas?'

Pierre said nothing for a moment, and Neville sensed a degree of embarrassment in his guide.

'Where is it?'

'Ah, nearby. Ten minutes, no more! Just down the hill, to the far side of Sacré-Cœur.'

Neville left the Cathedral behind and made his way down a side street. Pierre's directions took him to a small cobbled lane where the houses seemed to belong to a different age, their slightly misshapen windows and doors giving him an echo of Charles Dickens' London — something he dared not mention to Pierre for fear of offence.

After a few minutes, the crowd began to thicken perceptibly, and Neville emerged into a small vibrantly coloured square filled with people. At its centre was an inner rectangle defined by trees and lined with artist after artist working at their easels and surrounded by examples of their work. In the centre of the square — and all around its outskirts — dozens of café tables. Between artists and cafés, two streams of voyeurs made their respective clockwise and anticlockwise progress, watching the craftsmen in action and, in turn, being watched by those at the café tables.

Apart from the colour of the scene — which was quite unlike anything Neville had experienced before — he was struck by the volume of noise, which seemed quite extraordinary. It was the sound of conversation multiplied a hundred-fold, and backed by wave upon wave of music emanating from the buildings.

There were many different styles of work on display, many undoubtedly honed to exploit the market they were designed to serve. Certain styles seemed to appeal to the visitors, and the instant portrait in charcoal was a popular attraction. It did not take Neville long to realise that he was not looking at "great art", and the last thing he wanted to do was to spoil the day he had planned for tomorrow.

'Where's this café, Pierre?'

When no immediate response came, he looked to his lapel to see Pierre in conversation with the portrait of a pierrot resident on an easel by which he was standing. It could almost have been Pierre looking in a mirror.

'Pierre.'

'Pardon, Monsieur. An old friend.'

Neville accepted the apology, and though he did not quite understand it, decided not to push for an explanation.

'The café?'

'We are here, voila!'

The establishment Pierre was referring to appeared to be the oldest and shabbiest on the square. For a moment he thought to question his guide's judgement, but just then a little old man appeared from inside the café and ushered Neville to one of the empty tables. He sat down facing the painters, ordered a coffee and pastry (again in accordance with Pierre's suggestion) and settled to watch the crowds.

His time in Paris seemed punctuated by cafés, coffee and food, and he wondered if this was a reflection on him or on the city. When it came, the coffee was as reliable as always and — this time — the pastry remarkably good. Pierre chatted a little, but gradually became silent. Neville, relaxing in the warmth of the day, began to soak up the atmosphere.

Almost directly in front of him sat one of the charcoal portrait artists. He was busy at a new piece, but had no customers at present. Neville glanced over the examples of the artist's work on display and was suddenly surprised to notice a drawing of Mirelle staring back at him. It was not a recent work — she looked a little too young for that, a little too much how he would have liked to remember her — but there could be no doubt that it was indeed her. With a start, he suddenly realised that there were other people there whom he knew; there was even a drawing of Samuel (who until this moment had slipped from his mind) sporting a natty French beret and Breton shirt.

Neville took another sip of coffee and wondered if he should ask Pierre what was going on. And then he remembered that Pierre could read his mind so there was little point. Presumably, as he had volunteered nothing, Pierre had nothing to offer. Or chose to offer nothing.

In front of him, the artist rose from his small seat. As he did so, Neville saw the face of the woman he'd seen on Rue St Dennis staring back at him from a drawing which, until that moment, had been obscured from his view. He felt an arrow slice through him. She was truly amazing. For a second he froze.

'Magnifique!'

Pierre's voice interrupted him, and Neville looked up to suddenly find himself focusing on his own face, there in charcoal, being presented to him by the artist. Yes, it was his face, but it was a strange face too. There was something about it Neville failed to recognise, as if it were him from another time; past or future he was uncertain.

'Every visitor should have one,' Pierre extolled, 'and such value!'

Neville went to his wallet and offered the artist some cash, which he took with a slight smile and handed over the portrait in return.

'I thought you might like that, as a souvenir,' Pierre said.

'You asked him to do this?'

'Monsieur; it is my city, this café and this seat was my choice. I wanted you to have this.'

And Neville looked up to see that the artist — and all his works — had vanished, and now someone else occupied his place. He was not surprised, but began to wonder again exactly how much control Pierre had over him.

Neville rolled up the portrait carefully and slid it inside the cardboard tube he had also been given. Dusk was falling, and for the first time that day, Neville felt a slight chill in the breeze. The crowds had begun to thin, and one by one the artists were packing up their wares. Things seemed to disappear rather than be put away, their owners more like magicians.

He watched two portraits conversing in front of him: one was of an attractive, bare-torsoed young man; the other a young woman, tears welling in her eyes. The drawing styles were different, and they were obviously about to be parted.

'Good night, my Darling', said the woman, stifling a sniffle.

'Tomorrow, perhaps,' came the reply.

'Can you persuade him to stand here again?'

'I can't be sure; today we took very little money. He may want to try somewhere else.'

A woman appeared; evidently she was the owner of the female portrait, which she lifted from the ground.

'À bientôt, my sweet,' and in a moment the portrait had gone, gathered up in an armful of others.

'Monsieur?'

The familiar voice of Pierre broke into the closing of the scene. Neville rose, and threw some money on the café table.

'Monsieur?'

'Yes, Pierre?'

'She we go to la Pigalle now? There is much to see there.'

Neville walked into the centre of the now deserted square. All the artists had gone, all the café tables were empty, the lights hanging in the trees were dim. Without the magic, there was nothing. He felt the portrait in his hand.

'No, Pierre. I just want to go back to the hotel.'

Pierre remained silent. Neville wondered whether the pierrot was aware how tired he felt or if he recognised the sense of doubt — about Paris, about his future — that had suddenly come upon him.

Neville looked up, hopeful of seeing a battered old yellow bus waiting for him on the street corner, Samuel standing by its door. But there was no bus; and Neville felt strangely alone except for memories of the past and dubious premonitions of the future.

TEN

At breakfast the next morning, Pierre began to harangue Neville over their failure to visit La Pigalle the previous evening. There was nothing venomous in Pierre's nagging, but Neville began to wonder again if the visit Pierre had envisaged — or perhaps had already planned — was more for his own gratification rather than Neville's. Because of that he did not feel disposed to consider the wants and wishes of his porcelain companion.

Inclined to something a little different — and regretting his rather meagre intake of food the previous day — Neville ignored Pierre's advice and wanting some form of cooked breakfast, made his way down to the hotel's restaurant. He assumed such a request would not be unusual for an establishment catering for English tourists, but when the feast eventually arrived Neville found himself staring at a single, rather wizened sausage, and three fried eggs. Accompanied by two slices of rather under-done toast, the whole was somewhat indecorously arranged on a willow pattern plate.

With a slight sigh — 'Not what you had in mind, eh?' was all Pierre offered — Neville picked up his knife and fork and made for the sausage. As he did so, the sausage rolled out from under the knife as if to avoid any incision. Two small figures in the pattern on the plate — a "typical" Japanese scene common on willow-patterned plates — also moved just as Neville's knife made contact with the china.

He stared hard at his breakfast, then listened, waiting the inevitable voices. There ware none. The restaurant was virtually empty, and the only background noise came from the slurping of coffee at a table hosting two Germans. Neville prepared for another attack.

As his knife and fork once again made for the sausage, he heard the distinctive roar of an aeroplane (some kind of dive bomber) and then, unmistakably, the sound of anti-aircraft fire. It was an echo from Malvern. Again the sausage rolled away this time managing to get underneath one of the eggs, and the two figures — who had been standing on open ground — disappeared into a willow-patterned house. Again his unsuccessful knife hit the plate.

Frustrated, he dropped the knife and fork and grabbed one of the soft slices of toast, biting hard before it too could escape.

A waiter appeared at his side holding a small plate containing two hot croissants. He placed the these in front of Neville, removing the virtually untouched "English" breakfast with his other hand. Then — again unbidden — he topped up Neville's coffee. As he went away with the willow plate, the sound of an "all clear" siren wailed. Neville took up one of the croissants. It was warm and moist and the first bite melted in his mouth.

At this particular moment, Neville's desire was to talk about the things he had seen over the previous two days, but the only person he could really confide in he would not see until sometime the next day. Whatever he may have been, Pierre could in no way be considered a confidant. Neville no longer trusted him. It was hard to say why — or if his suspicions had been aroused by the shower head — but he could not help but question the course events seemed to be taking.

'Monsieur?' Pierre prompted, the tone of his voice showing no concern for Neville's state of mind. Indeed, there appeared no recognition that his present master might be in the process of rebelling.

'Yes, Pierre?'

'The croissants; they are good?'

'Of course. And the coffee.'

Neville sensed his small friend wanted praise or thanks, but he was in no mood to offer either. He wondered what today might have in store for him; where his Parisian roller-coaster might take him.

'Where should we start today? The Louvre or the other one?'

'The Musée d'Orsay, Monsieur. Bien sûr, the Louvre is the more famous, but she is — how shall I put it? — not so "moderne". I think you will find the d'Orsay more immediate.'

'You mean accessible?'

Pierre paused, weighing Neville's choice of word.

'Accessible, perhaps. But I think immediate is a better word.'

From somewhere in his past, Neville remembered a rare trip to a circus. He had seen a clown there, face painted white, tall conical hat. This clown proved to be more of a ring master than a fool, directing those about him into situations which brought them nothing but humiliation or pain. He rose.

'Shall we go?'

'The Musée does not open for another demi-heure; but perhaps a short walk along the Seine then would be good. The weather is very fine.'

Outside, Neville waited in the hotel doorway for a taxi. The two lions eyed him with a degree of suspicion, but without imparting any sense of danger. A yellow cab juddered to a halt and Neville, without regard for its driver, opened the rear door and got in.

As he watched the streets roll by, he was aware he had managed to cultivate an undeniably fatalistic attitude towards the remainder of his visit; perhaps even beyond that. He could not say if it had come to him out of choice or as a result of his recent experiences; he was aware of a new sense of wanting to get it over and done with — whatever "it" was.

The taxi spun round a corner and headed towards the river. Pierre was silent (as seemed his want now) and Neville was in no particular mood to talk. Outside, the weather seemed a little less bright than previously, with an intermittent layer of cloud partially blocking out the sun.

They came to a halt by one of the many bridges over the river. Neville paid and found himself once again heading off under Pierre's direction. Ahead in the distance he could make out Notre Dame, and his mind flitted back to the scene at the café and the disappointment that whole experience had given him.

Across the river, Neville saw a glimpse of the giant pyramid that was the remarkable entrance to the Louvre; an edifice strangely out of context with the solid and historic building to which it provided a gateway.

After a short while, Pierre pointed out the Musée d'Orsay; a large rectangular building on the other side of the road.

'It looks like a railway station,' Neville said, immediately unimpressed with its exterior appearance.

'Monsieur!' Pierre was pleased, 'Bien sûr! It *was* a railway station! Only in Paris would you find such a thing transformed into a palace of wonder.'

Neville thought "palace of wonder" a little strong, and, despite the tone of Pierre's voice being reminiscent of their initial few hours together, was not entirely convinced of its authenticity.

Having crossed the road, he joined the short queue that had begun to form. In the window, a poster proclaimed a special exhibition of works by a group of artists whose movement was known as Fauvism. Neville considered asking Pierre for a little background, but decided against it.

In the small square in front of the building, pigeons fluttered amongst the few tourists who were waiting on the seats, begging for crumbs from late breakfasts nibbled from anonymous paper bags. The sound of bolts being pulled back and keys being turned, drew Neville's attention to the doors which were now opening.

The queue shuffled forwards and in through the glazed entrance hall. Once inside, they filed through one of two booths collecting entrance fees. Having paid, Neville loitered for a moment looking for a guide to the museum written in English, then, suitably armed, moved into the core of the building.

He was greeted by a large and remarkably bright open space. The roof had been generously panelled with glass, and the day's light flooded in. Much of the interior of the building had been refurbished with white marble. The centre of the museum was dedicated to sculpture, and on this floor numerous alcoves opened off the central atrium, each boasting its own small collection of paintings dedicated to individual artists or schools.

Standing quietly, absorbing the breath-taking quality of the place, Neville found himself as thrilled by its interior as he had been non-plussed by its exterior.

Gradually he made his way from alcove to alcove. The ground floor seemed dedicated to Realists and Romantics, wall upon wall filled with both the famous and the unfamiliar. He was pleased he had come early as the gallery was still not busy, and he was able to relax as he toured in relative silence.

At the end of the building, an escalator rose to the first floor. Open to the body of the building, he was able to see others as they wandered below him, in and out of the alcoves just as he himself had done.

He consulted his guide. Each level existed as a ring about the central space, with balconies and walkways looking out across the museum and down to the sculptures below. The first floor was dedicated to more Realists and a few early Impressionists; the second offered the great and famous works of the Impressionists, and the Fauvism exhibition. Neville decided to try the special exhibition and work his way back down to the ground floor.

As he made his way up to the top floor, he pulled off his jacket and swung it over his shoulder, supporting it with his finger in the collar tab. Pierre, who had once again become silent, was lost amidst folds of cloth. 'Out of sight...' thought Neville.

Turning left at the top of the escalator, he found himself confronted by more of the posters he had seen at the entrance, then, turning right into the exhibition area, came face-to-face with the pictures themselves. There was a display on the wall offering a general introduction to the exhibition and the artists whose works were on show. Despite the paucity of Neville's knowledge about Art, he recognised a couple of the names.

As he wandered slowly to the first wall, his eye was caught by a number of paintings by Andre Derain. They were landscapes; bright, attractive pieces that Neville found instantly appealing. Here was the quality missing from the Place du Tertre! One piece in particular drew him. It depicted a number of trees in the foreground of a brightly coloured landscape. According to the display, it was painted in 1906 and called — appropriately enough — "Les Arbres".

He walked up to it and stopped three feet from the canvas. The trees were bright, wiry things in mauve and bold reds, and the landscape danced before his eyes with its bold brush strokes.

'Enticing, isn't it?' Pierre had emerged somehow from the folds of Neville's jacket and appeared to be admiring the work too. 'Derain has a certain vitality,' he continued, 'a certain rawness, perhaps. As if he is in touch with — something.'

Not bothering to reply, Neville leaned a little forwards and took one single step closer.

His foot came to rest on a surface that felt entirely different from the hardness of the museum's polished tiles. He looked down and found it softly embedded between great tufts of grass. But the grass was not green; it was amber and ochre. And looking up, he saw four trees immediately in front of him. The one nearest, to his left, was light purple deepening to a dark blue base; the others, various rusts and reds. He pushed out his hand and felt the firmness of the trunk.

About his body, he sensed the heat of a summer's day; the sun shone brightly in the pale blue and yellow sky, and there was a breeze which carried with it the hint of water. In the distance rose mountains of blue and indigo.

He took a another step and moved further into the field. Just beyond the clump of trees — in whose midst he now stood — the land slipped away slightly, down to a yellow field. Beyond this field and some more trees — was that the green of figs or dates? — the river.

Lured on by the shape of the land, its invitation to explore, Neville continued walking, down through the yellow field and across the pale blue shadows cast by the dark trees with their solid fruits, pink in the sun.

The river flowed in blocks of solid colour, purple, blue. Away in the distance, riding on a mass of red, the ferry — little more than a splash of brown — plied its trade to the far bank. Neville looked down. His shoes had become misshapen rectangles of blue, and his crimson legs were apparently suffering from years of exaggerated rickets. He felt fine.

Over his shoulder, the four trees he had first encountered were now away across the field and up the hill. Ahead, beyond the river, the mountains; and to either side, stretching away, the strange mosaic of the landscape.

As he reached the river, the ferry was making preparations to leave. The ferryman — a misshapen man of black and blue — beckoned him facelessly, and with confident steps Neville climbed on board the strange vessel. It seemed to have no definite sides or edges to it, just layer upon layer of reds and fleshy pinks. He could make out no definite hull or waist, but managed to find a seat (a spotted white oblong) on which to sit. Silently the ferryman pulled on his oars, and with the wind pushing at the magenta and cobalt sail, they moved out onto the river.

The journey to the far bank was over in moments. Neville had hardly time to take in the sensation of travelling across a rippling surface of blue — the boat trailing a wake of green and yellow — when they arrived. Immediately in front of him, the mountains rose ever higher, their mass darker and more solid now. A road — strangely white — beckoned him towards the mountain pass, and effortlessly he carried on.

As he moved further into the hillside, he noticed that the colours had become more solid; they had begun to be defined by black lines around their perimeter, as if to hold the colours in. Gone was the freedom and the flowing beauty from the other side of the river; now things seemed a little darker. The yellow had gone from the sky which was a deeper blue; the lightness of the fields had moved towards orange; and Neville noticed that in one or two places, deeper shadows had begun to appear. Where there had been nothing but colour before — the blue shadows of the green fruit trees — now came true shade.

The road began to sweep downhill, and Neville was carried onwards by it. He tried to look behind, to check his progress, but to no avail. His legs were no longer irregularly shaped, but solid and more exact things; and on the white road, he had begun to cast a shadow.

The road swept down through the mountain pass, and as he travelled onwards he moved further into a darker landscape. He had begun to feel a little cold, and donned and buttoned his jacket against a chill breeze which had sprung up. The sky menaced before him; now ebony, it bore nothing but the promise of storm.

He turned a corner and was suddenly out of the landscape and into a bleak monotone flatness. The earth was a dull grey now, and large rectangular shapes of buildings loomed on either side. Black windows offered him nothing, and their long shadows cast a deep cloth in front of him. On the wall of one building, a plain clock began to dissolve under his gaze, its numbers melting down the brown brickwork. Ahead on the horizon — and how far was that? — strange creatures appeared to be moving in his direction.

The empty space became swallowed up the shadows of the building, and he found himself in an ever darker alleyway. Ahead was a single door through which he seemed compelled to go.

From one place of desolation, he entered another. Now there was no sky, and no walls. All seemed to blend together. Even the definitions between things had begun to blur in a monotony of tones. He suddenly longed for a splash of yellow; for a hint of green. He looked to his lapel, but Pierre was invisible in this light.

Ahead, from what appeared to be some kind of kitchen, came the throbbing sounds of a boiler as it beat against an invisible wall. Neville tried to stop, to turn back, but his progress was remorseless. Suddenly the boiler wrenched itself from the wall, spewing black water in his path. Steam poured from its pipes as it lowered itself to the ground, then, uncertainly at first, began to walk towards him.

Neville could see the flames within it burning ferociously; but even these possessed little colour. The boiler began to make better progress, growing larger before his eyes. The noise it was generating had become almost deafening, and Neville began to wince at the intrusion. He looked for help, for an exit, stairway, anything; but there was nothing he could distinguish, nothing remained.

The boiler stretched out its pipe-like hands, spraying water and steam towards him. It roared monstrously, and all Neville could do was to find his voice and scream.

ELEVEN

When Neville awoke, he found himself lying on his bed. Judging by the light filtering through the faded curtains, it was morning. Moving, he discovered not only was he laying above the bedcovers, but that he was fully dressed — and in clothes he had not been wearing when he went out the previous day.

Unsure whether his head ached or not, he sat up slightly, leaning on his elbows. At the foot of the bed his two bags sat neatly side by side. In the far corner of the room, one of the doors of the wardrobe was open, revealing emptiness inside. Apparently his luggage had already been packed.

'Bon jour, Monsieur!'

Neville's jacket was lying across the back of a chair, and Pierre had been in prime position to watch his first stirrings.

'Your last day in Paris, and you must not be late!'

'Late?' Neville was now sitting on the edge of the bed, looking for his shoes. 'Late for what?'

'For la Tour Eiffel, of course! You are leaving around mid-day, n'est-ce pas? So you do not have so much time.'

Having found his shoes neatly placed beneath the bedside table, Neville was pulling them on as Pierre spoke. The noon deadline was news to him, but presumably all part of the plan. He remembered that he would be seeing Samuel again, and then — this time with a sudden chill which physically shook him — came a recall of his experience of the previous day.

'Pierre; did you say that this was my last day?'

'Oui, Monsieur.'

'Don't I have one more day to go — to visit the museums?'

'Again?!' Pierre gave a short laugh. 'Was yesterday not enough for you?'

Even though Neville could remember only the first part of his previous day's excursion, he decided not to press Pierre for a breakdown on the remainder. Somehow he felt better not knowing what had happened — and was encouraged that Pierre seemed up-beat about the coming day.

'Of course, yes.' He stood up and went to the window.

Looking out, the view was much the same as it had been the previous two mornings; Paris awakening. It seemed slightly busier, and the clock on the wall confirmed he was some half an hour later stirring than before.

There was a knock at the door which Neville answered without moving from his position. Only when he heard the door open did he look over his shoulder. The doorman filled the door frame.

'My bags?' Neville surmised out loud. The doorman nodded, and walked into the room. Turning away from the window, Neville went to pick up his jacket, but then decided that prudence demand he use the bathroom first.

Unzipping his trouser fly, he heard a familiar hiss from the bath.

'Leaving us then?' The shower head's observation sounded more like accusation than anything else.

'Apparently so.' Neville stared down into the toilet, and when he pulled the cistern chain, water began to swirl into the bowl and then away.

'Had fun?'

Considering the shower head had actually tried to be helpful, he had difficulty in deciding the true nature of this particular character. Was he misanthropic or philanthropic?

Neville pulled the bathroom door closed a little further.

'What you said, the other day. What did you mean?'

'What I said?' The shower head uncoiled itself and slid into the base of the bath. 'What do you mean, "what I said"?'

'About Pierre. The pierrot.'

'Ah.'

'You warned me about him.'

'Did I?' The tone of the reply was slippery in the extreme. 'I wouldn't say I warned you about him. Perhaps simply to be cautious; observant even. But not a warning. Why should I?' A pause. 'Did I need to?'

From outside, Neville heard a call of 'Monsieur!' and a reminder about the time. He looked back into the bath. The shower head was motionless, and its hissing had stopped. Neville decided he didn't like deliberately ambiguous characters; they thought they were so clever, but were nothing more than cowards.

'We must go!' Pierre said when Neville reappeared in the room. 'The taxi is waiting.'

'No breakfast?'

'Perhaps later.'

As he descended in the lift, watching the first floor creak past through the trellis-work gate, Neville wondered if he shouldn't be a little more authoritative; perhaps he should put his foot down, send the taxi away, insist on breakfast. Under other circumstances he may well have done so, but this particular morning found him more like a boxer the day after a fight rather than one feeling bullish the day before.

As he walked through the hotel entrance, he saw the doorman putting his two bags in the back of a taxi parked half on the pavement. The rear passenger door was open, and he was greeted again by the unusual aroma of the taxi's interior. The toad was leaning across the back of his seat as Neville got in.

'Leaving us then?' And the toad gave his croaky laugh. 'Had fun?'

'Not so fast today, please,' was all Neville could offer.

'Fast? Man, you English got no balls!' And with that, the toad crunched the taxi into gear and pulled off the pavement with a leap.

Pierre was slightly more talkative this morning; excited even. Perhaps he was making a special effort because it was Neville's last day. He pointed out minor things as the toad's amazing lane-changing antics threw them from side to side. It suddenly occurring to him that the small porcelain figure could never leave Paris, Neville wondered what would happen to Pierre when he departed.

He would have asked the question but for their screeching arrival at the Eiffel tower. The toad hit the curb with a bang and the doors — all four of them — sprang open with the impact. Neville paid and made to get out.

'Come back soon — and don't forget me!' And with that, the toad slammed the taxi into gear with such force that Neville's bags bounced out of the boot and onto the pavement of their own accord. A dust trail followed the toad as he sped off into the city hubbub.

'What do I do with those?' Neville asked, looking at his bags.

'There is a small office. They will take them.'

'Good.' And with that, Neville picked up his two bags and made for the ticket booth.

As he walked beneath the tower, he looked up through its centre, standing square between the four legs. All he could see was a pattern of steel repeated at each corner like some hypnotic mirror image. Above — and how high was that? — the first platform blotted out any residual image of the sky, and along one leg he could see a small lift making its way upward.

He walked on. It seemed that once again he was early, and because of this the queue was quite short. When he reached the booth he asked for a ticket.

'To which level?' came the rather short reply.

Neville glanced down to his lapel.

'Well?'

'Two,' said Pierre, 'there will be a long wait to get to the top.'

'Is two high enough? As I'm here...'

'Two,' said Pierre, adamantly. 'That should be fine.'

From behind the grille, the same question.

'Sorry. Second level, please,' Neville offered.

'Deuxième étage,' said the attendant.

'And can I leave my bags?'

'Of course, Monsieur. Please leave them at the door.'

Neville left his bags where he had been told and made his way to the lift. After ten yards or so, he glanced back to find the bags gone; efficiency was, to be honest, the last thing he had expected.

There was also a short queue — some twenty people or so — waiting for the lift. He looked up the nearest leg of the tower to see the cage on its way down, slowly descending towards them. From behind he heard the excited chatter of some Japanese tourists as well as the equally exited chatter from their cameras, the latter busily exchanging advice and tips on aperture sizes, filters, and exposure speeds. He remembered that he had wanted to buy a camera. He would ask Samuel about that.

Turning his attention to the front of the queue, he noticed a figure that seemed familiar to him, a woman he could only see in part-profile. She was wearing a white coat with a large grey collar, all of which contrasted with the darkness of her hair which was a mass of curls falling about her shoulders.

The sudden sound of a bell diverted his attention to the lift now upon them. It hit the ground with a small thump and immediately opened its doors on the far side, disgorging its passengers onto terra firma. Those arriving back seemed in good spirits, laughing and joking. He noticed one or two couples holding hands and talking half-secretively to one and other.

A nudge in the back prompted him to move forwards with the rest of the queue, and within a few strides he found himself on one side of the lift, pressed against its metal side by some of the Japanese visitors. Immediately to his left, the camera of one — slung casually across its owner's shoulder — gave him a conspiratorial wink.

'Guess what?'

'What?' Neville replied in a whisper akin to that in which the question was offered.

'She's forgotten to load any film!' And the camera winked again, and chuckled to itself. This was obviously a tremendous joke, as a number of the other cameras nearby joined in with the merriment.

Neville thought the camera was a bit mean, but refrained from saying anything. This was partly due to his general reserve and decorum, but more because he had now noticed that the woman in the white coat was none other than his vision from the Rue St. Dennis. She stood, here and now, no more than eight feet away from him, half-turned, her profile set against the Paris skyline as the lift moved upwards. Eight feet — yet completely out of Neville's reach as there were two Japanese, three Germans, and a Spaniard between them.

For two somewhat torturous minutes, the lift rose slowly towards the first level, all the while Neville trying not to stare at the woman — yet also trying to stare at her. The exit doors would open on the far side of the lift, and as they came to a halt, it occurred to him that she might get out here. If she did, he decided that he would follow. There was little else he could do.

In the event only two people got out, but a few more crammed in. The eight feet between them became squashed to around seven, and Neville faced the crawl to the second stage with the same dilemma of staring and not staring. The woman seemed to not be aware of him; at no point on their journey upwards did she look his way.

As they climbed, he allowed himself the occasional brief glance upwards to check on their progress — and outwards, in a faux show of interest — but there was really only one thing on his mind. Pierre had said nothing since they had stepped in the lift.

'Pierre?'

'Monsieur?'

But Neville's potential interrogation was halted by the stutter of them arriving at their destination.

The doors opened and the lift began to empty. The woman was out quite quickly and it took Neville about twenty seconds longer to exit. Once outside he went to the rail and looked about. He could not see her. The platform was not that large, so she had to be there somewhere.

Neville gave a cursory glance to the city. He could pick out Notre Dame from where he stood, and made a stab at a building which might have been the Musée d'Orsay; but these were now minor considerations. Far from the original intent of the tower providing him with a memorable panorama of the city, it had apparently become the climax of some obscure quest. Pierre had known what he was doing when he suggested that Neville leave it to last.

Moving away from where he stood, he slowly walked anti-clockwise around the edge of the platform. His searching took him in towards the centre of the tower rather than away to admire the skyline as was the norm, and his visage was wreathed in a frown rather than the smiles so abundant on the faces of others.

He had nearly completed a circuit when he turned the final corner and came across her standing immediately in front him, a slight smile on her face. It was as if she had been waiting.

He stopped instantly.

'Bon jour, Monsieur.'

She was, without question, the most captivating woman he had ever seen in his entire life. Her greeting seemed to drop from her lips with such elegant seduction that his ears felt unworthy to receive her words. Her eyes shone with a clarity that even the purest gem stones would have envied. And her beauty, would have defied the gods themselves.

From Pierre there came a slight whistle.

'You have been looking for me, yes?'

'I'm sorry.' Pathetic.

'I saw you the other day. I think you have perhaps been searching.'

Neville was now standing within two feet of her. His tongue felt glued to his mouth — and his brain hundreds of feet below, grovelling amongst the flower beds of the nearby park.

'Yes,' then, 'no.'

She smiled.

'I mean; I recognised you. From the street, the other evening.'

'And the café, perhaps?' she suggested.

So.

'And what do you want of me?'

Still the smile; but this was the sort of question Neville had never expected to face in any normal life, let alone now.

'Want?' He could think of nothing — and everything. 'Who are you?'

'Who am I? You mean, what is my name, perhaps? Can you guess?'

Neville, for a moment lost, realised that there could be only one answer.

'Mirelle?'

'Bien sûr.'

But she didn't look like Mirelle; she surpassed Mirelle in every way.

'I'm sorry,' he faltered, 'but I don't think I understand.'

He moved a step forwards. Her response was to lose the smile and to take a step away.

'Careful, Monsieur.'

'But, who *are* you?'

'I am,' she paused, 'I am all you desire. I am the embodiment of your dreams. I am all you would have me to be.' And as she spoke the smile returned to her lips, and a gleam came to her eyes. 'But I am not yours. I am mine.'

Again Neville moved forwards, this time his hands a little outstretched. Again she moved away, maintaining the distance between them. She was now more than the most beautiful woman he had ever seen; she had become something intangible, something for which he had been searching, chasing; that elusive thing to which he could not give a name. Possession was what he desired. But he could see that she was not one to be possessed. Yet if this was indeed the case then he decided he would have to touch her, for even the briefest contact suddenly seemed to represent some kind of achievement.

After a moment's silence he lunged forwards. It was step into the abyss. He was leaving behind so much that he knew, and throwing himself at the mercy of the woman that stood before him now.

As fast as he moved, so she retreated. In an instant, she was standing on the railing, suddenly towering above him. And as he looked up, his hands grasping nothing, she changed into a beautiful seagull. With one magnificent flap of her wings, she leant forwards and plucked Pierre from his lapel with her beak. Then, falling back, she was away from the tower and out into the air, sailing off into the city.

'A bientôt, Monsieur' came the feint cry from Pierre as he dropped out of sight.

It was only when he felt the hand on his waist that Neville realised he too was standing on the railing, preparing to throw himself into oblivion.

TWELVE

He had just missed him at the ticket office Samuel explained a few minutes later as they were descending in the lift. He had seen him arrive, buy his ticket, then deposit his bags by the office.

'If I hadn't grabbed them, who knows what might have happened to them!'

Neville was a little calmer now, though he had said nothing since his encounter with "Mirelle".

'You must have been very close. I mean; I turned around and saw the bags were gone.'

'I decided to put them in the bus and then come back for you. Unfortunately I was just too late.'

'You would have stopped me going up there?'

Samuel smiled. The lift had reached the ground with a bump and the doors rattled open.

'I think I might have come up with you, Sir. I don't think I could or should have stopped you.'

They walked past the refreshed queue — more Japanese, more winking cameras — and away from the tower. Neville took one last look up. He could make out one or two birds circling high above; the second level of the tower seemed a universe away.

'I'm glad you weren't *too* late.' He tried to smile, but it proved a little difficult. Samuel squeezed his arm and offered a silent nod of understanding.

The old bus sat waiting for them in a small lay-by just off the main road. It looked a little less battered, and now sported a bright red coat of paint. Samuel intercepted Neville's gaze.

'Thought I'd give the old girl a little treat. Well, she deserves it really.'

Neville offered nothing; he knew he wasn't supposed to. Instead, he let Samuel reach the bus first and open the door. Inside, his two bags were in their previous position, and his own seat — the one at the front alongside Samuel's — had been recovered in new fabric and accessorised with a large soft cushion. There was a small table beside it too, and on this a fresh mug of tea steamed.

'Tea,' Neville said in a rhetorical manner. 'Is that significant? I mean, it's not coffee.'

'I thought you might be just a little tired of coffee, Sir', Samuel said, and he turned the key and started the engine as if to add weight to his words.

Neville raised the cup and took a sip.

'Where to Sir?'

Samuel had that slight mischievous smile again as he glanced back at his passenger, then, without waiting for a reply, rolled the bus gently out into the traffic.

'I don't know yet,' Neville said. 'Perhaps we should just leave the city first, then decide. Is that OK?'

'That's fine, Sir,' said Samuel. 'How's the tea?'

The bus rumbled slowly on — once more at twenty seven miles per hour (the coat of paint had done nothing to improve the speed) — twisting through the streets of the city. Neville sipped his tea, expecting at any moment to feel the beginning of the long drag up the incline from which they had first approached three days before. But there was no hill; instead Samuel kept steering along flat and uninspiring roads. Eventually Neville realised that, without ceremony, Paris had simply slipped away behind them.

He wondered if one last look might have been in order. Thwarted by events at the Eiffel Tower, the promised panoramic view had been partially denied him. Perhaps that was just as well. Samuel seemed, as ever, fully in control of the situation, and was pressing on to their next destination — as much he could ever give an impression of "pressing on".

'Samuel.'

'Sir.'

'Where are we going?'

'Going? Well, that's up to you Sir, of course.'

'You appear to be going *somewhere* though.'

Samuel gave him a brief glance.

'Not quite. We are going *away* from somewhere. If you don't mind me saying, Sir, you have to do that before you can go *to* anywhere else. Especially if you don't know *where* it is you are going.'

'That's just semantics. They are, of course, both one and the same thing — simultaneously.'

'Perhaps.'

Neville, without the appetite to pursue Samuel's philosophical theory, drained the last of his tea and realised how much he had missed its unique flavour. He wondered what other things he had missed; days of croissants had presumably taken the place of something else too. The last time he drank tea had been in his office — perhaps just minutes before he became a "redundant" individual. It had only been a short while, but Neville already knew that his most recent job was one thing he was never going to miss. Perhaps Brian, Colin and David were managing things a little better than he had done; but quite frankly, he didn't give a shit.

After a while, Samuel slowed the bus and indicated that he was going to pull over. Ahead was a small lay-by, vacant apart from a solitary, simple vending unit. As they crawled to a halt alongside it (and in the process allowing the stream of traffic that had been growing behind them to race away) Neville saw it was a fruit stall.

'Fruit, Sir?' Samuel enquired, and then continuing in a rush, 'I hope you don't mind me stopping but I've something of a fad for bananas, and the urge has just taken me.'

The sentence trailed away into hopefulness as Samuel, the bus now stopped, turned to look at his passenger.

'Not at all.'

'May I get you anything?'

'Perhaps an apple.'

'French?'

'Whatever.'

As he watched Samuel descend and walk round the front of the bus, Neville marked the use of his word "French". He looked on the awnings of the cabin, and craned his neck to see inside, but could find no evidence of signage of any kind. The countryside had lost some of its Gallic charm and seemed to possess a kind of nondescript uniformity: the gently rolling hills; the hedges; the odd stone wall. The sky — blue but peppered with puffy while clouds — gave nothing away. Neville sniffed the air. Nothing. The fields were empty, and there was no music in the background.

'Samuel' —who was half way up the steps when Neville next addressed him — 'where are we? And don't say "between here and there".'

Samuel laughed, presuming a joke.

'Very good, Sir; very good!' And with that, he handed Neville a green apple.

Neville rubbed it on his jacket — force of habit — then took a bite. It was crisp and juicy.

'Well?'

Samuel was peeling his banana. He looked up.

'You weren't joking, Sir? About being between here and there?' Neville's silence confirmed as much. 'Oh, sorry. Pity.'

For a few seconds there was a kind of silence as the two of them chomped through their respective fruits. Samuel, finishing first, consigned his banana skin to the brown paper bag from which it had been produced.

'We are, of course, between here and there. It's a shame when you didn't mean what you said, Sir, because you are absolutely correct. In our present context, "here" was Paris, and "there" is wherever you wish to go next. Of course, the saying should be "between there and there", because we are most definitely *here* — but that doesn't sound so well, does it?' He waited for some kind of response. Neville took another bite from his apple. 'We could, of course, talk about Paris if you wanted to? I mean, if I can help with any outstanding questions? Historical clarification, perhaps?'

Neville lobbed his apple core forward, and Samuel caught it deftly in the brown bag. He looked at little disappointed at being called upon to perform such a facile trick. The look lasted but a moment.

'Paris? Clarification, yes; but not so much the historical.'

Samuel nodded, smiled, placed the brown bag down by his feet, and waited. Neville weighted his words.

'What actually happened?'

A small laugh escaped from Samuel — somewhat involuntarily, Neville guessed — even though his face showed nothing but considered respect.

'I don't think I could manage anything quite so challenging, Sir. Could you be a little more specific?'

'For a start, how about what happened on the Tower. Can you explain that to me?'

Samuel frowned.

'To be honest Sir, I was hoping you might do me the honour there.'

'Sorry?'

'I arrived to find you standing on the edge about to throw yourself off! If I were more demanding, perhaps I should ask for an explanation of that circumstance.'

'You didn't see Mirelle?'

'Your wife?!'

'No, another Mirelle. Or at least, she said she was.' He paused, looking for a subject that might be a little less contentious. 'Or Pierre, the Pierrot.'

Samuel offered an "old boy" shake of the head, suggesting a degree of bewildered confusion.

'I'm sorry, Sir. Perhaps if you would like to explain...'

Neville considered Samuel's offer for a split second. Either he was dissembling and knew exactly what had happened, or he was genuinely in the dark. In each case any explanation from him would probably be in adequate.

'Forget it.'

There was an uncomfortable silence. Neville picked over the images of his visit, thinking of morsels he might offer Samuel.

'The Musée d'Orsay. Can you explain what happened to me in there?'

'What was that, Sir?'

'Samuel!'

Neville thumped the small table in frustration. Even if Samuel was in a position to shed some light on things, would he be able to understand what was said, or would there be more phoney here-there mumbo jumbo to confuse him? And if Samuel could explain nothing, was it because he wasn't aware of what had transpired or because, for some reason, he was prevented from providing illumination? Neville knew he could resolve none of this.

'Have you checked your watch, Sir?'

'My watch? Do you need the time or something?'

'I was thinking of the additional information.'

For once Samuel's message was understood, and Neville remembered the display of his financial "balance". He looked down. The number 16738 greeted him. He tried to remember the initial figure.

'A little over nineteen thousand', Samuel offered.

'But that means I've spent a fortune!'

'Nearly two and a half thousand by my calculation.'

'We said Paris would cost a few hundred; a thousand at most! This can't be right, Samuel.'

Samuel's countenance became a degree more stern, verging on the school-masterly.

'Correction, Sir; *you* said you anticipated such a sum, not I. You must remember the cost of the hotel, and the travel.'

'Travel? But I only took a few taxis.'

'I'm afraid I must include myself in your budget, Sir. The old bus may not be particularly quick, but I'm afraid she is a little expensive to run — especially given her particular *talents*.'

The last work hung ambiguously in the air, demanding definition; but Neville missed it, and pressed on.

'And I bought nothing.'

'There is the portrait I collected with your bags, Sir. And the Pierrot, you mentioned...?'

'But surely...' Neville lost his argument. He could not reconcile his brief visit with such vast expenditure.

Samuel waited for anything further. When nothing came, he continued.

'Do you remember the General? The gentleman who purchased your car.'

'Of course.'

'He paid what you considered to be a ridiculous amount of money for it, did he not? But he had his reasons, as I explained. I also explained that what we were dealing with there was the concept of *worth*, rather than *value*. The General paid a sum matching the car's worth to him, not one in accord with its value.'

'Are you suggesting that, somehow, my visit to Paris was "worth" nearly two and a half thousand pounds to me?'

'Perhaps.'

'How come? Explain it, Samuel; I don't understand!'

Samuel offered a smile of sympathy.

'I don't think I can, Sir. It's not that I don't want to, it's simply that I fear it is impossible. It is a lesson to be learned perhaps; nothing more nor less.'

Neville checked his watch again. Sixteen thousand. Was that how much his life was now "worth"? And based on the last three days, how could he possibly know how quickly he was spending it, or when one thing might cost him more than another?

'I'm afraid you must trust us, Sir. We are, after all, on your side. I will help you all I can, but these are the rules we are playing with.'

'Option 3?'

'Indeed.'

Unable to comprehend exactly how things now stood, Neville looked out of Samuel's side of the bus at the fruit stall. The boxes of fruit which had stood in neat racks had now vanished, and the stall was decorated like a Punch and Judy show with brightly coloured curtains adorning the sides of what was — to all intents and purposes — now a stage.

From within the stall (there was no-one visible) came a brief drum roll, which was followed by the appearance of a banana peeping nervously round the curtain. With a sudden lunge — as if pushed from behind — it flew out and came to a sliding halt centre stage. It bowed low. From somewhere Neville heard a small ripple of applause. The banana bowed lower, and the applause was louder.

With this second ovation, two apples — one red, one green — rolled onto the stage from the opposite direction. They appeared to be in conversation, though how Neville could actually know this was vaguely mystifying. They stopped suddenly on seeing the banana. The red apple moved round the banana to its other side, so that the apples now flanked it. The banana tried as best it could to straighten itself. Neville sensed some tension. An orange appeared from one side of the stage, paused, then rolled quickly across and out of sight on the other side.

The apples sidled up to the banana, squeezing it between them. The banana tried to bow and failed. From either side of the stage various other fruits, evidently attracted by the drama, made their appearance; spectators rather than participants. By this time the banana was looking even more uncomfortable as the apples, both redder with their efforts, pushed against it. Neville could only watch, mesmerised by the strange show.

Gradually the banana peeled back its skin, and, as it did so, the apples backed slightly away. The audience in the wings also moved back slightly. Then, without warning, the banana spun viciously round, whipping the apples with its flailing skin as it did so, sending them flying from the stage and onto the ground. With that the curtain closed.

Neville looked at Samuel, intending to ask him for some interpretation of these events, but he appeared to be asleep.

'Samuel!'

The driver woke with a slight grunt, straightening himself in his chair in embarrassment.

'Sorry, Sir. Must have just dropped off; apologies.'

'Samuel,' Neville paused. 'Never mind. I think I'd like to go home.'

'Home, Sir?'

Neville sensed another discourse coming on; something he wanted to avoid at present.

'Birmingham. Let's go back to Birmingham; I need cheering up. Perhaps that meal.'

'And the tuxedo?' Samuel offered with a smile.

'The tux? Why not!'

As the bus crunched into gear, Neville felt a sudden chill breezing through his open window, and noticed that the sky had turned an angry grey. He sensed England might not be that far away, after all.

THIRTEEN

The weather broke after a few minutes' driving, the clouds Neville had seen indeed anticipated the brief deluge that was to follow. For a while, as they made their way towards Birmingham, visibility was seriously reduced. Samuel, concentrating hard, adopted a resolute silence which seemed to carry with it a warning that, should he be forced to break it, some kind of penalty would be incurred. He had switched the headlights on, and the windscreen wipers moaned across the surface of the glass.

Occasionally, another vehicle would approach them from the opposite direction, lights blazing, and generate a cloud of spray for them to drive through. Silhouettes seemed to pass by at random moments: he detected a small wood, the odd building. It was not until a little later that he realised they were travelling through a built-up area. He heard Samuel sigh, and sensed a degree of relaxation which signified it was now permissible to open communications.

'Where are we, Samuel?'

'Birmingham, Sir.'

Neville peered through the window again. The rain, now held back by buildings on all sides, appeared to be lighter, and Neville was able to see more of their present environment. He had lived in Birmingham for a while and assumed he knew much of the city, but evidently this was not so.

'You may not recognise this,' Samuel offered prior to the question being asked, 'but this area houses some of the best tailors in the city.'

'Indeed.'

Instead of being in a commercial district, Neville found they were making leisurely progress through what appeared to be little more than residential streets. Samuel's use of the word "houses" appeared to be doubly precise, as the buildings were indeed domestic — row upon row of terraced dwellings — and the only signs of entrepreneurial activity Neville could see was the occasional plaque above a door or window.

All the houses fronted directly onto the pavement, their small square windows adorned with net curtains of various persuasions and backed by multifarious draperies. Neville felt as if the dwellings were somehow leftovers from a previous generation; as if they should have been condemned years before and replaced by more modern constructions.

The bus swung from one identical street into another, then Samuel pulled the vehicle to a halt.

'Here we are, Sir.'

They had come to rest outside a dark blue door whose paint had begun to submit to the ravages of time and was retreating in flakes to the paving stones below. Above it, a sign in a slightly different shade of blue, proclaimed "A. Bossiman — Tailor".

Samuel opened the door and led Neville down the steps. As he knocked at Mister Bossiman's establishment, Neville tried to peer through the front window, only to find his gaze blocked by a heavy net curtain which, judging by its off-white colour, had also seen better days. He wondered about Samuel's assertion regarding "some of the best tailors in the city" and was going to challenge this when the door opened. Samuel stepped to one side to reveal a small man in a blue and white striped apron. He nodded to Samuel, then offered Neville a slight bow. Neville nodded back, then followed the man into the building.

'Mister Bossiman,' Samuel whispered, as Neville passed him on the threshold.

'Are you coming in?'

'I'll wait on the bus, Sir; if you don't mind.'

Mister Bossiman was, to put it bluntly, incredibly small. Neville followed him down the long hallway to where, at its end, Mister Bossiman turned through a door on the left and led Neville into a large and surprisingly bright room. At the far end was the net-bound window which opened onto the street, in front of which two small settees were placed facing inwards. Either side of the room, hanging on rack after rack, were suits, jackets and trousers, and near where he now stood, an evidently well-used tailor's cutting table. It was difficult to make out where the light that illuminated the room was coming from. The front window admitted next to nothing, and the bulbs hanging from the ceiling seemed so dim as to be extracting light rather than contributing to it.

Mister Bossiman turned, and smiled up at Neville.

'Pliss, your yacket.'

'I'm sorry?'

'Your yacket?'

'Yes, sorry.'

Neville pulled off his jacket and placed it across the back of a nearby chair. Mister Bossiman smiled professionally, and pulled a tape measure from his apron pocket. As he was only about three foot tall, Neville wondered how he would be able to measure him effectively. He looked towards a second door at the back of the room, expecting an assistant to emerge and assist with the task.

'Pliss, turn about,' smiled Mister Bossiman.

Neville did so. Instantly he felt an expert hand at the nape of his neck, and a second tracing the tape measure down to the small of his back. He glanced sideways and caught a glimpse of Mister Bossiman in a mirror on the wall. It was indeed the small tailor doing the measuring but with arms Neville could only describe as telescopic.

'Goud. Pliss, turn about', said the small tailor.

Neville turned, and Mister Bossiman extended his small arms to measure his shoulders, his chest, and then his waist in turn.

'Do you come from far away — originally, I mean?' said Neville, for some reason having the impression that a tailor was like a hairdresser and that small talk was de rigueur during a consultation.

'Yiss,' Mister Bossiman smiled, evidently pleased to make such intimate contact with his customer, 'I from Walsall.'

Neville's natural desire to laugh at the response — joke or not — was tempered by Mister Bossiman's manner, one which indicated that his reply had been given in all seriousness and with some personal import behind it.

'I see,' was Neville's only possible option.

After a few more extensions of his arms, the tailor had completed the measuring exercise and — though he had committed nothing to paper — appeared ready to continue with the next stage of the process.

'Pliss, you chooce fabric?' and with a wave of his arm (now back to its normal proportions) indicated a large rack of cloth near the cutting table. The rolls of cloth showed, not unnaturally, a predominance of greys, blacks and blues. There were narrow stripes and wide stripes, but nothing as adventurous as Neville would expect to find in his local high street "man's shop". Somehow this seemed in keeping with the general tenor of the place.

'Pliss, for what you wish suit?'

'Actually, I was looking to buy a tuxedo.'

'"Torpedo"? Pliss, what is "torpedo"?'

'Tuxedo', Neville corrected. 'Well, it's actually a very smart jacket; often velvety, I guess. Some kind of smooth fabric. A bit like a dinner jacket. You know; you can wear it with a bow tie and cummerbund. That kind of thing.'

'"Come-undone"? Pliss, what is this?'

Neville, amazed at Mister Bossiman's sartorial ignorance, was nonetheless disarmed by the naiveté of his smile. Under more conventional circumstances, he might have been inclined to storm off, but — considering Samuel had given Mister Bossiman his personal recommendation — felt such action would not only be churlish, but potentially unwise. He decided to compromise.

'A tuxedo is a very, very smart suit; and a cummerbund is a kind of wide belt made out of bright fabric. Is that OK?'

'OK, pliss,' smiled Mister Bossiman. 'Smart belt, I got.'

And with another wave of his arm, once again invited Neville to choose his material. Neville had decided against any of the plain greys or blues, and had — he was surprised to discover — something of an aversion to stripes. His ex-Boss had always worn suits with a stripe in them, and this had now invested such unpleasant connotations in the style that he could not countenance wearing it himself. Towards the bottom of the rack, he noticed some material that appeared to be vaguely green, yet, on closer inspection, seemed to even possess a degree of redness about it. He heard Mister Bossiman murmur to himself as Neville bent to consider it further.

'I like this,' he said, on straightening up, 'may I see it, please?'

'Pliss, remarkable fabric,' said Mister Bossiman who then, without bending, simply extended his arms downwards, and pulled the entire roll effortlessly from the rack.

In an instant it was on the table, a metre or so unwound for Neville's closer inspection. His first impressions — of a material that suggested both green and red — were not inaccurate. Neville struggled to identify exact what its base colour might be — grey? blue? something else? — but gave up almost immediately. Whatever it might be, it was certainly different enough to meet his requirements and taste.

'That's fine, thank you,' and with that offered to shake the tailor's hand and leave.

'Pliss,' suggested Mister Bossiman, and gestured to the settees by the far window, 'I make for you, suit.'

'Now?!' Neville was stunned.

'Pliss. You like tea, yes?'

'Thank you, yes.' And Neville walked to the settee where he discovered a cup of tea and small plate of biscuits awaiting him.

Mister Bossiman seemed intent on undertaking the construction there and then. Indeed, as Neville settled to his tea, he could see the tailor's arms already flying about the table, flashing scissors and tape measure amidst the folds of the material. Satisfied that his wait would not, after all, be an impossibly long one, Neville turned to look out of the window. Through the net, he could just make out the outline of the bus which was still parked outside. He felt a small flush of relief at this; knowing Samuel was on-hand gave him a feeling of security, especially after his recent escapade.

His attention was, however, almost immediately drawn back into the room by the sound of an unnatural cough. He assumed that it was Mister Bossiman endeavouring to get his attention — presumably for further measurements — but when he turned, he found, facing the settee, a dark pin-stripe suit standing to attention in front of him. The suit thrust out an arm towards its right when three other suits were now sitting, each in possession of a musical instrument. The trio, thus invited, began the introduction to a slow, drawling jazz number led by a saxophone, and backed up by a base and — of all things — a harp. Neville looked to the centre of the room to find the dark suit had vanished and the stage was now held by a pale yellow suit and a flamingo pink ball gown — though where this latter had come from, Neville had no idea.

The trio picked up the sleazy beat of their tune and the yellow suit slid over to the ball gown and began to dance around it. For a few bars the gown feigned indifference to these advances, but then, drawn on by the hypnotic nature of the music, soon gave way, and the two of them embraced. For the next few minutes (with Mister Bossiman's arms flying about in the background) Neville watched the yellow suit and the flamingo pink gown engaged in a remarkably stunning dance which reminded him of the Astaire and Rodgers routines he had occasionally seen in old movies. Gradually the trio — who were also remarkably accomplished — picked up the tempo of the piece to a thumping crescendo which climaxed in the yellow suit flinging the ball gown to the ground, then collapsing in a heap alongside it. Neville's applause was automatic and unreserved. The yellow suit and pink gown rose to take their bow, and the trio stood briefly in acceptance of their guest's appreciation.

Suddenly, from the far end of the room, there came a brief crash as Mister Bossiman's scissors hit the table, and in an instant all the entertainers disappeared. Mister Bossiman now stood, hidden by the new suit his arms were proudly holding way above his head. Neville rose and walked towards him.

'Pliss, is goud?' came the disembodied voice from behind the waist of the trousers.

Neville felt the material and examined the seams. The workmanship was, without question, of the very highest quality, and the suit seemed more a work of art than artefact.

'Very impressive.'

'Pliss, you try.'

Slipping off his shoes and trousers, Neville donned the suit. It fitted everywhere to perfection, and felt instantly comfortable. He turned to look in one of the mirrors. In this light the green in the material was emphasised, and shone lustrously. He turned to look over his other shoulder at another mirror, and discovered that the redness in the cloth now appeared dominant, and gave the suit a warmth that was remarkably attractive. Remembering that he had wanted a tuxedo — and backing a hunch — Neville closed his eyes then turned to the mirror directly in front of him. When he opened them, he found he was indeed wearing a quite remarkable tuxedo. He smiled to himself.

'Pliss, is goud?' said Mister Bossiman.

'Mister Bossiman, it is truly excellent!' And the small tailor blushed at Neville's praise.

'My fist "torpedo" I make. So pliss, you like him.'

After a further glance in each mirror, Neville slipped out of the suit which then, of its own accord, folded itself and climbed into a waiting bag. Once he had restored his old trousers and jacket, Mister Bossiman offered both the bag and his hand to Neville who took the former with gratitude and shook the latter with warmth.

'Thank you very much.'

'Pliss, the honner is all mine, Sur,' and the small tailor bowed low.

Samuel was waiting for Neville on the bus.

'Was your visit a successful one, Sir?'

Neville held the bag aloft.

'Yes, Samuel, it was. Thank you. Mister Bossiman is a remarkable tailor —
and he has an interesting establishment.'

Samuel started the bus and began to roll it forwards.

'Indeed, Sir; as you say, a remarkable establishment. Strange how, from the
outside, you would not image that such a talent could exist there.'

'But it does.'

'And has for years, as Mister Bossiman might have told you himself.'

Neville regretted he did not engage the tailor in any further discussion beyond
his place of origin.

'These other houses, Samuel.'

'Sir?'

'Do they hide similar talents?'

'"Talents"? Not necessarily. But they each have something about them I
suspect.'

It was one of Samuel's phrases which demanded nothing but silence and
contemplation in reply, and, as usual, Neville respected it.

They drove on through one or two more similar streets — the terraced
frontages, the fading signs — and then out onto open road.

'I have taken the liberty of booking a table for you at a restaurant this evening,
Sir', Samuel informed him.

'What sort of restaurant, Samuel?'

'I think you had something exclusive in mind Sir, did you not? This particular
establishment offers nothing but the highest quality in terms of food, service,
and atmosphere. I am sure you will not be disappointed.'

'Given your most recent recommendation, I am sure I won't be.'

'You will need, of course, to wear your new suit. It is important to create the
right impression.'

'Indeed.'

'And to that end, I have taken the liberty of selecting a number of bow ties for you to choose from. They are on the seat behind you.'

Neville turned and lifted a small tray containing seven ties to his lap. They varied in colour and style, but also appeared of the highest quality.

'Compliments of Mister Bossiman, Sir.'

'Ah.' Neville glanced up. 'Will we be there soon?'

'In a while, Sir. I suggest you relax; perhaps sleep a little.'

FOURTEEN

It was dark when Neville awoke; the bus was stationery. In the silence he could hear starlings about their early evening social activity, chaotic cries accompanying their manic business. From somewhere at the back of the bus, he could hear Samuel whistling gently to himself. He checked his watch: it was a little before eight.

'Ah, so you're awake, Sir! Good; I was worried that I might have to disturb you.'

Neville turned to discover that there had been something of a transformation to the interior of the bus since he had fallen asleep. All the remaining seats had been removed and the vehicle now appeared to be compartmentalised, with a narrow passageway running down one side. Curtains separated the various areas, but these were currently drawn back, so Neville had a full front-to-back view. The first two sections contained beds, each with a small cupboard by the headboard and a lamp on a tiny shelf set into the structure of the bus. Beyond the second of these arrangements, there appeared to be what could only be described as a small galley, and it was here Samuel was currently occupied. Beyond the galley was a door — not a curtain — and Neville assumed this could only be the bathroom. Samuel looked up from the small stove where he was tending his supper.

'I took the liberty of making a few minor adjustments while you were asleep, Sir. I thought it best to allow for any future circumstance, you see.'

'I'm impressed, Samuel; you have been busy.'

Neville left his seat and made his way towards the back of the bus. Passing the first compartment — 'That one is yours, Sir' — he felt the bed (it seemed remarkably soft) and opened the cupboard door. Inside hung his new suit, along with the remainder of his clothes. Samuel had evidently unpacked his bags too. Passing Samuel's quarters, he reached the galley which, despite its size, seemed rather well equipped. The driver was in the process of making some kind of vegetable stew for his dinner.

'Don't worry Sir, this isn't yours!'

Neville returned Samuel's smile.

'When will we get to the restaurant?'

'We are there already, Sir. I took the liberty of parking in their car park a little early; your table is booked for eight thirty.'

'I should be thinking about getting ready then.'

Samuel motioned to the door beyond the galley.

'The bathroom is through there, Sir. Everything should be ready for you.'

Neville opened the door. The bathroom, though compact, still boasted a full sized bath and toilet. The bath was full, steam rising gently from the surface of the water. Above the toilet, a small mirrored cabinet stood half-open, revealing appropriate shaving and washing products.

'I'll lay out your suit, Sir; you go ahead.'

Neville closed the door behind him. Two towels waited on a rail beside the bath, and a small chair was provided to take his discarded clothes. He checked his face in the mirror. He would need a shave too, and was pleased to find an electric razor in the cabinet. Samuel appeared to have considered everything. He undressed quickly, then felt the bath water with his hand. The temperature seemed fine. Within seconds he was immersed. The bath was surprisingly deep, and reclining in it, Neville found his body completely covered. At the foot of the bath — where, to his surprise, there were no taps — a yellow plastic duck bobbed in the water. On a small rack to the side, a flannel, a sachet of shampoo, and some soap awaited his attention.

'Comfy, ain't it?'

The duck bobbed a little closer towards him.

'Very, yes.'

'Can't stand those bloody shallow baths.'

'Indeed.'

'Can't get enough water in 'em. Sit down, but don't get your arse wet; know what I mean?'

'Yes, I do.' Neville leant forward for the shampoo. 'Excuse me.'

'Sure; no worries. Don't splash about too much though mate; can't stand it when I gets soap in me eyes. Odd, ain't it? A duck what don't like water that much. Well, it ain't the water so much as the soap, see? Makes me eyes smart. Ain't natural, is it ; a duck and soap, I mean?'

Neville, having doused his hair, began to wash it. The duck, evidently to avoid as much discomfort as possible, bobbed away from him a little.

'What you up to then?'

'Sorry?' Neville looked at the duck through the one eye that was not covered in soap suds.

'I mean, here. In this bath. Like, I ain't seen you before, have I? You ain't like the last guy.'

'Last guy?' Neville stopped rinsing.

'Yeah. Big feller; fat, know what I mean? Come to think of it, there was hardly room enough for me in here with him. Miserable sod too. Only saw him the once.'

'You've seen lots of people have you?'

The duck gave a quacky laugh.

'Course I 'ave. Well, what do you expect; it's a bleeding 'otel, ain't it?' — and the duck quacked again.

From outside, Samuel shouted through a reminder about the time. Neville's mind flashed back to the bathroom in Paris.

'OK, Samuel. Won't be long.'

'Sam. That's his name is it? The geezer who looks after the room. Sounds like an obnoxious git to me; always bossing blokes about. Can't stand that, being bossed about. Know what I mean?'

'Yes. Excuse me.' Neville stretched for the soap and began to wash.

The duck bobbed around in a circle for a few moments, attempting to whistle as he did so; something that, thanks to his physiognomy, proved impossible and resulted in nothing more than a largely silent dribble.

''Ere; ain't got any bread, 'ave you? Shit, I could murder a nice crust! Bloody hotel keeps you on tight rations, know what I mean? My dad used to talk to me about rations in the war, poor bustard. But it weren't like this though; eh?'

'I expect not.'

Again Samuel shouted a reminder, and this time Neville rose and stretched for a towel.

''Ere, you're quite a big bloke aren't you? Tall, I mean. Fit are you; I mean, play football or something? Some blokes look like shit; know what I mean?'

'I'm just skinny; that's all,' replied Neville through the folds of the towel as he dried himself.

After a minute or so, he turned his attention to his chin. The razor was fully charged and remarkably efficient. It seemed to take no time at all to remove the small amount of stubble that he had manage to accrue since Paris, and rubbing his hand across a now smooth face made him feel much more comfortable.

'Nice talking to you,' he said, turning back to the bath. But although the duck still bobbed, it did so lifelessly.

The door opened, and Samuel popped his head round.

'Everything OK, Sir?'

'Fine Samuel, thank you.'

'I've laid out your suit Sir, and a white shirt. The ties are there too, if you would like to choose one.'

'Thank you.'

And with a towel wrapped around his waist, Neville made his way back to his compartment through the now closed curtains. As Samuel had said, his clothes were ready for him, including a new pair of shoes and a selection of socks. Neville chose a rather flashy green patterned tie and green socks, hoping that the combination would bring out the best in Mister Bossiman's handiwork. There was a mirror on the door of the cupboard, and within a few minutes Neville was able to consider his overall appearance.

He was, without doubt, pleased with the final composition. He had not looked as smart as this for a considerable period of time. Indeed, he found it impossible to recall the last occasion when he had needed to "dress up", but felt certain that it would have had something to do with Mirelle wanting to impress someone. He checked his watch. It was nearly eight thirty. Pulling back the curtains, he found Samuel waiting for him.

'I say, Sir!' he said, warmly, 'you do look just the part. Very dapper.'

'Thank you, Samuel. You think I'll do?'

'I think you will do very nicely, Sir.' And with a slight bow, Samuel opened the bus door and stood aside.

At the foot of the steps, Neville was greeted by a rather distinguished edifice gently illuminated by low-level exterior lights. The building was detached, and there appeared to be no other nearby. The faint breeze Neville felt on his cheek suggested they were out of the city and somewhere in the country. He looked for a nameplate to identify the building, but found none. Indeed, without knowing it to be a restaurant, one might be forgiven for assuming it was a small stately home and not open to the public. He made his way across the gravel car park to the front of the building where a large well-lit porch invited him on. In the hallway, an elegant man in evening dress moved forward to greet him.

'I have a reservation for eight thirty.'

'Ah, yes Sir. Very pleased to see you this evening. I trust you will enjoy your meal with us.'

'Thank you; I'm sure I shall.'

The elegant man clicked his fingers, and another dark-suited man appeared.

'Gustav; show this gentleman to table eight.'

'Eight?' said Gustav, 'certainly.'

Gustav leant forward and whispered something in the Maîtres' ear. The latter stiffened slightly.

'I'm sorry, Sir,' he said addressing Neville, 'but it appears that the last diner is just finishing her coffee at your table — which, apart from that, is of course ready for you. Would you like to follow Gustav, please.'

Neville was about to suggest that he take a different table or that he might wait for the previous diner to finish, but there seemed some insistence that he follow Gustav, and this he did. The hallway opened out into a small dining area which was lit with a subtlety and elegance that matched the Maîtres' own. It was not large — perhaps containing no more than ten tables — but furnished impeccably. Around half the tables were occupied, the remainder boasted "Reserved" notices. The diners already there looked remarkably smart. He followed Gustav to a table in the far corner of the room. Its current occupant, looked up from her coffee at their arrival.

'Pardon, Madame; but this gentleman has arrived for his booking. I wonder if you would mind if he sat with you for an aperitif while you finish your coffee?'

She shot Gustav a strange look which seemed to display some kind of disquiet, though this was quickly superseded by a return to a more relaxed demeanour and even the beginnings of a smile. She glanced at Neville.

'Of course not. I won't be very long. That is, if the gentleman doesn't mind?'

Neville returned her smile. 'My pleasure,' he said, and took the seat offered him by Gustav.

'Drink, Sir?'

'Gin and Tonic.'

Gustav nodded, and left.

As he scanned the room, Neville noticed a mural adorning the wall. From the back of his chair, it rose about two feet, and circumnavigated the whole of the room. Its theme appeared, appropriately enough, to be food. Neville was taking this in, when the woman spoke.

'I'm awfully sorry about this. Perhaps I eat slowly. They came and started relaying the table, but I didn't realise...'

'Please, there's no problem, really.'

The woman was, Neville supposed, a little younger than himself. She was on the interesting side of plainness, with an open smile which suggested a positive outlook on life and a bright eye confirming as much. He was surprised she was alone. Gustav returned with Neville's drink, and placed a menu on the table in front of him. He was inclined to begin his selection immediately, but the woman seemed keen to make a little conversation.

'You'll like it here; the food is excellent.'

'Good, I hope so. I have a very reliable recommendation.'

She nodded, still smiling slightly.

'I would tell you what I had to eat and recommend that, but I don't wish to influence your choice. In any event, I'm sure it is all wonderful.'

Neville smiled, raising the cold gin to his lips. The woman sipped her coffee then, after looking away, turned back to him.

'I hope you don't mind me saying this, but that's a rather fine suit.'

'Why thank you. It's new, actually; the result of another recommendation.'

'Your tailor has done you proud, I must say.'

The woman's dress — a vibrant pink, Neville now noticed — was also quite exceptional; and when she stood (having now finished her coffee) he could see the cut of it. The skirt was quite full, and the bodice — which was strapless — decidedly flattering. He rose to allow her to move past him. She offered her hand.

'It's been a pleasure to meet you.'

'The pleasure is all mine,' he replied, a little taken aback.

And then, after a brief handshake and a further smile as she reached the door, he was left alone at his table. In a moment, Gustav was back at the table clearing away the coffee cup.

'Perhaps Sir would like to take the seat vacated by Madame. I think you will find it more comfortable. I will return for your order in a few minutes.' As Neville thanked him, Gustav turned on his heel, and moved away.

FIFTEEN

Neville opened the menu and was confronted with two pages, listing — in a highly stylised script — the dishes on offer. Unable to resist habit, he scanned the pages for looking for prices but found none. There was also no mention of wines, and Gustav had failed to leave him a wine list. Undeterred — and already slightly relaxed by the gin — he decided to press on with his selection.

The left hand page of the menu summarised the Entrees; the right, the main courses. As he scanned for his starter he was immediately impressed by not only the range of dishes available, but their sophistication. He was not in the mood for fish, nor the more traditional starters such as pate or soup — even though these, as described, encouraged selection. Consequently he expected to find making the final choice difficult, but this proved not to be the case. One dish stood out: Salad of Roast Duck, served on a bed of wild rice; dressed with a light pepper and gherkin salad, and finished with a Cherry and Rose glaze. Thus decided, he turned his attention to the second page.

Over time he had become aware that, in certain circles, there was a kind of etiquette regarding the "construction" of a meal. Starting with duck, for example, would in theory limit the number of dishes available for a main course. But things were not, of course, subject to the "norm" at present (in almost any sense, as far as Neville could see) so he immediately decided to consider all options fair game. In Paris, Neville had seemed to take his food "on the run" as it were, and — to his chagrin — failed to take any advantage of the city's distinct cuisine. It felt as if he should have been in a similar situation to this whilst there — sitting in a restaurant, choosing a meal — but this had not materialised. On the basis of his entrée, he bypassed the chicken dishes and the fowl; this left him with meat, fish, or vegetarian.

Neville had dabbled with vegetarianism in the past, but unsuccessfully. For him it felt like something he would have to work at rather than instinctively adopt. For this reason, if none other, he was drawn to either the meat or fish. Logic having taken him this far, he took another sip from his gin, and undertook the final selection. As before, the task seemed simpler than he imagined possible; and once again the choice was obvious: Fillet of Monkfish pan-baked in fresh cream, dressed with a subtle dill and thyme sauce, and complemented with nuggets of honey-glazed carrots, buttered mange tout, and lightly dusted mustard potatoes. Satisfied, he closed the menu.

'Great choice! "On the money", Bob!'

The voice game from his side, and he turned to find a large, bright blue fish addressing him from the mural.

'Monkfish; great! They do it so well, it's "out of this world".'

The fish had large, bulbous eyes that were slightly out of alignment, giving it a peculiar stare. In addition, the artist — whom, Neville judged, could never profess that painting fish was his strongest suit — had given the creature a strange lop-sided leer. Neville glanced along the rest of the mural. The style throughout was similar, but this fish a shade exceptional. Gustav returned.

'Sir?'

'Yes. The duck, followed by the monkfish, please.'

'Sir.'

'Is there a wine list?'

'We are proud to think that we know our wines at this establishment, Sir, and it is our policy to provide our customers with precisely the correct wine for each of their courses. That way, you do not have to worry over the selection, and we ensure you get the best experience. Is that satisfactory, Sir?'

'Sounds fine. Thank you.'

As Gustav removed both the menu and himself, Neville was left impressed with the restaurant's efficiency.

'Really "on the ball", isn't it?' — the fish again — 'taking all the hassle out of it. And he's right, Bob; the wine's exceptional.'

'I'm sure.'

Neville glanced round the room. All the other diners appeared to be eating and drinking with such an air of satisfaction to suggest that there was some truth in what the fish had said. One well-dressed middle-aged lady glanced across from her table, and gave him a slight smile. She looked vaguely familiar.

'And yep, "you know your onions"! The duck; wow!'

Neville glanced back at the leery fish, frozen in the mural.

'It's exactly what the woman had; duck and monkfish.'

'Woman?'

'Yes; the broad who was here before you. The one with the pink dress.'

'Really?'

The fish lowered his voice.

'If I'd had been just a few inches further that way Bob, I could have spent the entire meal looking down her cleavage!'

Neville was taken aback. Perhaps that kind of attitude went with the fish's rather lascivious look.

'"You bet your boots", she had a great pair of...'

'Enough, I think, don't you?'

'Sorry, Bob; just "passing the time of day".'

'And don't call me Bob!'

'"Keep your hair on", Bob. "Can't teach an old dog, new tricks", eh?'

Neville returned the leer with a little contempt, but refused to respond to the fish's last remark. In addition to the continual reference to "Bob", he was beginning to be annoyed by the fish's ruthless use of cliché — even where marginally appropriate. He thought about changing his seat, but recollected that there was unlikely to be an alternative available. Perhaps, if it was in danger of spoiling his meal, they might like to paint out the fish on the wall.

'Hey, Bob; "horses for courses". I can't help being me, can I? How much choice did I get, "hear what I'm saying"? Shoot the artist if you like, but "don't shoot the messenger".'

Neville felt vaguely guilty at being hostile, and his desire to obliterate the fish altogether.

'OK; just be a little quieter, maybe.'

'Quiet, Bob? "Like the grave"!'

A few moments later, Gustav returned with a trolley on which were Neville's Entree and a half bottle of red wine. He laid the plate on the table with a slightly extravagant air.

'Your duck, Sir.'

The food presented looked nothing less than sculpted: slices of duck nestling on their wild rice bed, couched within the pepper and gherkin salad, all on the shoreline of the red cherry dressing. It was — as the fish might have said — "too good to eat".

'White is normal for the Entree,' Gustav said, pouring the wine, 'but as you were having the duck followed by fish, we felt that this red — a light Beaujolais — would best suit. If Sir would care to taste...'

Neville lifted the wine to his lips. It was smooth, and skipped lightly across his palette.

'Very pleasant, thank you.'

Gustav nodded and withdrew. For a short while Neville began to delicately dismantle the food on this plate. The duck was immaculate, and the combination offered with it such a stunning mixture of flavours and textures, that his taste buds were thrown into something of a frenzy.

'A little better than you're used to, Bob? "Home cooking", eh?'

'Yes', Neville looked at the fish, deciding to be a little nicer to him. 'And you were right; the food is truly excellent.'

'The smell gets me every time. Well, the taste can't, can it?! Turns me "green with envy"'. And is if to prove it, the fish flashed from blue to green, and then back again.

Neville sipped the wine. With the remnants of duck and peppers still on his palate, the Beaujolais tasted better than before.

'"Compliments to the chef", eh Bob? That's exactly what the Broad said. She called Gustav over and said "Compliments to the chef". People always do.'

'I don't blame them. The food is wonderful.'

Gradually the first course disappeared, and it was with some satisfaction that Neville closed the knife and fork on his plate, and poured himself the remainder of the red wine. On cue, Gustav came over to remove the plate.

'That was excellent,' Neville hesitated. 'Compliments to the chef.'

'Bob!', the fish said, after Gustav had gone, 'I knew you'd say that! Didn't I say they always say that!'

'Who?'

'Customers. They are always so impressed; that's what they say.'

'Just like they say other things?'

'Sorry, Bob?'

'Perhaps "don't shoot the messenger"; or "can't teach an old dog new tricks"; "horses for courses"?'

The fish was silent for a moment.

'OK; yes, like those things. Those are the sorts of things people say, OK? Don't take the piss out of the way I speak, Bob. How else am I supposed to learn except by listening to others; "leading by example", "hear what I'm saying?" That's all there is: "day in, day out". I listen, I learn. OK? Sure, I'm just some dumb fish, but that's it.'

'OK, sorry.'

'Sorry? Shit, you people, you've all got attitudes; "know what I mean?" That broad wasn't quite as bad as you, but I bet the next guy will be; I can tell Bob, I've seen them all.'

Gustav's arrival with the trolley once again interrupted them. Neville, who had become uncertain as to the direction the conversation with the fish was taking, found himself needing to refocus on food and the principle purpose of the evening. The waiter, having removed the red wine bottle and glass from the table, deposited a chilled bottle of white wine and fresh glass.

'A Chablis, Sir. I think you will find it quite perfect for the monkfish.' And then, with an even grander flourish than before, he removed the silver dome from Neville's plate to reveal the glory of his main course.

The monkfish sat proudly in the centre of the plate, mange tout radiating outwards. In the segments created by the mange tout, the carrots and potatoes alternated, the whole arrangement encircled by the gentleness of the sauce. Neville simply nodded at Gustav, preferring this time to say nothing. He took a sip of the Chablis before picking up his knife and fork. Deciding where to start was not easy, as the very first incursion would disrupt the symmetry of the plate. He chose mange tout, and then everything followed from that. The fish kept a respectable silence for a while as Neville savoured the exquisite meal. It was difficult not to eat at a breakneck pace, and he found himself needing to be disciplined in order to progress at an acceptable speed. The monkfish simply dissolved in his mouth, and each of the accompanying vegetables were cooked to perfection.

Movement across the room attracted his attention as one of the parties stood up to leave. This was the table containing the lady who had smiled briefly earlier on. She was a largish woman with well tonsured hair; the kind of blue-grey perm so favoured by ladies of a certain generation. She glanced at him again as she moved away, and Neville once again had the sensation that he had seen her somewhere before.

'So it's OK then, the food?'

Neville would have expected that sort of question to come from the Maitre or Gustav, but it was the fish again.

'Superb, of course.'

He expected more from the fish but there was no follow up. He looked at the large blue body, the strange eyes and the leer, and felt vaguely sorry for him.

'What kind of fish are you anyway?'

'Me? That's tough. I've been "kept in the dark" over that one, Bob, so I'm not sure I can say. Does it matter?'

Neville paused, fork paused before his mouth.

'No, I guess it doesn't.'

'No? That's good. Hey, thanks.'

And Neville was sure that, had he been able to, the fish would have given him a wink of one of his bulbous eyes. He carried on eating, though there was little left now. Another couple entered the room and took up their places at one of the reserved tables, and another waiter — one Neville had not seen before — made an appearance. He checked his watch. It was nearly nine thirty; obviously they closed quite late here.

'So where are you off to next, Bob?'

'Next?'

'I mean, once you're out of here. Tomorrow, when the sun shines; what does the day have in store for you?'

Neville finished the last morsel from his plate and poured another glass of Chablis.

'I don't know; I guess I hadn't really thought about it.'

'See if "something turns up", maybe?'

'Maybe.'

Neville thought of Samuel outside in the bus, and wondered if there were plans for tomorrow about which he as yet knew nothing.

'What's on the schedule?'

'Schedule?'

'Yes. You guys always seem to have plans; "things to do, people to see". People always talk about their plans — to each other, to Gustav, to me even.'

Gustav came and recaptured the now empty plate.

'Take that broad who was here before you; she talked to me. She had plans, she said — though from what I could see, there was little left on her list.'

Neville began to wonder about the fish's interest in the previous occupant of his seat. Perhaps there was a little more to it than lechery.

'So where was she off to, then?'

He tried to sound as disinterested as possible, but from the tone of his reply the fish must have realised he had Neville hooked.

'She said something about a Cruise; and another trip abroad, I think — though she wasn't sure about the order in which she'd do things. Why?'

'No reason.'

Neville's concentration was now taken again by Gustav, who had reappeared at his table and — having presented him with some coffee — was beginning to relay it. He showed little interest in Neville.

'What are you doing?'

'Laying the table, Sir. For the next customer.'

'But what about dessert?'

'I'm sorry Sir.' Meaning to complain, Neville looked up for the Maître. Gustav left the table and walked away to the hallway.

'It's always the same, Bob', said the fish, attempting to console him, 'there's never enough time.'

'What?'

Gustav appeared through the door, accompanied by a large, fat man. They approached Neville's table. Gustav bowed, slightly.

'Pardon, Monsieur; but this gentleman has arrived for his booking. I wonder if you would mind if he sat with you for an aperitif while you finish your coffee?'

Neville looked hard at Gustav. Those had been the very words he had used to the woman when he himself had arrived at the table. For a moment he felt a degree of panic, of uncertainty over what exactly was going on; and then, in an instant, the fog cleared. He looked from Gustav to the new arrival.

'Of course not. I won't be very long. That is, if the gentleman doesn't mind.'
He offered a smile to the newcomer, who nodded.

'See what I mean, Bob?' whispered the fish.

'Drink, Sir?', said Gustav to the man.

'Beer, ta.'

Neville smiled to himself. They were all in the same boat; him, the woman, this
new chap. He could spill the beans now if he choose; let the big man know
what was in store for him — even down to the leery-eyed fish — but that
would not be playing the game. Hadn't the woman toyed with the idea of
recommending her own choice of meal, but not done so? Had he not chosen it
anyway? He looked at the suit the newcomer was wearing. Although he was a
very large man, the suit managed to make the best of what was there. In doing
so, Neville recognised the handiwork of a certain A. Bossiman. With this,
there came a flash of memory, and Neville suddenly knew where he had
previously seen the woman's pink dress.

SIXTEEN

Neville spent a short while attempting to establish some kind of rapport between himself and the newcomer. The fat man was, however, ill-disposed to his efforts, possessing a level of taciturnity which blocked all attempts at social chit-chat. Neville wondered if he was facing another of those who had chosen Option 3; and guessed — perhaps rather unkindly — that if he had, this particular adventurer was surely destined for '3B'. He felt suddenly sorry for the big man because of this; yet things were never certain, and he could well be wrong. Who was to say how his experience might turn out?

He glanced at the fish. Judging by first appearances (which he knew to be an unwise move) he felt certain that the fish's words regarding the "next guy's attitude" were likely to be correct. As he left the restaurant, he wondered how 'new' the large man was to the particular game in which they were both engaged. How would he react to the fish, or at ten thirty, when the next customer would presumably arrive at Gustav's elbow and be invited to share the table for a short while? For his own part, Neville felt he had tried to vary the script a little, perhaps to put a modicum of his own personality into the game in an attempt to make what was to follow a little easier for the subsequent diner. Perhaps? For all he knew, the woman — in that pink ball gown from Mister Bossiman's — might have been doing exactly the same thing to him.

Samuel was sitting on his bed reading when Neville boarded the bus. The lighting had been changed and was a degree more practical. Samuel looked up, then placed his book — still open — face down on the bedside cabinet.

'How was your meal, Sir?'

There was a hopeful tone in Samuel's voice, rather than the air of certainty Neville had convinced himself he would find. He wondered how best to respond. He pulled off his tie as he thought of a reply.

'The food was excellent, of course.'

'Good; I was confident it would be. Perhaps you would like a little night-cap before retiring, Sir. I have a little brandy in the galley.'

'That would be good — and please have one yourself, Samuel.'

Samuel smiled.

'Thank you Sir, I think I might.'

By the time Samuel returned with the two glasses of brandy, Neville was sitting on his bed in his dressing gown. The suit hung over the door of the cupboard, and Samuel's first move was towards this.

'Samuel, please sit down.'

'I thought I might put this away first, Sir.'

'It can wait; please.'

Samuel responded by depositing himself in the driver's seat which he swivelled round to face into the bus. He read Neville's surprise.

'Oh, just another little modification I made while you were out, Sir.'

'You are a very ingenious man, Samuel.'

'Thank you, Sir. I like to think I can turn my hand to most things.'

'I hope you are not also ingenuous.'

'Sir?'

Neville sipped his brandy and felt its warmth contrast the chilled Chablis he had so recently sampled. He was uncertain how to progress this conversation. There were many questions he wanted to ask; things that needed clearing up. He had his own theories too, and was looking for some form of confirmation. As he looked at Samuel, he wondered just how much the latter was in control — or knew, come to that. And how much he was still master of his own destiny.

'Samuel, I have a feeling that this evening I met two other people who are in the same situation as myself.'

'"Situation", Sir?'

'People who have chosen Option 3. You see?'

'Indeed.'

'And...'

'And?' Samuel offered a slight frown, suggesting clarification was needed.

'Is that possible?'

Samuel paused. His eyes remain fixed on Neville's as he too sipped his brandy. The earlier image Neville had conjured equating Samuel to his grandfather was back again and, because of this, he felt no sense of peril in the conversation to come. Neville pulled his legs up onto the bed, and crossed them beneath him.

'Yes, it is possible. There are, of course, many people who may — at one time or another — find themselves in a similar situation to yourself. I think you might be surprised to find it is remarkably common.'

'And do you know them all?'

'Know them, Sir? No. Some perhaps, over time; but how can I know them all when I am with you?'

'OK; what about the restaurant then? How come there were at least three of us in there this evening, sitting at the same table, eating the same food?'

'You are certain of that?'

'Yes.'

Samuel tipped his glass, and took a little more of the Brandy. He looked hard at Neville.

'What if I told you that I was not aware of that being the case? Would you suspect me of not telling the truth?'

'If you were in my shoes...?'

'Yes,' Samuel smiled, 'point taken.'

Neville finished his glass and placed it on the cupboard. Almost before his hand had left it, ruby brown liquid had filled it again. He looked at Samuel.

'Mere trickery; it is not important. Really.'

Neville nodded, prepared to let it go.

'The restaurant,' he pursued, 'you use it a lot, I assume.'

'Yes,' Samuel nodded.

'Because of the fish?'

'The fish? Well, I hear that the fish is good there, but then the whole menu is supposed to be excellent.'

'Samuel, that's not what I meant — and you probably know it!'

'I'm not sure I follow, Sir. If our clients decided — as you did — that they want to experience a high quality meal, then this is one of the restaurants we can suggest to them. That is all.'

'So it has nothing to do with what happened to me inside?'

'What happens to you inside is — to be blunt — entirely of your own making. What happened to you in Paris was also entirely of your own doing.'

'OK, let's forget Paris for a moment. In there,' Neville nodded his head to indicate the restaurant, 'I met — Bob. Bob told me that the lady who had been sitting at my table before me — and who I met — had ordered exactly the same food as me, was planning to do exactly the same sorts of things I was planning to do… There's too much coincidence.'

'I see.' Samuel paused. Outside all was quiet, the silence only broken by their conversation. '"Bob" told you this, did he? And did you believe him? Was he telling you the truth, and about something that actually happened?'

Neville could not answer.

'You assume so, yes? But you cannot know, Sir. Perhaps you wanted Bob to tell you these things.'

'So what about her dress?'

'Her dress? Whose dress?'

'The lady at my table. Her dress. It was a flamingo pink ball gown; I saw the same dress at Mister Bossiman's.'

'Are you sure?'

'Positive.'

'It is true that, like the restaurant, we make full use of Mister Bossiman's services; but I think you may be overlooking one thing?'

'Yes?'

'Mister Bossiman is a gentleman's tailor. He has nothing to do with ladies' garments.'

Neville wanted to tell Samuel about the dance he had witnessed, about the dress, the band. But he realised quickly enough that he might be on uncertain ground. If Samuel was right — and why should he not be? — and everything that happened to him was actually within his control, then why should Samuel know about these things? What influence could he have over them? He thought back to Paris, and to Pierre. He had assumed that Pierre was something out of his control — something with a degree of power over him. If Samuel was being completely frank with him, then this might not be the case. Pierre might actually have been a manifestation of some part of himself.

This was difficult. Neville took a large swig from his brandy, and allowed it to burn slowly down the back of his throat. All the while Samuel was looking unswervingly at him.

'I'm not sure I understand, Samuel.'

There was a note in Neville's voice that caused the smile to leave Samuel's face.

'Please don't think that you are — how shall I say it? — going mad, Sir. You are not. Really.' He paused, then with a small note of relief, said 'Mrs Morris.'

'Sorry?'

'Mrs Morris. I saw her leave the restaurant while you were there. Do you remember her?'

Neville tried to regroup his thoughts.

'Largish, well-dressed lady. With silvery hair?'

'Indeed. Did you recognise her?'

'Vaguely, yes.'

'She was in the tea shop the day we met.'

'The Conservative Lady.'

'Sorry, Sir?'

'Yes, Samuel, I do remember her.'

'I see her about from time to time. She's a pleasant enough character, don't you think?'

Neville nodded. He was uncertain where he should place Mrs Morris in the general scheme of things. Perhaps it was enough for now that she was there in the restaurant and that he recognised her. As he sat pondering, he could almost feel night descending about the bus. Samuel, for the first time in a while, took his eyes from Neville and concentrated on finishing his drink. There was a sense of an averted crisis in the air; that the reality of Mrs Morris, both in Samuel's world and his own, had anchored him somehow.

'As a matter of interest, Sir, have you consulted your watch lately?'

Neville looked to his wrist, but the watch had already been put away in the cupboard.

'No, I haven't to be honest.'

'And did you while you were in Paris?'

'I can only recall looking at it once I was back on the bus; why?'

'Do you not think it strange, Sir, that given your reasoning that your original situation arose because of money, you should be so unconcerned with how you are spending it now?'

'But you said that it had nothing to do with value, and was all about worth.'

'Indeed; but you still have a finite stock with which to play. And yet you seem unconcerned about it.'

'Is that wrong?'

Samuel smiled again.

'No, Sir; I am not saying it is wrong, I am just trying to understand your apparently more relaxed attitude.'

'Perhaps it doesn't seem so important any more. Perhaps there are other things that matter. Maybe, I was wrong…'

Samuel's smile broadened.

'That it's not money that is the problem — and never was?' Samuel followed up.

'That perhaps it got in the way. Or the lack of it got in the way. Yet maybe that wasn't the case after all.'

He wanted to go to his cupboard and check his watch. He wondered about the worth of his dinner, or of the brandy they were drinking now — or even the "worth" of this present conversation with Samuel. He guessed it might be expensive. A thought crossed his mind.

'If I am right, Samuel…'

'Sir?'

'Do the rules change? Does money become irrelevant?'

Samuel shook his head.

'I'm afraid not, Sir. The rules cannot change. You made your bargain with Hans, and that is the bargain to which you must adhere. Your search — for whatever it is you are looking, or whatever it is you need — has been underway for a little while. Perhaps only now are you beginning to realise just how things stand. Or how you stand. But, you have defined your limit; you cannot dishonour that.'

'Cannot?'

'Cannot.'

Finishing the remnants of his brandy, Neville nodded slowly. He was now quite tired — and, to be truthful, a little drunk. Their conversation had given him much to think about. Despite what Samuel said, it was like throwing away the rules of a game and being given a new set for the same game. Perhaps he had a new goal to consider. Perhaps he had never had a real goal at all. As he slipped out of his dressing gown and into bed, he wondered how much clearer things would be in the morning.

SEVENTEEN

He was eventually roused by Samuel's cheery 'Good Morning!' and the aroma from the cup of tea which simultaneously landed on the cupboard by his bedside. It seemed one of those unfair awakenings: being disturbed before one was well and truly ready. He had managed to get some sleep, though for how much of the night it was impossible to say. All Neville knew was roughly the time he went to bed, and that it was now a little after seven.

Having checked his watch, he replaced it on the cupboard by the tea.

'Isn't this a little early, Samuel?'

His words felt blurred as he spoke them, crawling tiredly from him, as if they too were exhausted by a lack of sleep.

'Early, Sir? I don't think so. I suspect we may need to make an early start today.'

It was a comment which Neville failed to register. Unwittingly, he found himself returning to the root cause of his disturbed night, his trying to understand recent events; but he could only come up with things that seemed dream-like in themselves: "Mirelle" turning into a seagull; 'Bob', the talking fish.

'Don't let your tea get cold, Sir.'

Neville watched Samuel disappear round the edge of the curtain, and reflected on how his Mother had, for countless years, contrived to use those same words at least once a day. And if you substituted 'dinner' for 'tea', then he had heard it more often than that. Just now, however, it seemed a reasonable command to take seriously. It forced him to sit up a little — to 'shake himself', as Bob might have offered — and think about the day ahead.

The first few sips of tea (which was actually *very* hot) somehow placed a frame around the night, parcelling it up, and allowing Neville to file it away. It was something that was over, there was nothing residual left; it was time to move on. As he half-lay there, he contemplated the inside of the bus — a mobile home which, by the day, was becoming more like a home and less like anything mobile!

Neville drained the tea and climbed out of bed. Pulling on his dressing gown, he made his way through the curtains and towards the smell of bacon that was, under Samuel's command, frying on the galley stove.

'How are we this morning, Sir?' Samuel said, as Neville reached him.

'Fine, Samuel. A little tired, but fine.'

'I have taken the liberty of running your bath.'

'Thanks.'

Neville deposited the tea cup on the small sink unit and went through into the bathroom. The filled bath awaited him, but this time there was no duck floating on its surface. Neville looked for it briefly, but it was not in evidence. As he slid into the water, he wondered if it might have been pleasant to have spoken to it again — but then again, perhaps its absence suggested it had served its purpose.

As it was, Neville emerged a few minutes later after an undisturbed and relaxing bath. Samuel was still at the stove, though now tending sausages. The bacon had disappeared, though its smell lingered.

'Everything all right, Sir?'

'Fine, Samuel; thank you.'

'I've put your clothes out on the bed.'

Neville nodded and walked through to his small compartment.

As Samuel had said, Neville's attire for the day awaited him: slacks, a polo shirt and light cardigan. He pulled back the curtain at the window and looked out. It seemed a little too grim outside for such light clothes, but then presumably Samuel knew what he was doing — or, indeed, what they both would be doing.

At the foot of the bed, Neville noticed the suit trousers he had worn the night before lying there, awaiting return to the small wardrobe. He was surprised to find them, partly because he thought he could recall some form of discussion from the previous evening about putting them away, and partly because, given Samuel's faultless efficiency, it seemed something of an anathema to find them still out.

He thought about calling to Samuel, but decided it would be simplest to just put the trousers away himself. As he lifted them from the bed, a small rectangle of white paper fell from one of the pockets and down to his feet. Neville, with the trousers resting over one arm, bent to pick it up. In the moments between bending and standing upright again — just about to open the folded paper — he tried to imagine what it might be: a receipt for the meal? Had the fat man given him something? He could recall nothing.

The paper, which was of reasonable quality vellum, was folded accurately into halves and opened easily. Neville could tell by the pristine state of the paper, that it had been folded once — firmly and with conviction — and no more; there had been no unfolding to reconsider its content. It was headed with the crest of the restaurant, and its contents were formed in a free-flowing hand. About half-way down, Neville read:

I hope you enjoyed the Duck and the Monkfish - they were really very good, weren't they?! I wonder if your evening turned out anything like mine; something of a "sting in the tail"...?

I am going on a cruise — but perhaps you know that already! S.S.Pilgrim; leaving Southampton tomorrow.

Perhaps we might meet again one day...

M.

The note could only have had one author. Neville, rather than digest its content, was intrigued as to how it could have found its way into his pocket. The woman — "M" — must have written it on her way out; on that basis, did Gustav slip it into Neville's trousers at some stage? Or perhaps it had been the fat man? Neville could not reconcile himself to the latter option; at least Gustav would have had the chance — and the "agility" — to perform the required operation.

He turned his thoughts to the content after a moment. They threw an interesting light on the discussions he had had with Samuel the previous evening. "M" was obviously "in the same boat" as he, and their shared experience — even down to Bob (surely "sting in the tail" was a reference?!) — was patently real enough. He raised the note a little higher, as if doing so would confirm its authenticity, and prepared to call Samuel.

In the instant between raising his hand and engaging his vocal chords, Neville's reaction to the note shifted from the intellectual to the emotional. Questions savaged him from all sides: why was this woman, "M", telling him where she was going? What did she mean by "perhaps we might meet again"? Was she really part of his plot — that pink dress! — or had they somehow become entangled?

'Samuel!'

The curtain drew back and Samuel, holding a tray containing Neville's cooked breakfast, stood before him.

'Sir?'

'Southampton, Samuel. We're taking that cruise of mine.'

'Very good, Sir. Would you like me to keep your breakfast hot for you while you dress, or will you eat it now?'

'I'll be dressed in a minute; you can leave it with me.'

Samuel put the plate by the side of the bed.

'Shall I get us underway, Sir — if you'll pardon the nautical turn of phrase.'

'Please.'

'Can I enquire the name of the ship?'

'The S.S.Pilgrim; why?'

'Just so I know where to go when we get to the docks, Sir. That's all.'

'Presumably you know where she's sailing, Samuel?'

'I believe it's the Mediterranean, Sir.'

Neville looked at the clothes laid out for him on the bed.

'And presumably you also knew we were bound to be going there?'

Samuel smiled.

'I'll get us moving, Sir; I don't think we've too much time to spare.'

EIGHTEEN

When Neville made his way to his customary seat a few minutes later, the bus was already in motion. He put the plate containing his bacon, sausages and eggs down on the adjacent table and looked along the road. They were in the country, presumably south of Birmingham, though as he knew it was difficult to tell exactly where the bus might be at any one time. Samuel acknowledged his arrival with the merest glance, then returned his attention to the road ahead. Neville fell to his breakfast.

He believed he had managed to instil a degree of urgency into their prospective journey; indeed, he assumed this was confirmed by Samuel's apparent willingness to get the bus underway immediately. Despite this however, their progress was limited to the mandatory twenty seven miles per hour, and as they meandered through the countryside Neville felt inclined to ask Samuel if he couldn't possibly manage to go a little faster.

History — thus far, at any rate — suggested Samuel's judgement in terms of timing was impeccable, and Neville had no real cause to doubt they would arrive in Southampton in plenty of time to board the boat. He speared the remains of his last sausage and raised the fork to his mouth.

'I take it you have made reservations for the voyage, Sir?'

'Reservations? I thought you took care of that sort of thing. There don't seem to have been any problems in the past.'

The sausage segment became suspended three inches from Neville's mouth.

'When I can. But you seem to have taken this decision rather suddenly.'

'You're telling me you didn't know where we were going?'

'Of course not, Sir. How could I?'

'But the clothes you laid out seemed so suitable. And your attitude. You weren't at all surprised.'

Samuel glanced round. In the brief pause, Neville pulled the sausage from the fork with his teeth.

'I like to think that I am prepared for anything, Sir.' Samuel took a breath, allowing for any potential contradiction. 'The clothes? You had talked about a cruise. Perhaps I made a lucky guess.'

'Perhaps.' Neville was doubtful. 'Does that mean the cruise is off?'

'Oh, not at all, Sir. If we can make a quick stop, perhaps I might be able to phone ahead.'

This seemed a strange departure from the ritual as Neville had experienced it thus far. Samuel seemed perfectly genuine, yet something about the situation ran contrary to the general pattern of the adventure. Neville — whose desire to make the boat had been steadily growing since the idea first struck him — was powerless to do anything except concur.

Five minutes later the bus was stationery, and Neville was watching through his window as Samuel rang Southampton docks from a roadside telephone kiosk. There was little spectacle in this, Samuel remaining motionless and non-expressive for the duration of the call apart from a slight inclination of the head at one point, and a more definite nod immediately before he put the phone down.

'All booked, Sir.' Samuel announced on his return. 'The S.S.Pilgrim sails on this afternoon's tide, which doesn't leave us too much time — but I'm sure we'll make it.'

The last remark was offered with one of his knowing winks which meant that, when they set off at their snail's pace again, questioning their progress was the last thing on Neville's mind.

Slowly they rolled through the countryside; the roads were quiet and, apart from the occasional flock of sheep or herd of cattle, the scenery was relatively bland too. Samuel had retrieved an atlas of the world from somewhere, and presented it to Neville with the suggestion that he might like to study the islands of the Mediterranean in order to familiarise himself with them prior to their arrival.

'"Our" arrival?' Neville had echoed.

'Yes, Sir. I think it might be wise if I were on hand, don't you?' Neville recalled Paris and reflected on how valuable Samuel's ultimate intervention had been.

As he took in details of Malta, Corsica and Sardinia, he felt the bus gradually descending downhill. It seemed a hill without a bottom, and without any adverse gradient to counter it. He could hear Samuel in his driver's seat reciting poetry —

I must go down to the seas again,

to the lonely sea and the sky,

and as he spoke it seemed the bus was — quite literally — going *down* to the sea as there, in the distance, the Solent shimmered in the early afternoon sun. There were no tall ships — at least not as John Masefield would have known them — but Neville could make out one or two large vessels and the jibs of the tall cranes working them.

The bus turned a corner and Neville lost sight of the docks. He wondered which of the two ships he had seen was the S.S.Pilgrim — or if neither, then where on the docks she might be. Samuel would probably know, but Neville was ill disposed to disturb him as he feared they had come as close to "racing against the clock" as they were ever likely to.

When they reached Southampton it seemed as if humanity had descended on the town. The roads were full of cars, and the pavements packed with people.

'Must be some kind of event, Sir,' Samuel said after they had been stationary in a traffic queue for a few minutes.

'Is there any way out of this, Samuel? How much time do we have?'

'I've been following the signs for the docks, Sir. We'll get there as soon as we can.'

Neville spotted a policeman walking their way; he was chatting with other pedestrians, apparently unconcerned by the congestion. Neville — who was by now on his feet and leaning against Samuel's seat — pointed him out. Samuel lowered his window.

'Excuse me, Officer. We're trying to get to the docks, and I'm afraid we're in rather a hurry.'

'Hurry, eh?' The Policeman laughed. 'Well you won't get there through the middle of the town; there's a big "do" on, see? It's where all these people are going.'

Neville, although intrigued to know what kind of "do" would bring people out in such numbers, had his mind firmly set on making the docks in the shortest possible time.

'Can we go some other way? Not through the centre of the town?'

'Well, Sir; let me see.' And the Policeman paused long enough to effect a professional frown before replying. 'You might try going west, and then back in from that side. I think it should be less busy that way.'

'Thank you, Officer. Now, which way's that?'

'Why, over there.'

And as the Policeman pointed, a gap appeared in the traffic to the right, just where another road branched off. Samuel swung the bus out of the main stream.

'Try a couple of miles or three,' the Policeman shouted after them, 'then head back in!'

As they headed west, cutting across the threads of traffic and people all aiming for the town centre, their progress — though still not rapid — improved. After two miles, Samuel began to look out for signs that indicated "Docks" and, on finding the first one, took the designated route. The Policeman had been correct in his judgement, and, though they were now in a position where Neville would have been glad of twenty seven miles per hour, at least they were making forward progress.

When the "Docks" signs eventually drew them out of the throng and away downhill once again — and back to twenty seven miles an hour — it had been nearly an hour since they had lost sight of the Solent, the ships and the cranes. Samuel had been silent for virtually all of that time, and even now — with open road again ahead of them — remained quiet. Neville, having returned to his seat, felt a degree of tension in the air undoubtedly caused by Samuel's unspoken concern that they might actually be late.

The first entrance they came to proclaimed Dock Gate Twelve. Neville looked at Samuel.

'Which one do we want, Samuel?'

'Three, Sir.'

The gates seemed impossibly far apart, and although they were no longer hampered by traffic, it was taking an age to get from one gate to the next. When they reached Four, Neville thought he could see a gentle plume of smoke rising from beyond the wharf-side sheds ahead, and wondered if that might be the Pilgrim making ready to get under way.

On finally pulling through Dock Gate Three and driving down to the pontoon, they discovered the smoke was indeed coming from the S.S.Pilgrim —

however, the ship was not making ready, she was actually sailing away. Perhaps by as little as ten minutes, they had missed the boat. Samuel shut down the bus engine, and the two of them sat in silence watching the S.S.Pilgrim grow ever smaller, churning a white wake with seagulls dancing in the foam. The cawing of the gulls carried back to them, mockingly almost.

'I'm sorry, Sir.' Samuel broke the silence, though without taking his eyes off the ship. 'I don't know how this happened. I don't think I have ever been late before.'

Neville wondered about the Eiffel Tower, but admonishment never occurred to him.

'You couldn't have known about the traffic or the crowds, Samuel. Otherwise we would have made it.'

Samuel choose not to reply. Again they both stared after the boat. The dockside was deserted apart from them.

'I guess that's it then,' was all Neville could offer, as he struggled with the disappointment of not making the boat, of not taking the cruise, and — most importantly — of not renewing his acquaintance with "M".

Samuel rose from his seat.

'Excuse me, Sir; I won't be a minute.' And with that he was off the bus and out of sight.

For some reason, Neville had a brief image of Captain Oates at the South Pole — "I may be some time" — and wondered, not without some concern, why Samuel had left the bus.

The minute Samuel promised to be away extended to thirteen, but when he returned — boarding the bus as suddenly as he had left it — the smile on his face immediately suggested that all was not lost.

'We are in luck, Sir!' he said as he started the bus.

'Samuel?'

'The S.S.Pilgrim is making a special stop in the Channel Islands before she heads for Gibraltar. There is an airport just north of the town and I have arranged a plane for us. We can overtake the ship and board her in Guernsey.'

Neville could say nothing. He sat back in his seat as the bus moved away from Gate Three and out into the city again. Might his hopes not be dashed after all? And what should expect to find once he stepped on board the ship?

The bus began the steady incline away from the docks, occasionally offering a view of the sea and the speck the S.S.Pilgrim had now become. Samuel had taken to whistling, evidently relieved that all was not yet lost, and Neville — to take his mind off their renewed chase — had picked up the atlas again and was contemplating the rather complex geography of the Caucasus Mountains.

They left the city behind and, for a few miles, travelled once again through open country. The aerodrome — signified by its tower, radar and windsock — came upon them suddenly: one minute they weren't there, the next they were. Samuel steered the bus through the main gate, past the car park, and out onto the fringe of the runway. As they descended the bus, Neville looked for the plane that would speed them to the Channel Islands and his longed-for rendezvous. Expecting a small jet or some such, the only plane he could see was an old World War One bi-plane.

From a building which housed hangars and administration as well as the control tower, a figure emerged and began walking towards them. As the man drew closer, Neville, recognising the portent of his leather helmet, handlebar moustache, white scarf and jodhpurs, put two and two together. He looked back at the old bi-plane. Could that get them to Guernsey in time?

The pilot and Samuel were in conversation when Neville turned to them again. The pilot smiled and walked towards him, offering his hand.

'"Binky" Bingham's the name!' he boomed in a B-movie accent. 'Hear you chaps want a quick recce over the water, what?'

Neville smiled as he took Binky's hand, then winced politely under the pressure of the cast-iron grip.

'Have you over there in a jiffy!' Binky continued, 'No Huns about today, what?' And with that, he marched off to the plane.

Neville looked at Samuel. He refrained from articulating the questions — and fears — which were bouncing around in his head. Samuel's silent nod of understanding and meek smile of acknowledgement were sufficient. They followed Binky to the plane, where, after the appropriate degree of "Boy's Own" bonhomie, they were installed in the two passenger seats. Ahead of them, Binky planted himself firmly in the pilot's seat and, pulling his goggles down, bawled "Chocks away!" to no-one in particular.

The bi-plane's archaic engine spluttered into life and with a cavalier wave from their pilot, they began to bump roughly across the apron to the end of the runway. As they paused for the engine to work up the appropriate enthusiasm,

Neville noticed another hanger near the tower outside of which numerous modern aircraft sat idle. He tapped Samuel (who was sitting in front of him) on the shoulder, ready to suggest they abort Binky for something a little more modern, when the bi-plane suddenly lurched forwards.

Rather than smoothly, they accelerated along the runway in pulses. Binky appeared to have several goes at yanking the joystick to lift the plane into the air, but each of these met with failure. Indeed, they came within a few yards of the end of the runway — and Neville contemplating the failure of his quest in some "total" sense — when the plane's wheels hit a large bump (almost, he would reflect later, like a Sleeping Policeman) which threw the craft from the tarmac and up into the air.

For a few seconds, the plane seemed suspended, uncertain as if it would manage the rest itself; but then, roaring like a wounded lion, the single engine pulled them upwards and towards the heavens.

NINETEEN

After the initial scare, the flight began to feel a little more like a conventional excursion. They ascended to something in the order of a thousand feet, at which point the engine seemed to give up its quest for more height and insisted on levelling off. As far as Neville could tell, Binky had managed nothing as yet to suggest he had any control over their fate. He wanted to talk to Samuel about arrangements for their immediate future, but was forced to abort any such plans when his first and only attempt was completely thwarted by the noise of the engine. Powerless to do anything but sit there and wait, he decided to make the most of the flight.

The plane banked over Southampton Water — though whether this was due to Binky it was impossible to say — and began to follow the Hampshire coastline west. Neville felt reassured that, for the first time since he had met Samuel, they were travelling between two distant points *and* were using a means which allowed him to verify the nature of their progress. Although they were not flying particularly high, Neville soon began to feel cold as the wind rushed about him. Binky, at one stage, turned and gave them a "gung ho!" kind of wave, apparently oblivious to the conditions his passengers were facing. Samuel had, very soon after take-off, rummaged around in the cockpit he was sitting in and managed to retrieve a leather flying jacket and hat, both similar to Binky's. Within minutes, from the rear view he had of them Neville found it impossible to tell the two apart.

With Samuel proving the benefit of initiative, minutes later — and a fair distance along the coast — Neville decided it could be worth his while to see if there was additional clothing secreted somewhere for him. A few seconds searching around where he sat rewarded him with a rather tatty white scarf which, despite its somewhat careworn appearance, was soon adorning his neck. He tried to tie it in a manner appropriate for an aviator, but suspected all he managed was a clumsy kind of knot. In any event, it was a little warmer, though still insufficient for his present needs. As he looked about, craning his neck to examine every reachable space, he discovered a small lever on the side of his seat which, when depressed, allowed him to rotate a complete 180 degrees. In doing so, he was rewarded by two things: first was the welcome sight of a sheepskin jacket in a recess by his feet; second was the realisation that the plane boasted a primitive anti-aircraft gun mounted on the fuselage and pointing to the rear. He pulled on the coat, wondering as he did so, how he

had managed to miss the gun; presumably this had been due to excitement —
or fear.

Warmer now, Neville rotated in his seat again, then looked out in a more
contented frame of mind. They had progressed along the Devon coast and,
banking left, ahead of them lay the western half of the English Channel. It was
a bright, clear day, and Neville thought he could make out their destination. If
that were the case, then surely at some stage they might also fly over the
S.S.Pilgrim. He turned to the east, scanning the surface of the water,
attempting to discern the cruise ship from the various other craft plying their
respective trades. Tankers were easy to spot because of their bulk; yachts easy
to miss because of their lack of it. The S.S.Pilgrim should, from what he could
remember, reveal herself as something between the two.

He had just caught sight of a ship that met his expectations — right sort of size
and steaming in the right direction — when his view changed instantly and he
found himself looking at nothing but water. Worse than that, it was water that
seemed to be getting closer, and rather quickly. They were in something of a
steep dive. Ahead, Binky's scarf flew stiffly behind him as they accelerated
downwards. Neville was about to tap Samuel on the shoulder when a sudden
manoeuvre from the pilot resulted in them being thrown back in their seats; all
he could see now was the blue of the sky.

If the engine had roared on take-off, its complaint now was less feline and
more like that of a dinosaur. Up and up it pulled them — certainly higher than
before — until it they began to lose momentum. At the last minute, just as they
seemed about to stop dead still, the plane banked and began to swoop away to
the right.

Neville — who by this time had not only lost all sense of direction, but was
beginning to wonder if he might not lose his breakfast too — doubted such an
extreme exhibition was part of the normal in-flight entertainment; though with
Binky at the controls, anything might be possible. Indeed, he was beginning to
search for other reasons for their present course when a second roar greeted
his semi-deafened ears; another bi-plane appeared suddenly ahead of them,
crossing their path.

Although they were not travelling particularly fast, the two planes seemed to
cross in a split second, and Neville had to rotate in his chair to follow the
progress of the newcomer. His tracking of this second red plane revealed the
presence of a third; the latter now bearing down on them from behind and
slightly above. He could not be exactly certain what first confirmed it —

perhaps it was the fact that these new planes were bright red; perhaps it was their markings; or perhaps it was the flashes from their forward-mounted machine guns — but Neville knew they were in trouble.

He felt Binky begin to steer the plane into a dive again, and as they began to drop, Samuel tapped him on the shoulder.

'What!' Neville shouted, convinced Samuel could not hear him.

'The gun!'

Samuel must have made a superhuman effort to get himself heard above the din, but hear him he did. He turned back to the gun and took its butt in his hands. It was heavy and cumbersome, and at first Neville could do little but wave it round.

As they dived, the second red plane buzzed above them. Neville could see the first turning their way, preparing to attack again. No way was this a simple drama. Remembering to aim away from the rudder, Neville tried to fire off a couple of trial shots. He pulled the trigger and nothing happened.

'Safety catch!' came Samuel's voice again.

Glancing along the gun, Neville found a small lever that appeared might do the trick. He flicked it and tried again. The gun kicked into life, the recoil far stronger than he expected (despite its mounting), and he simply sprayed the rounds in a broad arc. This would be more difficult than he had anticipated.

As the first of the intruders swooped towards them, Neville took careful aim and fired. After a short burst, the gun ended up pointing at least twenty degrees away from the target, Neville just able to make out the fading traces of his initial attempt falling tamely away. The red plane opened fire. Neville could not see the traces of the bullets as they came towards him and, although he had nothing to back this up, he sensed their adversary's shooting was a little better than his own.

The planes crossed again as Binky slipped into a slight dive, then pulled up and away to the right. Considering its age, the bi-plane was performing remarkably well, and Neville was beginning to re-evaluate his opinion of Binky as an "Ace". Samuel was once again silent, watching helplessly as the drama unfolded either side of him. Neville hoped that a little instruction might come his way, but there was nothing further.

In the distance — it seemed miles away — the two red planes came briefly together then began another attack. They were faster than Binky's old crate and, it appeared, could out-manoeuvre them too. Neville flexed his hands and prepared to pick up the cudgels again. He had learnt much from his first attempt and had decided that it would undoubtedly be best not to aim directly at his target but away from it, allowing the gun's natural travel to strafe the plane's path.

From either side the red planes began their swoop. Closing in, it appeared that they would cross on completion of their attack, peel away, and come in for another run. Neville licked his lips. Fire spat from the oncoming bandits before Neville opened up — "don't fire until you see the whites of their eyes!" He aimed well to the right of the plane attacking from that side and pulled hard on the trigger. The gun swung violently around, spraying a wide array of bullets which, in its enthusiasm, peppered their own tail before coming to a glorious end by hitting the plane on their left-hand side — the one Neville had *not* been aiming at.

There was a slight puff of black smoke, a cough, and then the stricken plane began to fall out of the sky like a wounded bird. Neville's exhilaration was immediate and intense; he had just about enough time to imagine Samuel reciting some war poem or other, when he realised that they too were beginning to lose height. He looked about; he could see no sign of smoke. Turning to face the front of the plane once again, he failed to see the cause of their present predicament immediately — though the fact that they were in trouble was evidenced by the increasing rapidity with which they were losing height and the slight spin they also seemed to be adopting.

Past Samuel's shoulder, Neville noticed Binky slumped forwards. He thumped Samuel on the shoulder, and pointed ahead. He could see nothing of Samuel's face, nor hear any reply that might have been forthcoming; but what he did see was Samuel raise the thumb of his left hand. Was this reassurance or understanding? Or did he have a parachute?

As his mind raced to find some kind of solution, he felt the spin steady then stop. Then he felt the plane's descent ease. He craned his neck in an attempt to see round Samuel's body. His bus driver was now proving that he was something of a pilot too — or was it all the same thing? A second set of controls adorned the portion of the cockpit where Samuel sat and, for a while at least, things were back under control.

Samuel's other hand jerked out over the side of the plane and upwards. There, above them, the second red devil was beginning another run. Neville swung back into his firing position and prepared himself. There was a flash, then another. He heard a strange "whing" then saw — in slow motion almost — a small hole appear in the body of the plane just by his left leg. Driven on by anger, Neville pulled the gun round and opened fire. This time it remained steady and his aim unswerving.

A puff — the tell-tale smoke — and then the beginnings of a spin. The enemy pilot leapt from his cockpit to abandon the dying craft. Again Neville's burst of joy was short-lived as the red plane began to hurtle towards them. He spun round and thumped Samuel on the back of the head. Samuel looked round and Neville closed his eyes.

The asthmatic cough of the attacker's dying engine was the next thing of which Neville was aware, then the rush of the red plane as they themselves fell from the sky in the opposite direction. He opened his eyes to see the second plane spinning harmlessly away like a broken toy. The two parachutes of the defeated pilots looked like flowers above a sea-green flower bed; and there, just where he would have expected it to be, the outline of the S.S.Pilgrim — no doubt oblivious of the drama being played out in the skies above it — making its way towards Guernsey.

Samuel levelled the plane and banked to head in the same direction. After a few minutes flying, the island presented itself as a welcome haven. It seemed ridiculously small, and the runway — when Neville eventually made it out — an impossibility. They circled twice before there was suddenly silence.

From ahead, Samuel shouted one word — "Fuel!" — and, almost on command, they began to lose height.

As the ground gained on them — Neville now able to make out individual houses and fields, the old fortifications and the new hotels — he closed his eyes once again. It was not lack of faith that prompted such an action, but cowardice. It seemed an age for nothing to happen. And then there was a bump. And then another. And then, in the silence, the sound of squeaking wheels on less than smooth tarmac. Neville opened his eyes; they were down.

Their arrival was greeted by a small crowd of airport staff who, to their credit, behaved as if having a slightly wounded bi-plane landing on their runway without fuel was an everyday occurrence. Once they had come to a complete halt, Neville sat motionless and silent. Samuel, flicking a lever on his own seat, turned to face him.

'Sir? Are you all right?'

Neville looked into Samuel's concerned face.

'Thank you, Samuel.'

At the front of the plane, a moan escaped from Binky.

'I didn't know you could fly.'

'I learned in the war, Sir.'

Again a moan from Binky.

'I didn't know you could shoot, Sir.'

Neville laughed.

'I can't!'

'Tally Bloody Ho!'

Binky was now standing on his seat, waving his arms and sending his scarf into spasms. Unsteadily he turned to face his two charges.

'Bloody good show! Bloody good...'

But the rest of his words were interrupted by him losing balance and falling out of the plane completely. Three airport hands prepared to scrape him from the runway.

'Is he OK?'

'Probably just a scratch, Sir. Couldn't stand all the excitement.'

Neville caught Samuel's smile.

'He wasn't the only one!'

TWENTY

There were no formalities at the airport. Neville and Samuel simply walked away from the plane and towards the waiting taxi in which Binky was already installed. Samuel had divested himself of his flying gear, returning it to its place of origin before leaving the plane. As Neville watched him, he realised that he had forgotten his companion was essentially an old man; how old it was difficult to say, but his reference to "the war" was intriguing.

Binky was sitting on the back seat of the cab, nursing a shoulder wound.

'Hah! We showed those rotten blighters, didn't we boys! Blasted the bounders from the sky!'

Neville caught the scent of medicinal brandy on Binky's breath.

'Are you all right?'

'Me? Never better, old boy! Just a spot of shrapnel in the shoulder, you know. Always gets me there. Fainted clean away! Thank God for the skipper, what!'

Binky turned to offer Samuel a congratulatory thump on his shoulder, but as he did so the pain from his wound sent him swooning in a heap to the floor of the car. Neville bent forwards.

'I'd leave him Sir, if I were you. He's probably better resting there.'

As they pulled away, Neville wondered how close Binky's "resting" had been to finding a permanent heavenly abode — and how long it would be before he was plundering the skies again in his ancient machine. He looked out of the back of the cab to see the old bi-plane being pulled from the runway to a waiting hanger. Presumably it would sit there until Binky had recovered sufficiently well to fly it home.

'The hospital; then the docks, please.' Samuel gave the instruction to the driver, then turned to Neville. 'Are you OK, Sir? Would you like to take that jacket off?'

Neville was still wearing the sheepskin from the plane.

'I'd like to keep it — just for a while, if that's OK.'

'Still cold?'

'The shivers. That's all.'

It was a half-lie, but sufficient to allow him to extend his loan of the garment. He was uncertain as to his exact feelings at that precise moment. There was, he suspected, a degree of shock yet to emerge as a result of the flight, and he was unsure how that might manifest itself. It was certainly warmer on the ground than it had been in the air, but Neville was taking no chances.

Half-way to the hospital, Binky roused himself with a cry of "Blighters never fight fair!" followed by half a chorus of "There'll always be an England" before passing out again. Locating a cushion, Samuel pushed it under the pilot's head.

'Has that happened to you before, Samuel?'

'What, Sir?'

'That; the dog fight.'

'Why do you ask?'

'I don't know; you seemed quite "natural" as a pilot. And you said something about the war.'

Samuel smiled.

'Yes, I did.' He paused. 'Let us say that I have flown an aeroplane on more than one occasion — and something not dissimilar to that we flew in today.' He paused again. 'But you, Sir; you have a fine eye, if I might say so!'

Neville, buoyed by Samuel's praise, abandoned his original line of enquiry.

'I was just lucky, that's all.'

'Nonsense Sir. The way you took out that second chap; most impressive. Most impressive.'

'Well, perhaps I'd got the hang of it by then.'

The conversation trailed off, and the journey was soon broken by their arrival at the hospital. Three porters were waiting to haul Binky from the floor of the cab and onto a waiting trolley. His cry of "Give my love to Blighty!" was the last they heard as he disappeared through the swing doors of the casualty unit.

With Binky taken care of, they were off again, the taxi rolling sedately through the narrow streets of St. Peter Port. Neville had lost track of time — was it Thursday or Sunday, he had no idea — and was consequently uncertain whether or not to be surprised by the relatively small number of people out and about.

The volume increased a little as they came to the waterfront. In the marinas, dozens of boats bobbed hopefully in the water, criss-crossing their masts in animated — if silent — conversations while their owners discussed the state of the tides or the winds whilst knotting ropes or sipping pink gins. Further along the quay, a large and impressive vessel was moored: the S.S.Pilgrim.

As they approached the ship, Neville could see a few people walking the various decks and hanging over the railings looking back into St. Peter Port. He tried to remember what "M" looked like, but could only conjure a vague image in pink; certainly insufficient to locate her among those he could see now.

A couple of taxis pulled away as they drew up. There was a single walkway up to the deck, and this was covered with a white cloth awning which rippled in the breeze. Neville expected this to bear the name of the ship, but it displayed the name of the port instead. At its base a young dockhand stood, his hands in the pockets of slightly grubby overalls. He looked up at their approach, and seeing them get out of the taxi, walked over.

'You the two daft gits who missed the boat in Southampton then?'

It was not the sort of greeting Neville would have expected. The Channel Islands had a certain reputation, a certain image in his mind; this man did not match that.

'We did miss the boat in Southampton, yes.' It was Samuel who replied.

The young man looked after the retreating taxi.

'No bags?'

'I believe everything has been taken care of. May we board?'

He shrugged his shoulders.

'It's up to you, Daddio. I mean, we've only been waiting for you, haven't we?'

Neville sensed Samuel stiffen, ruffled by the abusive treatment they had just received. Neville noted the man's last comment which suggested he was one of the ship's complement, rather than an islander.

'Come along then, Samuel,' Neville prompted, 'let's get on.' And as they walked past the dock hand, Neville managed to tread — with a deliberate degree of force — on the young man's left foot. 'Sorry; my fault.'

The look Neville received in consequence was sufficient to suggest he might not have seen the last of this particular character.

They passed under the awning, and began the climb up to the deck. At the top, one of the ship's officers was waiting for them; this time the greeting was a sharp salute.

'My name's Porter; I'm the Bursar. Glad to have you on board, Gentlemen. May I show you to your cabins?'

And with that he turned on his heel and began to walk away, safe in the knowledge that Neville and Samuel were bound to follow him. Voices now rose from somewhere else on the ship, and Neville looked back to see the insolent dock hand running onto the ship from the walkway just as a crane began to haul it away. From the jetty, men appeared to be suddenly busy with ropes, and a "whoop, whoop" from the ship's whistle set the seal on their preparations for departure.

As they followed the Bursar along the deck, a number of the passengers leaning on the rail waved towards the shore, but Neville could see no-one to wave back. Perhaps somewhere in the town — and armed with binoculars — there might be relatives invisibly signalling.

Porter took a sharp turn through an open doorway and into a corridor.

'Mind your head, Sir,' said Samuel, indicating the slightly low lintel.

'I'm fine Samuel, thank you.'

A few yards along the corridor they came to a stairway leading upwards. Porter, this time after a brief glance behind and a slight, professional smile, took these stairs to the next deck. At this point they came across another corridor and another set of stairs. Once again Porter ascended.

At the top of the second set of stairs, the Bursar waited for his two new passengers.

'If I can explain,' he said, once they had joined him, 'you arrived on-board on deck "C". We have just come through deck "B", and are now on "A" deck; this is where your cabins are.'

He began to walk along the short corridor, a little more slowly this time, talking as he did so.

'You gentlemen were quite lucky with your bookings, as it happens. I understand you arranged passage a little late? We had a couple of cancellations and both twenty seven and twenty eight became available.'

They had arrived at two doors, set close together, with numbers on them Porter had indicated.

'They are adjoining cabins, with a door between them should you require such a facility.'

'Thank you', said Samuel.

'You take twenty seven, Samuel,' Neville suggested, thinking instantly of the bus. 'Is that OK?'

Both other men nodded their approval.

'Your baggage is here I believe,' the Bursar said. 'I'll let you get settled in, then arrange for Bursar, the Porter, to come and check that everything's "ship shape".'

'"Bursar"?' said Neville.

'Yes?'

'No; sorry, Bursar. I mean the Porter; his name's Bursar?'

The uniformed man smiled.

'Yes; and my name's Porter, and I'm the Bursar! Don't worry; it confuses everybody, especially the Captain!' And with that, the Bursar bowed and left them.

Samuel opened the door to his cabin to reveal a rather spacious interior which looked, for the most part, like a very expensive hotel room. Neville followed him in. The adjoining door to his own room was open and, having had a brief scan round twenty seven, Neville walked into twenty eight. This cabin was identical to Samuel's, with the sole exception of the door's location.

His bags were at the foot of the bed. He wondered how they had managed to get here before him, whether there had been some other way of getting across the Channel, or if, at the end of the day, it was another of Samuel's "tricks". It seemed unimportant.

'Nice cabins, Samuel.'

'Very nice, Sir. We should be comfortable here, don't you think?'

Neville felt the ship begin to roll slightly underneath him as they got underway.

'Do you want to have a wander round on deck, Samuel? Wave Guernsey goodbye?'

'If you don't mind, Sir, I think I'll just have a rest. A little nap perhaps. I suspect they will be calling us for dinner in a couple of hours or so.'

'Fine. I'll see you a bit later then,' and with that Neville closed the door dividing the rooms.

His first instinct was to go searching for "M", but practicality suggested it might be wise if he unpacked his bags first and then perhaps freshen up. It was a little after five and, as Samuel had suggested, they had no wish to be late for their first evening meal on board.

The two bags on the bed were familiar to him, though, on opening them, he discovered some new items of clothing: bright T-shirts, some shorts, and a pair of sandals that had obviously been included as a nod to the Mediterranean. His suit was there (of course!) as were the other items of casual wear he had expected. There were also two new pairs of shoes: one in smart black leather; the second, a kind of blue canvas deck shoe.

As he toyed with the idea of slipping into the naval shoes, there came a knock at the door.

'Yes?'

The door opened to reveal an exceptionally tall man, dressed in a uniform similar to the Bursar's. The first thing Neville noticed about this new man, as he bowed low in order to be seen, was the large bandage he wore around the top of his head.

'M-m-m-may I, Sir?'

'Please.'

As the man stooped to enter, he failed to duck low enough and banged his head right about where the bandage was.

'F-f-f-flaming doors,' he muttered. Neville wondered if the bandage was there to tend an old wound or prevent a new one.

'Can I help you?'

'N-n-n-no Sir; c-c-c-can *I* help *you*,' the man bowed, showing Neville the full extent of the bandage which, from this new angle, resembled nothing less than a full turban. 'I'm B-b-b-bursar; the P-p-p-p...'

'Porter,' Neville offered.

'Is there anything I can d-do for you, Sir? Would you like any d-d-d-drinks, or anything?'

'No, I'm fine thank you, Porter.'

'C-c-c-call me B-b-b-bursar, Sir, if you would. P-p-p-porter's the B-b-b-b...'

'Bursar. Yes, I've met him.'

'N-n-n-n....'

'Nice chap; yes.'

Bursar looked around a little helplessly.

'Well Sir, if that's all. J-j-j-just to t-t-t-tell you that the C-c-c-c...'

'Captain?'

'Has invited you to d-d-d-d...'

'Dine?'

'With him this evening, Sir. Eight o'clock; main b-b-b-ballroom, Sir.'

Neville smiled.

'Thank you Por — Bursar; I dare say we shall see you later.'

The Porter considered replying, thought better of it, then bowed again. Neville watched him as he left, waiting for what he assumed would be the inevitable dull thud as his skull hit the door frame on the way out. Bursar paused at the door, then made a special effort to bow low. It made no difference: "thump!"

'F-f-f-f....'

And the door closed with a naval "click".

Neville went back to his bags and completed the remainder of his unpacking. The voyage to the Mediterranean would, he assumed, take a few days; after that, they would spend some time visiting the islands themselves. The clothes available to him would seem to be adequate to cover that period, but what about after that? As he sat on the bed, once again he recognised there was no clue as to what might happen at that point, nor where he would be going. Had there ever been such clarity, he wondered? Presumably there might come a time where there would be no "next" for him to consider.

As he slipped closer to philosophy, a voice whispered '"M"' at the back of his brain, and he decided to take a quick tour of the ship before dinner. He donned the canvas shoes and opened his cabin door.

TWENTY ONE

Once outside his cabin, Neville paused. He looked right to the stairwell from which he, Samuel, and Porter had emerged a little earlier, then left to the end of the corridor which was delimited by a single door. He decided to walk left.

The numbers on the cabins continued ascending until forty was reached, this being the last cabin before the grey door. Neville looked back. He guessed from the length of this particular passageway that there were perhaps twenty or so rooms — presumably much like his and Samuel's — leading from it. He placed his hand on the handle of the exit and pushed it open.

He was immediately hit by fresh sea air which carried with it the hint of salt spray. The front of "A" deck was not a large affair, boasting a few recliners and deckchairs, and the odd wrought iron table welded to the superstructure. Neville walked to the front rail and leant over. Just below him he could see both "B" and "C" decks, and beyond them the bow of the ship complete with capstans, ropes and the like.

The two lower decks were kitted out for a number of pastimes; Neville could make out the markings of games' courts of various kinds, including one he assumed was used for some form of curling. There were a few people milling around, fewer than he had expected, but the weather was not as brilliant as it might have been.

Despite the flying jacket, he now felt a little chilly. Turning, he noticed a second door leading back inside from "A" deck and, as he walked towards it, couldn't fail to see the bridge of the ship above it. Neville looked up. He was greeted by a sharp salute from someone behind the glass; he guessed the Bursar, though he could not be sure.

The corridor beyond this second door was much like his own; indeed, the similarity was so great that Neville immediately remarked to himself on the enormous potential for confusion. The first door to his right bore the number one, and — as he suspected — ascended from there; the numbers proving to be the only distinguishing feature of this passageway from his own. At twenty there was a stairwell down to "B" deck — presumably in parallel to that he had so recently climbed on the other side of the ship — and once there a further set of cabins.

Rather than another door at its end, this passage bore round to the right by ninety degrees and revealed another, shorter corridor. At the end of this, another turning which mimicked the "U" shape of the "A" deck walkway above. From the bottom of the "U", a single, much larger double staircase dropped down to the deck below. Neville checked his watch. He had enough time before he needed to prepare for dinner to push on with his exploration.

The bottom of the stairs opened out into a large lobby, adorned with soft sofas and parlour palms. There were one or two notice boards, and a place specifically designed to leave messages. Neville scanned this. It was much like the pigeon-hole system used in hotel lobbies. Finding his own room — "A-28" — and the empty slot assigned to it, he then decided to take a brief rest on one of the sofas. The lobby was deserted at present, though he had seen a couple leave just as he arrived.

From his new vantage point, Neville noticed again the remarkable degree of symmetry the ship possessed. Indeed, here it was not only left-right symmetry as he had already noticed on "A" deck, but fore-aft symmetry too. In each corner of the lobby, an archway led off in its own discrete direction, yet all appeared identical.

He had not been studying the ship's architecture for long when a voice assailed him from behind the settee.

'Bastards!'

Neville turned. An exceptionally large Venus fly trap was leaning towards him, its two major leaves open like a single eye complete with lashes. The leaves suddenly snapped shut with a vengeance, and another pair became the plant's mouth.

'Bastards!'

'I'm sorry; but who are you referring to?'

'You. Them. Everyone,' the plant snapped back, swaying slightly closer to him with the motion of the ship.

'Who is "everyone"?'

'The bastards who put me here, on a bleeding ship, miles from anywhere.'

'Is there something wrong in that?' Neville asked, moving away to the edge of the settee and relative safety.

'I suppose you'll be having dinner tonight with the Captain, won't you? Stuffing your bleeding faces, I bet!' The plant snapped open and closed again. 'And me? Starving bleeding hungry. Not a fly in slight. Stuck on board a bleeding ship; don't they know I'm supposed to be carnivorous?'

Neville was beginning to feel vaguely uneasy about his aggressive companion.

'I'm sure they must have flies here somewhere, if only to feed you.'

'And my mates.'

Neville looked nervously around, but could see no evidence of any similar species.

'Of course; and your chums.' He paused, eyeing the plant with a degree of mistrust; just how carnivorous could one of these things be? 'Look,' he said rising, 'if I find any flies, I'll keep them for you. OK?'

'Sure,' snapped the plant, 'that's what they all say!'

Without waiting for a more suitable conclusion — if there could be any such thing — Neville made a move down the nearest corridor.

There were cabins on "B" deck too. Neville noticed that they also bore numbers in the same range as the level above, but here the doors to the cabins appeared to be slightly closer together and just along the outside of the corridor. On the inside there were other doors that bore legends such as "Staff Only" and "Laundry Room: B3". As he continued his stroll, he even came across one marked "Bursar: A.Porter". "B" deck was obviously not quite so desirable as his own. There would be more comings and goings here, more noise, and the cabins were probably less spacious.

After a few strides he came to the end of the corridor. He had evidently been walking towards the rear of the ship as the corridor now gave way to another lobby, this time with large glass doors opening out onto the aft deck. This lobby was also deserted, though out on deck a number of people were standing at the rail, wrapped up warm against a strengthening breeze, and watching the wake of the ship as it pointed back to the now invisible Channel Islands.

Neville contemplated joining them, but decided against it. Checking his watch, he decided that it was probably time for him to return to his cabin. As he walked back — exactly the way he had come to avoid getting lost — he realised he had not been given a map of the ship. This would have been useful at this present moment — and would probably be so in the future should he wish, say, to find the ship's Doctor. At some stage, he would ring for Bursar and get him to fetch one.

When he got back to the Venus lobby, there were a few people at one of the notice boards. Neville joined them and discovered that they were examining the seating plan for that evening's dinner. A large diagram, filled with circles representing tables, had been annotated in a practised hand with the names of the passengers. He found his own surname next to the Captain's on the top table. He recognised none of the others on his table, and wondered which of them — if any — belonged to Samuel. There was also — of course — nothing which said simply "M". Neville nodded politely to his fellow passengers as he left the lobby, and made his way back up the staircases to "A" deck.

When he reached his cabin, he found the adjoining door open and Samuel moving between the two. On his bed, a white shirt lay ready for him to wear at dinner, and Samuel was currently making sure his suit trousers had a sharp crease in them.

'Hello, Sir. Had a nice stroll?'

'Just a quick wander, that's all.' Neville took off his flying jacket and threw it on a chair. On the small table near the porthole, steam rose from a pot of tea.

'I've just made that Sir; please, help yourself.'

Neville went to the table and began to pour the tea.

'It is a nice ship, don't you think? Have you seen very much of it?'

'I just wandered down to "B" deck; had a look round the lobby, you know.'

'Porter said he saw you at the front of "A" deck, outside.'

'Porter?'

'The Bursar, Sir. He just popped in to let us know where we were sitting for dinner.' Samuel, having finished working on the trousers, placed them on the bed alongside the shirt. 'The Captain has invited us to dine with him.'

'I know,' said Neville, between sips of tea, 'I saw a plan of the tables and where everyone is sitting.' He realised that one of the names on top table had to belong to Samuel. 'There seemed to be quite a few tables too.'

'Oh, I think this is quite a large boat; probably a couple of hundred people on it.'

'It seemed very quiet when I was out, that's all. Hardly anyone about.'

'Perhaps they were all unpacking, Sir.'

This seemed reasonable enough. Neville caught sight of an open drawer and realised that Samuel had completed the job he himself had started half-heartedly. He sat on the bed, sipped his tea, and watched Samuel as he finished brushing his suit jacket. Samuel, aware that he was being watched, offered a slight nod and smile. It was more a fatherly kind of gesture rather than that of a manservant, which is what he seemed to be half of the time. Neville felt he was being protected by this old man, as if — an addition to everything else, "tricks" included — he was offering him the benefit of his wisdom.

'Is that all right, Sir?' Samuel had finished with the suit which now hung on the outside of the wardrobe along with the shirt. 'I've given your shoes a bit of a polish too, so you should be all ready.'

'Should I choose the tie?'

'Second drawer down.'

'Thank you, Samuel.'

Again the older man nodded, paused as if he wanted to respond to Neville's suddenly inquisitive gaze with something solid, but then turned silently back into his own cabin, closing the door behind him.

Almost simultaneously there came a knock at the main cabin door. It was a hesitant kind of knock, and sounded like one which had difficulty getting going; "k-k-k-knock, knock"! Neville walked to the door and opened it to reveal almost all of Bursar.

'S-s-s-sir,' the Porter said, bending his head beneath the level of the door to effect the greeting. 'I've g-g-g-got you these.'

He extended his hand, and presented Neville with a number of small pamphlets, the topmost one was entitled "Your Ship".

'I thought they m-m-m-m-'

'Might?'

'B-b-b-'

'Be?'

'Useful, S-s-s-sir.'

Neville took them and nodded.

'Thank you Bursar; just what I was looking for.' He felt as if he was patronising this tall man in some way, almost without intention; as if there was something in the other which brought such an attitude out of him. A brief pause ensued, during which time Neville became a little unsettled by the thought.

'Is that all?' he asked somewhat brusquely.

Bursar thought for a second, then nodded.

'Enjoy your d-d-d-dinner, S-s-s-sir.'

'Thank you.'

Neville watched the porter as he turned, straightened, then banged his head on one of the lower ceiling beams as he walked away down the corridor. Neville closed his cabin door on the sound of Bursar's "F-f-f-f-" as it came back up the corridor. Throwing the pamphlets on the bed, he decided to take a quick shower before dinner.

The bathroom was compact, boasting only a shower, a toilet, and a washbasin. Neville would have preferred at bath — indeed, at that particular moment, he had a strange desire to be back on the bus, bathing in the company of the yellow plastic duck. As he switched on the shower, he remembered the shower head in Paris and wondered — for the briefest of moments — if he were to be in for the same kind of experience here. There was a splutter and a hiss, but then that was it.

He got into the shower in a rather disturbed frame of mind. He felt slightly angry now, though unable to locate the root cause of this emotion; it seemed to be flapping about inside him, without a focus, looking for something to scar as it lashed around. Bursar had been an easy target, and Neville was angry with himself for that. Samuel might have been a target once too, but there was now a little too much between them to allow Neville to even consider it.

As he stood under the jets of hot water — refreshingly strong and slightly stinging — Neville tried to imagine the force of the shower cleansing the anger from him, washing it out of his body, and away down the plug hole. He looked down at where the water swirled away and had an image of someone, somewhere — perhaps the overalled man from the quay side — waiting with a watering can to catch all his anger ready to feed it to the Venus fly trap. He smiled to himself at the picture — as if any more anger were needed there! — and the tension left him.

It was replaced, without any conscious bidding on Neville's part, by the rather blurred image of "M" as she turned to wave goodbye at the restaurant. He could remember pink, the colour that dominated the image; and if he tried hard, he kidded himself that he could remember her shoulders too. This was a lie, he knew; he remembered Bob's words, and that was about it. If she were to walk past him in the corridor and he not realise it, then what kind of a crusade was he embarked on?

He thought about that single, neatly folded sheet, and tried to imagine how he might fit into *her* plans; if she too was on her way to Option 3 — "A" or "B" — where did he come into the frame?

From outside he heard Samuel open the adjoining door and walk into his cabin.

'Just coming, Samuel,' he called out, beating the other to the punch. Then, pulling the soap from its holder, he began to wash himself vigorously.

Ten minutes later, he was sitting on the edge of his bed. He could see Samuel in the other cabin looking remarkably smart in a pale grey suit with a rather magnificently patterned tie. Neville wondered what people meeting him for the first time this evening would think of him, of what he did, of his history. And what would Samuel say, to introduce himself?

Neville, in shirt and trousers, had chosen a rather brilliant red tie from the small collection presented to him by Mister Bossiman, and had already remarked on how the suit seemed to be able to complement the colour; however, his immediate concern had become the location of his shoes.

'What did you do with my shoes, Samuel?'

'In the bottom of the wardrobe, Sir,' came the reply from the other room.

Neville checked where directed. The only suitable shoes there were the new ones he had seen earlier, and he had been looking for comfortable old shoes. As he was about to turn away, a voice from the floor called him back to the wardrobe.

'Hey! Try us!'

'Yes,' said another, not dissimilar voice, 'try us; we're tailor-made for you, honest!'

The shoes — in bold and shining black leather — had a subtle brogue pattern in them which, to Neville at least, resembled something of a face; or at least, half a face in each shoe. This impression was endorsed when the left shoe — the one that had spoken first — winked knowingly at him.

'You won't regret it, will he?'

'Never!' exclaimed the right shoe, 'can't regret it, can he?'

'Ever danced, Mister?'

'Sorry?' Neville was again sitting on his bed, though with the shoes now in front of him.'

'Danced,' said the left shoe again.

'You know, the old quick step; one-two, one-two-three.'

'Ah the thrill of the ballroom!'

'Sorry,' Neville interrupted, 'but what's this got to do with me?'

The shoes winked conspiratorially at each other.

'You'll see!' they said in unison.

'Ready, Sir?' Samuel had popped his head round the door, 'I think we should be going.'

'Yes, OK; I'll be right there.'

Neville slipped on the shoes, and stood to get his jacket. As he took a pace forwards he needed to look down to check that he was indeed wearing the shoes. They felt so comfortable, it seemed as if they were not there at all.

TWENTY TWO

They reached the lobby on "B" deck almost without Neville realising it. During the brief walk along the corridor and down the double stairway he had been concentrating on the sensation the shoes had given him — or, more accurately, had *failed* to give him. He was roused from this rather vague introspection by the sudden realisation that the lobby was now remarkably busy.

Each of the sofas was now home to a full complement of backsides of various shapes and sizes; all the notice boards were faced by people giving the table plan varying degrees of attention. Behind the settee on which he had been seated earlier, he noticed the Venus waving with the roll of the ship, snapping ferociously; if ranting "Bastards!" at any passer-by, this time it would go unheard.

Neville scanned the lobby from the second step where he had paused. Everyone was dressed for dinner: the men in smart suits or tuxedos, bow ties abundant; the ladies were all finery and lace, and Neville sensed a layer of perfume about six inches deep hovering in direct competition with cigarette and cigar smoke a few inches below his nose. Samuel had pressed on into the throng, and Neville plunged through the pungent layers to follow him.

There appeared to be a general movement in one particular direction, although it struck him that Samuel's own course appeared to be charted with a degree more knowledge than that of someone simply following the herd. Samuel glanced over his shoulder to check on his progress — he was already several bodies behind — before moving on again. After a short while the corridor turned to the right and, as with the deck above, revealed the bottom of a "U" shape and another stairway. These stairs however, boasted not two, but three sets of steps and descended into a lobby much grander than that on "B" deck. There was a sign indicating the ballroom at the entrance to which — having negotiated the stairs and a 180 degree turn at the foot of them — Neville found Samuel waiting for him.

'There you are, Sir.'

The Bursar was there also.

'If you gentlemen would care to follow me, I'll introduce you to the Captain.'

Porter led the way into a large, expansive room which seemed to extend the full width of the ship and twice the same distance lengthways. At the far end, a small stage was occupied by a number of musicians evidently preparing to play some form of accompaniment for the meal. Nearest the entrance, tables were laid for dinner, with one, slightly larger than the rest and closest to the stage, set slightly apart.

Some people were already seated as Porter led them towards the top table. A number of rather elegant ladies made cooing noises to the Bursar as he walked by. He nodded professionally and courteously, even promising dances with some of the women in order to smooth his progress. Neville remembered his new shoes' enthusiasm for dancing, and could not fail to notice the large expanse of ballroom floor between the Captain's table and the stage.

The Master of the ship was not yet present. Porter showed Samuel to his seat first, then Neville to the one he would occupy next to the Captain. Neville smiled at Samuel who was virtually opposite him, then began to take in the room.

There were two other people already on their table, one either side of Samuel who, with simple ease, had already begun to engage in conversation. Apart from the Captain, that left three places vacant. Neville's seat placed him with his back to the stage, and thus with a full view of the rest of the ballroom. Watching people enter, he could only compare the experience with that in the minutes before a theatre performance where the only thing one could do whilst waiting was to observe the other theatre-goers and comment mentally upon them.

Any impression of his fellow travellers which might have been derived from the ladies accosting the Bursar a few moments before, proved to be as unfounded as would any lazy theory in relation to a cruise ship's paying company. He had expected the voyage to be populated almost entirely by wealthy, retired people who, having spent an entire lifetime working, were now out to enjoy the fruits of their labour. That there were some of these he was certain; indeed, as he sat there, he could pick out couples who might have fallen into such a category. But there were also those — of varying ages — who were obviously travelling alone; there were also young newlyweds on honeymoon, and those who he felt unable to describe in any way other than to call them "professionals".

Such categorisation — which had begun to take on the shape of a game show — accounted for perhaps three quarters of the people he could now see. The remainder were made up of a mix who, although they may well have fallen into one of the previous groupings, defied immediate identification.

A tap on his arm pulled him from his reverie.

'Good evening. My name's Watson; please call me Audrey.'

The speaker was an elderly lady with fine grey hair and smilingly bright eyes. She had arrived at the table — as had the other two missing guests — without Neville being aware of it.

'Neville; pleased to meet you.'

'Is this your first cruise, Neville?' Audrey asked, her voice the kind of sing-song he imagined all Grandmothers are supposed to possess.

'Yes, it is actually.'

'Oh, you lucky man! And at the Captain's table on the first night too!'

Any reply Neville might have made was cut short by the sound — distant at first — of applause, which gradually became louder. From the entrance to the ballroom, a tall, uniformed figure was making his way towards the top table, bowing as he did so to acknowledge the applause. The smile on the man's face was restrained, cultivated, and Neville was uncertain as to the degree of pleasure or satisfaction which might lay behind it.

Porter, who had stayed in the vicinity of the table, began to introduce the Captain to his dinner companions as soon as the applause had died down and normality restored. Neville — by now standing — was the last to be introduced.

'Captain Hook,' said the Bursar.

The Captain offered Neville his hand.

'My pleasure,' said the Captain cordially, taking Neville's had firmly within his own. Without breaking his smile, he turned to Porter. 'Thank you, Bursar.'

Porter, offering a sharp salute, turned and left.

'Please, be seated.'

Neville, who had been struck almost dumb by the appearance of the Captain, sat as ordered. Hook was not merely tall, he was statuesque. He boasted a dark thatch of hair and a true naval beard, mature by any standards. He had the appearance of a rugged man; a man who had seen action and lived to tell the tale. And he sported a black eye patch. For those first few seconds, Neville could think only of Peter Pan and this Captain's namesake. How accurate were the parallels Neville found himself drawing? Even if revered by his guests, how close might a man such as this come to embody the very opposite of goodness were he given to a slight twist of attitude or inclination? Or was he indeed already malevolent, eye patch and all; some kind of pirate in disguise?

Looking across the table — Hook being in conversation with the lady to his right — Neville saw Samuel looking his way. There was a glass raised in his direction which, on being recognised, Samuel raised a little higher.

'Here's to you, Sir!' — and with a wink, its contents were downed in one.

Neville picked up his own glass (which had been filled without his realising it) and took a sip. It was a fine white wine. He nodded back to Samuel, but he was once again in conversation with his neighbours.

'So, your first cruise, Sir.'

The Captain's voice drew Neville's ear like a magnet. The face bore that same perfect "professional" smile; the inclination of the head, displayed the correct degree of interest. Neville knew that Hook must have done this hundreds of times before.

'If you don't count crossing the Channel to France a few times, then yes, this is my first cruise.'

'Don't dismiss the Channel, Sir; it can be something of a vicious mistress. You can be lulled and lured in the Channel, then, in an instant, ripped asunder!'

Neville sensed a dead end in that track of the conversation. In order to play the game — whatever it might be — he tried something of his own.

'But you must have done this hundreds of times.'

'This?'

'I don't know: crossed the Atlantic; sat down with dinner guests; docked in foreign ports.'

The Captain nodded solemnly. One or two others on the table were looking his way.

'Indeed, as you say, Sir.'

'And the Pilgrim?'

Hook stiffened slightly.

'Do you mean this ship?'

'How long have you been its Captain?'

'She,' Hook corrected with a strange emphasis, 'has been my home for several years. The S.S.Pilgrim is a fine ship, Sir; she will do for me — and, I suspect, she will do for you too.'

Although there was no change in his demeanour, Neville sensed something other than a Captain's cordiality in Hook's reply. Perhaps there *was* menace there, he could not be sure; then it occurred to him that much about the boat suggested hostility: the dock hand; the Venus fly trap; even its geography. Was this dark figure another?

'And what does the "S.S" stand for, Captain?'

Audrey, intruding delicately, offered the conversation a little steering.

'It stands for "Steam Ship", ma'am,' came the prompt reply, and with it a brief history of commercial sea-borne transportation.

The completion of Hook's monologue coincided with the arrival of the first course of that evening's dinner, and within a few minutes the ballroom was filled with the general clatter of cutlery and china, the clink of glasses and bottles, the thrum of chit-chat and laughter. The Captain's table was by no means an exception to this, except perhaps in the rather restrained demeanour of the host who, though not dampening spirits, imposed a degree of sobriety not in abundance elsewhere.

Somewhere between the first two courses, a man from a far table rose, banged the table with his fist, and shouted "Here's to the Captain!" before downing a full glass of red wine. There was a general shout of approval, and Hook stood, raised his glass to the assembled throng, and sipped his drink. There was broad applause. Neville looked to Samuel who had, for the moment at any rate, ceased his conversations and was now taking in the general scene in his own quiet way. He noticed Neville looking his way.

'The food is good, isn't it?'

Neville nodded.

'Excellent.'

'Though not as good as some restaurants we know, eh?', and Samuel offered a slightly more exaggerated wink than usual as an accompaniment.

Samuel's reference brought back to Neville the reason he was actually sitting here at all. He scanned the room in a hurried fashion. There were waiters moving between the tables; people getting up and sitting down; toasts being made, and toasts being answered. The general picture presented a blur of activity within which it was pretty much impossible to distinguish anything or anyone specific.

Another plate of food arrived in front of him. Suddenly not hungry, he fell to eating it more as a mechanistic response than anything else.

Hook, having completed another conversational round of the table, turned to him again.

'Have you been to the Mediterranean before?'

Neville imagined him with a catalogue of hundreds of questions he could trot out in order to wow his passengers with his concern for their well-being. Neville had decided that he didn't particularly like Hook that much — he only hoped he could do his job.

'Never, Captain. In fact, I've never been further south than — Paris.'

'Well you are further south than that already. I think you should enjoy the Mediterranean; the sea is as clear a sea as you would ever wish for. Warm and calm and blue.'

Neville waited for an anecdote about the islands, the voyage, or the people, but there was nothing else. Hook glanced away, then fell to eating again.

From the stage, the trio of musicians began to raise the volume. Neville presumed that they had been playing for some time now, but had failed to hear them above the general din. The fact that they were now insisting on being heard — perhaps triggered by completion of the main course — suggested something was at hand. Beneath the table, Neville's new shoes sensed it too. They began to tap gently to the rhythm of the band, alternating beats between them in a subtle and accomplished manner. As he was doing nothing himself, Neville felt as if his feet were getting a free massage, and so eased himself back a little in his chair, content to enjoy it.

Dessert proved to be over and done within a matter of moments, and soon all the tables were adorned with cups of coffee, bottles of Port, and smoke rising from dozens of cigars. There was a general movement away from the tables to the lavatories and back again; ladies checking their lipstick, gentlemen emptying their bladders. From somewhere there came a crash as a waiter was sent flying by someone hastily backing out from their table.

Gradually, and without orchestration, the hubbub began to subside; the movement in and out of the ballroom diminished to a trickle; a kind of expectant calm descended. Hook rose from the table and walked slowly to the stage. By the time he reached it, the room was silent. He was handed a microphone by one of the musicians.

'Ladies and Gentlemen. May I take this opportunity, on behalf of the crew and myself, to welcome you on board the S.S.Pilgrim. There are one or two faces I recognise from the past, and I would like to offer a special welcome to those old friends.'

From the back of the room a small cheer went up from one table. Undeterred, Hook went on.

'I trust you will all have an enjoyable and rewarding time with us. Please be assured that we will do all we can to make your time on board as memorable as possible.'

His short bow was greeted with cheers and applause. Neville looked at Samuel who, though listening intently to Hook's words, had not joined in the approbation. The Captain raised his hand.

'Thank you. For your entertainment this evening, we have with us — to accompany our resident trio — a young lady who comes to us with the highest reputation and who, I'm sure, who is already known to many of you. Please welcome, Miss Tracy Vaughan.'

And with his last words and the rising applause, the ballroom was plunged into darkness.

TWENTY THREE

For a split second, just as the applause faded, Neville sat in the darkness, his expectation heightened. Was this why he had come to this boat, for this moment? From somewhere near the stage, a woman's voice started humming through the blackness, picked out a rhythm which was taken up by the trio with sleazy laziness. "Tracy Vaughan", Hook had said; but all Neville wanted to see was "M".

A light suddenly picked out a bare spot at the front of the stage and became fixed there. The woman's voice grew louder, the trio's backing more defined; then two stilettoed feet appeared in the spotlight, moving slowly forwards. Next, legs could be seen through the exaggerated split of a blue sequinned ball gown. Gradually the singer moved into the light. Neville, who had taken his napkin and was now crushing it in his left hand, was mesmerised by the spotlight and its contents. It seemed as if a genie was about to appear. He thought, in a haphazard way, about magic and miracles. Then, with the rising last note of her introduction, Tracy Vaughan stepped fully into the light.

She was not "M".

As the song began, Neville realised that, even in this dim light, both Samuel and Hook were looking his way, rather than at the stage. He released the napkin from his hand and let it fall to the table. He was not aware that he had been other than silent during those last few seconds, but could not be certain. He offered Hook as casual a smile as he could muster, which he knew was not returned.

Tracy Vaughan was sliding through a smoky version of "Up A Lazy River", which Neville assumed, was supposed to have some reference to the fact that they were on a ship. He was trying hard to focus on the singer, on her words, on the trio behind her; indeed, almost anything to relieve him of the pressure that he had managed to heap on himself during those few brief moments of her introduction. The rest of the song passed off without incident. Vaughan's low bow at the end of the number was greeted with appreciative and enthusiastic applause. Neville, although he had not actually heard of her before — even if Hook had implied that he should have — recognised she had a fine voice, and that her style was sufficiently out of the ordinary to be her own.

When the second number started, the trio led the way. This was a much more upbeat introduction which instantly had Neville's shoes tapping beneath the table. The tune was an old Fred Astaire number, and as he listened to the first few bars, he heard an echo in his head. There was something familiar about this particular tune, about the way it was being delivered. The mannerisms of the bass player reminded him of another who had played exactly that same piece.

Realisation hit him in a sudden flood which left him instantly shipwrecked: the band was playing the music he had heard at Mister Bossiman's.

If there were other parallels Neville might have been inclined to draw, the effort to do so was not required of him. At the left of the stage, in another, softer spotlight, a figure in flamingo pink stood motionless. He had not been prepared for this; having just had his expectation crushed, he was still on the way down, still trying to regain his equilibrium. But exactly as the ball gown had stood at the tailor's, now "M" stood waiting.

Neville looked around, expecting to see her partner glide into view from somewhere nearby. As he did so, he noticed everyone on his table staring intently at him. Samuel was smiling almost benignly; and Hook had left behind that professional study of his, and was staring at Neville with an almost malicious desire. Under the table, someone kicked him. He looked down. It was not someone, but something. The shoes, now frantic, were rapping his ankles to get him to rise. It dawned on Neville that *he* was supposed to partner "M" for the dance, and that what he had seen at Mister Bossiman's was nothing less than a rehearsal for this moment. But he could not dance. How could he make a fool of himself in front of all these people?

Then, without any effort on his part, he rose from his chair. More of Mister Bossiman's handiwork. The suit had taken over.

The initial movements were awkward, jerky. Neville's arms, uncertain of their place in all of this — as indeed was his whole being — fought the persuasive tugging of the sleeves. The shoes, demonstrating a surprising degree of power, moved him towards the edge of the stage; his efforts to keep his balance gave them all the edge they needed. For a brief moment, he was stationary. "M" — role-playing to a tee — stood head bowed, ignoring his presence, yet waiting.

Neville knew he had no choice. He was powerless against the combination of cloth and leather; his only option, the only way he could save himself from humiliation — which was suddenly what he feared most of all — was to give in, to relax; to let the flow of things carry him forwards. He tried to recall that image from the front of Mister Bossiman's house; and then, more obscurely, he tried to imagine that he was Fred Astaire.

The next movement — a slow turn and a lazy dragging of the feet — came much easier to him. He endeavoured to concentrate on his attitude, his frame of mind, and to ignore what his body was actually doing. He suddenly found himself spinning, then stopping suddenly, as if he had just noticed "M" for the first time. He tried to look surprised, or stunned; anything which seemed to fit his role in a play whose script had been hidden from him.

"M" looked up. Neville thought that, in the half light, he caught a glimpse of recognition in her eyes; but it was obvious that she was playing the game too. She turned slightly from him. He wheeled across the floor until he was suddenly beside her, and, in that instant, she became his focus. Images of the rehearsal, of Fred and Ginger, fled from his mind; all he could do was to look at her.

He spun around her body, following her head as she turned it first one way then the other to avoid his stare. The music drawled out the tempo; his shoes now transmitting their exhilaration to him through his legs; the suit displaying supreme subtlety.

And then his arm was out, and he caught her hand.

She looked at him now, eye to eye. It was a play, a dance; and yet it wasn't. She made to move away, and he held her hand more tightly. This was not the suit; this was Neville, acting for himself. Whether it was the suit or his own volition that pulled her towards him he could not say; in the drama they were enacting it had become impossible to distinguish anything. In any event, gradually, and with no real hesitation, she began to respond, and they began to dance.

The next few minutes passed in a blur of sensations: the brightness of the spotlights as they were caught in their beams; the vibrant pink of her dress, as she flashed before his eyes; the heat of the trio, whose steaming rendition of the song defined the moment; the invisible eyes, drawn into the tension; the touch of her skin. Defeated, and yet victorious, Neville simply gave in and let it happen.

With the climax of the number, "M" — who, playing the role to perfection, had become more and more enmeshed in the dance — spun once, then collapsed in his arms like a puppet whose strings had been cut. There was a sublime moment of stillness and silence, and then the ballroom exploded with applause.

For an instant he was uncertain what to do. A faint movement from "M" gave him the clue to lift her into a standing position. Holding her hand, they turned to face the body of the room, and bowed. Neville could see Samuel on his feet applauding, the smile on his face echoing the pride of a parent. Elsewhere, others stood too. Then, from the side of the stage, a young girl ran on and presented "M" with a large bouquet of flowers.

Neville glanced at his partner. She squeezed his hand slightly.

'Shall we sit down?' he offered.

'You know,' she spoke between breaths, 'I have always wanted to do that! Thank you.'

Neville kissed her hand, and led her towards the top table.

TWENTY FOUR

As they returned to the table, they found an extra chair awaiting them set between Neville's and the Captain's. Samuel, who was still standing, offered Neville his hand.

'Well done, Sir!'

Neville, having freed his right hand from "M", placed it on Samuel's shoulder.

'Thank you, Samuel.'

Having accepted the verbal approbation from those already at the table, "M" had walked round to take her chair alongside Hook. Neville looked round to see the Captain graciously addressing himself to "M" and her general comfort.

'Remarkable performance, Miss. Remarkable.'

He looked up as Neville prepared to sit.

'And you too, Sir. I must say I was surprised by your elegance.'

Neville, whose euphoria was sufficient to keep him floating, was not going to allow anything negative to spoil it.

'No more than I, Captain; no more than I!'

The Captain nodded at the joke, adopted his normal smile.

'And what's your name, my Dear?'

Audrey, having offered her own enthusiastic congratulations to "M", was effecting her standard introduction. Neville sat down between them. "M" glanced at him before replying.

'Mirelle,' she said, 'but I prefer Mita.'

'Mita?' Neville had hardly been surprised by her answer. Indeed, he was beginning to wonder why everyone he met wasn't called Mirelle. Was he undergoing some form of semantic torture that would follow him through his entire life? Mirelle's qualification was, perhaps, his first break.

'It was my Grandmother's name', Mita explained. 'She was Italian, from Tuscany. My Father, who was French, was adamant that I should have a French name. Of course, I couldn't protest until I became old enough to make my own choice; but he still calls me Mirelle to this day.'

'Mita', Audrey paused, 'yes, that's quite a nice name, isn't it Neville?'

Neville nodded.

'And didn't *you* dance wonderfully well too!' she carried on, placing her hand on his arm and squeezing it gently. 'Mita; didn't our Neville dance superbly?'

Mita smiled at Audrey, then Neville.

'Indeed; I could not have wished for a better partner.'

Neville smiled back. Beneath the table he felt his ankle being kicked. He looked down. The left shoe gave him a wink.

'Was that OK?'

'That was brilliant!' Neville replied in a hushed voice.

'See!' said the left shoe, 'we were brilliant!'

'Of course,' confirmed the other, 'we're always brilliant. Didn't we say you wouldn't regret it!'

A waiter appeared to replenish the wine glasses. In the background, under the umbrella of Tracy Vaughan's voice, there seemed to be a general movement of couples to the dance floor. Samuel's voice suddenly sounded nearby.

'Excuse me.'

Neville looked round, expecting to find the remark addressed to him; however, Samuel was — with a rather fine, if discrete, bow — talking to Audrey.

'Would you care for this dance?'

Audrey, whose hand was still resting on Neville's arm, rose. She glanced at Neville.

'Is your friend to be trusted?' she said, with a mischievous note in her voice.

Neville feigned a serious expression, and glanced at Samuel.

'With my life. I think you will find Samuel to be an honourable gentleman, Audrey.'

'In that case; Samuel, I would be delighted!' and with that, she exchanged Neville's arm for Samuel's, and they walked a few steps to the edge of the throng and began to dance.

Neville watched their cautious and sedate movements for as long as he could, but soon they were subsumed into the general melee. He turned to Mita. She had been watching them too. Hook's chair was vacant.

'So, we meet again!' Mita smiled warmly. 'Something of a coincidence — though I can't say I'm surprised.'

'You're getting used to coincidences?'

'Something like that.'

There was a code underlying all of this. Neville chose to approach Mita as if she knew much of his secret and had already experienced many of the same things herself.

'How was the monkfish?' she asked.

Neville laughed. Bob had been telling the truth, after all.

'The monkfish was fine, but I don't suppose you managed dessert? I mean, I must have interrupted.'

'I was a little surprised, yes.'

There was a brief pause. Neville noticed Hook making his way towards them from the far side of the room.

'You dance remarkably well.'

Mita smiled.

'It was something I always wanted to do; something dramatic like that, ever since I was a little girl.'

'Fred Astaire and Ginger Rodgers?'

'Or Cyd Charisse. She was my favourite. I remember seeing her in films with Gene Kelly. I took dancing lessons as a child because I wanted to be like her; to dance in empty ballrooms with elegant men.'

'I'm afraid that this ballroom was not particularly empty, nor your partner very elegant.'

'What nonsense!'

'If only I could take the credit.'

They were interrupted by Hook, who, on his return, immediately asked Mita if she would care to take a turn.

'I am afraid dancing with some of our guests is one of my chores; but before the chores begin, I should like to have a little pleasure.'

Mita took the arm he offered and, with a smile for Neville, left the table. As they walked to the dance floor, they crossed with Audrey and Samuel on their way back. Audrey returned to her own seat, while Samuel took that just vacated by Mita. He followed Neville's eyes to the Captain and his partner.

'She is a very attractive woman, Sir, if I may say so.'

Neville saw how Bob — because of his lascivious leanings — had ignored the Mita's essence and done her a gross injustice. Typically, Samuel had missed nothing.

'And how was your own twirl, Samuel?'

'Ah, I'm afraid I am a little rusty, Sir; but I believe that Audrey still has all her toes intact!'

Neville glanced at Audrey to confirm this, but she was now engaged in another conversation and he chose not to disturb her.

The dance finished with applause for the singer and the Trio. After a few moments, the latter picked up another tune and the dancing began again. Neville expected Mita to return, but caught a glimpse of her on the far side of the ballroom, still in the custody of Hook.

'And what do you think of our Captain?'

Samuel's question came as something of a surprise. It wasn't that it was an illogical question — indeed, just then, it was *the* most logical question to ask — it was rather the manner in which it was phrased; the tone of the words; the weight behind them. Neville looked at Samuel. He was not smiling.

'He's seems popular enough, doesn't he? I mean, consider the applause when he came in to dinner.'

'But what do *you* think of him?'

Neville paused, but only for a moment.

'I don't like him, Samuel. And I don't trust him. There's something about him...'

He paused feeling a hand resting on his left arm. It was Audrey; she had been listening. She gave him a slight squeeze, but said nothing. Neville looked back to Samuel. He had the feeling that he was sitting between two guardian angels; and from their manner, he was beginning to think that there was something very definitely amiss.

'Why?'

'Sir?'

'Why do you ask, Samuel? Is there something… is there something I should know?'

'As you say Sir, Hook is a popular Captain. He steers his ship, entertains those who sail on her, and people come back to the Pilgrim time and again. What could be wrong in that? And yet,' he gave Neville no time to intercept him, 'as you say, there is something about him, something you do not like and do not trust. I have nothing to tell you, Sir. I think you know all you need to.'

Samuel looked out onto the dance floor; he appeared to be looking for something in particular. When he fixed his gaze, Neville knew he had located his quarry. Neville followed Samuel's line of vision. There was Hook; fine and upright in his uniform, dancing in the manner of a trained, professional seafaring Captain. He "cut a dash"; he was "a fine figure of a man"; and yet…

Neville could only see his back at first, but when Hook turned he saw his dance partner. It was not Mita.

It was neither the suit nor the shoes, but rather Neville who propelled himself from his chair. Staring into the body of the dancers, he searched for Mita. He had no concrete reason to panic, no reason to suspect that something might be awry. She was no longer dancing with Hook, and she had not returned to the table. Simply that. Perhaps she had slipped out to "powder her nose", to "take the air", or to watch the moonlight on the sea. There could be a dozen reasons why she was not there with him and nowhere to be seen. And yet.

Samuel and Audrey remained seated. Neville glanced at each of them, but they said nothing.

As he made his way to the exit, a number of people tried to stop him to offer their congratulations on his earlier performance. He did not hear them. On his feet, his dancing shoes felt again like normal shoes; perhaps they had no liking for this kind of drama. On his body, his suit hung like dead cloth. At the door he paused to look back.

At the top table, Samuel and Audrey — both standing — occupied it alone. On the dance floor couples turned. There were officers in uniform, ladies in dresses. But there was no flash of flamingo pink, and now there was no Hook.

Out in the lobby a few people were milling. Neville had to hurry to get wherever he was going (though he had not yet decided where that was) whilst being observant enough to miss nothing. He saw the Bursar who began to prepare his sharp salute. If it was delivered, it was not seen; Neville was away, up the stairs to "B" deck.

At the base of the 'U' he paused. Left or right? Both appeared the same. He decided to go left, walking quickly now towards the corner of the corridor. He turned. Ahead a long stretch of rooms. He moved on, not knowing what he was looking for. He had no idea of Mita's room, or even the deck on which her cabin was situated. Perhaps there would be something that might give him a clue. He paused briefly half way along at a stairwell leading back down to "C" deck, then made for the "B" deck lobby. Where this had been throbbing with people a few hours earlier, it was now deserted. Behind the sofa, the Venus fly trap was still. He was about to move on, then remembered the pigeon holes. He checked the slot for "A-28", but it was empty.

Again he faced a decision: up to "A" deck, or along "B" deck. The corridors which ran off the lobby gave him no help. In mirroring each other, they seemed only to compound the fruitlessness of his task. He decided to carry on, and aimed for one of the "B" deck corridors heading for the bow of the ship. Half way along, he came to another stairwell leading downwards. Perhaps these were the stairs that led up from "C" deck; the stairs that he and Samuel had first climbed on their arrival on board. Would it make sense to try outside? What could "B" deck offer him except locked doors to potentially empty cabins?

He decided on the stairs, almost slipping half way down and grabbing the handrail to keep himself upright. At their foot, he turned out onto the deck. The night was black, darker than he had expected; and though there was a moon, the light it threw across the sea seemed reluctant to illuminate anything. There was a breeze, and the ship rolled gently as it made its way into the darkness. Ahead, a couple leaned on a handrail, looking out across the sea. No-one else was visible. He decided to push on; to do a complete circuit of the ship if necessary. If he did not find Mita here then he would try once again inside, for he had now convinced himself that she desperately needed him to find her.

Reaching the bow of the ship — or as far as he was allowed to go — he turned and looked up. "B" and "A" decks rose above him. There were three people talking on the deck above; "A" deck appeared empty. Beyond that, in a strange white silhouette against the sky, Neville could make out the lights of the bridge. He thought he could see a figure standing at the window looking out; he imagined it might be Hook.

A couple wandered by and bade him "Good night". When he looked back to the bridge, the figure had gone.

Turning again, Neville set off for the other half of the ship. The deck was empty, and few lights were on in the outside cabins. Ignoring any stairs leading upwards, he walked the full length of the ship before finding himself at the stern. The rough white wake frothed as it left its temporary snail-like trail behind. Two men smoked cigars by the swimming pool; a young woman sat on a deckchair talking to one of the ship's crew. He could hear the sound of music from the ballroom and found a door into the lobby.

At the ballroom door he stopped again. The Captain's table was deserted, and, judging by the number of people dancing, many had left the festivities for the night. A few nodded as they passed him on their way back to their cabins. There was nothing else he could think of doing. He had walked the ship; searched as much as he was able. Could he knock on every door, hammer on every cabin? And on what pretence? Should he challenge Hook and demand — what of him?

Heavy legged, he ascended the stairs once again and made his way up, through "B" deck, towards his own cabin. When he entered it he found the adjoining door open, and Samuel waiting for him.

TWENTY FIVE

It was not until Neville had spent a few minutes explaining his recent movements to Samuel that he remembered the pamphlets the Porter had so recently left him. Without a second thought he had discarded them on the bed where the one titled "Your Ship" now lay uppermost. Although his searching for Mita had been a little frantic, the navigation had not been complex; yet thanks to his ever-growing sense of urgency, he was finding it almost impossible to describe his route to Samuel. In order to outline where he had been, he had begun to wonder if there might be paper an pen in the cabin somewhere, and, in looking for this, had noticed the pamphlet.

The document was an A4 sheet of paper that had been folded twice to form a small booklet. Neville had picked it up on the assumption that it would contain a floor plan of the vessel. The front page contained the pamphlet's title and a colour picture of the ship, evidently taken in some exotic port: the sky was clear; the sea, a brilliant blue; the backdrop heavenly. Neville partially opened the pamphlet, drawn to the text thanks to its rather enticing typeface:

WELCOME aboard the S.S.Pilgrim! The Directors of Total Leisure Incorporated would like to take this opportunity to introduce you to the ship that will be your home for the next few days as you relax on your ultimate holiday experience.

NOTHING is too much trouble for us. You will find our crew — led by the indomitable Captain Hook — only too willing to meet your every need, whatever hour of the night or day.

INDULGE yourself in your dreams, your fantasies. Our trained personnel will be on-hand to arrange and assist wherever they can.

EVER wanted that famous shipboard Romance? Or to win thousands at Roulette? Ever wanted to stumble across an impossible crime, yet solve it to the amazement of all?

TOTAL Leisure Incorporated specialises in making your wildest fantasies come true. Speak to those who have travelled with us before — they just keep coming back for more!

YOU don't have a fantasy? Nothing you'd want to act out? Think you're coming along for just a quiet cruise? Don't you believe it! We ALL have our hidden desires. Total Leisure Incorporated — your passage to fantasy land...

He handed the leaflet to Samuel, then walked to the porthole and looked out onto the blackness; all he could see was a reflection of himself.

'Were you aware of this?' He asked the question of Samuel, yet all the while staring at himself in the glass. Samuel said nothing. 'Was that what your warning about Hook meant; the fact that he wasn't what he seemed?'

He turned. Samuel had fully opened out the pamphlet to reveal the deck plan on its inner face; this now lay visible on the bed. Neville glanced at it, then back to the other man.

'Samuel?'

'I wasn't sure, Sir.'

'Not sure? Since when have you been unsure of anything? Tell me that! And Mita. Is she just one of the cruise's guests acting out her fantasy with my help? If so, then what am I in all of this?'

'Mita?' Samuel seemed shocked at the suggestion. 'How could she be just a guest, Sir? You met her at the restaurant; like you, she has her own quest. That has nothing to do with this ship.'

'Unless you are part of it too.'

'I'm not sure I get you, Sir.'

'"Total Leisure Incorporated".' Neville almost spat the words out. 'What if it's bigger than just this ship; if all that's happening to me is just some fucking game!'

Samuel moved towards him, placing an arm on his shoulder.

'No, Sir! No. I can only ask you to believe me. The fact that you are on this ship is...'

'A coincidence?'

'You are here because Mita is here; because she chose to be here. She wanted a cruise; she had her fantasy about the dance. It might have happened elsewhere, but it has happened here. And you are here because you decided that you wanted to be where she was. Is that not true?'

Neville said nothing.

'Do you think me evil, Sir?'

The question hit Neville like a slap across the face. He straightened, and looked his friend square on.

'No, Samuel; of course I don't think you're evil!'

'This is a dangerous ship, Sir. Some of the things they allow to happen here... Even considering what I have seen elsewhere — or have been party too, I confess — even I could not condone them.'

'But Mita's dance; surely that was harmless.'

'Indeed. But where is she now; now that she has finished acting out her dream? Is she now part of someone else's fantasy? Has she herself become an innocent victim?'

Samuel's words triggered a thought in Neville's mind. If she had indeed become entangled in another's game, wouldn't it be possible for the present scenario to be *his*? For him to have — however subconsciously — drawn up the framework for a plot they were all now part of?

'I know what you are thinking, Sir; and I do not know the answer. But I think it might be possible.' There was a pause. Samuel turned away from him, and walked a little further into the room. 'My dance with Audrey, Sir.'

'What about it?'

'That was not prearranged; it was not part of my plan, or your plan, or any plan of which I was aware. Perhaps it was something that I have wanted to do for a long time. A simple dream; to dance with a lady during a moonlit cruise. Innocent I know, but although I did not will it to happen, it still happened.'

Neville walked to the foot of the bed and stared down at the map.

'I think we had better find Mita. How quickly can we be off this ship, Samuel?'

'I will find a way, Sir — if you can find Mita.'

The first three decks on the plan — "A", "B" and "C" — were much as Neville had already experienced them. With the map to help him, it took no time at all to outline where his initial search for Mita had led him and, in doing so, to confirm that, without searching all the cabins and storerooms on the top three decks, he had covered as much ground as he could during that first sweep.

'Perhaps we should try elsewhere, Sir.'

'Elsewhere?'

'Higher or lower.'

Neville sat down on the bed and lifted the map in his hands. Samuel manoeuvred behind him to see.

'Higher? There's only the bridge and some officer quarters.'

'And lower?'

Neville traced an outline with his finger.

'Presumably we should call this "D" deck. There isn't too much detail here is there? These large blocks are probably the holds. And there are some storage rooms, by the look of things. These stairwells look as if they go even lower.'

'To the engine room, perhaps?'

'Probably, Samuel; yes.'

There was a "k-k-k-knock, knock" at the door.

'Sounds like Bursar,' Neville said automatically.

Samuel opened the door. The tall bandaged figure of the Porter dipped into the room.

'So *your* dreams don't come true then, Bursar?'

The Porter looked confused.

'S-s-s-sir?'

'Never mind. What do you want?'

'I was p-p-p-passing by the p-p-p-pigeon holes, Sir, in the l-l-l-l-'

'Lobby.'

'When I s-s-s-saw this in "A-28".' From behind his back, Bursar produced a lady's glove. It was flamingo pink. 'I thought you m-m-m-m-'.

Neville was off the bed in an instant, and snatched the glove from Bursar's hand without even bothering to finish his sentence for him.

'Was there anything else?'

'S-s-s-sir?'

'Any note, or anything like that,' Samuel suggested.

'N-n-n-no, Sir.'

Neville examined the glove. There was a moment of uncomfortable silence — Bursar's trademark it seemed.

'W-w-w-will there b-b-b-be anything else?'

'No.' Neville was suddenly preoccupied.

'Wait.' Samuel called the Porter back, just as he was about to leave. 'Perhaps you could explain something on this deck plan for us.'

Neville looked up, his focus back again.

'Yes,' he said, 'here.' He pointed to the plan. Bursar walked over to where he could see the map. 'Would we be right in thinking that this was "D" deck, Bursar?'

The tall man rubbed his chin, as if to indicate that he was thinking about the answer — and one which might not be perfectly straightforward at that.

'W-w-w-well, Sir.'

'Quick as you can man, if you could. Please.'

Bursar nodded.

'In that this d-d-d-deck here is called "C" d-d-d-deck; yes, Sir. B-b-b-but we don't c-c-c-call it that, Sir.'

'Why? What do you call it?'

The tall man turned and looked round the room; he seemed nervous in case someone else had joined them without him realising it. To Neville it was something of a theatrical gesture — but in this instance, perfectly appropriate.

Porter, the Bursar, stood in the doorway.

'Dismissed, Bursar! I'll help the gentlemen out.'

'S-s-s-sir.' The Porter tried a rather untidy salute, turned and left the room, banging his head on the door frame as he did so.

The Bursar, having closed the door behind him, now stood smartly at the foot of the bed. He glanced at the map.

'We call it "the Games deck", Sir. That's where many of our guests enjoy the best moments of their holidays. Those large rooms used to be holds, but they have been converted to "activity areas"; perhaps a little like stages on a film set. One is permanently set up as a Wild West Saloon — you'd be surprised how many would-be gunfighters there are in this world!'

Neville said nothing.

'We chose not to label them on the plan Sir, for fear of giving our little secret away. We find the element of surprise is part of the fun.'

'So why are you telling me this?'

'Because you have lost the young lady you danced with. Is that not so? When I saw you leave the ballroom I knew that something must be the matter. The lady at your table — Audrey — told me who you were looking for.'

Neville glanced at Samuel, who said nothing.

'And I understand that you are concerned. So, I have come to see if I can be of any assistance.'

'Yes, there is something.' Samuel smiled at the Bursar, then looked at Neville to assure him that he knew exactly what he was doing. 'The one area we didn't check was the bridge.'

'You would not be allowed up there, Sir.'

'Of course not. Now it may be — and we don't know how, of course — but it may be that the young lady has found her way up there. Or,' Samuel paused, then glanced at Neville, 'I'm sorry Sir, but I have to say this. Or she may have gone to one of the Officers' cabins...'

Samuel allowed the suggestion to float in front of the Bursar. Neville knew — because he knew Samuel, and because he already had an inkling about Mita — that this could not possibly be the case; however the suggestion had to feel realistic to Porter.

'I see,' said the Bursar after a moment, 'you could be right.'

'So in that case, would it be possible for you to check for us?' On Samuel's words, Neville turned away from the two men and walked back to the porthole. He hoped that this would have the desired effect. 'If she is there, shall we say "of her own accord" — if you could let us know, then we will no longer have cause to worry.'

Neville watched the Bursar in porthole. Samuel waited patiently.

'Gentlemen,' Porter said with the air of a man charged with duty, 'I'll go topside myself and see if I can find her. If you would care to wait here, I'll bring you news as soon as I have any.'

'Very kind,' said Samuel, 'thank you.'

Seconds later, the cabin door closed and Neville and Samuel were left alone again.

'Now Sir, I don't think we've much time.'

'Do you think she might be up there, Samuel?'

'Not a chance, Sir. If I were a betting man — and I have had the occasional flutter in the past, I must admit — I'd put money on her being down below.'

'Agreed. Are you coming?'

'I'll sort out our means of escape, Sir, if I may. We should arrange to meet somewhere.'

'How about "C" deck; where we came on board?'

Samuel thought for a moment.

'That should be fine.'

'How much time do you think we've got, Samuel?'

'I'd say it depends on the Bursar. Is he genuinely trying to help us? Or if not, does he suspect anything regarding our plan?'

'Fifteen minutes?'

'It's not long, Sir, but it should be enough for me.'

Neville gave Samuel's arm a brief squeeze and, deck plan in hand, made for the door. As he reached it, Samuel called him back.

'Here, Sir.' In his arms he held Neville's flying jacket. He threw it across the room. 'You might be needing this.'

Smiling, Neville pulled on the jacket then opened the door.

TWENTY SIX

The way down to "the Games Deck" was concealed behind two doors on "C" deck, both cunningly labelled "Dry Stores — Crew Only". Within moments, Neville had made his way down two flights (choosing to bypass the "B" deck lobby) and was standing outside the first of the two entrances. If they were to make good their escape as arranged, this would be the exit Neville had to take in order to effect the rendezvous with Samuel as quickly as he could.

The corridor was empty. He consulted the map, then slipped it into the inside pocket of his flying jacket. Apart from the stairwell, the map showed him nothing on the other side of the door and would, therefore, be virtually useless. He glanced along the full length of the corridor before trying the door. It opened easily.

A single lightbulb hung from the ceiling just beyond it. Neville closed the door as quietly as he could and took stock. Immediately in front of him was another set of stairs; with bulkhead on either side, there was no room for anything else. It was dark at the foot of the stairs, and peering down he could see nothing.

There was no time for contemplation or second thoughts. His first step echoed slightly in the stairwell. He hoped his shoes might lend a hand, but they remained inert. Treading carefully so as to limit the sound he made, he descended to the deck below. As he did so, he found himself counting the steps; "thirteen" greeted his arrival on the Games Deck.

He paused, wanting to be sure that no-one had heard him approach and to allow his eyes to adjust to the somewhat subdued lighting. From the map he remembered that the passageway he was in extended both fore and aft with a few doors on either side. Being nearer the bow, he had already decided he was going to try aft first. He was surprised by the silence. There was nothing apart from the distant rumble and reverberations of the engine. Dim lights adorned the walls of the corridor at irregular intervals, and Neville began to wonder if he hadn't missed something; if elsewhere there might be a slightly more "passenger friendly" approach to this deck, as opposed to the dim service-way he now found himself in.

Cautiously he moved forwards. He had only gone a few feet when he realised that, should anyone suddenly appear either in front or behind him, his only chance of concealment would be to throw himself through the nearest door without any heed for what might lay beyond.

He came to the first door and paused, inclining his head to it, listening for any sound from within. There was none. Cautiously, he tried the handle. It moved silently, and — as the "Dry Stores" door above had done — opened easily requiring little effort on his part.

Beyond, was a small, well lit room. In its centre was a large dentist's chair. Around the walls were various cupboards and cabinets, and in one corner a wheelchair and sink unit. He wondered what kind of a game might go on in here, and recalled Samuel's warning that dark things might happen on a ship such as this. He shivered involuntarily; this was something he had no desire to contemplate.

Back at the door, he paused long enough to check that the corridor was clear before stepping out of the room. Closing the door behind him, the passageway was subsumed in darkness, and he had to wait a few seconds to allow his eyes to adjust once more. Again there was the dull thumping of the engine somewhere below and, somewhat closer, the thumping of Neville's heart.

He pushed on to the next door, a little further ahead: a pause, the listening, and then the opening of the door. This room was also lit, though less well compared to the previous one. It was also slightly larger. There was deep pile carpet on the floor, and the walls had been decorated in such a way as to give the space a warm feeling. In the centre was a long padded couch, and, along one wall, another of similar appearance which resembled a bed. In the corner nearest the door, an elegant wooden cabinet stood with its top drawer slightly open. Neville pulled it towards him. Inside was a pile of soft towels, and a number of dark bottles.

He lifted one of these out. The label read "Natural Massage Oil". Any temptation he may have had to delve into any of the other drawers was rendered unnecessary by his realising the exact purpose of this particular room — one which was obviously more closely aligned to conventional pleasures.

The corridor was still quiet when he regained it. As the second room had been less bright than the first it took him a little less time to re-adjust to the lack of light. He knew he had spent at least four or five of his allotted minutes, and began to worry that the fifteen minute window he and Samuel had allowed themselves would be woefully inadequate for him to complete his task. Neville's impression had been that Samuel knew how he would resolve his problem, yet he was still — almost literally — in the dark.

As he walked forwards, he became aware of an additional sound that had begun to echo in some vague harmony with the turbines. He paused. It was difficult to establish the exact direction from which it was emanating. He checked behind; all was clear. The sound became perceptibly louder. For a moment it seemed as if it was being generated above him somewhere, and Neville looked up to where the bare bulbs hung uncertainly down. What was that noise?

The realisation that it was the sound of someone's footfall as they descended the very same stairs he had so recently traversed hit Neville hard. Why had he not been counting? How close would the count have been to thirteen?

He had just enough time to react. The next door was only a few paces away. Without regard for the sound he made — and without the cautious pause at the previous two rooms — he ran to the door and opened it.

Expecting to find another small room, he was surprised to find himself in a large cavern of a place. Perhaps this was one of the holds he had noticed on the map, though he could not recall where or when he was supposed to encounter the first of these. Having closed the door behind him, he pushed his back flat against it and listened. The footfall outside seemed to have ceased; there was still the sound of the engines, but now this was being embellished by another new noise.

It was difficult to make this out at first. Somewhere in the room, a dim light glowed, seeming to cast its beams upwards from the floor. He could see the shadows of a number of objects which appeared to be crates of some kind; there appeared to be little else visible. The sound he had heard was undoubtedly metallic; not the sound of solid metal, but rather the fragmented jangling of small objects.

Neville looked up. Overhead, suspended from the ceiling above — which seemed remarkably and incongruously distant — were a succession of chains. Having nothing suspended from them, they dangled loosely, and with the gentle rolling of the ship, sounded like crude wind chimes. Given the presence of the chains and the crates, he began to wonder if this particular hold might still used for the purpose for which it had been designed. An image of old black and white gangster movies popped into his head; a tried and tested formula full of old clichés.

Then, a sudden noise echoing from beyond the crates was the first indication he was not alone.

Cautiously, he left the relative security of the door, and made his way towards the first crate. It was large and, by crouching down, offered Neville a degree of shelter from the sight-line of anyone beyond. Again he heard the noise, this time the unmistakable sound of someone struggling; they were breathing heavily, and a sudden curse uttered with a degree of frustration was sufficient to persuade him that he should press on.

Peering around the edge of the crate, the remainder of the hold was open to his view. The dim light was emanating from two spot lamps that were situated on the floor by the far wall; they had been angled upwards, and thus threw a strangely diffused and shadowy light upon the contents of the space. There were a few more crates, and, quite near the lights, a figure in a chair. Even in the half-light, Neville could see sufficiently well to spot the vague glow of pink.

'Mita!'

He had not wished to reveal himself, but his relief at the sight of her escaped from him before he could contain it. She stopped struggling in the chair and looked his way, attempting to make out the origin of the voice from the deep shadows.

'Neville?'

Straightening, he stepped out from behind the crate and into the open.

'Are you OK?'

'What are you doing here?' Neville moved forwards in response to her question. Her shout halted his progress. 'Stop, Neville! You should get out of here!'

'Indeed; you should listen to the young lady — if only it weren't too late.'

A second voice — deeper, solid, masculine — rolled out from near where Mita sat. Frozen, Neville scanned the darkness for its owner.

'Where are you?'

It was the only thing he could think of saying. The voice responded.

'Here.'

From only a few feet behind Mita, the outline of a man appeared. He placed himself between Neville and the spotlights, casting a vast shadow the length of the hold. Neville moved forwards, then paused.

'Who are you?' he repeated.

The answer to his second question came, not in the form of a verbal response from the silhouette, but as a vicious shove in the back which, taking him by surprise, sent him sprawling to the floor.

Momentarily stunned by the presence of a second assailant, Neville looked up at the man towering above him.

'On your knees!'

Looking over his shoulder to the speaker, Neville realised that the footfall he he had previously heard on the steps belonged to the man from the Guernsey quayside. He did as he was told, then obeyed the pointing of his assailant and shuffled towards where Mita sat. As he approached, he could see she had her hands tied behind her back and her feet were strapped to the chair which appeared to be welded to the deck. The shadowy man moved a step closer.

'That's far enough!' he said. Neville was almost within touching distance of Mita; spitting distance of her captor.

A swift kick in the ribs from the quay-hand instantly doubled Neville up, and he collapsed to the floor again. There was a brash and vengeful laugh, followed by the commencement of soft whistling.

After he had recovered his breath, he sensed one of the men standing over him. He looked up nervously, half-expecting to find himself the recipient of another blow. The shadowy man was standing much closer now; so close, indeed, that even in the poor light, Neville could make out the features on his face. They were familiar to him; he tried to assemble the appropriate image in his mind.

'Are you all right?'

Mita's voice was soothing despite its tremulous tone.

'How touching!' The first man laughed — and the laugh completed Neville's image.

'Binky?!'

There was a brief moment of silence during which Neville heard the turbines and the chains again. Binky had stiffened slightly, and the other man — now sitting on a nearby crate — stopped whistling.

'Is that you, Binky?'

'Why do you call me that?' There was only caution and hostility in the voice.

'"Binky" Bingham. You flew me across from Southampton. Shit, it was only this morning!'

Bingham smiled slightly.

'So the old fool's still flying, is he?'

'The old fool?'

'My twin brother. Mad as a cow. Thinks he's some fucking World War One Ace! Never could handle reality.'

Neville looked from Bingham to Mita, then to the man on the crate (who had begun whistling again), and back to Bingham.

'Your brother?'

'I'm Monty. The whole family's from a long line of failed war hero types. We tried fighting; disaster for all of us. Yet Binky's reaction was to simply carry on pretending.'

'And you?'

'Kicked out of the army. Bastards! Ungrateful sods! This country doesn't deserve the likes of me. Unwanted; cast aside; chucked out.'

Neville was struggling to put together the pieces of the jigsaw Monty seemed to be offering him. There were clues, but no picture to fit them to.

'So why the girl? What's she done? What's going on?'

A feint smile played briefly across Monty's face. He looked at Mita, extending an arm to touch her cheek as he did so. Neville motioned to rise, ignoring the dull pain in his chest, but the thug was off his crate in an instant. Neville became still at the threat.

'This young lady?' There was almost affection in Monty's voice. Perhaps a trace of regret too. 'She found out.'

'Found out?'

'Neville, he's mad! Get me...'

Her plea was cut short by Monty's hand across her face. He looked hard at her, now half-slumped in the chair, then turned back to Neville.

'Ever since the army rejected me, I decided that I'd work for someone who *was* interested in utilising my services. Binky tried to stop me, presumably out of some misplaced loyalty. He still does. In fact, we've this little rivalry going; you could call it a family feud. He tries to stop me, and I...'

Neville picked up another jigsaw piece.

'The planes that tried to shoot us down today?'

'Failed again, eh?'

'They were designed to look like German aircraft, just to keep Binky's fantasy alive; and all the time...'

'And all the time they're actually working for me.'

'And you are working for "the other side".'

Monty laughed, amused that Neville had managed to put some of the pieces together at last.

'It's a shame about you two; considering you dance so nicely together.'

He could not be certain exactly what sparked his next action: perhaps it was the threat; or that his allotted fifteen minutes were nearly over; or even some deeply buried sense of national pride. Sensing the thug still was close at hand and had been distracted by Monty's discourse, Neville attempted to spring to his feet.

The sudden movement, combined with the lack of grip between patent leather shoes and the metal deck, led Neville to launch himself forwards rather than upwards; the result of which was for him to bury his head in the deck hand's groin with such force that the latter collapsed to his knees. This unexpected success brought Neville quickly to his feet, from where he followed up his initial strike by a more measured swing of his right instep into the deckhand's midriff.

Monty took a step back, seeing his aide now helpless on the floor.

'A lucky blow; but not lucky enough!'

From his belt, Monty pulled a small handgun. Neville had missed this in the gloom and now appeared to be completely at the other's mercy. Then, hearing a metal rattle close to his ear, he turned to find a large chain dangling just within reach. He swayed to his right, grabbed the chain, and hurled it towards Monty.

Like a heavy pendulum, it caught Monty on the side of the head on its upswing. He tottered, the gun now hanging limply in his hand. Moving forwards, Neville — still with images from Thirties' gangster movies resounding in his head — swung his fist, and with a "crack!" made solid contact with Monty's jaw. The body and the gun went spinning in different directions.

Neville turned to Mita.

'Come on' he shouted, as he bent to untie her bonds, 'we've got to get out of here!'

The ropes and straps gave way after a little fussing, and soon Mita was on her feet. There was no time for a romantic embrace, just a squeeze of the hand and then Neville was running for the door with her trailing behind.

'Samuel should be waiting for us — let's hope we have time!'

The corridor was empty. Neville paused to check for sounds. There were the turbines again, and, in addition, the sound of metal scrapping against metal.

'This way!'

Running along the corridor, their steps echoed loudly. It sounded as if there were twenty people running rather than two. Neville knew there was no time for caution now. The Bursar must have completed his check of the bridge and would surely be heading for "A-28" — if he had not arrived there already.

They climbed the stairs, Neville two at a time and not bothering to count this time, bursting out onto "C" deck just as an elderly couple were walking past the "Dry Stores" door. They froze, amazed to see two young people appear from nowhere and barge past them without a word.

Outside, Neville stopped, Mita coming to a halt beside him, her hand holding his again, her quick breathing making clouds in the chill night air.

'Where is Samuel?'

Neville heard a shout from above. He looked up. Two decks above, a figure in a uniform was leaning over the rail. He had expected to see the Bursar, but it was Hook.

'Sir; over here!'

Samuel stepped out of the shadows to join them.

'Samuel; are you OK?'

'Fine, Sir. Are you all right, Miss?'

'Mita's fine! Did you see Hook up there? How do we get out of here?'

Samuel smiled and pointed to the deck rail. A small section had been removed, and Samuel led them to the gap. Neville could see a rope ladder hanging over the side of the ship, and there, scraping against the hull as it bobbed in the water, a midget submarine.

TWENTY SEVEN

Any immediate questions Neville might have had — like "Where the hell did you get a midget submarine!" — were interrupted by the intrusion of a cry from the bridge deck followed by the distinct sounds of boots on steps. It was a sound Neville had heard recently enough for him not to have forgotten it.

'Samuel; you go first. Mita, follow Samuel down. And quickly!'

He had never had the chance to take control of a situation such as this, and, apart from adrenaline, was functioning based on a notion of how he was supposed to behave, a model formed from countless different experiences — and movies — for such a situation as this.

He watched Samuel go over the side and then, when the older man was about a quarter of the way down, helped Mita onto the ladder. No histrionics; no panic. He dashed to the foot of the stairwell. There was still no sign of their pursuers, though the sound they were making indicated that it would not be long before they appeared. Neville checked up and down the deck before lowering himself onto the rope ladder.

The last time he'd used one of these had been at school. He remembered that, if there was someone else climbing it at the same time as you, it could feel unstable. Once, he had frozen and refused to move until he was on the ladder on his own. If his present experience was similar, the circumstance most certainly was not. After a few seconds he looked down to find Samuel already at the foot of the ladder, standing on the top of the submarine waiting for Mita. As he continued his descent, Neville continued to check both upwards — for a sight of those chasing them — and downwards — to make sure Mita was safe.

Gleaned from black and white movies relating war-time heroics, popular legend told him that midget submarines were craft designed for two. However, as he watched Mita safely board, it appeared that this particular vessel managed to cater for at least four: not only were Samuel, Mita and — soon, he hoped — himself on board, but he could also make out at least one other person already in situ.

As he placed his left foot on the submarine, Neville felt a tug on the ladder from above. He looked up to see the thuggish deck hand, Monty, and — it appeared — the Bursar, yanking at the ropes. The force with which they were able to pull it almost sent him toppling into the ocean.

Taking his cue from Samuel, Neville lowered himself into the last place in the submarine's cockpit, a long narrow affair. Mita was already installed immediately in front of him, and — to Neville's immense surprise — Audrey in front of her. Samuel occupied the position between the two women.

Suddenly the craft lurched away from the ship and out into a sea roughed-up by the liner's bow as it ploughed through the water. A curtain of spray enveloped the sub, covering its occupants with a fine layer of water.

Samuel turned in his seat.

'Put on this headset,' he waved a strange helmet in the air, 'it contains an oxygen supply if we need it, and a radio so that we can talk. Then duck!'

Neville saw Mita pull her headset from the side of her chair, and found his own in the corresponding place near his left hand. He had completed Samuel's first instruction and was just about to question the second when, from the corner of his eye, he saw the submarine's canopy appear from its housing in the side of the craft. Within seconds, the perspex dome had spun over their heads and enclosed them. There was a strange hissing sound as aseal was made, and Neville then felt his ears complain at a sudden change in pressure.

He looked back to the S.S.Pilgrim. Already she seemed far away. He could make out a small crowd on "C" deck, some of whom appeared to be pointing in their direction.

'Samuel,' he said, having faced forwards again. He got no response. 'Samuel!' Again nothing. Not even Mita turned at his shout, and she was only inches away from him.

On the back of Mita's seat was a small panel with five lights on it. The light numbered 'three' was flashing. Beneath was a button, and, assuming he was meant to, Neville pressed it.

'Are you all right, Sir?'

Samuel's voice came to him through his helmet.

'Did you hear me calling?'

'No, Sir, I didn't. We can't actually speak and be heard in this particular vessel; hence the need for the radio.'

'I see.'

'And it's merely a one-to-one radio, I'm afraid. Which means you can only talk to one person at a time.'

'Where on earth did you get this tub? And why is Audrey here? And who's driving this thing?'

He heard Samuel give a little laugh.

'Three questions, Sir. Well, as to the first, let's say that it's just a little tr...'

Samuel's voice was cut off by the flashing of the number 'one' light, and the corresponding voice which cut across the conversation.

'G-g-g-glad to have you on b-b-b-board, Sir.'

'Bursar?!'

'Of c-c-c-course!'

Neville thought of the enormously linear Porter and the general dimensions of a midget submarine.

'How did you fit into this thing? And where are you?'

'It's q-q-q-quite easy, Sir. I'm lying underneath your f-f-f-feet. There's a little glass w-w-w-window at the f-f-f-front, so I can see.'

'And you know how to steer a submarine?'

'Steer a submarine? Don't be silly dear.'

It was Audrey's voice. The second light was now showing. Neville realised that he would need to keep an eye on which light was on in order to have some idea as to who was listening in. Or talking, come to that.

'Audrey?'

'Yes, Dear?'

'How come you're here? I mean, why are you here?'

'She looks after me,' this was Mita now, 'a bit like Samuel looks after you, I guess.'

'Are you OK?'

'Me? I'm fine. What about you?'

'Sure. Never felt better.'

It sounded like a lie, but in some respects Neville knew it was the honest truth. The fourth light was still on.

'Was that little adventure part of your plan? Something Audrey had "arranged" for you?'

Mita laughed a little uncertainly.

'No; not me.'

'Me neither,' Neville wondered if he sounded convincing — to himself, let alone Mita.

'All I wanted was to have that one dance, which was just about the last thing on my list.'

'Your list?'

'Of things to do. Didn't you make one; at the very beginning, I mean? When you first met Samuel?'

Neville recalled the Menu and the cheese straw. And he recalled the reasons behind him drawing up the list, the motivation for which, as it turned out, seemed to have been proven to be a falsehood. He glanced at his watch to check his "bank account". It showed a little over eight thousand. Neville could not remember the previous figure from the last time he had checked it, but assumed that eight-two-three-three was correct and included everything to-date.

He was about to carry on his conversation with Mita when he noticed that the second hand on his watch was sweeping backwards. It was going very slowly — slower than a normal second-for-second sweep, but perceptibly backwards.

'Sorry, Mita; I just need to check something with Samuel.'

Neville pushed button number three.

'...and then North after that. I think that should be suitable.'

'Samuel.'

'Oh, hello, Sir. I was just giving our course to Bursar. We'll be diving in a minute; you'll hear a little bell to warn you when it is going to happen.'

'Fine.'

'What can I do for you, Sir?'

'Samuel, why is my watch going backwards?'

'Backwards, Sir?'

'Backwards, yes. The second hand is sweeping backwards, and, for all I know, the other hands are probably doing the same thing. So why? Do you know?'

There was a slight pause. Neville checked his lights to make sure that he was still connected with the right person.

'Do you recall, Sir, when you discovered that it wasn't really money which was the — how shall I put it? — the "Holy Grail" of your adventure?'

'I do.'

'And you asked if that meant that the rules of the game had changed?'

'Yes. And you said that they hadn't; that I was still bound by the amount of money I had, and that I could spend no more.'

Again a pause.

'Samuel?'

'Well, Sir; I'm afraid I lied a little.'

'Lied?'

'The rules did change — not in the sense of the money, Sir, which (in my defence) is exactly as I suggested.'

'How then?'

'You see, you could — in theory — take as long as you wanted to spend your remaining money. You could, for example, invest it somehow and try and live off the income. If you did that, it would mean that you could go on for a long time without ever having to face up to the issues which will decide your fate.'

'Issues? What issues?'

'Those elements, Sir, which decide on "A" or "B". The things you need to find or discover which, all together, give you your answer.'

Neville had a thought. He checked the lights before his next question.

'And is Mita one of those things?'

'Mita?' Samuel paused. 'That is a difficult question to answer, Sir. She is on her own path; your paths happened to have crossed. If she is, as you suggest, intimate to your own plan, then you would need to be so in hers. Do you see?'

'So what about the watch?'

'Yes, the watch. Given what I just said — about spending money — and the fact that there has to be some kind of limit, some target for you to reach your goal, there is a need to ration another of your limited resources.'

'My time?'

'Indeed, Sir; yes.'

Neville looked at the watch again. He could not say that he was particularly surprised, however the challenge he was facing was now further constrained by even stricter boundaries. Not only were his finances limited, but it appeared his time was too — and both tied to a search for "things" about which he was unclear and could not readily identify. There was nothing against which he could tick off any achievements.

'How long do I have, Samuel?'

'What do you mean, how long do you have?'

Light four flickered brightly. Having intercepted his question to Samuel, there was a note of fear in Mita's voice. Was she really one of the things for which Neville had been searching?

'Neville?'

'Sir?' Samuel was back.

'How long, Samuel?'

'What does your watch say now?'

Neville checked. It was still going backwards, slowly.

'A little after eight.'

'If you assume that hours are days, Sir, you won't go far wrong.'

Eight days. A little bell rang, and moments later the submarine began to descend. Water soon encircled the dome, then began to flood over it. The sky became hidden by a layer that looked like ever-thickening opaque glass. Soon there was nothing left to be seen. From the sides of the submarine, small spotlights shone as brightly as they were able, challenging the darkness of the ocean to a duel they could never win.

Neville pulled off his head set and switched off his radio. Watching the darkness pass, he tried to contemplate what the next week might have in store.

TWENTY EIGHT

Having made contact with Mita again, the last thing Neville expected was to lose her so soon.

After a few minutes watching the dark ocean and some of its inhabitants occasionally slip by, Neville — no longer preoccupied by the radio — simply fell asleep. When he awoke, they were once again on the surface of the water, and now within sight of land. However, the fact which scared him the most was that two seats were now empty.

He shouted for Samuel before remembering the radio.

'Samuel,' button three glowed, 'where's Mita?'

'Ah, Sir. You are awake! We weren't sure whether or not we should disturb you, but considering your recent exertions, decided not to.'

'Who decided not to, Samuel?'

'Well it was Mita actually — though I must say, I did concur with her judgement.'

'Where has she gone?'

'She and Audrey were "put ashore" I believe the phrase is. The young lady said that she had one more thing to do; something about her list I believe. And then she was going back.'

Neville, who still imagined that he might be in a dream, rubbed his eyes and looked out of the window. Rocky cliffs passed on their left side, large tankers were ahead on the horizon, and in the distance an island loomed.

'Back? Back where?'

'To where she started. To find out.'

'Samuel, stop talking in riddles for Christ's sake! Find out what?'

There was a brief pause. The number two light went out, then a few seconds later was on again.

'Where were we? Oh yes, Sir, I recall. Going back; indeed. Well, Sir, that is the only way to discover the outcome of the — what shall I call it — "quest". Is that all right?'

'Do you mean "A" or "B"?'

'Indeed, Sir: "A" or "B". The only way to find out which is your destined route is to go back — in some sense or another — to where you began. To cast a fresh eye over yourself, if you will; to see how things stand.'

'That's not very clear, Samuel.'

'No Sir, I'm afraid it isn't. But it is rather difficult to explain; especially if one hasn't experienced it oneself.'

'So I too will have to "go back" somewhere?'

'Or to something, Sir; yes. Or even someone.'

'And Mita? What will happen when she goes back? Does she know?'

'Know? Oh no. It is impossible to know until that final moment. Why, I have known people who believe that they have found what they were searching for and that their life has been saved; only to find out that, at the last, they were hopelessly wrong. And I have known the reverse too.'

'Does Audrey have a view, about Mita.'

Samuel paused. Neville could imagine him smiling gently to himself.

'Yes, Audrey does. She thinks Mita will do very well. But even she could be wrong, as I have said.'

'And do you have a view, Samuel, on how I might be doing?'

This time there was a slight laugh.

'Sir! I will have a little nearer the time. But for the moment let us say that I think you are progressing quite well.'

Ahead the island was growing larger, and the cliffs had given way to a flatter coastline. There were clumps of buildings here and there, and Neville made out the larger conurbation of a town.

'There is a note, Sir.'

Samuel's voice suddenly came back to him just as he was thinking about Mita's progress — and how he was as uncertain about her future as he was about his own.

'A note?'

'Yes, Sir. the young lady left you a note. It is, I believe, in the pocket of your jacket.'

Neville felt in the side pocket of the flying jacket he was still wearing over his suit. He pulled out two pamphlets — the top one was "Your Ship" — and then an small envelope. He replaced the first two in favour of the latter, which bore no inscription. He pulled it open. Inside were several sheets of blue writing paper dressed with neat lines of blue ink.

Dear Neville,

I wasn't sure whether or not I should wake you, but then decided if I did it might make leaving more difficult. I have one more thing that I need to do, and I'm afraid I have to do it on my own. I asked Audrey if you might be able to be there, but she said (as I knew she would) that such a thing wasn't possible. Don't worry, it's nothing to do with you; it's something I set out to do a few days ago and that's the end of it. I won't explain as it isn't relevant to you — and it would take too long to do so anyway.

Audrey says that she can't promise what happens after that. I've asked her of course. I guess you'll also be asking Samuel the same question soon. He seems like a nice old man, and I don't think he'd lie to you, not about something so important. He and Audrey have a lot in common I think, don't you?

We haven't really had much time to get to know each other have we? Just a few minutes in the restaurant, and then the dance on the ship. Even after my note, it was a real surprise to see you there. I'm happy that it was you though; if my dream dance needed to have a dream partner, then I think you fitted the bill very nicely.

There isn't much time really; not to tell you about why I came to be in the situation I am in, nor — more importantly — what I've been running away from and what I'm going back to face. Audrey says that whatever it is — the thing that has brought us so much grief — we have to go back and confront it; that's the only way of knowing really. I must confess I'm scared. I think I've taken a long hard look at myself and I've tried to address those things I've needed to; but I don't know how I've done — not for sure — and not knowing, I can't be certain of the outcome.

Audrey says that you've only just found out about your watch. Mine says a little before one o'clock, so by the time you read this — well, it may be all over, one way or another.

I asked Samuel if I came through the ending okay whether or not I'd be able to see you again. He said that you still had a few days to go yet, but that he couldn't see there being a problem with me being around. I mean, apparently as far as you're concerned I can't influence things any more than I have already (I hope that's for the better!), and provided I was prepared for "the worst", then it was up to me. But then we both know what "the worst" is. I've a theory it means that one minute you're there, and the next minute you're not... Maybe we shouldn't think about it.

He said something about you going to the Derby at Epsom. Were you planning that? I said it would be nice if I could arrange to meet you somewhere; you know, something definite that we could both hang on to. (And now I'm assuming that you actually want to

When he finished reading, Neville was surprised to find that his eyes were filled with tears. There was a slight ink stain at the top of the final page, so perhaps he had been in that condition for longer than he imagined. Mita's note seemed sad, more like a farewell letter. He wished for a little more hope, a little more fight; but she was scared and unsure, and, it seemed, preparing herself for "the worst".

'Are you all right, Sir?'

Neville coughed, trying to clear the lump that had risen in his throat before replying.

'Fine, Samuel,' he said, his voice deep, hoarse, and brim-full of emotion. 'I hope she'll be OK.'

There was no reply. Neville guessed that Samuel could say nothing without sounding either patronising or morbid, so perhaps silence was the best response. In any event, he chose to interpret it as "So do I, Sir; so do I".

Since he had been reading Mita's letter, the submarine had made significant progress and appeared to be heading towards a small harbour at a river's estuary. Thanks to the rocks feature known as "The Needles", the island they were passing Neville now recognised as the Isle of Wight, and in doing so understood that Samuel had brought them back to England rather than continue on to the Mediterranean.

He checked his watch. It was a little before seven thirty, so the journey in the submarine had taken them over twelve hours, most of which — it would appear — he had passed in sleep. Neville wondered if he might not have preferred a couple of days in the sun before his time ran out, but, under the circumstances, he was happy to defer to Samuel's judgement.

'Samuel.'

'Sir?'

'Where did we drop the ladies off?'

'I'm not sure I can say, Sir. You understand?'

'Yes, of course. But can you tell me if it was England? Would that be OK?'

Samuel paused.

'Let us say that we did not get any closer to the Mediterranean. Would that be enough for you?'

'Is that all I'm getting?'

'I'm afraid so, Sir.'

'Then it will have to do.'

Samuel's light went out and then, with a loud "hiss", the submarine canopy suddenly popped from the top of the superstructure and tucked itself away to the side. Neville felt the fresh air stinging his face. Ahead, Samuel pulled off the helmet, then turned to him.

'That's better, isn't it?'

'Feels good, Samuel, yes.'

The quayside was now rapidly approaching and two or three groups of people had gathered to witness the arrival of their rather unusual craft. Bursar — whom Neville had not heard from for some time — slipped the submarine between the fishing boats and pleasure craft that bobbed gently at anchor, evidently aiming for a small jetty at the far end of the harbour.

As they approached, a man who had been sitting on a bench mending a fishing net, rose and gestured for them to throw him their mooring rope. From somewhere near the front of the sub, Samuel produced the appropriate length of hemp and — with a degree of accuracy which surprised his shipmate — threw it to the man on the quay.

'Good throw, Samuel!' Neville shouted.

Samuel turned and smiled.

'I threw the odd rope or two in the war, Sir.'

'Yes, of course. Why am I not surprised?'

With a bump, they came alongside the jetty. Samuel, first out of his seat, stepped onto the hull of the submarine and then up to the pontoon's timbers. Neville followed suit. From an open hatchway at the front of the submarine a bandaged head suddenly appeared, and with it the unmistakable visage and shoulders of Bursar.

'Thank you Bursar,' said Samuel.

'M-m-m-my pleasure.' He looked at Neville. 'How are you, S-s-s-sir?'

'I'm fine, Bursar. Thank you very much.'

There was a brief pause, as Bursar looked around at nothing in particular.

'W-w-w-well,' he said with sudden emphasis, 'I'd b-b-b-better b-b-b-be off!'

'You take care!' Neville shouted back, as the former Porter — with his customary cry of "F-f-f-f..." — dropped down through the hatchway once again.

Neville, Samuel, and the man on the jetty, watched as the small submersible moved away and headed out towards the open sea. After a few moments, the perspex dome flipped over the cockpit once again, and gradually the craft slipped down into the water and out of sight.

'Will he be all right?' Neville asked.

'Bursar? I should think so, Sir. He seems quite a capable chap when all's said and done.'

The smile on Samuel's face assured Neville he knew more than he was letting on. It was the smile of a man who had an edge, who knew the game and the way to play it. But it was a benevolent smile too, and whatever lay in store for him over the next seven or so days, Neville was pleased that smile — and its owner — appeared to be firmly on his side.

'Shall we take the bus?'

Samuel had turned and was leading Neville towards the steps at the end of the jetty.

'The bus? Isn't it at the airport?'

The smile remained on Samuel's face as they climbed the quay steps. The bus — now painted a deep metallic green — was parked just a few yards from where they emerged. Neville placed a hand on Samuel's shoulder, and Samuel gave a little chuckle. And as they walked to the bus, Neville suddenly wondered where Mita might be at that precise moment, and whether, at some time in the future, he would see her again.

TWENTY NINE

Returning to the bus, Neville was expecting to find that in addition to the colour of the exterior, things would have changed on the inside too. However, this was so much *not* the case that he noticed the old mug containing the dregs of his last cup of tea still resting on the small table at the front. Samuel gave an audible sigh as he stood by the driver's seat, with his right hand resting on the steering wheel.

'You know, Sir,' he volunteered, 'I do miss the Old Lady when we're separated.'

'Prefer it to a midget submarine, eh?'

Samuel smiled.

'Just a little.'

Neville wanted to ask how the bus had found its way to this coastal inlet from an airport some ten or fifteen miles away, but he knew that the answer — although in all probability an honest one — would not tell him anything material. He made a move towards the closed curtain that defined the boundary of his compartment.

'Well, I don't know about you Samuel, but I'm going to get changed.'

Pulling back the curtain, Neville expected to find the bags that had been on the ship awaiting him on the bed. Such sleight of hand was one of the things he had become used to, Samuel's "little tricks". So when facing his bed and finding the covers exactly as he had left them prior to their departure on the S.S.Pilgrim — and not a suitcase in sight — he was a little surprised.

'Tea, Sir?' Samuel said as he walked past him, carrying the now empty cup.

Neville wondered about the clothes but refrained from asking.

'Good idea, Samuel. Why not?'

As Samuel made his way to the galley, Neville silently questioned whether the non-appearance of his clothes had something to do with the fact that the game was now being played against a countdown, as if this was another aspect of the rule changes he seemed to be facing: he had limited time, and now a limited wardrobe. He pulled open the relevant cupboard; at least there were sufficient clothes there to prevent him from finishing his adventure stark naked.

Despite the not inconsiderable sleep Neville had enjoyed on the submarine, he once again felt rather tired; in consequence his bed seemed quite inviting to him. He stretched, and pulled off the heavy flying jacket it seemed he had been wearing for ages. From an inside pocket the edges of the envelope were showing. Neville removed both Mita's letter and the remainder of the pocket's contents. He thought about re-reading the letter, but it already felt familiar enough to him and, at the present time, it seemed sufficient that his thoughts were with her. He needed no prompting for that.

'Souvenir, Sir?' Samuel reappeared just as Neville deposited Mita's letter in a drawer, and was holding out the guide to the S.S.Pilgrim.

Neville looked at the "Your Ship" pamphlet: "Total Leisure Incorporated". Something else he was not likely to forget in a hurry.

'Should I keep it as a souvenir, Samuel? Or rather, can I keep it? Is that the more appropriate question?'

Samuel smiled.

'Your tea. I'll leave it here, shall I?'

Neville tapped the guide on his hand, then put it in the drawer with Mita's letter. This left him holding one other item. It was a pamphlet of similar size as that relating to the S.S.Pilgrim's configuration. He had been aware of it since Bursar had left it with him, but had lacked the opportunity to pay it any attention.

'Hey! Hey, Mister!'

A small voice of complaint rose from the floor. Neville looked down at his shoes.

'Come on! We're dog tired. Take us off!' moaned the left shoe.

'Yeah; give us a break!' added his partner.

He sat on the bed.

'OK guys, fair enough.'

Neville united the laces and slipped the shoes from his feet. Both they and his feet sighed at their freedom. He leant forwards and placed the shoes at the bottom of his cupboard; then, before sitting back to drink his tea, also took off his suit jacket and laid it along the bed. In so much as it had seemed a barometer of his own moods and situations, the jacket now looked rather grey and lifeless as it lay crumpled at his side.

He picked up the second pamphlet again, and considered its title which he now noticed for the first time. The cover design was a somewhat abstract pattern. Despite the rather random nature of the shapes from which the image was comprised, Neville had the rather definite impression that it was meant to depict something.

From the far end of the bus, he heard Samuel's voice — 'Just going to have a quick bath, Sir!' — and the sound of running water. Had he wished to consult Samuel on the pattern or — more importantly — on the title of the pamphlet, the opportunity was to be denied him for a few minutes. Neville stared at the words now attracting his attention:

CROAK: *A Guide to the Game.*

It seemed a strange title for a game, "Croak"; and it was certainly one he had never come across before. He turned to the next page of the booklet.

1 — Introduction to the Game

The Board. *CROAK is played without a board. If it were however, it would be a multi-dimensional affair, with — in all probability — at least seven levels. Each level would contain either squares or hexagons which, in the full game, would need to contain in excess of twenty seven segments. With each level slightly offset from both its predecessor and its precursor, the game would offer movement complexities far in excess of comparable board games.*

The Pieces. *CROAK is played without pieces. If it were however, the set would consist of a number of different constructs, each of which would obey its own particular rules of movement. Although the set would need to be multi-coloured (with each colour representing a different "family" within the game) the pieces would, as a whole, form the total capacity of the single side which took part in the game. As such, the struggle for control and mastery — and the ultimate goal of victory — would rival the stratagems required to complete tasks of impossible complexity.*

The Dice. *CROAK is played without dice. If it were however, the die (or dice) would need to be multi-faceted, and of colours similar to both the board and the pieces (although this would not necessarily imply any strict relationship between the elements concerned). The faces of the die (or dice) would contain more than one value (though not in all cases) and the score applied when the die (or dice) were thrown would depend on the particular circumstance of the game at that moment and would, in any event, not necessarily correspond to an equivalent move — either laterally or vertically — on the board. Given such potential variations, the use of the die (or dice) would render the most powerful computer impotent in the calculation of all the variations available at any one time.*

Neville turned away from the booklet for a moment and picked up his tea. As he sipped it, he tried to conjure up an image of "Croak": the rather eccentric board, the colourful playing pieces, and the complex die (or dice). From the description given — this pertaining, of course, to exactly what the game was *not* — Neville thought he could see a vague relationship between how the game might look and the rather abstract cover to the booklet. Beyond this he was fundamentally lost. There would, he assumed, need to be some kind of rule book for the version of "Croak" described, and he could only envisage this as some enormous volume of ordered and numbered statements which, he suspected, would be no more than a series of "hints and tips" rather than a comprehensive set of game-playing instructions.

As he put down his tea, he tried to imagine the game without the board, its pieces, and the dice required to move them; but all that left him with was the booklet.

2 — Object of the Game

One. *CROAK has a number of objectives, or goals, which the player may attempt to achieve. The first of these relates to the duration of the game. Any player of CROAK should endeavour to make the game last as long as he or she possibly can. Depending on the circumstances within the game at any one time — and any circumstantial factors relating to the player's own interpretation of the rules — the game may or may not be played beyond the point at which it ceases to be enjoyable. Indeed, many of the finest exponents of CROAK ensure a game of limited duration by confining themselves to strict boundaries. If CROAK were a board game (as described above) then such a player might choose to confine his pieces (having chosen a restricted set) to a single level, and play the entire game with perhaps only one or two die (or dice). Such a stratagem, whilst popular in that it would make the game more accessible, would not provide for a great deal of excitement nor post-game analysis.*

Two. *The second objective of CROAK is to obtain mastery of the entire game-playing scenario. This is the most difficult of the game's objectives. The player must attempt to arrive at a position in the game where, irrespective of any move made by the player himself (or herself) or, as a result of any external influence — such as an unexpected roll of the die (or dice), or a mistake on the part of the player in the execution of a move or moves — the player must be able to retrieve the situation to such an extent that, not only is there no loss in terms of his or her overall control of the game, but that the resulting position of the player is undeniably strengthened. If CROAK were a board game (as described above) then such a situation might occur if the player had deployed his pieces with such skill and foresight that, irrespective of any subsequent move or action, the player would have all options covered, and be able — in any situation — to move his or her* *pieces to such an effect that they would obtain a position of increasing irresistibility.*

__Three__. The third objective of CROAK relates to the way the game is played, rather than the specific outcome of the game itself. CROAK is renowned as a spectator sport and, irrespective of the style of play chosen by the player, he or she should endeavour to provide some degree of entertainment to those watching. In the majority of cases, games of CROAK which are the most exciting tend to be of shorter duration than the norm; they can be quite frenetic, with a player sacrificing overall control of the game in the pursuit of this particular objective. If CROAK were a board game (as described above) the player attempting to maximise the enjoyment of those watching would be most likely to choose a game with a large sub-set of the available pieces and/or to conduct the game across the full range of playing surfaces. Irrespective of this inevitable complexity, the game would still need to be tackled at speed and, by utilising the majority of the die (or dice) available, the player would be accepting and taking risks, having little or no control over their outcome.

With the end of the page, Neville once again turned to his tea, this time finishing it in one swallow. From the back of the bus he could hear faint splashing from the bath and Samuel's rather broken tenor as he fumbled his way through a famous Puccini aria.

Neville wondered if Samuel might be able to shed any light on "Croak". The fact that the booklet had been given to him by Bursar, and that Bursar was — to some extent — an acquaintance of Samuel's, led him to put two and two together. This was, Neville knew, akin to his overall relationship with Samuel. Often there was little definition, little precision; Samuel liked to offer limited suggestions or chose to remain vague — as evidenced by his use of words such as "perhaps". Indeed, Neville realised, despite their occasional chats relating to his own situation and where Samuel was presumably endeavouring to pass on relevant information, in the end he often felt as much in the dark as he had been before they'd started talking.

He weighed the booklet in his hand. This little document seemed to be much in this vein too; it appeared to be aiming to give information, yet as much as it gave, it seemed to take away again. Neville struggled with the concept of "Croak". Having been offered the board and all its pieces — whatever they looked like! — he was unable to fix an image of them in his mind and thus permit concentration on what the game *actually* was. The rules gave nothing away, either. A picture, a diagram, or even some form of chart laying out — something — would have been of use; as it was, Neville struggled with the words, lacking a suitable context within which to fit them.

Readjusting his pillows in order to allow a more comfortable sitting position —
his legs, along with the rest of his body, now on the bed — he decided to press
on.

3 — The Opening Position

The Set-Up. *The player, on first starting a game of CROAK, finds himself
confronting the opening position. It is important to note that, although there are
many similar initial set-ups in the game — and that many of these could be seen
to form themselves into particular groupings or styles of game — there are no
standard openings in CROAK. The player enters the game as if it has already
been in progress for some time, the maturity and complexity of the situation he
finds himself in dependant on factors outside of his or her gift, yet which are totally
relevant to the individual concerned. In the hypothetical case of CROAK being a
board game (which it is not) the player would come to the board with a number of
pieces already dispersed. The number, make-up and variety of playing pieces laid
out, as well as their location in terms of not only the levels occupied but also their
precise positions, remaining outside the control of the participant.*

The First Move. *Given the variability of the opening position, the player should
initially attempt to evaluate the situation he or she faces. This is important as a
first step in that, by doing so, the player may make an assessment of the type of
game he or she is going to play and, more specifically, which of the objectives they
will pursue throughout. In order to make an accurate assessment of the situation,
the player will need to spend a considerable amount of time in studying the
position before them. At this point in the game the player is at his or her most
vulnerable from a) external influences and b) making mistakes in their own
game-play. It is often the case that a player's assessment of the situation — and
the strategic direction consequently decided upon — is proven to be incorrect, and
as a result they are faced with the difficult decision of attempting either a) to
change their strategy or b) to make the best of the sub-optimal position in which
they find themselves. In the hypothetical case of CROAK being a board game
(which it is not) the player might choose — based on the initial position — to
decrease the number of pieces they are playing with and confine themselves to a
single level of the board, only to discover that during the early stages of the game
additional pieces suddenly appear and in locations which undermine the player's
overall strategy. As the first moves in such a game of CROAK are also
representative of a familiarisation period, many players might choose to follow a
course of play which falsely suggests itself as being a safe set of opening moves
(should such a thing exist). It is important to remember that, should any such
"safe" moves appear to be available, there are none, no matter how apparent risk-
free or inoffensive they appear.*

*We will now go on to consider the **Method of Play**, and the **Conclusion of the
Game.***

'Sir?'

Neville glanced up. Samuel, now dressed in a tweed dressing gown, stood by his curtains. He looked fresher and somehow younger after his bath.

'Hello, Samuel. Nice bath? I heard you singing.'

'Oh, sorry about that. I'm afraid I do have a minor weakness for breaking into song when in the bath.'

'It was fine — Pavarotti would have been proud!'

Samuel laughed, recognising that the very opposite was likely to be the truth.

'I just wondered if I could get you something as a night cap.'

'A night cap?'

'It is nearly midnight, Sir. I assumed that you were planning to turn in.'

Neville looked at the small clock that stood by the side of his bed. Progressing in a clockwise direction — as all normal clocks should do — it confirmed Samuel's statement. He realised that, since their escape from the S.S.Pilgrim he had lost all sense of time. There was the trip in the submarine; that had taken a few hours. And then the journey along the Solent to here; presumably that was a few hours more. It did not seem to amount to a little over a day; but then again, he had been feeling tired, and the reading had made his eyes a little sore.

He closed the booklet and placed it on the small cabinet.

'Ever heard of a game called "Croak", Samuel?'

'"Croak", Sir? No, I don't believe I recognise the name. Why?'

Neville considered explaining the pamphlet and its contents to Samuel, and — considering the booklet's origins — perhaps challenge him on his last statement. However, he decided that it might be prudent to finish reading the last two sections before indulging in any debate.

'Why? Oh, I'll tell you later. It isn't important right now.'

'Very well, Sir.' Samuel paused. 'And did you want anything?'

'No thank you.'

'I'll say Good Night then, Sir.' And in doing so, Samuel turned towards his own compartment.

Neville called him back.

'Sir?'

'Samuel, do you ever know what happens to other people?'

'Other people? I'm not sure I follow.'

'Mita, for example. Would you know — would Audrey tell you — what had happened to her?'

Samuel paused, tugging at the tie of his robe as he did so.

'To be honest Sir, I might never see Audrey again. If we meet in the future it will be by chance; so I have little or no prospect of Audrey telling me anything.'

'I just thought... Actually, I'm not sure what I thought. Perhaps that you saw each other regularly, somehow. I don't know.'

Samuel smiled gently.

'I'm afraid we don't belong to some kind of club; even though it might seem that way at times.'

Neville waited; and Samuel waited too.

'But will you know about Mita, Samuel?'

Samuel leant forwards and placed a consoling arm on Neville's shoulder.

'No Sir; I'm afraid I won't.'

THIRTY

'Is there anywhere you particularly wanted to go, Sir?'

This was — after the usual early morning routine of waking up, getting dressed, and eating breakfast — the first question of any note Samuel asked the next day. Neville sat on his stool in the galley, the empty plate which had contained his bacon, sausage and eggs, pushed to one side in front of him; his hand rested on the small breakfast bar, cradling a half empty mug of coffee. Samuel was standing by the sink.

Neville looked at the questioner. He had been staring out of the window watching early-morning fishermen as they returned to port. It was not a large fleet here — perhaps three or four boats — but they gave the impression that the small harbour was a working one, and thus all the more authentic for that. He had been feeling restless since rising, and despite the opportunity for a bath and a hearty breakfast to refresh him, remained at something of a low ebb.

'Do I have a choice, Samuel?'

'Don't you always?'

Neville chose not to reply, primarily because he was still uncertain of what the correct answer to that particular question might be.

'What do I need to consider? Given my present constraints, what parameters do I have to work within?'

Samuel put down the cup he had been drying and hung the tea cloth on a hook by the taps. He pulled his own stool a little closer and, with a small but perceptible sigh, sat down. Reaching to his side, he picked up his own tea and took the first draught from it.

'You are not happy, Sir?'

'Happy?' It seemed an emotion totally out of place given the context of Neville's immediate situation, and Samuel's choice of word surprised him a little. 'You could say that I am not happy. In fact I'm not sure I can remember the last time I was.'

Samuel paused for a little more tea.

'I am not surprised you say that. I know things have been a little difficult; and especially near the end, people forget things, lose their way.'

Neville wondered exactly what "near the end" meant, but chose not to challenge Samuel on it.

'You ask when you were last happy? On the ship perhaps, when you were dancing with Mita? Or on the submarine later, once we had effected the rescue?'

Neville could only concede this, and he knew that Samuel knew it too. He checked his watch.

'Apparently I have something like six and a half days left. But "left" before what? I mean, presumably I have to go somewhere at the end? Mita talked about "going back" to face something. Is that what I must do? And if so, where do I need to go? How much time do I need?'

'There are a lot of questions there, Sir, aren't there?' Samuel tried a smile to ease the tension that was beginning to build. 'I can't give you too many answers — but I do know that you are closer to answering them than you think.'

'Really?'

'Yes, really.'

Both men returned to their teas. Outside on the quay side, one of the boats was unloading its morning's haul. Crates brim-full of fish gleamed in the sun as the light reflected off the scales of the dead fish. Neville thought of Bob; and thinking of Bob thought of Mita.

'I understand, Sir,' Samuel had been watching Neville as he stared out of the window, 'but I'm afraid that all you can do is hope and have faith.'

'Faith? In what should I have faith, Samuel?'

Samuel smiled.

'You see; I told you that you were closer to finding the answers you needed.'

'How so?'

'Because you begin to know the questions to ask.'

Neville finished his tea. Perhaps there was something in what Samuel had said. Perhaps he had been approaching his situation from the wrong angle; looking for the wrong things; expecting to find *something* tangible that would solve this inexpressible riddle for him. Perhaps understanding was the first step. But if it was — and understanding *what* indeed? — would that be enough over the next six days to save him?

'Do I go back to Malvern?' He asked the question as one might a fortune-teller.

'Why?'

'Because that's where it started. "It". All of this.' He swept his arm out in a gesture through the air, trying to encompass the bus, the harbour, all the dead fish.

Samuel shook his head slightly. He was still smiling that benign smile of his.

'Is it? Is it really?'

The last day. Neville wondered if he had that long — five and a bit days — to work out where he supposed to return to. Maybe he should aim to "go back" to the day before, just in case he was wrong; just in case he might be horribly mistaken. At least then he would have a day's grace; a second chance.

So what else should he do? He tried to remember his original list.

'When's the Derby, Samuel?'

'In three days I believe, Sir.'

'Then we should go there, don't you think? I did say that I wanted to; and I told Mita that I would be there, so I have to don't I? Because...'

Samuel cut-in before he could elaborate any further.

'Indeed, yes. I would recommend that we get there the day after tomorrow; that will give us plenty of time. I wouldn't like to risk the traffic, not on Derby day.'

'And after that; will I have enough time to "get back" to wherever I'm going — wherever that might be?'

Samuel tapped the side of the bus.

'I think we should be able to get you wherever you wanted to go, Sir, yes.'

'Good.'

Neville, who had begun to feel a little better, returned Samuel's smile, boosted in part by the other's confidence. He wanted now to be doing something; he wanted not to be sitting idle and waiting for whatever it was that was coming his way. It was suddenly important for him to be occupied. He wanted to vanquish any fear about the future, and he wanted not to think too much about Mita. Going to the Derby was the only thing to do, and if Mita was there, and if she found him — well that could be another question answered.

'Shall we get underway then, Samuel, off in the general direction of Epsom perhaps? Maybe we could go via Winchester. I would like to see the Cathedral again; I haven't been there since I was a boy.'

'The Cathedral?' Samuel thought for a moment. 'That sounds like a good idea, Sir. Yes, let's do that, shall we?'

They both rose and Neville handed Samuel his empty mug for washing. As Samuel busied himself at the sink, Neville replaced the two stools in their slots beneath the breakfast bar. The bus suddenly seemed a remarkable piece of engineering; everything with its own place, all fitting together remarkably well. He could think of nothing wasted, nothing extraneous.

'Will you be travelling up front, Sir, or in your compartment?'

Neville paused.

'Up front I think; mind you, there is something I need to finish reading, so I may not be much company for you.'

'Don't you worry about me, Sir; I'm happy enough just to be behind the wheel.'

A few minutes later, Neville heard the familiar sound of the old bus being persuaded into life as he stood by his bed pulling on a loose lambs' wool cardigan. The brochure he was half way through sat in the open drawer where he had left it the previous evening. In a way he was a little surprised to find it still there, as if it would have been fitting for it to somehow have disappeared before he had a chance to finish reading it. Armed with the booklet, he made his way to the front of the bus.

Samuel gave him a quick glance as he settled in his seat but remained silent, making no reference to what he might be reading nor passing any comment on their progress. Neville, having done up his seat-belt, took a few moments to reacquaint himself with the sensation of being driven in the bus. Though he knew that it was not, it seemed a long time since his previous experience of Samuel's cautious twenty seven miles per hour; so much had happened in the intervening day or two.

Outside, they had already rumbled through the fringes of a tiny village and were in open country. Inside, Neville opened the pamphlet and began to read.

4 — Method of Play

Strategy. *The player of CROAK should endeavour, at the earliest opportunity, to furnish themselves with the strategy they will try to follow for the duration of the* *game. As has already been indicated, the strategy should be allied with the attainment of one or more of the game's objectives. However, this is not always necessary, and the player may, if they so desire — and if the position in the game is such that the alternative is both feasible and attractive — choose to adopt a strategy which is essentially open-ended and without allegiance to a pre-defined goal. Such a strategy, which is essentially flexible both in terms of game play and the options available to the player, is, of course, the most difficult to master. In addition to this, it has a fundamental drawback in that the player may easily find himself or herself suddenly in an end-game without having established any potential route to victory. In this case, the entire game becomes an anti-climax, and many famous — and infamous — games of CROAK have ended in much disappointment. Given the illustration of CROAK as a board game (obviously out of the question) the player would need to have established a wide variety of pieces across all levels of the board, and with such a balance in their strengths and mobility, that they would be in a position to easily counter any situation which may occur. The difficulty arises when the player discovers that they have insufficient power in one area or level of the board, or an inappropriate mix of pieces, to deal a decisive blow at the conclusion of the game.*

Levels of Play. *There are numerous ways to approach the play-by-play mechanics of CROAK. The player may endeavour to plan their moves well in advance, even to the extent that they have identified a chain of dozens of moves which they plan to execute one after the other in the pursuit of their defined strategy. Alternatively, it is possible to play the game on a move-by-move basis, where the consequence of any individual move is never considered. These two methods of play — from the extremes of pre-planning to the cavalier and liberated — both have weaknesses. In the first instance, certain events may force the player to deviate from his or her planned sequence of moves to such an extent that they must to take time to re-plan a new sequence of moves. A possible outcome of this is that the player may actually end up making an insufficient number of moves and thus achieve nothing by the end of the game. In the second example, the player may make many moves — certainly more than he or she needs to — with the issue arising that, as none of the moves bear any strategic relationship to each other, the player may drift through the game aimlessly. Given the illustration of CROAK as a board game (obviously out of the question) the player will need to strive for balance at all times, weighing the state of the game with their relationship to both strategic aims and the challenges and opportunities presented to them at each turn. Dependant on the immediate situation (which could, of course, change in an instant) they will need to be able to adopt either a fully planned sequence of moves or a number of spontaneous moves, as necessary.*

Neville looked up from the booklet. Outside the countryside was passing them by as they made their casual way northwards. On both sides of the bus, large areas of forested parkland opened up, and occasionally he could see deer or ponies amidst the trees. Samuel was aware that he was now looking out of the window.

'Finished reading, Sir?'

'Nearly Samuel.'

'I was wondering if you might like to stop for a cup of coffee in a little while, before we get to Winchester.'

'Yes, that might be nice. Any idea how long it will be before we get there?'

Samuel's smile reminded Neville that, in the context of his present adventure, there could hardly be a more redundant question to ask. Still, his driver humoured him.

'Shouldn't be long, Sir, I expect.'

Neville checked the booklet. He had only one more section left to read, though he was — now, as much as at any time before — still not sure why he was continuing to read the guide, let alone attempting to make any sense of it. "Croak" seemed to defy logic as far as he could see, though the booklet did appear — and at every turn too — to present itself as if it were a rational and logical exposition of a game that anyone could pick up and play.

5 — Conclusion of the Game

The End-Game. *At some point in the game, a position may be reached where one of a number of potential situations arise. In this event, the game comes to an end. Forewarning that the end of the game is at hand comes when CROAK enters its final phase, or end-game. The end-game — which cannot be identified by any particular occurrence, position, or manoeuvre — may last as long again as the entire game up to and including the point at which it is reached, or it may be over in a single move. The actual duration of the end-game will depend upon the type of game being played, the player's strategy, the situation at any particular point in time, as well as any number of external factors. Once the end-game is entered, it is usual for the game to progress to its conclusion. However, under certain exceptional circumstances, it is possible for the player — either though their own efforts or otherwise — to leave the end-game and return, quite legitimately, to the game proper. Under such circumstances, the player may expect to enter another phase of end-game at some stage in the future, the timing and duration of which will be no more nor less calculable than was the original. In the board game scenario — where CROAK might manifest itself in an appropriate format — the end-game could be triggered via a number of individual situations or circumstances ranging from a) an individual move, b) through a combination of pieces and their physical locations, to c) a particular result of a die (or dice) roll.*

The conclusion of Neville's reading of the booklet coincided with a gradual deceleration of the bus, accompanied by a plaintive moan from the ancient gear box. Neville, looking up and expecting to find Samuel preparing for a coffee break in a quiet lay-by, was surprised to find the facade of Winchester Cathedral rising not three hundred yards ahead of him.

THIRTY ONE

After a brief debate, they decided to have coffee anyway. While Samuel prepared it and opened a packet of biscuits (chocolate cookies he said he had been "saving") Neville returned the "Croak" guide to the drawer. Back in his seat and with the bus parked in the Cathedral square, he was once again able to cast his eyes over the building that, as a child, he seemed to have visited almost every weekend.

However, he was certain his memory was inaccurate and that, as he had been so young at the time, events associated with the cathedral — which were never particularly pleasurable to him — had spawned a legend of almost weekly torture. As the bus filled with the rich aroma of fresh coffee (Samuel obviously in an expansive, non-instant mood) Neville was able to consider the external architecture of the building with fresh eyes. The negative sensation from his childhood amused him, and he found himself intrigued rather than daunted by his notion of the place.

'Intrigued?'

Samuel had come in on the end of his thoughts and was obviously interested in the line of thinking he had been taking.

'Perhaps that isn't the right word, I don't know. But the fear has gone.' Neville smiled. 'I used to hate this place, just coming here. For a while we lived quite nearby — in Twyford, by the river — and my Aunt would insist on visiting regularly, normally on Saturdays when we came to town to shop. Even though she may have only been enduring these trips for me, I suppose I was too young to protest.'

'Or to know why you hated it?'

'Well, it wasn't the Cathedral I hated; it was most likely the being dragged around, lacking the freedom to do what I wanted.'

'To stay at home and play with your model cars?'

Neville laughed.

'Something like that!'

Samuel placed a mug of coffee and a small plate of biscuits in front of him.

'And intrigue?' he said, as he resumed his own seat and began to munch on a cookie.

'Interest; a lack of understanding, maybe. About what it stands for — the church, I mean. Church in the "big", general sense. Why is it here, the cathedral? What made — and makes — men build things like this?'

'Is it something you don't understand?'

'Something I don't think I comprehend, rather than fail to understand. Is there a difference?'

The square was quiet. Two old ladies left the Cathedral, walking arm-in-arm away towards the shopping centre. It was mid-week, mid-day, and the weather had encouraged the tourists to stay at home. Against the dull sky, the building — still impressive as a structure — seemed to blend its greyness with the day itself. Neville looked for a spiritual beauty and seemed to find none.

'Why now, Sir — if you don't mind me asking.'

'Now what, Samuel?'

'Why Winchester Cathedral now? Is there any reason for you to be here?'

Neville, still looking at the building and its square, tried to locate some kind of context for it.

'I don't know. As we were passing, I thought it might be nice to see it again; to lay an old ghost to rest, if you like. And you said something about faith, too; do you remember? Perhaps there is a question there I need to answer.'

'About what, Sir; Christianity?'

Neville laughed gently.

'No, Samuel, I don't think so. My Aunt managed to put me off *that* very early on — not that she was particularly devout or tried to force it on me. Not that I remember anyway. I guess I saw her give a lot to her faith and receive nothing in return. Not as a child, anyway. So it has never appealed; nothing has, really.'

'And now?'

'And now I'm not sure if that's right. Or if it *is* right — right for me that is — whether or not I understand why that is. Do you see?'

There was silence as the two men drank coffee, a silence broken only by the occasional crunch of a biscuit or the "clink" of mug on saucer. Neville, having finished first, rose from his chair.

'Are you coming, Samuel?'

Samuel smiled.

'I don't think so, Sir. I need to get one or two provisions. I thought it might be nice to have a bit of a picnic at Epsom, so I really ought to go and get the things we will need. So you go ahead. I will probably be back here before you, anyway.'

Neville imagined that Samuel could — if he put his mind to it — probably acquire all the things he needed without even leaving the comfort of the bus. In any event, having made the offer, he was quite pleased that Samuel had declined as he fancied seeing the place on his own. Returning to his compartment, he buttoned up his cardigan and pulled his overcoat from the cupboard. Momentarily he toyed with the notion of wearing the flying jacket, but this seemed somehow inappropriate with a visit so far removed from any idea of "action".

As soon as he had left the warmth of the coach, the wind — which was certainly stronger than it had initially appeared to be — bit hard into him, even through the fabric of his coat. In the grey sky, lumps of dense and threatening cloud chased each other in their hurry to get somewhere else and soak someone. It did not seem like early June, and Neville — as he walked across the green — hoped that the weather would be kinder at Epsom.

He paused in the entrance vestibule and scanned the notices, including one for a local bell-ringing group, another proclaiming the advent of a Bring-and-Buy sale in Twyford in aid of the village school, and — largest of all — the rather imposing sign which requested (in a vaguely threatening way) that visitors make a donation to Cathedral funds. Religion with menaces. Perhaps there was nothing new in that, but he was sure — all those years ago — entrance used to be free.

'But it still is free,' said a deep voice, surrounding him with a kind of quiet echo: 'free, free, free...'

Neville looked around and could see no-one. He checked the walls and the ceiling, but could find no source for the voice. Undaunted by something which might have struck terror into those instantly interpreting it as God, he pushed open the semi-glazed entrance door and walked into the cathedral proper.

His first footfall gave off a quiet echo of its own, and once inside he stood still for a moment. There was no other sound. He could see the small gift shop was closed, and guessed from the absence of any other sound (except perhaps the occasional whistle from the wind outside) that he pretty much had the place to himself. They had always walked the Cathedral the same way when he had been young, and now — habit still strong even after all these years — he began the same anti-clockwise rotation.

He had not gone far — past the first few stained glass windows — when he became aware that he was being watched. He paused by a memorial stone to an early Bishop of Winchester, stared up at one of the windows, and waited to see if the sensation would pass. It did not. Indeed, he now felt the feeling augmented by a sound which he could only identify as slow but deep breathing.

'Well, it *has* been a long time, time, time…'

It was the same deep voice, only now coming from behind him and within the body of the building. Neville turned expecting to find that he was being addressed by a member of the clergy or a parish warden, or even the old pensioner he recalled and who used to arrange the flowers; but the Cathedral was empty.

'Here, here, here…' said the voice, the same slow echo bouncing off the pillars and pews.

A little over twelve feet from him was a monument to the crusades. On a stone plinth, was the figure of a Knight, one hand holding his sword, shield on his chest, dog at his feet; his other hand was usually clasped in that of his Lady who lay at his side — except that the Knight was sitting half-upright, leaning on his right arm, and looking directly at Neville.

'I saw you come in, in, in… You haven't been here for a while, have you, you, you..?'

Neville took a pace or two forwards then stopped. The Knight slowly swung his legs over the side of the plinth, the movement of stone on stone making a deliberate grinding sound. Lowering himself to the ground, the floor seemed to shake as he made contact with it, and Neville looked round involuntarily to see if the noise had roused anyone.

The Knight left his shield and the dog to guard his place and took two solid, heavy steps towards Neville.

'Shall we walk, walk, walk..?' There was the echo again, now accompanied by breathing and the rather powerful sound of flexing stone.

'Do you remember everyone?'

'No, no, no...' said the Knight, 'but more than people might imagine, imagine, imagine... After all, what else is there to do all day when you are lying there but look at people passing, passing, passing..?'

'And you remember me?'

They had started walking, still anti-clockwise and still slowly, their progress accompanied but the sound of the Knight's stiff movements across the stone floor.

'Yes, yes, yes... Of course I remember someone who I saw week after week, week, week... That was your mother who brought you, you, you..?'

'My Aunt. We lived nearby, in Twyford.'

The Knight looked puzzled.

'That is not a name I know, know, know...'

Neville chose not to elaborate; after all, it was quite likely that the Knight would be unfamiliar with many modern place-names — and it was not a subject about which he knew enough to do justice. He returned to his previous theme.

'But I was only small then; and it was probably thirty years ago. How could you recognise me now?'

'Because I expected to see you again, again, again... Because I have come to recognise those who will once more cross my path at some stage in their own future, future, future...'

'So all those years ago, you knew that one day I would come back here?'

'Not one day, but this day, day, day... And I have been waiting — as I wait for all others — for you, you, you...'

They had walked nearly the length of the Cathedral and had reached the entrance to the crypt. Often, Neville had used to try and persuade his Aunt to let him go down into the crypt; more often than not she had refused. Neville paused, but the Knight continued in his slow pace, giving the impression that if he stopped once he would not be able to move again.

'You go down, if you want to, to, to... You can always catch me up, up, up...'

Neville thought for a moment, then decided to give the crypt a miss. He joined the Knight at his side.

'How do you find this, being' — Neville hesitated, thinking about using the word "stuck" but then deciding against it — 'being here after your exploits in the wars?'

'Wars, wars, wars..?'

The Knight's granite face showed little expression. Neville looked at it, trying to find some degree of humanity in it, but there was none. Yes, it was a benevolent face and not that of a cruel man, but the Knight had lost all power of expression except that carried in the resonance of his stony voice. Just now he seemed a little displeased.

'We were on a righteous and glorious crusade, crusade, crusade... We were fighting for God, God, God...'

All the candles throughout the Cathedral suddenly burst into flame ignited by the power that seemed to underpin the Knight's last words. He was, however, unfazed. If recent experiences had taught him anything it was not to be surprised — and also that the Knight, whatever his own motivations or desires, was undoubtedly there for a specific purpose in relation to his own quest.

'But only your view of God, surely. Were you not fighting to impose your God on another race?'

'We were right, and we were chosen, chosen, chosen...' The Knight's right hand tightened its grip on his sword.

'But a lot of people died, didn't they?'

The Knight paused. His words, when they came, were filled with sorrow and grief.

'Yes, a great many died, died, died...'

'And for what? Things have moved on now.'

'Did we not win, win, win..? Were we not victorious, victorious, victorious..?'

And then it occurred to Neville that the Knight might have died during the Crusades and returned home a dead and unfulfilled man; that the sorrow he had just sensed was in part the emotion of a man grieving for himself.

'They have God there now, and they are a civilised people.'

'But the God they have is not our Master, Master, Master..?'

'Who can say?'

There was a brief pause. The Knight, with his hand once again relaxed at his side, moved slowly on. They had reached the far end of the Cathedral and were walking behind the altarpiece. As they did so, the Knight turned his heavy head and looked directly at Neville.

'And what of you, you, you?'

'Me?'

'You are embarked upon your own crusade, are you not, not, not..? That is why you are here, today, as God has willed it, it, it...'

Neville wondered about the Knight's assertion that he was expected to be here, and on this day too. How much of this was down to the Knight's blind faith and ignorance of the twentieth century calendar?

'I don't know about God's will, but I suppose you could say that I'm on a crusade of sorts.'

'Ah, Ah, Ah...'

'But it's no holy war; not in my case.'

'Then you are seeking the Holy Grail, Grail, Grail..?'

The laugh escaped before Neville could stop it, and although he tried desperately to cut it short, it reverberated uneasily about the building. He sensed the Knight stiffen — if such a thing were possible — and saw his hand return to his sword once again.

'I'm sorry; forgive me.'

The Knight said nothing, and Neville tried to remember that he was walking with someone whose myths and legends were centuries older than this own and untainted by decades of discovery, cynicism, and counter-truth.

'Yes. Yes, you're right; I suppose you could say that I am searching for a Holy Grail of sorts.'

'For what do you search, search, search..?'

Neville paused. When it came, the answer was blissfully simple.

'For myself.'

The Knight lifted his left hand. Slowly it rose, the stone complaining with the stress of movement, until it hung a little above Neville's head. Then, equally slowly, it began to descend until it was suddenly at rest on Neville's shoulder. It landed lightly, more as a feather than a ton weight. The Knight nodded.

'And God, God, God..?'

'God?'

'Have you come here to find Him, Him, Him..? Or to ask for His help on your quest, quest, quest..?'

Neville now wondered exactly why he had come here. Was there more to his decision than simply "looking up old friends", or because it was on the way to somewhere else? How much had Samuel's words influenced him, or was he looking for inspiration, for motivation?

'To be honest, I don't think I have come to find God or to get His help. I think I need to find myself first. Perhaps God comes later.'

'Then in what do you have faith, faith, faith..? In what do you believe, believe, believe..?'

'I think I need to believe in myself.'

They had reached the end of the Cathedral and were now only a few yards from the entrance. The Knight had removed his hand from Neville's shoulder and was looking up and along the nave to the altar. Slowly he crossed himself. Neville sensed that the interview was over.

'Now I must rest, rest…' said the Knight, the echo now weary and faltering.

'I may be back again,' Neville suggested, hopefully.

'I wish you well on your quest, quest... May you prosper, prosper...' And with that the Knight turned away from him and walked slowly back to his plinth.

For elsewhere in the Cathedral, Neville heard the sound of a door closing and then footsteps; sharp, quick, human footsteps. He looked towards the altar but could see no-one. Then there was the sound of another door, more muffled footsteps, then — for a moment — silence. Gradually, almost without beginning, the sound of the organ began to fill the Cathedral. Its notes were quiet and mellow, all-pervading and peaceful. Neville looked back to the plinth. The Knight was at rest again, his dog at his feet, and once again clasping his Lady's hand.

THIRTY TWO

Samuel was standing in the galley unloading two carrier bags of shopping when Neville returned to the bus. After the Knight had resumed his silent vigil on the plinth alongside his Lady, Neville had decided on another turn around the Cathedral though this time accompanied only by the sound of the organ.

Gaining the exit, Neville found the gift shop was open and a man busy inside. He decided to pop in for a quick look before returning to the bus. An elderly couple entering the Cathedral nodded in his direction as they passed him. The gift shop was, much like the fabric of the place itself, little changed from his memory of it; the range of goods for sale was the same — bookmarks, postcards, miniature imitation stained glass windows — though each was of a higher quality than twenty-odd years before.

He had been uncertain as to his ground when he decided on the purchase of a small memento to remind him of his visit; uncertain because the rules might not permit him such temporal fancies. Still, he argued to himself, he had his suit and his flying jacket; were they not some form of inheritance? Thus, when Neville emerged out into the square, he began walking towards the bus with a small brass effigy of a Knight of the Crusades resting in the pocket of his overcoat.

'A bit nippy out there, isn't it Sir?' said Samuel looking up from his bags.

'I can't say I noticed it.'

'Ah, well, perhaps that augurs well for Epsom then.'

Neville left Samuel with his bags and went to his cupboard to hang up his coat. As he did so, he noticed the hangers that had held both his suit and flying jacket were now empty.

'Samuel.'

After a brief pause, the older man joined him.

'What is it, Sir?'

'My suit; it's gone. And the flying jacket.'

'Oh, yes. I meant to tell you. I thought your suit was looking a bit grubby — probably all that rushing around on the boat, I should imagine — so I thought I'd have it cleaned for you. And, while I was at the cupboard, I thought you might as well have the jacket tidied up as well.'

'I see. But there were things in...'

'In the pockets? Yes, Sir; I removed them. They're safe and sound.'

'Fine.'

'Would you like some tea?' Samuel had already turned and was on his way back to the galley. 'I was going to pop the kettle on once I'd put the shopping away.'

'Thanks, yes.'

He wondered where to put the small replica of the Knight. Would it make sense to hide it away somewhere, just in case? He looked about then quickly came to the conclusion that, apart from beneath the mattress or under his pillow, there were no suitable hiding places. Perhaps it would be best left where it was; the overcoat was clean enough, and Samuel would be unlikely to make another trip to a dry cleaners in the immediate future.

'Has it changed, Sir? The Cathedral, I mean.' This when Neville re-joined Samuel in the galley.

'Changed? No, I don't think so. Not structurally anyway!'

Neville's small joke went unrewarded. Samuel, busying himself over the tea pot, continued with what appeared to be a predetermined line of enquiry.

'Same old faces, I suppose?'

'Sorry?' Neville thought of the Knight; surely not the face Samuel was referring to.

'You tend to get people working in places like churches and Cathedrals for years. Often until they are past working. You know, Sir; the little old lady who tends the flowers, or the old chap who sorts out the Bibles. That sort of thing.' He looked up, awaiting a reply. Neville thought of "the Old Boy who drives the bus", and wondered again just how long Samuel had been doing what he was doing.

'There was a chap in the Gift Shop. I didn't pay much attention to him, but I guess he could have been an "Old Timer".'

The lie hung limply in the air, and for a moment Neville imagined Samuel might simply swat it away and crush it against the wall. But he said nothing, merely nodded and began to pour the tea. Neville wondered why he had bothered to avoid the truth, especially as Samuel could just read his thoughts anyway. The Knight was no more fanciful than Mister Bossiman or "Bob", and yet he felt the desire to keep a hold of him, to retain the secrecy of their exchange and the privacy of his own response.

'We'll go for'ard, shall we, Sir?' Samuel, mugs of tea in hand, offered the suggestion using misplaced nautical vernacular. He nodded too, offering his beguiling smile. Neville wondered if he might patent it — "Samuel's Soother", he could call it — and sell it to old Grandfathers and Great Uncles who needed a little something to keep young relatives in check.

As he followed him to the front of the bus, Neville wondered if, somehow, their relationship had begun to change; if his dependence on Samuel was beginning to diminish. As they sat down, Neville decided to try a little test.

'Can I ask you something?'

'Of course, Sir.'

'My suit; and that flying jacket.'

'Sir?'

'I'll never see them again will I?'

Samuel opened his mouth to protest, but immediately thought better of it. He looked out of the bus for a moment, then back to Neville.

'They have served their purpose, Sir. You wanted a tuxedo to wear to an expensive restaurant. You got a suit that served not only that purpose but another too.'

'The dance on the ship?'

'Indeed.'

'And you're now saying that I will no longer have any need of it, whatever happens?'

'You are going to the races Sir; to the Derby! You will need something different for that.'

'And after the races? Are you telling me you know I won't need them?'

'Perhaps an educated guess.'

Neville wondered how much of his experience — and the tangible things which contributed to that experience — was expendable. He wanted to go back to his compartment and check to see if the "Croak" guide was still there; if it was then he knew he had at least one other lesson still to learn. But it went further than that. How much of this entire fabric — even down to incidents like the dogfight and (he could not avoid thinking it) people like Mita — were injected into his reality just to serve a specific purpose, to enable him to work things out for himself?

'What shall we do for the rest of the day, Sir?' Samuel called him back. 'I don't think that there is any point our heading to Epsom until sometime tomorrow, do you?'

'Sorry? I was miles away.'

Samuel smiled.

'I just wondered about the rest of the day; assuming we go to Epsom tomorrow.'

'Yes, of course. Tomorrow should be fine, don't you think?'

'And today?'

Neville, finally getting his mind to re-focus on the conversation, took up his side of it.

'Today? I don't know, Samuel. Perhaps a lazy kind of a day. Things seem to have been so hectic. I think I might like to wander around the town this afternoon. More old memories, that kind of thing. And perhaps we could "eat in" this evening.'

'Or I could get a take-away, Sir. Do you like curry?'

Within a few minutes they had settled the plan. Neville was to take a stroll around the town (especially as the weather was beginning to improve) while Samuel took the bus to check its water, fuel and tyres. Then they would have a Chinese meal to round out the day.

After a quick sandwich — rustled up by Samuel in double-quick time — Neville found himself stepping off the bus (though this time without his coat) and heading away from the cathedral.

Between two old cottages there was a small discrete exit which led towards the town centre. Neville, emerging at the far end of the ginnel, found himself facing a scene which had changed little since his childhood. Indeed, the first of the small shops he came across — tucked away as they were — bore the same names and sold the same goods as they surely had all those years before. Indeed, he even suspected that, on the exterior of one or two of them, the paintwork — which had been looking jaded back then — was still awaiting the touch of a handyman.

From one such shop — selling trinkets, postcards, and sweets — a lady emerged as he was standing at its window. She nodded, then walked off. Neville was struck not that she chose to acknowledge to him, but because her overall manner and demeanour seemed strangely out of place. Then, watching her until she disappeared from view round a corner, he realised that the way she was dressed fitted not his present time but the past he could still vaguely recall.

Another figure crossed his line of vision. The old fashioned cut of the jacket, the hat — peculiar to a time when he was a child — all gave weight to a theory he was in the process of formulating. For an instant he was gripped with panic, and, intending it as some form of retreat, abandoned himself to the shop. The owner, standing behind the counter, gave his new customer a slightly wary look. Neville nodded, then pretended to look at the postcards. He glanced down at his own clothes. They were not ostentatious or outrageous certainly, but he was certain that they would appear unusual to an inhabitant of the nineteen sixties.

Deciding on a plan of attack, he pulled a postcard from the rack and walked with it to the counter.

'Hello,' he said to the man, attempting a fake and indistinguishable foreign accent in the hope that this would allow some excuse for his mode of dress.

The assistant smiled and, in true British tradition, shouted "Hello" back, loud and slow.

As Neville reached for his wallet, he suddenly realised that although he was relatively "cash rich" at the moment, none of it would be of any use. He might try and palm the shop keeper off with fifty new pence, pretending it was Italian or something — but then the Queen's head would give the game away. He fumbled around and then, staring at the man waiting for the money, shrugged his shoulders, left the postcard on the counter, and walked out.

A few yards further up the street he looked back. The shop keeper was standing in his doorway looking after him. Perhaps it had not been as convincing a performance as Neville might have wished.

In a way he was disappointed to find himself having regressed some thirty-odd years and to be walking the same Winchester streets as he had when a child. On leaving the bus, part of him had been looking forward to seeing how things had changed so that he could compare and contrast; it would have been an opportunity to measure progress, to see how some other part of the realm had managed without his intervention. However, he was now acutely aware that, trick or no trick, there *had* to be a reason for finding himself walking the same temporal streets as he had all those years ago, staring in through the same shop windows at the same goods. Yet even though nothing had changed, Neville knew this still gave him a sense of perspective, of measuring what had happened to *him* with the passing of time. He was now something of an alien being of course: strange clothes, and with money that couldn't even buy him a cup of tea. At least the language was the same.

He had reached the end of the street and was about to turn the corner, when, from the direction of the bus station, he saw a woman and a child walking towards him. He stopped dead, causing a man who had been following him to bump against him heavily. The man muttered something indistinguishable; Neville failed to apologise.

It had been the woman he recognised first. Or rather her coat. It was a little lighter than bottle green with a dark brown imitation fur collar and devoid of any semblance of "cut" or style. A little above knee length, he could see the muddy tan trousers and brown court shoes which, as an ensemble, had come to symbolise his Aunt Maggie. And now here she was again, marching towards him with her heavy Christian steps and heading for the Cathedral. Neville realised that as well as striding *towards* him, she was also marching *alongside* him; for there, in those slightly ill-fitting corduroy trousers he'd always hated, *he* was walking too.

There was little harmony between these two figures (they were just across the road now, waiting for the traffic) and Neville recognised the feelings he'd once had of prisoner and jailer reconstituted physically before his eyes. The child looked sullen, unhappy; reluctant to cross the road, reluctant to take his Aunt's hand when she insisted. As he watched, Neville caught the boy's eye. It was a dull lifeless stare, lacking any of the vibrancy he'd always imagined children possessed; indeed, that he assumed he'd had too. This was the face of child who was not interested, who did not care, and who — though without realising it — was letting his life slip by.

Margaret stepped into the street, dragging the boy — dragging *him* — after her. Neville stepped back a little, and they passed within two feet of him. Neither looked up. He caught the tail end of a sentence his Aunt was completing but missed the specific words, though the tone and the manner of its delivery made his spine tingle. The boy ignored her, wrestling his hand free.

He had always imagined himself a lively child (this as he followed both Margaret and his younger self back down the street towards the Cathedral). He could remember playing football in the playground, chasing girls; he remembered snowball fights with Spotty Johnson, Long Preston, and Big Jim, and how they used to beat him up if scored more goals than them at Subbuteo. He remembered how he liked to draw planes and build model ships from Airfix kits, and how — despite years of trying — he was never very good at conkers. He thought his teachers liked him, even though he was never quite at the top of the class; and he knew his parents loved him. This was the package, the memory of himself he had chosen to take forwards into his adult life. Consequently, he had settled on the fact that he'd been an okay kind of kid, one who was building a solid foundation for the future. But now he had looked into those cold and empty eyes; his own eyes.

Neville allowed them to get a few yards ahead. Margaret, judging from her manner, was still talking — how she could talk! — and occasionally *pointing* or pulling or tugging. The boy — *he* — was not responding. They passed the small shop in which he had so recently sought refuge; the boy tried to dawdle to look at the postcards, but Margaret was having none of it. In a whisker they were into the alleyway and through to the green.

As he reached the shop, Neville — perhaps it was habit from all those years ago — again glanced in the window. It was changed from his most recent experience of it. He stopped and stepped back. The paint work was a little different, a little brighter; and in the window, prices no longer bore labels marked up in shillings-and-pence. He looked through the archway. He could see no-one.

Stepping inside the shop, he received a cheery "Good Afternoon" from the man behind the counter. This was not the same man who had tried to serve him earlier. Neville looked at the postcards, at their quality, at the simple *difference* in them from thirty years earlier. He picked one up and took it to the counter.

'Twenty seven pence, please.'

Neville took out his fifty pence piece, handed it over and waited for the change. Twenty three pence was duly returned. He thanked the man and left.

As he walked towards the alleyway and the Cathedral green beyond, he knew that his Aunt and the boy would be long gone. In fact, as far as the boy was concerned, he was just about to walk through the alleyway once again, only this time carrying a small paper bag containing a postcard of Winchester Cathedral.

THIRTY THREE

Emerging into the Cathedral square, Neville checked that the bus was there rather than pursue any faint hope — if hope was indeed the appropriate emotion — that he might see his Aunt and the boy walking ahead of him. That the bus had moved was certain, as it was now parked facing away from the Cathedral; that his relations (if he might categorise them as such) were not in sight was evidenced by the square being deserted.

'You were gone a while Sir,' said Samuel as Neville climbed onto the bus again.

'Was I?'

'A little over three hours, by my watch.'

Neville checked his own. It felt as if he had been gone no longer than fifteen minutes or so, but Samuel's estimate appeared to be pretty accurate. Did time have a worth then, in the same way that money did; something unconnected with its empirical and relentless progress? If this was so, then the time his watch was telling him he had left might vanish in the blink of an eye.

'I was about to go out for the food, but thought I ought to wait for you.'

'Thanks, Samuel.' Neville moved through to sit on his bunk. Samuel followed him.

'Did you have any preference for dinner, or shall I get a range of dishes?'

'I don't mind. Go for the selection; that might be better.'

'I agree, Sir. I've opened a bottle of wine in readiness. It's breathing in the galley.'

'Fine.' Neville stood up again. 'I'm going to have a bath before dinner, if that's OK.'

Samuel smiled.

'I thought you might Sir, so I ran one for you. It may be a little hot still, but it's all ready.'

Neville nodded and began to pull off his cardigan.

'Well, I'll be off. Shouldn't be too long, Sir. I've been recommended a suitable establishment in the town centre by a gentleman at the garage.'

Left alone, Neville removed the rest of his clothes and donned the blue and red striped velour dressing down that Samuel had laid out for him. Opening the top drawer of his small cabinet to retrieve some clean underwear, he saw the "Croak" guide still in its place, though he suspected that — no matter how hard he might try — he would now be unable to find the "Your Ship" guide to the S.S.Pilgrim.

Walking through the galley he could hear laboured puffing from the bottle of wine as it breathed heavily on the work surface, readying itself for the meal.

'Evening,' it said as he passed.

'Keep it up,' said Neville encouragingly, then went through the door and into the bathroom.

The surface of the water was almost totally covered in suds from the bubble bath Samuel had obviously put into it. Neville pushed his hands through the surface to test the temperature of the water. It was a little hot, as Samuel had suggested, but nothing he couldn't stand. Disrobing, he placed his right foot into the bath, then the left; eventually lowering himself in.

'Hey! Careful, chum!'

From beneath the surface of the bubbles came a voice, followed by the yellow plastic duck which bobbed Neville's way.

'Sorry,' said Neville.

'Ain't I seen you before?'

'Yes, a few days ago.'

'Sure, I remember you. Never forget a — face. Know what I mean?'

The duck laughed its peculiar laugh.

'How are you?'

'How am I, mate? OK except for all these bleeding bubbles! I saw that geezer — Sam, in't it? — come in here with that foamy stuff and I just knew he'd put too much in. Now look at me!'

'Can I help?'

'Na. I'll be OK, ta. It slips off after a bit; I got the right sort of skin, see?'

Neville picked the soap from the side of the bath and began to lather around his neck and arms.

'You rich?'

'Rich?' The question surprised him.

'Yeah, rich. Most guys I only see once, but this is the second time I've seen you. Staying long in the 'otel, are you? Must be rich if you're still here.'

'I don't think I'll be here much longer, actually. Maybe another day or two, that's all.'

The duck bobbed off into a little circle, skirting the edge of the bubbles, while Neville continued washing. Having rinsed himself, Neville slid a little further down the bath and tried to relax. He listened for sounds from outside, but could only make out the faint puffing of the wine. With the water now up to his chin, the duck bobbed up closer.

'So, what you been up to then? Since I last saw you, I mean. Had a good time, eh? Seen the sights; that sort of stuff?'

'In a way, yes.'

Steadying himself about six inches from Neville's chin, the duck eyed him directly.

'What's the matter, mate? You look pretty pissed off, like you've lost a biscuit and found a breadcrumb.'

Neville smiled.

'I like that, it's clever.'

'Clever; that's what I am see, though people don't pay be me no attention. Like, they think that 'cos I'm just a duck all I do is float around all day, know what I mean? They don't give you credit, see?'

'I think I understand.'

'Sure, I ain't never gonna be no brain surgeon — ain't got the qualifications for that for a start — but that ain't the point. I know who I am, I know what I'm supposed to do; that's it. I just gets on with it, being a duck; but it don't mean I'm stupid!'

Neville watched the duck as it bobbed gently backwards, its big eyes unflinchingly wide.

'I don't think you're stupid; not in the least.'

'See,' said the duck, coming closer again, 'that's what I mean. You're all right, you are. If you can take a guy for what he is, you know, and just let him *be*; shit, that's all there is to it!'

There was a slight pause as the duck quack-quacked gently away down the bath. Neville eased himself up in the bath, making slight waves as he did so.

'Hey, don't mind me mate!' said the duck, obviously happy that he had been gifted a degree of respect from his fellow bather. 'You make all the bleedin' waves you like; I'm OK.'

Careful not to hit his yellow companion, Neville raised his left leg out of the water and began to wash it. The lather from the soap had started to disperse the bubbles, and the surface of the water was now relatively clear. Having finished his left leg, he moved on to the right.

'Where you off to then?'

Neville paused.

'Next, you mean?'

'Yeah.'

'Actually I'm going racing, to the Derby at Epsom.'

'That's horse racing, ain't it? I've heard of that.'

'That's right.'

'Yeah. 'Cos I've got a cousin who works on a farm near a place called Newmaster.'

'Newmarket?' Neville suggested.

'Sure; Newmarket, Newmaster — what's the difference? Anyhow; there's this horse riding place next to his farm, see. Sometimes — or so he says, anyway — he gets to hear things about the horses and the races they're in, like.'

'Really?'

'Yeah.' The duck bobbed closer and lowered his quacky voice to the equivalent of a whisper. 'Look; as you and me's mates, I'll have a word with him and see if he knows anything about this 'ere Derby thing. Might be able to tell you somethin', eh?'

'Indeed.'

Neville was uncertain how the duck might be able to communicate with his relative in Newmarket; but then, seeing as he had — in some sense or other — just managed to communicate with his own self from a previous generation, perhaps nothing was impossible.

From outside, he heard the sound of the bus door being opened, and immediately the smell of Chinese food came wafting his way.

'Heads up,' said the duck, 'it's Sammy!'

'It's only me, Sir!' Samuel called when he reached the galley. Neville heard him put a bag on the work surface, then a "sniff-sniff" as he checked the wine. 'Dinner shouldn't be long; I just need to put the plate warmers out. That sort of thing.'

'You'd better get goin' chum,' said the duck with a playful quack, 'else old Sammy'll be after you, and no mistake!'

'Samuel's OK, actually. Something of a gentleman to be honest.'

'That so?'

Neville nodded.

'Well, if that's what you says, then it's good enough for me.' The duck paused. 'But tell him to chuck a little stale bread my way, OK?'

And with the duck still cheerfully bobbing around at the foot of the bath, Neville hauled himself to his feet and reached for a towel. Within a couple of minutes he was standing by the side of the bath, once again in his dressing gown. He looked down at the bath and the duck still mobile within it.

The duck saw him looking.

'Hey, don't worry about me! Just pull the plug; I'll be fine!'

'Sure?'

'Sure I'm sure!' replied the duck, adding, just as Neville leant forwards, 'Listen; I won't forget about the horses, OK?'

'OK.'

'And take care of yourself.' And with those words the duck became rigid plastic once again, transformed as simply as if someone had flicked a switch.

Neville left the bathroom and walked through the galley (where Samuel was sorting out plates and tin foil containers) and back to his compartment where he dressed. From that point on, the evening passed off without incident. The food was acceptable, without being exceptional (despite the King Prawns scoring quite highly) and then, after dinner, Samuel suggested that they try a few hands of rummy to pass the time.

It had been a while since Neville had played rummy, but, apart from a few "local rules" as Samuel called them, they embarked upon a version of the game that was quite familiar to him. Familiarity was not, however, enough for him to triumph over Samuel's exceptionally strong play.

'I put it down to my memory, I'm afraid', he said, half way through the game, when he was leading by nearly two hundred points, 'I suppose it gives me something of an advantage, but I hope it doesn't spoil it for you.'

'Not at all; I actually enjoy seeing someone play the game well — even if I am on the receiving end!' Neville's complement was only half true: he did enjoy seeing the game played well, but as for being on the receiving end... 'and anyway, it's only a game!'

After a second game, they decided to call it a day. Samuel went to make coffee while Neville cleared away the cards and — at Samuel's request — found a road atlas of Britain. As they drank coffee, they plotted the best route to Epsom, planning to arrive in the early evening, after the departure of that day's race-goers. Samuel had already phoned ahead to book their parking place — 'in the centre, near the fair' — which meant that was one thing they wouldn't have to worry about.

Having chosen the route and estimated both departure and arrival time — the length of the duration between the two suggesting that Samuel would not be pulling any "tricks" the next day — they finished their coffee, chatted for a short while, then retired to bed.

Neville did not sleep well. His dreams were contorted with visions of himself as a young child drowning at the hands of a malevolent duck who — as a bookie's runner — was getting revenge for an account that Neville had failed to settle. Having flitted in and out of sleep, at around seven Neville gave way to the inevitable, and decided to get up.

He drew back the curtains in his compartment to reveal that the weather was indeed on the change and the day had dawned as all June days should, bright and blue. Judging by the trees, the wind had not yet totally abated, but it was a step in the right direction. Driven by the need to go to the toilet as much as anything else, Neville donned his dressing gown and went to the galley where he put the kettle on. Then, while waiting for it to boil, he went into the bathroom.

As he stood urinating into the bowl, his eyes inadvertently focused on the mirror above the sink. There, in barely legible writing, was a message evidently meant for him. It took Neville a little while to decipher the rather strange script which was probably inevitable given the words had been scribed by someone with webbed feet. Eventually he made out the soap-scrawled note thus:

Mate, this durby thing. My cusin says that somefin called Restrant Rendevoos *is the nag to be on, an no shit. OK?*

Neville had yet to see a list of the runners for the race, and consequently had no way of knowing if *Restaurant Rendezvous* was a horse, let alone entered into the Derby. However, the duck appeared to have been as good as his word, and Neville — at this stage of the game — was not going to turn down anything that might resemble a "hot tip".

THIRTY FOUR

Samuel appeared in the galley as Neville was making the tea, and immediately their day began. There was a strong air of routine about the performance of breakfast which followed. Neville was beginning to get a handle on Samuel's way of doing things — for example, the sequence in which he made toast, fried sausages, and poured orange juice — and how he had been able to augment the overall process so that the composite article materialised in double-quick time.

The breakfast ritual became, from Neville's perspective, an appreciation as to how one should go about its cooking and what it should eventually look like. The product of his recent domestic experience with Mirelle invariably led to a plate of food which at best resembled the crude attempt made by the hotel in Paris rather than anything which an Englishman would want to be served. His mother had, at various stages, gone through phases of cooking "a proper breakfast". These usually coincided with either fits of depression or happiness and, as far as he could tell, these moods were initiated by his Father (though after his vision of himself the previous day, he could no longer be truly certain of that).

The two men ate in relative silence, passing only the most superfluous comments on the state of the weather, the condition of the bus — which was, according to Samuel, far from excellent — and Neville's prospects for Epsom. He chose not to mention the duck's tip.

'What happens if I win, Samuel?'

'If you win, Sir? I'm not sure that I understand.'

'Well,' Neville put down the glass he had been holding, 'let's say I get lucky. I have a couple of bets and win a few quid.'

'I'm with you so far.'

'What happens to the money? I mean, I may well not need it.'

'In what sense?'

'In that — well, it depends on the outcome of Option 3, doesn't it?'

Samuel nodded.

'Yes, I see.'

'And secondly; if I've decided that money isn't as important to me as I once thought it was...'

Neville let the sentence finish itself there, confident that Samuel would be able to fill the blanks. There was a short pause, before Samuel responded.

'I would suggest — if I may — a slightly different approach, Sir.'

'Which is?'

'Firstly, maintain your new-found assertion that money is not as vital to you as you once imagined it was. That is important because — as I think you now see yourself — it is a healthy attitude to have.'

'And secondly?'

'Secondly, do not scorn it either. You cannot know what will happen to you in the future. If the goal you seek is achieved, then it may well be that money will be of considerable use to you in the future. On that basis, I would not worry about being successful. If you win — well, so much the better, whatever the outcome.'

'So, go to the races prepared to lose, but try to win?'

'Indeed. I think that may well serve your purpose.'

Neville had heard his Uncle (Maggie's husband, who had been an inveterate gambler) advocating that same philosophy every Saturday morning before he left the house to make his weekly pilgrimage to Ladbrokes. 'My boy,' he used to say, 'I only go prepared to lose what I can afford, and if I win, well that's a bonus!' The problem was that Freddie had, over the years, lost track of what he could actually afford to lose, driven on as he was by an ever-inflating target of the actual amount he was trying to win. More than once — when he was older — Neville had accompanied Freddie on some of his last sorties to "church" (as he called it) and had discovered during those smoky afternoons that the "church" was filled with "Freddies", each of them an incarnation of their own peculiar variety of the same fundamental human strain. It had been enough to quash any danger of him becoming an addict himself, but he had learnt enough to know the difference between a "Yankee" and a "Canadian", and the pluses and minuses of a "Round Robin".

Yet now, and for the first time, Neville felt his "tuition" — as Freddie might have liked to call it — might prove useful. Under the circumstances there was no way that Neville could fail to put money on "Restaurant Rendezvous"; a gambler's predilection toward coincidence and superstition would not allow him to let it pass. Indeed, the very experience he was going through had much in common with the craps player whose attitude was to throw the dice, say "to hell with it", and then ride his luck for as long as he could. It was difficult to know how benevolent Lady Luck was being just at present, but Neville felt willing to ride with her a while longer.

After breakfast they set off for Surrey. The route they had chosen allowed for a stop in Farnham for late elevenses and then a brief sojourn at a nearby beauty spot, Frensham Ponds. Here, despite the improved weather, Samuel chose to remain on the bus while Neville walked off the early lunch they had just consumed in the town. For an hour or so he wandered around the lakes, giving way to horses and their riders as they jogged along the bridle paths.

On his return, Samuel — who had been taking in the general scene through the windows of the bus — suggested that it might be useful if the horses Neville chose to back the following day went a little bit faster.

'But you don't know my luck, Samuel!' Neville had replied.

'Indeed. Perhaps that makes two of us!'

His laughter signalled that he was intending a joke, but Neville was still wary of Samuel's penchant for the cryptic, and, as they drove away, the literal meaning behind those last words remained with him.

The traffic increased the closer they got to their destination. Neville wondered if this might be owing to the crowds leaving the course for the day, but Samuel's theory — and one, he said, based on painful experience — was that the volume of traffic increased in proportion to one's proximity to London and the M25. Indeed, for a short while, the bus was actually stationary, a mere cog in a seized-up chain.

Consequently, they arrived at the course a little later than planned. It was still light, but apart from a few cars belonging to course officials, deserted. Samuel paused alongside a man who was patrolling one of the main entrances to receive directions to their overnight parking space. As he had promised, they made their way to the centre of the course, finally parking close to the running rail about two furlongs from the winning post.

Neville got off the bus as soon as they arrived in order to "soak up the atmosphere". Behind them, the fun fair — normally a bright, colourful and bustling arena — was quiet and dark, the only signs of life in the occasional shadows of the stall holders and ride mechanics as they went about clearing up, checking equipment, and generally preparing for the next day. Across the other side of the course, the grandstand — itself in darkness — loomed high into the air. Tomorrow, it and the vast space in front of it, would be thronged with a seething mass of spectators; a congregation which would come together and, as a single body, rise up with one voice to provide the inevitable crescendo to the big race. Neville had never been to the Derby yet could only imagine how, after the race was over, the rest of the day might be nothing more than an anti-climax.

He and Samuel had not talked about what might happen after the racing finished. Neville guessed that, if necessary, they might be able to stay another night; but if not, then he was fairly certain that Samuel would have something in reserve. If they were reliant on him coming up with their next destination, then Neville was currently in the dark as to where that might be. Or whether, indeed, there would be another destination at all.

THIRTY FIVE

Derby day dawned bright and clear. Neville, once more beating the alarm clock and Samuel's call, was roused not so much by the light but rather by a sense of excitement, of place, and the feeling that something dramatic was about to happen. His first thoughts were of Mita and the question which had been hounding him on and off over the previous couple of days: would she be there? Speculation was, of course, pointless, and he had been trying hard to adopt the stoic approached advocated by Samuel: if she was she was, and if she wasn't... Well, who knew what else might turn up?

Neville was conscious such a Micawber-like approach to life might get a little out of hand. He could see dangers in merely waiting for things to happen, and he knew he had not been pro-active enough in the past — how many times had he heard that complaint in his working and private life! Now recognising the trait and striving to be a little less passive, perhaps he was finally in with a chance of gaining a degree of control over his destiny — however slight. Samuel — obviously possessed by a sense of occasion as well — excelled himself at breakfast, and it was with a solid sense of well-being that Neville descended the bus and propelled himself into the day.

All was much as it had been the night before: the fair stood un-illuminated and motionless; the grandstand still loomed large, grey and empty. However, there were the beginnings of activity to be witnessed, activity that carried with it a growing sense of urgency. Amid the stalls and rides, men in lumberjack shirts and jeans could be seen hauling tarpaulin, pulling ropes, and carrying boxes; occasionally they would pass within feet of each other and share suitably cheery greetings. Across the course, others could be seen moving around the various buildings; occasionally a car would arrive in the officials' car park. Once or twice, thundering out of the quiet, a horse would gallop by having a last work-out prior to the big race.

As he stood against the rails cradling a mug of hot coffee in his hands, an elderly gentleman in a bowler hat approached from the other side of the running rail.

'Morning, Sir!' he said brightly, the tone of his voice echoing the day's importance.

'Good morning.'

'Just walking the course, you know; checking it out. Going's a little on the soft side of good, wouldn't you say?'

Neville watched the man dig the heel of his boot into the turf, testing to see how easily the ground gave way.

'Presumably the rain,' Neville suggested.

'And just in time too! Last week it would have been bone hard; terrible, really. Watering every night; didn't make the slightest damn difference! Still,' he examined at his boot again, 'look at it now! Well, must get on. Good day, Sir; and good luck!'

Samuel joined Neville at the rails.

'Who was that Samuel; one of the Stewards?'

'I should think so, Sir. What did he say?'

'"On the soft side of good" apparently.'

'Perfect; just perfect!'

A new voice joined their conversation. A second man, who had evidently been walking just a few yards behind the Steward, now drew level with them. He nodded in greeting.

'That's what the Steward said.'

'Eh?' said the man, pausing.

'The ground; just about right.' Neville clarified.

'Aye — and it's perfect for my little beauty!' The man gave a slight wink in their general direction.

'You are hopeful of success today then, Sir?' asked Samuel.

'I am. But don't judge our chances by the bookies. They don't think my little girl's got any chance in this kind of going. They think she needs to hear her hooves rattle. But mark my words, she'll prove 'em wrong!'

'Who was that?' Neville asked once the man had resumed walking and was out of earshot.

'Harry Simpson,' said Samuel, 'or "Happy" Harry, as he's known. Local trainer. Doesn't have a big stable, but he's got one going in the race after the Derby; *Second Visit* I believe.'

'How do you know so much; I didn't realise you were into racing?'

'I'm not, Sir. But as we were coming here, I thought I'd do a little homework; research if you will.'

'Any "hot tips" then?'

Samuel laughed.

'Ah, that might be asking a little too much!'

For the rest of the morning Neville wandered about the course observing as magically — like a photograph — the scene developed before his eyes. And with the visual changes came the additional sounds and smells that accompanied them. The rides in the fun fair were tested, lights flashed, music boomed out; then the hot dog and burger stands were prepared, with smoke rising from the early fries cooked as reward for the hard-working men. Across the course, the tannoy blared out "One, Two; One, Two; Testing, Testing", and the huge television screen panned through an image of Tattenham Corner. Pulleys clanked as the number boards rattled up and down, finally raised with the names of the jockeys in the first race slotted into place; even the "Stewards' Enquiry" and "Weighed In" flags were run up and down.

The crowds began arriving early too, staking their claim for a place near the running rail or up in the Grandstand, marking out their territories and always leaving Granny or Granddad on guard while the rest of the family went exploring. Samuel had set up a couple of chairs in front of the bus near the rail, effectively sealing off a very small area as if it were a private enclosure. Neville had been a little surprised that they had not stayed in a hotel overnight and then taken one of the better spots in the Grandstand. Now however, with the atmosphere building, he was pleased to be at the heart of things, and near people whose earthy attitude to the day seemed to make it even more real.

After lunch, Neville went off in search of a race card. He had decided it was time to get serious — and for that a list of the day's runners was needed. He found a man in a small booth selling the day's official programmes.

'How much are they?'

'Quid, mate.'

'Thanks.'

Neville went to his wallet to retrieve some cash only to find it was strangely full, and that the reason for its increased size was it now contained a large number of fifty-pound notes. Instinctively he checked his watch. The small display read zero.

'Quid, mate, please,' the man in the booth said, still holding out the small booklet.

'Sorry,' Neville smiled apologetically, found a pound coin in his pocket, and took the race card.

Once away from the booth, he located a quiet spot and checked his wallet again. It seemed impossible, but there were eight bundles of fifty pound notes, each bundle with a little wrapper on which "£1000" was inscribed. In addition, there were some loose notes. He replaced his wallet in his button-down trouser pocket and contemplated the situation.

All he had in the world — apart from his clothes and things on the bus — was represented by what he had in his back pocket. Everything. He was free to do with it as he would. There could be no come-back if he lost every single penny on the first race; there would simply be nothing more after that. The responsibility — and it *was* a responsibility — was suddenly quite daunting. If he lost everything, he knew he would not be able to rely on Samuel to work some kind of miracle; perhaps there might be no more miracles. And what did this imply about what followed today, or what happened tomorrow? Did it mean that he had no further use for money? That, somehow, his fate was sealed? Or was what happened on this one day key to his future?

He contemplated this last thought then rejected it. Money was not the answer. Even if he lost it all, it meant nothing — or at least not as much as he had once imagined. As he stood and thought, he felt a tug at his arm.

''Scuse me, Guv.'

Neville looked round. A man, perhaps in his late fifties (though it was difficult to tell) stood at his side. He was shabbily dressed in a torn jacket and with the souls of his shoes hanging from their uppers by a literal thread. The man was not particularly clean, and his fingers were stained with nicotine. But it was none of this which stunned Neville as much as the man's resemblance to his Uncle Freddie.

'Guv; ya couldn't spare an ol' hand a Sov', could ya Guv?' Not getting any response, the man lowered his demands. 'Or a few bob even. Just a few bob, God bless ya, Guv.'

As he stood looking at the man, he thought of Freddie's maxim about what you could afford to lose. He knew this man was not Freddie, but none the less it seemed he had a chance to give him a break; if he wasn't his Uncle, that didn't really seem to matter. Neville thought about the next day, and he thought (all in a fraction of a second) about Mita and about how he didn't have a clue what was going to happen to him. Much was unanswerable and out of his control; almost everything, but not this.

He pulled his wallet from its pocket and opened it. Then, without a flicker of hesitation, pulled out one of the wads and handed it to the man.

'Here. It's a bit more than a few bob, I know; but that's just your luck, isn't it?'

The man stared at the twenty fifty-pound notes now lying flat in his dirty left hand, then looked up at Neville. His fingers gradually closed round the money until it was scarcely visible in his fist. Slowly he extended his right hand.

'By God, Guv, ya must be some fuckin' angel or somethin'; but, by Christ, I thank ya; by Christ I do...'

Neville smiled and shook the hand offered him.

'This ain't no joke, is it Guv?'

'No joke; no. Let's just say you remind me of someone, OK?'

'Whatever ya say, Guv. God bless ya. Jesus Christ!'

By now, tears had begun to well in the man's eyes and he relinquished Neville's hand in order to brush his grubby cuff across his face.

'I'm sorry, but I should go now.'

And with a final smile, Neville placed his hand on the man's arm and then left him. After he had gone thirty yards or so, he looked back over his shoulder. The man was standing in the same place, staring down at his still closed fist.

'There you are, Sir.'

Neville turned to find Samuel now beside him.

'Hello, Samuel.'

Samuel looked at the scruffy beggar.

'I saw that, Sir; and may I say what a magnanimous gesture it was.'

They began walking back towards the bus.

'He reminded me of my Uncle Freddie. The poor bugger never really had a lucky break; I guess I was just trying to even the score a bit. And I don't need all this anyway.'

He felt Samuel's hand once again on his shoulder.

'Maybe so, Sir, but shall we see if we can find the winner of the first race in order to get your little donation back?'

Once on the bus, they settled in their chairs and began to study the form for the first race of the day. After a short while, Neville had narrowed his choice down to two; *Thunderer*, and *Hard in Places*. Samuel, having stated his intention to put a small wager on *Dunmail*, offered to take Neville's bet for him.

'It's OK Samuel; I'll manage. See you back here in a few minutes?'

The two men walked together to the bookmakers but were then quickly separated. Neville had decided on *Hard in Places*. Checking a few of the bookies' boards, his horse was generally quoted at four to one. However, one chap — an elderly man, in a rather dated tweed suit, and sporting the name "Dick Springs" — was offering nine to two. Neville walked over to him and pulled a wad from his wallet.

'Can I have a thousand on *Hard in Places*, please.'

Neville expected to be turned away or told that the amount was too great. Instead, Dick took the money, muttered "Four and a half grand to one, *Hard in Places*; ticket four one eight" to his clerk, and handed Neville an oblong card with "Dick Springs — 418" printed boldly in green. He then crossed out the nine to two offer and changed it to five to one. This was unusual. Neville would have expected the price of the horse to shorten having laid such a large bet on it. As he made his way back to the bus he checked the other bookies; sure enough, all were now offering *Hard in Places* at five to one.

Samuel was already back when Neville returned. He thought about describing what had happened, but decided that it might be best to wait for the outcome of the race first.

Having watched the horses gallop past on their way to the five furlong start, Neville waited with mounting excitement for the race. They could see nothing from where they were apart from a few hundred yards of the track immediately in front of them, and even so, given the angle from which they would be watching the majority of the race, they were reliant on the racecourse commentator for a description of the action.

Within minutes "They're Off!" was called to great cheers. *Hard in Places* was apparently quite well away at the start, but soon faded from the commentary. *Dunmail* took up the lead at about half way and, as they sped by, Neville could see that a challenge was being thrown down by another of the runners. This turned out to be *Thunderer* who, having collared *Dunmail* in the final furlong, went on to win by two lengths; *Dunmail* was second, *Hard in Places* seventh.

'Any good, Sir?' asked Samuel.

'Afraid not. Did you back yours to win?'

'Each way,' Samuel smiled, 'so I should make a little bit of a profit.'

The second race followed a similar pattern to the first. Neville was torn once again between a choice of two and, having made his choice — *Wood Kits* — went off to the bookmakers. Again, Dick Springs was offering the best odds on his horse, and again, as soon as he had placed his bet, the odds on *Wood Kits* lengthened. However, with Samuel also putting money on *Wood Kits*, Neville felt a little more hopeful of his chances; but this time the horse made no show at all, and trailed in last.

Samuel was philosophical, but Neville was beginning to lose his "it doesn't really matter" attitude.

The third race was the one before the Derby. This time the winner looked clear cut to Neville, and, for the first time that day, his choice — *True Mischief* — was favourite. When Dick Springs was once again offering the best odds and, having placed the bet, the horse's odds lengthened to such an extent that it ceased being favourite, Neville assumed the worst.

For a while however, it appeared that things were going to change. In a muddling race, the field bunched as they came past the bus. Neville could see *True Mischief*'s jockey flashing his whip, attempting to drive the horse through a gap on the rails. As they came towards the finish, the commentator suddenly announced *True Mischief*'s arrival on the scene and, by the time they reached the line, its apparent victory.

Neville's excitement was short lived however. First the "Stewards' Enquiry" flag was raised; then the board containing the numbers of the first three horses was lowered. On the giant television screen, the replay of the race showed *True Mischief* barging two other animals out of the way as it forced its way through on the rails. The could only be one possible outcome; the horse was disqualified.

After three races, Neville had now lost three thousand pounds, and his wallet felt decidedly thinner. He had also lost much of his good humour, and the philosophy he had possessed before racing began — and which had permitted him to give some of his money away — was now being put to the test.

THIRTY SIX

'Next one's the big one, Sir,' said Samuel when he returned from the bookmakers. Having placed a bet on the horse which, with *True Mischief*'s disqualification, was promoted to first place, he was consequently in something of a lively mood. Indeed, the entire crowd had been gradually building in anticipation of the next race, and the course was now a mass of colour and noise. Behind them the fun fair rides whirled and bucked, accompanied by screams and music, and in the grandstand a sea of heads bobbed continuously.

Neville was sitting in one of the chairs staring rather vacantly at the turf. He had seen Freddie in moments such as this when, having backed three successive losers, felt himself approaching that point which he had defined as "as much as I can afford to lose"; at that point there was usually a moment of crisis — especially in the later days — before Freddie would simply sail right across the line he'd drawn and embrace oblivion.

Despite the rather casual — if not cavalier — attitude he had displayed earlier with regard to the contents of his wallet, Neville was beginning to wonder if he shouldn't have set himself a limit beyond which he dared not cross. Given that he was here at the Derby under less than normal circumstances, perhaps he had assumed — and quite wrongly it appeared — that by some form of divine right he should win.

'Is something the matter, Sir?'

Neville looked up as Samuel sat down alongside him.

'Up? Not really. I just didn't expect to lose, I guess. And now I'm not sure if I know when I should stop.'

'Stop?'

'I can't blow all my money Samuel can I? And you do know that I have got *all* my money, don't you?'

Samuel nodded.

'Things haven't gone as I had planned, that's all. And maybe I don't want to take any more risks. Just in case.'

'"In case" what, Sir?'

'I don't know Samuel. Just *in case*. In case I need the cash tomorrow, maybe. Assuming that there will be a tomorrow, that is.'

Samuel leant across and handed him the race card.

'Why don't you just have a look at the runners in the Derby, Sir? I'm sure that you are quite all right at the moment.'

Samuel's words did not have the instant healing effect that they might have once possessed. However, Neville took the card and opened it up to the centre pages where the runners — all seventeen of them — were detailed.

Once upon a time, Neville would have studied form for an hour or so before a race like this in order to try and pick the winner, but not today. Indeed, after his experience in the first three races he was even tempted to close his eyes and choose something at random; this was just as likely to be successful. However, a little over half way down the card he spotted *Restaurant Rendezvous* and remembered his tip. He wondered if the limited knowledge of a yellow plastic duck could be any better than him trying to glean the full benefit from years of experience — and then almost immediately decided that it could.

He stood up and threw the race card back onto his chair.

'Decided, Sir?'

'I have Samuel.'

'That was quick, if you don't mind me saying so.'

'A little inspiration, perhaps.' Neville had wanted to say "A little bird told me", but decided against it, firstly because it would have required an explanation and secondly, the duck might well have objected to being referred to as "a little bird".

At the bookmakers, *Restaurant Rendezvous* was on general offer at ten to one. Neville spotted a couple of boards showing it at twelves, one at nines. He deliberately left Dick Springs to last, and, as he approached, hoped that this time Dick would not be offering the best price. The board showed fourteen to one. Neville's heart sank. For a moment he toyed with the idea of simply walking away, accepting that the outcome was already decided and that he must lose again. However, there were a number of forces at work inside him which prevented this: he'd had a "tip" for one, and Dick already had three thousand pounds of his money and he wanted it back. He pulled out his wallet.

'A thousand on *Restaurant Rendezvous*, please.'

Taking the money, Dick mumbled to his "Bag Man" and handed back ticket twenty six. Neville stood and waited, and — just as he expected — Dick rubbed out the fourteen currently against *Restaurant Rendezvous* and replaced it with the number sixteen. Neville remained motionless.

'Another thousand on *Restaurant Rendezvous*, please.'

'Sorry?' Dick looked at him eye-to-eye for the first time that afternoon.

'A grand on *Restaurant Rendezvous*, at sixteens. Please.'

'You sure?'

'Look, are you going to take the money?'

Dick held out his hand.

'Sixteen to one, the *Rendezvous*; ticket twenty seven,' he said over his shoulder, and handed Neville another green ticket, "027" the number brightly embossed upon it.

Neville, not caring what Dick did to his horse's price now, turned and made his way back towards the bus. He now had a little over two thousand pounds left. If he was unsuccessful this time then, he told himself, he had reached his limit.

It was now difficult to walk anywhere in a straight line, or without physically bumping in to people as you tried to do so. Things were beginning to reach fever pitch, and as he walked through the crowd his ears were assaulted by the names of horses just about to run, tips on their form, and fragments of stories relating how "if only the jockey had held the whip in his *left* hand" a different animal would have won an earlier race.

He realised how futile his suggestion had been to Mita that they should try and meet at the Derby. If she were here — indeed, if she were only a few feet from him — she would be impossible to spot, pink dress or no pink dress. He knew he couldn't hold out any hope of seeing her. If she were there, then perhaps she might get a message to him; perhaps Samuel might come up with one more trick.

Samuel was leaning against the rails when Neville reached the bus again.

'OK, Sir?'

There was a note of concern in Samuel's voice.

'If you've wondering whether I've bet all my money, Samuel, I haven't — though it did cross my mind, I have to say.'

Neville wasn't sure whether it had or not. In fact, he had become pretty uncertain about everything — all except the thoroughbred which was to carry his wager.

Within a few minutes the horses emerged from behind the grandstand and began their parade. They would walk towards the two furlong post, then turn and gallop away to the start. It seemed as if everyone on the course was now crushed against a running rail. On both sides of their small area — where Neville and Samuel still enjoyed the luxury of just a few feet to themselves — hundreds of people were craning their necks to get a glimpse of the horses.

As they came out in race card order, the first horse Neville saw was number one, which also happened to be the favourite. Samuel tapped his arm as the horse and jockey (the latter in bold black and white colours) came to a post temporarily placed in the centre of the course, walked round it, then headed off towards the start.

'That's my one, Sir.'

'The favourite?'

'I can't see it losing — not that I know anything about racing of course. And I met a gentleman a little while ago who put forward a most convincing case.'

Neville nodded, although he wasn't really listening. Across on the other running rail he could make out the green and gold colours worn by *Restaurant Rendezvous*. The horse seemed slightly smaller than the others; but then this seemed to be a fault Neville found in all the horses he backed, so probably said more about his perception of them than the horses themselves. It certainly seemed to move well (though how he could justify such a statement he wasn't sure) and as it turned at the post and galloped off, he had no reason to think any less of his horse compared to the others.

There were a few minutes of hiatus as the crowd moved away from the running rail a little, some endeavouring to get to a position where they would have a better view of the race itself. On the large television screen, the image showed the horses arriving at the start, having their girths checked by the green-uniformed handlers at the stalls, and then milling around, waiting for three forty to arrive.

The race course commentator describing the scene at the start elaborated on the pictures being shown. A great deal of attention was being paid to *Thatched Twine*, the favourite. On Dick Springs' board, Neville had noticed it being quoted at five to two, which seemed less generous than usual. As he watched the television, occasionally Neville caught a glimpse of the green and gold colours he was looking for, but his horse was denied any specific attention by either the camera crew or the commentator.

"They're going behind" echoing around the course raised the expectation level another notch. The horses were moving around to the back of the stalls and were beginning to be loaded. The electronic clock above the screen showed "3:39". Coverage of the loading process concentrated on *Thatched Twine* and another animal — *Silver Madam* — which was proving difficult to install. There was a moment's tension as a blindfold was applied, but then, on "3:41", the words "They're off!" were greeting with the cheers and shouts of the collective mass.

'*Thatched Twine* gets away to a good break on the inside, but its *Zynman* who immediately goes into the lead, with *Sea Castle* moving up on the outside.'

Neville listened to the commentary as he, like everyone else, became glued to the images on the huge screen. From what he could see, *Restaurant Rendezvous* was somewhere in the middle of the field which was being led by *Thatched Twine*'s pacemaker.

The first few furlongs followed the usual pattern for the race: the runners sorting themselves out; jockeys finding their favoured position, trying either to get to the running rail or away from it — even, in some cases, trying to remember the instructions given to them by their trainers a few minutes before in the parade ring.

'Coming to the top of the hill and beginning the sweep down towards Tattenham Corner, its *Zynman* still with a commanding lead. He's followed by *Sea Castle* and *Hokum*; *Silver Madam* is improving after a slow start, with *Thatched Twine* tucked in nicely just off the pace.'

Neville could just see *Restaurant Rendezvous* a little way behind the black and white of the favourite. It seemed to be going quite well, but, as yet, had warranted no mention from the commentator. As the horses made their way to the home turn, the crowd once again pressed to the rail, forsaking the television screen in the hope of catching a glimpse of the live action.

'Rounding Tattenham Corner, and now *Zynman*, under pressure, is beginning to drop back, and *Silver Madam* has been rushed up on the outside to take it up. *Hokum* is trying to respond, and now *Thatched Twine* is being shaken up on the outside. Just in behind these, *Restaurant Rendezvous* is making a little headway.'

Neville wondered exactly what "a little headway" might be. As he leant over the rails — the horses now a couple of hundred yards away and racing towards him — he could see the black and white of *Thatched Twine* looming on the outside. He knew that *Restaurant Rendezvous* was there, but could see no sign of the green and gold.

'And *Silver Madam* is now coming under pressure as he's joined in the lead by *Hokum*. But here comes *Thatched Twine*, cruising on the outside! Two and a half furlongs out, and *Thatched Twine* now comes to challenge!'

With the horses now thundering towards him, Neville saw the favourite's black and white colours ahead of the field, the jockey waving his whip and urging his horse on. But there, just behind him, *Restaurant Rendezvous* was still in touch. As they flew by in a blaze of colour, Neville knew that the green and gold was on the move.

'And its *Thatched Twine* over two lengths clear. Hokum is second with, on the outside, *Restaurant Rendezvous* moving into third and beginning his run. Just over a furlong to go, and its *Thatched Twine* still with a two length lead, *Restaurant Rendezvous* moves into second; *Hokum* looks beaten in third. These three are clear of the field. Coming to the final furlong, and its *Thatched Twine* now only a length in front from the *Rendezvous* in second. It's between these two. *Thatched Twine* is being challenged by *Restaurant Rendezvous*. Into the final hundred yards; *Thatched Twine* by half a length, but the *Rendezvous* is gaining. Coming up towards the line. *Thatched Twine* from *Restaurant Rendezvou*s. They're stride for stride! *Thatched Twine* and *Restaurant Rendezvous*, neck and neck! At the line — they've gone by together!'

Neville closed his eyes.

'It's a photo finish, between *Thatched Twine* and *Restaurant Rendezvous*! *Hokum* is third, with *Gold Cove* running on to be fourth.'

Samuel tapped Neville on the arm.

'My, Sir, that was a close one! Yours nearly managed it, didn't it?'

'Do you think *Thatched Twine* has held on Samuel?'

'Don't you, Sir?'

Samuel seemed slightly surprised that Neville could contemplate any other outcome.

'Do you *know* your horse has won?'

'"Know", Sir?'

Neville knew very well that Samuel had caught his drift. The giant screen was now showing a replay of the finish. The two of them — along with thousands of others — watched as the colours of *Restaurant Rendezvous* clawed back the favourite. Fifty yards from the line there was still no doubt that *Thatched Twine* was in front; but on the line it was much closer.

'Perhaps you're right, Samuel — but would you want to bet on it?'

Samuel smiled, and gently shook his head. On the screen, the pictures showed a still frame of the two horses as they hit the line. For Neville, this result had suddenly come to symbolise something about his relationship with Samuel: specifically that here, for the first time, he might actually have the chance to *beat* Samuel at something; to get ahead of him, to be one step up.

The air was charged with the silence from the public address and the large black and white "P" hung in the frame. There was a crackle from the tannoy, and the "P" began to be descend.

'And the result.' Thousands of people were suddenly silenced, conversations chopped in half, drinks half-swallowed. Neville placed both hands on the running rail and stared down at the turf. This was it. It was victory he wanted; proof that he could be a winner on his own. He wanted to go back to Dick Springs and redeem his tickets — and in doing so, redeem himself. It was not the money, it was more than money.

'First, number thirteen...'

The remainder of the announcement was lost as thousands of voices rose in one great cheer around the course. There were shouts, spontaneous bursts of applause; from those who had backed the favourite, there were harsher words.

Neville waited for a few seconds, then looked up. Samuel was smiling at him, his hand extended.

'Congratulations, Sir. Well done!'

THIRTY SEVEN

It took a few minutes — and the rather remarkable feeling of holding thirty two thousand pounds in his hands — for Neville to rationalise his success. His appearance at Dick Springs' pitch and the exchange of tickets twenty six and twenty seven for such a large sum of money caused something of a stir. As he walked away, one or two people even raised a cheer in his direction, thankful that someone had managed to get one over on a bookmaker.

There was, he guessed, something of the heroic in what he had managed to achieve — or at least that was how it seemed to him as he re-joined Samuel on the bus. For his own part, Samuel had chosen to mark the occasion by producing a bottle of chilled champagne (from where, Neville had no idea) and filled glasses were awaiting the return of the victor.

'Do you want me to look after that for you Sir? I could put it somewhere safe on the bus.'

Neville contemplated the large wad. He counted five thousand off, and handed the rest over.

'I'll just keep this, Samuel; I feel my luck may have changed.'

As Samuel disappeared into the relative security of the bus, Neville wondered whether — considering the champagne appeared to have been waiting in readiness — Samuel had expected *Restaurant Rendezvous* to win all along. If so, Neville remained as uncertain as ever where the blurred line which defined the border between Samuel's realm and the "real world" might lie.

With the passing of the Derby, Neville was aware that for many the drama of the day was effectively over and anti-climax was now beginning to come into play. Indeed, it was only the announcement from the tannoy that the runners for the next race were coming out onto the course that prompted Neville to once again check his race card.

The sight of *Second Visit*'s name towards the bottom of the list reminded him of his brief encounter earlier that morning. Having had one successful tip thus far, the last thing he was going to do was to turn down another one.

Returning to the bookmakers, Neville made straight for Dick Springs: if he was set to duel with Mister Springs all afternoon, so be it; he had the upper hand now and was determined not to relinquish it. However, arriving at his destination he found the place vacant, with a small painted mark on the tarmac the only indication that a bookmaker had once plied his trade there.

The bookie next door eyed him nervously.

'You've cleaned him out, mate. 'E's buggered off; had enough.'

'I see,' Neville turned to the speaker, 'It was nothing malicious; just one of those things.'

'That's as maybe. We've all got to take our chances, ain't we?'

Neville began to look for *Second Visit*'s price. Her trainer was undoubtedly correct in his forecast that, given the state of the ground, she would not be well supported. As he stood in front of one board, he heard another punter explaining to his companion that *Second Visit* needed firm ground or else she wouldn't last out the trip. Neville checked the distance of the race; it was nearly two miles.

The general offer on the horse was sixteen to one, but there were a few bookies offering twenties. Neville picked out five of these and placed a thousand with each of them; then, clutching five tickets, he returned to the bus.

'Feeling lucky then Sir?' said Samuel.

'I was just following the advice of that trainer we met this morning.'

'Harry Simpson?'

'That's the one; *Second Visit* he said.'

Samuel checked his own card.

'What price did you get, Sir — if you don't mind me asking?'

'Twenty to one.'

A little after four fifteen the commentator announced "They're Off!", and once again another small drama began to unfold.

Neville watched the beginning of the race on the giant screen. *Second Visit* — it appeared — was a confirmed front-runner, and bounced out of the stalls to build up an immediate five length lead. The remainder of the pack seemed quite content to settle in behind, and let her do most of the donkey work. As they turned into the straight, *Second Visit* was still clear in front, but the remainder were beginning to prepare a challenge.

As he leant over the rail and stared down the straight towards the field, Neville asked Samuel which horse carried his wager.

'None, Sir. I feel I've had my share of the day.'

Neville glanced at him, then back to the horses as they drew ever closer. The scarlet colours of *Second Visit* were still visible ahead of the field, but her jockey was beginning to work hard.

'And it's still *Second Visit* in the van, four lengths ahead of *Ernest's Story* and *Nunnery* who are making a move on the outside. As they come towards the final furlong, *Second Visit* still leads but by only three lengths now from *Nunnery* who goes second. It's *Second Visit* into the final furlong, being driven hard in the lead. *Nunnery* is closing in second. There's about a length in it. *Second Visit* from *Nunnery*. The leader's beginning to fade, but still has the upper hand. It's *Second Visit* from *Nunnery*. *Nunnery*'s not going to get there. At the line, *Second Visit*'s the winner, *Nunnery* second, *Gallic Crunch* third.'

After the horses had gone passed the post, Neville, fist clenched in victory, looked at Samuel.

'How much Sir?' Samuel asked.

'Did I win?'

Samuel nodded.

'It's the fact that I won at all which seems the most important.'

Samuel's smile showed that he accepted Neville's response, but at the same time indicated a desire to have his question answered.

'A hundred thousand. That's the answer to your question. Why do you ask?'

'No reason, Sir.' Samuel paused. 'There's one race to go. Are you stopping now, or have you had a tip for that too?'

All the way to the bookmakers and all the way back (this time clutching an even larger bundle of winnings) Neville tried to answer that single question. He had won a hundred and thirty thousand pounds in two races, but he knew he couldn't kid himself: the reason he had been successful was because of information he had received from different of sources; it almost seemed like cheating. This time he was on his own.

He thought of quitting. When Samuel held out his hand for the portion of the money to be secreted in the bus, Neville paused, uncertain how much — if any — he should keep back. He thought about looking at the card first, deciding on his horse, getting a "feeling" for it, then deciding on the wager; but this seemed out of spirit with the day. He kept ten thousand back, handed the rest to Samuel, then picked up the race card.

The last race was for two-year-olds having their first run in public, consequently there was no form for Neville to go on. In races like this either you knew something or you didn't; and if you didn't, you either followed the market, or had a favourite trainer or jockey. Neville was inclined to disregard all three of these factors, which left him, he knew, with nothing to go on but the horses' names.

He was beginning to think that there might be something in the fact that his success had come with horses called *Restaurant Rendezvous* and *Second Visit*, and having registered the possibility that their names might be significant, allowed the idea to sit quietly at the back of his mind. If he was right, then there would be something in the last race — a five furlong sprint, with eight runners — which should also fit the bill.

On the card, the eight names we baldly printed in front of him, unembellished with distinguishing form figures or handicap weights:

1 — *Dance Rail*

2 — *Flying Fashion*

3 — *Go Candidate*

4 — *Gurl Burl*

5 — *Harawa*

6 — *Mareda*

7 — *Pharaoh's Tomb*

8 — *Return to Work*

There was a great deal of money on *Harawa* which, Neville knew, would start a very short priced favourite, but — using his rule that the name must be significant — could be ruled out as far as he was concerned. He was also able to rule out nearly all of the others immediately, and left himself with *Return to Work* as the only possibility.

In spite of the logic he had applied to making his selection, Neville was disappointed with the outcome. He had been expecting to find something that would be more *obvious*; in fact, he was expecting to find something called *Mita's Message* running! *Return to Work* was hardly inspirational. And what did it mean? Was this, the name of a racehorse in a small newcomers event at Epsom, telling him what to do with the rest of his life?

As he walked towards the bookmakers — and the five additional vacant pitches he had inadvertently created as a result of the last race — he began to doubt that *Return to Work* would win.

Return to Work was generally quoted at six or seven to one, along with a number of others behind the hot favourite. His presence amongst the bookmakers had been noticed however, and having seen six of their clan wiped out by him already, a number of them had placed hastily-written signs saying "£100 max" on their boards. The consequence was that Neville was unable to get a decent wager on his horse, so he decided to try the Tote.

He knew this was another risk; that he was changing another variable and moving away from the pattern: first it had been a single bookie and a tip, then a range of bookies and yet another tip, and now it was the combination of both the Tote *and* not being able to rely on any tip he had been given. If he were to win, he knew there was nothing but a hunch behind it.

There was a slight delay at the Tote window when Neville announced his bet, "Ten thousand on number eight". The staff there were only used to dealing in five or ten pound units, and it required the personal attention of the manager to produce a ticket to the required value. Wandering back through the rails bookmakers, Neville noticed that *Return to Work*'s price had now fallen to five to one, and he wondered if that might be in part due to the interest he had shown in the horse.

Many people around the bus were beginning to gather up their picnic things and assorted belongings in preparation for a speedy departure after the last race. Samuel was sitting in one of the chairs reading.

'Should we think about packing up, Samuel?'

He looked up.

'Is there any need, Sir? I wasn't aware that we had anywhere to rush off to, and on that basis assumed that we might let the crowds disperse first.'

Neville remembered that, as yet, he had not decided their next destination — and it seemed that the decision rested entirely with him. Samuel was giving no hints.

Their conversation was interrupted by the commentator's announcement that, for the last time that day, the runners were on their way. Neville went to the rail and leant over, staring at the specks of colour half a mile away. He had been unaware that the runners had even come out onto the course, let alone gone down to the start and were now ready to race.

From the first strides, the race appeared to be between *Harawa* and *Return to Work*. After a couple of furlongs — and nearing the place where Neville was standing — *Go Candidate* flattered on the outside, but that effort was short lived. Class appeared to be telling, and as they flew passed him, he could see both jockeys at work on their horses.

The commentary seemed a little low key compared to previous races, and the cheers from the crowd — especially when *Return to Work* got its nose in front — were the most muted of the day. For the first time, instead of leaning over the rail and trying to follow the horses all the way to the line, or standing head down and eyes closed, Neville watched the conclusion of the race on the big screen.

He felt a kind of numbness spread over him during those closing moments as he watched *Return to Work* — in slow motion almost — just get the better of the favourite and pass the post first. He wondered if he had always known that his horse was going to win; and then debated that, if there had been a horse called *Mita's Message* on which he would have placed his money, *Return to Work* might still have won. What would that have told him?

'Any good, Sir?' Samuel asked from the chair.

'Afraid so, Samuel; my luck really does appear to have taken a turn for the better.'

There was a slight delay at the Tote window when Neville returned with his ticket. The manager, who seemed to spend much of the time on the telephone, was apologetic about the delay, and it was some ten minutes later when he was able to place a cheque for seventy thousand pounds in Neville's hand.

Walking to the bus, Neville was surprised to see how quickly the course was beginning to empty. Apart from a few punters collecting their winnings, the rails bookmakers' area was now a desert of torn-up tickets and crushed plastic beer glasses. There was litter everywhere, and all across the course lines of cars had begun to edge and honk their way out of the various car parks. In the fun fair, a few families were still making the most of the day, giving the children one last ride before they fell asleep on the long and tedious journey home. The tannoy limped out one final message about the Tote Placepot and was then silent. The numbers board showed the "8", "5" and "3" result from the final race but there was nothing else; the "Weighed In" flag had been taken down. Suddenly the day was over.

Samuel was pouring tea as he got back to the bus.

'So, what was the final tally then, Sir?'

Neville sat down, feeling suddenly tired.

'Another seventy thousand. I guess that makes about two hundred — though it doesn't seem particularly real, or particularly important.'

'I had a feeling you might be that lucky,' Samuel smiled.

'That lucky?'

'Win that much. Or I hoped you would, Sir, let's put it that way. I wanted you to be successful today.'

'Whatever happens?'

Samuel passed Neville his tea.

'Have you decided where you want to go next? I believe we could stay here overnight if necessary.'

Neville took a sip of tea and looked out across the course to the grandstand. A number of men in overalls had already appeared and were beginning to sweep up the debris of the day. He wondered if any fortunes had been won or lost over there, and then remembered the man — "Freddie" — to whom he had given the thousand pounds. How had he managed? Did he have any of the money left? Had he gone away a new man, to start a new life? It would have been nice to think so, but Neville knew that it was out of his hands; the man would decide for himself, it was up to him.

Picking up the race card, Neville flicked through its pages, pausing at the last three races, and staring at the names of the animals which had provided him with such a considerable expansion of his personal wealth. He thought of Mita and looked up, half expecting to see her suddenly walking towards him, her flamingo pink dress startling against the lush green of the turf. She was not there of course and, he suspected, she never had been. He thought of asking Samuel if he "knew" anything, but decided against it. There seemed little point.

Restaurant Rendezvous had, he realised, triggered this particular thought. He had hoped that he might get some clue as to his future rather than a reflection of his past, and the name appeared to be nothing more than that. But then he turned the page. *Second Visit*. What if he were to combine to two names? What if "Mita's Message" was in fact an amalgam of these two? He stiffened slightly in his chair. Samuel looked his way. Was he to meet her once again at the restaurant?

If he felt an urge to leap from his chair and demand that Samuel get them there immediately so that he could make that evening's meal, logic and a surprising degree of self-control (coming from where, he was uncertain) kept him in his chair. If this was indeed Mita's message, she would surely not expect to see him at the restaurant for a couple of days, so it would be ludicrous to rush off immediately. And, in any event, there was one slightly more pressing reason to wait.

Neville decided that the only way he could be prepared for such a rendezvous would be if it was undertaken on his own terms, and with all the unknowns about his future resolved. He did not want one fleeting evening with Mita and then oblivion. It would not be fair to either of them.

'Samuel, we're going to Birmingham,' he announced.

'Birmingham, Sir?'

'Back to the restaurant.'

Samuel nodded, slowly.

'Do you want us to leave now, Sir?'

Neville looked down at his race card.

'No, there's no hurry. There's something I have to do first.'

And on the last page of the booklet he stared at the words *Return to Work*.

THIRTY EIGHT

It was a little later when, as Neville sat at the front of the bus watching its headlights carve their way through the darkened countryside, he checked his watch.

Having made his decision to return to Birmingham and the place where just a few days previously he had been a conscientious employee, he and Samuel had discussed their departure time. Neville had been adamant that he had no wish to re-enter the building during the working day. It was not confrontation he was looking for, at least not in the sense of re-engaging with those who had once been his colleagues but then became his usurpers. There was nothing to be gained from that. What he was searching for — and what he wanted to experience one final time — was the *place*, the atmosphere; he wanted to be able to re-evaluate the environment which, for so long, had almost been more of a home than the dwelling he shared with Mirelle.

Since he had been fired he had been given the chance to come face-to-face with his feelings about money and, having done so, uncovered the delusions of his past and what amounted to a new-found independence in his present. He suspected there were other things — taboos relating to the world of work for instance — which also needed re-examination. It was, he sensed, a time for cleansing.

They had debated travelling the next day, but Neville was keen to strike while this particular iron was hot — and, if he was honest with himself, while he felt his luck was in. Samuel was of the opinion that, provided they made good time, they could be in Birmingham around three in the morning. Given such an estimate, Neville suggested they set off at once.

Having delayed their departure to indulge in a brief snack (Samuel was unwilling to undertake the journey on an empty stomach and had suggested it might be wise if they *both* ate something before getting started) they eventually left Epsom a little after eight o'clock. The racecourse was eerily still, the queues gone, and rumbling out of a deserted car park they found themselves on relatively quiet roads.

They talked little during the first part of the journey. Samuel had passed a few comments on the day's proceedings, and they had joked in a quiet, understated way about how Neville had seen his luck change to such a dramatic effect. The amount of money he had won was never mentioned, and Neville knew that somewhere on the bus it was safe enough.

Gradually the light had begun to fade, and on the horizon the sky deepened to a soft red glow. The presence of sunshine was, however, the last thing on Neville's mind as he stared out of the window, watching the ever-darkening trees go by, these occasionally lit by the headlights of a passing vehicle. Samuel had earlier suggested that he try to sleep and, suddenly roused by a bump in an uneven piece of road, Neville realised it had grown dark and therefore he could only assume that he had indeed slipped into a brief but restful slumber. Without thinking, he raised his wrist to check the time.

It took a few seconds for him to realise that staring at a watch showing a fraction before one he was not be registering the actual hour.

'What time do you make it, Samuel?'

The other man checked his own timepiece.

'A little after eleven thirty, Sir. We're making quite good progress.'

Neville looked down again, saw the second hand sweeping slowly backwards, then remembered. Surely this could not be right. The last time he had looked, his watch had said at least four o'clock, and now it was telling him that he had entered his "last" day.

'Samuel?'

Samuel turned briefly, put on alert by the rather tremulous tone Neville had used.

'Sir?'

'My watch. It says twelve fifty three, Samuel. I have less than a day to go; *less than a day*!' Neville's voice betrayed a degree of fear which had supplanted any sense of apprehension. He had not expected this. Although he had no concrete plan, he had wanted to allow himself a little contingency; to "go back" early, to give himself some time to get it "right". But now it appeared that there was no time to be had, and that — like it or not — he was perhaps embarked on his final journey.

'Where has it gone, Samuel? Where has all the time gone? I've lost days! Gone. Why?'

Samuel put his hand to his driver's mirror and adjusted it so that he could see his passenger in it, rather than the road behind. Neville looked at those old eyes in this new oblong frame as they flitted between his face and the road ahead.

'Sometimes it just goes. Time passes. We are never in control of it; there is nothing we can do about it. Today it may drag, tomorrow it may fly...'

'But I've less than a day! This is it; now, here. By this time tomorrow... And I'm going back to an empty building in Birmingham. Should I be? Shouldn't I be somewhere else, doing something?'

Samuel's eyes offered a consoling smile.

'"Doing something", Sir? I think you are doing something. And if you are going back to an empty building, as you say, then perhaps that is what you were meant to do all along.'

'But I've so many unanswered questions. A day! There isn't time to answer them all!'

'But at least you have them, Sir. And perhaps there are only one or two you truly need to address just now. Do you expect to solve them all; to have *all* the answers?' Samuel paused, to allow Neville the chance to speak. He did not. 'No-one has all the answers, Sir. Indeed, no-one knows all the questions. You have your set; they belong to you, are yours to live with, to work at. Perhaps — perhaps, mind — there will be others; perhaps not. Who can say? I know you cannot. And I? I know nothing...'

Neville watched the headlights paint splashes of colour on the night, then saw the colour swallowed again by darkness. He had less than a day — and that without knowing what would come at the end it. Just when he thought he knew where it was going, the roller-coaster he was riding had suddenly taken a sharp turn and was plunging towards its climactic end; it was gathering speed, and there was no way to get off.

Had it been like this for Mita, he wondered? Had the end come suddenly upon her too and caught her unprepared? Neville remembered her note; there had been a degree of calmness about it, as if she knew what might be round that final bend and what she expected of herself. He'd had the impression that nothing had been sprung on her — but who could say? He wanted to ask Samuel, but his last words — "I know nothing" — implied for once a kind of impotence, the suggestion that his power — whatever it might be — had gone, was used up, could affect nothing else.

Suddenly tired, Neville tried to sleep. Debate, with either Samuel or with himself, would get him nowhere. There was, he supposed, something final ahead.

He slept fitfully, occasionally waking to find Samuel still intent at the wheel, the bus still pushing its wedge of light along the road. Breaking from sleep, he would look out of the window almost unconsciously, attempting to catch a glimpse of a road sign for an indication as to where they might be. The journey seemed to take forever. As he tried to sleep he remembered the drive to Paris, how it had been over in an instant; and how they had returned from France almost as quickly. Things had been taking longer recently, and Samuel's twenty seven miles per hour had become nothing more nor less than that.

Samuel announced their arrival on the outskirts of Birmingham a little before three. Neville roused himself and tried to locate them in his old home town. This was not easy in the dark, but as they drew closer to the centre, the lights and shapes of familiar landmarks offered some certainty. Samuel requested directions when they reached the centre, and Neville — feeling himself involved once again — began to perk up a little. This was no time to be passive.

The block Neville had worked in was twelve storeys high; a large square monolith. As the bus came to rest in the car park outside, Neville looked up with both of an air of expectation and fear of the unknown. The building was in darkness, apart from a small light visible in the entrance lobby.

'How will you get in, Sir?'

'I know the guys on Security. I'm make up some cock and bull story; there shouldn't be a problem.'

Samuel scanned the building.

'Do your firm own all of it?'

Neville laughed.

'No. They lease floors seven and eight; that's all.'

There was a brief silence as the two men contemplated the structure ahead of them.

'Would you like some coffee, Sir?'

Neville shook his head.

'No thanks. I just want to get this — whatever it is — over and done with.'

'I understand, Sir.'

Neville rose from his seat and moved to the top of the steps where he paused. Samuel, pushing a button, opened the door for him.

'Samuel?'

'Sir?'

'When I come out — and I'm assuming that I will come out of course!' — Samuel gave an encouraging laugh — 'will you still be here?'

'I fully expect to be, yes.'

As he made his way the short distance from the bus to the building, Neville guessed Samuel could offer no more of a guarantee than that. He had given him an opportunity to challenge the assumption that he would even emerge from the office, and Samuel had let that slide too. Things had certainly turned around.

The Night-watchman had evidently seen him approaching and was unlocking the front door as Neville mounted the three large flat steps that led up to it. He could sense in the posture of the man — and in the way he carried his torch — that his training would prevent him from being immediately inclined to niceties; perhaps he had been prepared for the moment when, out of the blue at three in the morning, he would be accosted by some villain.

As Neville walked into the light cast by the lobby, the Watchman visibly relaxed, pulling the main door open wider than he had allowed it thus far.

'Hello, Sir! I wouldn't have expected to see you here; certainly not at three in the morning!'

'Hello, Cliff.' Neville offered his hand, which was taken warmly.

'I was sorry to hear they chucked you out, Sir; and after all these years too.'

'One of those things Cliff, I'm afraid.'

Cliff ushered him into the lobby, locking the door behind him.

'That's as may be, Sir; but it's still a bastard thing to do to a bloke. How's it going, anyway?'

Neville stood by the front desk, waiting for Cliff to join him there.

'Oh, so-so. You know how it is. Takes a little bit of time to adjust to things. As you say, it's been a long time.'

Resuming his seat behind the desk, Cliff glanced out to the car park.

'So what are you doing here then Sir; at this time of night — if you don't mind me asking.'

'Well, it's actually quite a long story.' Neville leant on the reception desk with the air of a man about to tell a story or to let someone in on a great secret. 'Let's just say that my friend and I — that's my friend, out there in that old bus; Samuel his name is. Nice bloke; you'd like him Cliff, really.' Cliff nodded. 'Anyway, believe it or not but Samuel and I are actually on our way back from the Derby.'

'Have any luck, Sir?'

Neville smiled.

'Managed to get the winner actually.'

'Get away! Have a few bob on it, did you?'

'A little tickle, yes.'

'Well good on you, Sir; that's what I say!'

'Thank you, Cliff. So, anyway. Samuel and I were on our way home, when I realised that we'd be passing through town and that I'd left one or two things in my old office. I'd thought about coming back during the day but, well, that might prove to be a little awkward; you know what I mean?'

'Awkward? Yes, Sir; I can see that.'

'So I said to Samuel that we'd try and stop by here. I was sure I'd see someone I knew on duty — and I'm pleased it's you Cliff — and that I'd be able to get the rest of my stuff.'

There was a pause as Cliff wrestled with the decision.

'I'm not sure, Sir. I mean, it's not exactly regular.'

'I was thrown out in a bit of a hurry, that's all. Look, Cliff; you can search me if you want to, just to make sure I'm not carrying a bomb.'

Neville pushed his hands into the air and spread his legs wide, making himself ready for an American-style body-search. Cliff laughed.

'That won't be necessary Sir! Lifts one and two are out of action tonight, so if you'd like to take lift three.'

'Thanks Cliff.'

'I'll be on my rounds in about forty minutes; so if you could be down here before then I'd appreciate it.'

'I'll see what I can do.'

It took Neville just a few seconds to reach the lift and then a little longer before — with a "ping" as the door opened — he stepped out onto the seventh floor. The hallway was in darkness, but knowing where the light switches were (years of familiarity!) he had soon illuminated the hallway leading away from the lifts and down to his old office.

Once through the open-plan section, his Boss's office was the first door on the left. There was one door after that — his old room — and two corresponding doors on the other side of the short corridor. As he passed the first of these, he noticed David's name stencilled in bold letters on it; next to David's office was Colin's, his name also similarly garish in large red script. Coming to a halt, Neville then turned to face what used to be his own door. Brian — to whom he had never given much credit on the simple basis that the man lacked talent — was evidently now the proud owner of his old desk and filing cabinet.

He took one step forward, then placed his fingers on the familiar door handle. He paused, looked back down the corridor, then twisted. The door eased open with all its accustomed fluency.

THIRTY NINE

The room was dark. Neville's fingers felt along the wall for the light switch which they found with certainty. He pressed it, but nothing happened. A little further into the office there was a whiteboard on the wall and a small strip light above that. Provided Brian had moved nothing, its cord-pull was just two paces away.

As he edged forwards, Neville reminded himself that Brian was the kind of man unlikely to make major changes to an office layout, so the chances of him running into an out-of-place chair was remote. Indeed, Brian had been praised more than once — and within Neville's earshot too — for his methodical approach to his work: their Boss liked the way he ordered and filed things, everything cross-referenced, and all within a fingertip's reach. Internally Neville argued that this was the approach of a man frightened his limitations might be exposed, and who chose to conceal them behind a facade of order.

His fingers found the wall, then his arm brushed the cord. He traced the small plastic knob at the bottom of the cord and tugged. There were one or two pulses of light from above which threw a strange strobe effect across the room. It was not much to go on, but Neville was sure — even in those temporary flashes — that he had spotted something different.

With a hum, the whiteboard light finally popped into action illuminating the office. As Neville had surmised, the desk and its chair were in the same location as he remembered them. Indeed, he would have sworn that they were in *exactly* the same places as when — on his last day — he had picked up his briefcase, loaded it with his personal items and walked out; along the corridor, past their manager's office, and along to lift two and then down to the car park. It was as if Brian had moved neither of them an inch.

For a split second this was Neville's impression of the room — partly because it was what he expected of Brian — however the desk became insignificant, *invisible* almost, when he noticed the far wall. His filing cabinet had gone and in its place Brian had erected shelving from floor to ceiling. Each shelf was around a foot deep and some fourteen feet long — and each one was filled with lever-arch files.

There wasn't a single inch of shelf space free. The first file in the top left corner was neatly labelled "CD-CH" in bold, over-large Dyno-tape; the one next to it "CI-CN" and so on throughout the entire alphabet. Neville bent to check the bottom right-hand corner; sure enough he found "ZO-ZZ". Each spine also carried the initials "BJF" — for Brian's name — and the year. Neville knew the Boss would love it.

Along the far wall a long window looked out onto the car park, and beneath this, another single shelf ran its full length. This shelf was not home to more binders but to an assortment of books, mainly paperback. Neville walked to the window. The bus was just visible in the car park, a small glow coming from the window of Samuel's compartment. That made him feel better.

Curiosity forced Neville to pull a few books from the shelf. These appeared to have nothing in common apart from their alphabetic ordering by author. Thus, a DIY Manual by a chap called Griggs, was preceded by Graham Greene's *It's a Battlefield* and followed by Hardy's *The Return of the Native*. They seemed a strangely apt trio considering his present circumstances.

As he slid the books back — in reverse sequence, something which would piss Brian off no end! — Neville remembered that the lever-arch files had begun with "CD". He checked the walls of the room again. There was no other shelving, and the desk — not surprisingly — was tidy to the point of being spartan. Where then, were the volumes that contained "AA" through to "CC"?

It was precisely at this moment Neville noticed a narrow door in the corner of the room between the window and the shelves. There hadn't been a door there during his period of occupation and, as far as he was aware, there was nothing at all on the other side of this particular wall; it was the end of the building. He knew he might be mistaken — though there was only one way to find out. He tried the handle, but the door was locked.

Undaunted, Neville went to the desk. Brian was a creature of habit. The key to the door would be in his desk drawer, but his desk drawer would be locked. Neville tried; it failed to move. He'd always stuffed the key to the desk drawer down the seat cushion of the chair so decided to try there. He felt between the cushion and the frame — on the left-hand side, as Brian was left-handed — and sure enough his fingers found metal. Neville unlocked the desk drawer and then pulled a second key from the small desk-tidy compartment usually reserved for paper clips. To someone who didn't know Brian, placing the key there might have seemed like a diversion from his regulated personality, but it was not: Brian didn't believe in paper clips; things could become detached, lost, and in consequence would never find their true place in his ordered and catalogued scheme of things. So, paper clips were banished from Brian's world — which left a nice little slot in his desk tidy for this small key.

Neville slid the key into the narrow door's lock and it turned with a positive "click". He pushed it open. In the half-light cast from the whiteboard, Neville could make out some sort of cupboard and felt for a light switch on the wall beyond. There was nothing on the wall, but as he was withdrawing his hand, his fingers brushed another cord. He pulled it. Again there was a strobe of neon as it kicked into life. In front of him Neville caught a glimpse of more binders and the letters "ERG-AL" caught his eye. Confident he had found Brian's secret store, he took a step forward but immediately found there to be no floor beneath his feet and he suddenly tumbled forwards.

He came to rest against the bottom shelf, partly on his back, the impact with the wall having dislodged two of the files which now lay by his side. Neville looked to the doorway and saw two small steps leading immediately down from the office. He felt a slight twinge in his left side, but apart from that seemed unharmed.

Picking up one of the volumes, he checked the spine: "BT-BZ". Opening the cover, he revealed a number of index cards inserted throughout the folder running in sequence from BT to BZ; he could have expected nothing else. Loosening the folder's document grip, Neville pulled back the BT partition and revealed the first paper. It was a letter from a firm of solicitors relating to a complaint from a member of the public who had tripped in the car park and was suing for damages; apparently they had torn their trousers. Neville read the letter, then, having done so, realised that there was no obvious reason why this had been filed under BT, even though it had "BT" scribbled in the top right hand corner. He turned to the next page, only to discover that it was blank. The next page was blank too, as was the one after that. Indeed, all the pages were blank except those that immediately followed an index card. BU heralded a gas bill; BV, a summons from the County Court; BW, a shopping list.

For years Brian had been peddling his "method", displaying his "system", and all the while it was — as Neville had suspected — nothing more than a sham. He'd always been vaguely suspicious of a display of such rigour, dubious about using any kind of straightjacket as a means of controlling things — even if he possessed a secret envy for the order they implied. He had never been particularly organised himself, but had occasionally felt a craving to be almost robotic. However, since his most recent experiences, he had come to realise that, although there was a place for some consistency in the world, one could not be a slave to it. Brian had evidently welded himself to his "method"; a system which had ceased to function as anything other than a cover for randomness.

As he stood, the two files in his hand ready to replace them, Neville noticed a small spiral staircase about six feet in front of him. He restored Brian's folders — again in an incorrect order — and made for the stairs.

They wound their narrow way upwards towards a hole in the ceiling, and — Neville could only assume — to the eight floor. As he ascended, he tried to remember what had been directly above his office. One of the lavatories was thereabouts, and also a store room. He hoped the stairs led to the store room.

On the bannister a few steps from the top, there was a small light switch. Neville pressed it and light flooded down to him from above. It appeared too dark in the room above for him to be heading for a porcelain-populated cubicle — unless the toilets had been recently decorated in something akin to Royal Blue mixed with Earth Brown.

With his head a little above the level of the floor, Neville found himself in a cavern of boxes; brown and blue boxes stacked floor to ceiling, at least eight deep. On each of the boxes was a small label annotated with an untidy scrawl; often the scribble had been crossed out and usurped by another. Once fully upright in the room, he pulled a box from the top of one tower. The label had "April 1991" in blue ink; but this had been crossed through in red and "January 1992" written above. Neville flicked off the lid. Inside was a pile of papers. He pulled out a few sheets; they had been aligned carelessly. Browsing through the first few, he could see no connection apart from the date.

'Had to come back, didn't you?'

A voice, not devoid of anger, assailed him from the far corner of the store. Neville dropped the papers in surprise.

'Had to come back, eh? Why? Why d'you come back? To find me out, eh?'

From behind one pile of cartons, Brian stepped half into the light. Neville moved a pace backwards, stepping on the dropped papers as he did so.

'Come to prove that you were right all along? I heard the stories and rumours you used to spread about me in the canteen, you bastard!'

'Brian?'

'I've been waiting, see. I knew you'd be back. I knew you'd try and get your old job back by trying to get me kicked out.'

'Brian.'

'Well you can't, you bastard! The old man loves me, see. He thinks I've got it licked. He likes to see my files; he thinks I've got all the angles covered, and I'm not going to let some little shit like you spoil it for me.'

Brian moved forwards. In his hand he held a large four-hole punch with which he appeared intent on doing some damage. Neville took another step back, his foot finding the top step of the staircase.

'Brian, I don't want my job back. I don't want to get you kicked out. I'm happy now.'

The last words escaped from him. There was no reasoning behind them. Brian scoffed at him.

'How can you be happy, you miserable shit! You were never very good at anything; how can you be happy out of here? How can you function without this place? Don't give me that crap, OK?'

'I mean it,' as he spoke, Neville moved down a step; Brian was gradually approaching across the room, 'I don't care about this place. You can have it. Keep my job; keep it, I don't want it.'

'Fucking bollocks!'

'Look' — the next step — 'I'm sorry about the things I may have said about you in the past. Really. We each have our own ways of dealing with things, that's all.' Neville cast his eyes over Brian's crates; the accumulation of his professional career. 'You have your system; it works for you...'

Brian suddenly let fly with a scream. The hole-punch missed Neville's head, becoming embedded in a carton labelled "May 1991".

'You sarcastic shit! "Works for me" does it?' Brian was now wild-eyed; he cast about, picking up the nearest crate. 'Works for me, eh? Of course it doesn't work! Look!' And with that, he tipped the entire contents onto the floor.

Neville found another step.

'Perhaps if you spent a little time — sorting things out...'

'The only thing I'm going to sort out is you!'

As Brian made a lunge across the store room, Neville turned and bolted down the stairs. A carton — still fully laden — followed him down, catching the back of his legs three steps from the foot of the staircase. He missed the final eighteen inches in consequence, and landed with a thump on his knees. He could hear Brian beginning his descent.

'Come here, you little shit! You were never any good at anything! I'm not letting you jeopardise my fucking pension!'

Neville got to his feet just in time to avoid another box as it flew towards him. As he reached the door, Brian's legs were just visible coming down the steps. The time for negotiation — had it ever existed — was now over. Neville leapt up the two steps he'd missed earlier, tugged on the light cord, and dashed into his old office. Closing the door behind him, he locked it and threw the key into the waste paper basket.

There was a bang on the other side of the door. Neville heard Brian turn on the light.

'You wait 'til I get out of here, you shit! I'll be after you, mark my words!'

Neville waited, not sure what to expect. There was an unnatural pause, then a howl from the other side of the door.

'My files! My files are out of order! You've put my files out of order, you bastard! I'll get you, you sodding bastard! You sodding...'

Brian's anger suddenly gave way to the sound of sobbing. Neville waited. In seconds there was nothing other than quiet sobbing. Brian moaned "my files" once or twice and was then silent. Neville guessed that at some point someone would release him. Perhaps he should mention Brian to Cliff on his way out. But then again — this thought as he turned out the whiteboard light — perhaps he shouldn't.

FORTY

There was a question uppermost in Neville's mind as he stood in the corridor contemplating his next move. The encounter with Brian amounted to something of a close call and, with Colin and David's offices still ahead of him, there was an argument — growing in strength — that he should simply turn around and leave. He checked his watch. Twelve fifteen; he had a few hours left at best.

As the lift had been rising to the seventh floor, he'd tried to understand exactly why he had returned and what he was to do. The decision to invade the offices of the three men who'd outlasted him had only been made as he walked the corridor towards them. If he had been looking for retribution or revenge he could simply have ransacked his old Boss's office; but Neville knew there was nothing to be gained from that beyond temporary satisfaction. In any event, recently he had learned enough about himself to conclude that he'd been ousted from his job because the three juniors had, as a cohort, been able to offer the company something it needed and which he obviously lacked. It felt (and all of this rationalised within a few paces) as if, by now going into their individual domains, he was facing head-on an earlier insufficiency in himself. If anywhere, that was where the confrontation existed.

The theory was fine; it fitted nicely and gave him a degree of comfort knowing that his action could be justified — or at least explained away. Perhaps he was looking for something he could present to Samuel too, for even now he still believed that Samuel held at least one more ace in that invisible hand of his.

He paused before Colin's door, staring hard at its name plate, almost trying to see through it and into the room beyond. He had not been prepared for Brian — though, on reflection, the nature of the office and their encounter didn't surprise him. Colin was a character who liked order too, though not in any mechanistic sense. He was — to use a popular consultancy term — something of a "Starter-Finisher"; he was definite and precise, liking things to be procedural, black-and-white almost. Neville knew that Colin regarded himself as an intellectual and tried to play up to a kind of "boffin" image; it was not a particularly impressive piece of role playing, but had proven to be sufficient to dupe the Boss.

Neville expected to find Colin's office in darkness just as Brian's had been. Had he been required to do so, he believed he had sufficient recollection of the room to be able to undertake a similar — if less confident — negotiation of the furniture. However, this proved to be unnecessary on two counts: firstly the light was on; and secondly, because he appeared not to have entered an office at all.

The door had opened out into an incredibly small, almost square room devoid of any furniture. There were one or two pictures on the walls — Colin liked to display a taste in art and make pronouncements on music — but apart from these, there was nothing to break the monotony of the void except another door in the opposite corner. There was just room for Neville, once inside, to close the first door behind him and open the second.

This anti-chamber was evidently new. Neville, his capacity to be surprised now almost entirely worn away, could see no reason why Colin should require construction of such a useless buffer between himself and the outside world — and then immediately wondered if it wasn't related to Colin at all, but something constructed as a one-off for his visit. There was a degree of hesitation in his opening of the second door, but this was so marginal as to be almost imperceptible.

Neville was half-expecting to find darkness beyond this second portal, but again he was wrong. The presence of light, however, was the least thing to surprise him. He appeared to have stepped out onto a pavement. Beneath his feet, grey and uneven paving stones stretched the width of the office. On both end-walls, murals had been painted to give the illusion that he was standing on a public highway between a milliners and a jewellery shop. If this were not surprising enough, ahead of him was the facade of a shop selling musical instruments. Had he been trying to convince himself that there would be no more tricks, that 'reality' was beginning to assert itself again, this new 'room' — which was certainly *not* Colin's day-to-day office environment — was a retrograde step.

From the shop ahead, he heard vague strains of music. In the window — which was only a window in name, as there was no glass in evidence — two rows of cellos hung, three to each row. They were brightly illuminated by individual spotlights, and, alongside them, a large double bass made up the display.

The music, which had been vague and indistinct on his entry, suddenly rose in volume; the tune — a familiar one he was however unable to place — blasting out accompanied by bells of various kinds. Neville had not heard the theme for ages, but it was something not to be forgotten. As it echoed around the small room, the sound of applause joined in and the six cellos and the bass began to fidget on their stands. Neville leant back against the wall, preparing for what was apparently going to be some kind of show.

The bass made a stiff attempt at a bow, and the music began to subside.

'Hello, good evening, and welcome.'

The words were delivered in a deep and resonant voice, the cellos all leaning towards the larger instrument.

'This evening we have the first semi-final in Symphony Challenge, with the French Violas taking on the Dutch Cellos.'

Neville now recognised that the instruments on the upper row — the violas — were slightly smaller.

'First the Violas.'

'A above middle C,' said the first smoothly, 'reading Nardini's Violin concerto in E flat major.'

'G above middle C,' said the next, 'reading Bach's Violin concerto number two in E major.'

'E above middle C, reading Grieg's Holberg suite.'

'C above middle C, reading Rimsky-Korsakov's Symphonic Suite, Opus thirty five.'

As the violas introduced themselves, they did so in gently rising voices as they moved up the scale from G, through D and A, and onto C. There was a small ripple of applause as the introductions ended.

'And the Cellos,' said the bass.

'E below middle C, reading Mahler's Symphony number five, in C sharp minor.'

Neville noticed the very different tone of the first cello.

'G below middle C, reading Elgar's Cello concerto.'

'A below middle C, also reading Elgar's Cello concerto.'

'C below middle C, reading Vaughan Williams' Sinfonia Antarctica.'

As Neville listened to the applause, he noticed how the tone of the cellos had fallen during the introductions, their overall mood seemingly more serious and determined. The bass waited for the applause to die down.

'Well, there they are and here we go. A starter for ten, with a bonus of ten to follow. Which Polish composer died in 1849?'

A bright, clear note rang out from the upper row.

'Viola, D,' prompted the bass.

'Frederic Chopin,' came the reply from the said viola.

'Correct. Your bonus for ten; you may confer. When was Anton Bruckner born?'

The violas leaned together, a strange, inharmonious combination of four notes rising from them as they conferred. After a few seconds there was silence.

'1824,' came the reply from Viola A.

'Correct. Another starter for ten, a bonus of twenty to follow. Which conductor became the biographer of Delius?'

There was a pause, and then a hesitant note from a Cello.

'Cello, C.'

'Sir Thomas Beecham?'

'Correct.'

The contest continued in this vein for a few minutes. Occasionally, the bass would remind the teams of the scores which, although never very divergent, were beginning to suggest a win from the Cellos in spite of the Violas taking an early lead. The questions, although demonstrating a rather heavy musical bias, also strayed into other areas of the arts, particularly painting. When this happened, one of the Cellos — C — was particularly outstanding and, had he been counting, Neville felt certain that this contribution was the critical difference between the teams.

With the scores at 145 to 125 in the Cellos' favour, Cello C, in making a rather over-hasty attempt to jump in on a question, sounded an unhealthy "Twang" rather than its customary professional note. There was a gasp from the invisible audience as the strings of the instrument snapped and the cello fell lifelessly forwards and onto the pavement.

'Where is the substitute, please,' said the double bass, evidently unruffled by the incident. The three remaining cellos hummed slowly and nervously to each other; above them, the violas were showing signs of excitement, sensing their chance to get back in the game.

'The substitute, please,' said the bass again, and with those words, Neville felt the sudden heat of a spotlight on him. He stood away from the wall stiffly.

'Come on then,' said the bass.

'Not me,' said Neville.

'Who else?'

'But I know nothing about music.'

The violas now chattered with even more excitement on hearing this news.

'Please,' said the bass, insistently, 'take your place.'

There was applause from somewhere as Neville, sensing he had little choice in the matter, moved forwards. There was a small ridge upon which the fallen cello had been resting, and Neville perched himself on that as best he could.

'And you are?' The bass leaned his way, wanting an introduction.

'Neville.' He looked apologetically along the line of the three remaining cellos.

'Reading?'

'Reading?' echoed Neville.

'Reading, yes. What are you reading?' The bass was beginning to get a little cross that his show seemed to be getting out of hand.

Neville tried to think quickly.

'Rhapsody in Blue, by George Gershwin.'

It was all he could think of. The audience greeted the news with a gasp; his team mates could only moan.

'On we go then. A little over ten minutes to go, and here's a starter for ten.'

The competition continued, but with the questions still majoring on classical music and Neville's team effectively being outnumbered four to three, the gap in the score began to diminish. As it became even more evident that Neville was unable to contribute anything, his team mates began to ignore him.

The violas had established a fifteen point lead, when the bass asked:

'Which mythical game is played on a number of levels with an infinite variety of pieces and moves?'

There was silence from the instruments.

'I'll have to hurry you,' hinted the bass.

Neville wondered what noise he needed to make which would be comparable to the instruments'. Giving in, he faked a cough.

'Cello, Neville.'

He felt the pressure of expectation upon him.

'Is it "Croak"?'

'Correct.'

There were murmurs of approval from the three other Cellos, and, although Neville could not answer the follow up question, he felt had made something of a contribution.

A few minutes later, Cello E had correctly answered a starter, but the subsequent question — "Who played in both *Genesis* and *Mike and the Mechanics* — had them flawed. Neville leaned towards them.

'Mike Rutherford,' he whispered.

The cellos were instantly silent. They conferred briefly again, then all leant his way. He was evidently expected to offer the answer.

'Mike Rutherford.'

'Correct,' agreed the bass.

With the cellos still fifteen points adrift, the bass announced that they were entering the final round. There was to be a starter question, and then three follow up questions, all worth five points. If Neville's team were to win, they must answer all four questions correctly.

'What do Vaughan Williams and the song "Cry Me A River" have in common.'

He had not wanted to say anything. He did not want to be responsible for the outcome of the contest; but as the word "London" suddenly slipped from his lips, he knew the die was cast.

'Correct,' said the bass, 'the symphony by Vaughan Williams, and the singer, Julie London.'

Assuming Neville's intervention had sealed their fate, the cellos groaned a discordant and low moan. Above, the violas suddenly let fly with a volley of cheery notes.

'Quiet, please,' demanded the bass. 'Here is your bonus, three questions worth five points each. Remember, no conferring. You are ten points behind. Good luck.'

Neville prayed there would only be music questions.

'These questions all relate to lessons learned from modern mythology. Firstly, what was the purpose behind the General's purchase of the motor car?'

Unsure he had heard the bass correctly, Neville asked for the question to be repeated. The bass did so. As he had suspected, the question was related directly to himself. Was this to be another reason for his return?

'To illustrate the value and worth of money.'

There was a pause.

'I'll need a little more,' said the bass.

'In buying the car for an inflated sum of money, the General displayed that money has both an accepted value and an intrinsic worth. The value is a universal norm, accepted by all; its worth is related to an individual and cannot be measured except by that individual against their own particular circumstance.'

'Correct.'

There was a small ripple of applause, and the cellos let out a low note. Neville knew that if he were able to answer the next question, then at least they would not lose.

'Second. What was the purpose of the excursion through the painting in the Musée d'Orsay?'

This was a question he could never have expected. Neville remembered how the experience had developed, moving from the pleasurable to the nightmarish, but had not — until now — ever been forced to consider it. He wished he had taken the opportunity to discuss it with Samuel after all.

'I must hurry you.'

'It was an illustration of the relationship between life and art.'

It was desperate, but all he could think of.

'Go on.'

'Well. It showed how life and art are different things. How art can imitate or depict life, but that it is something else.' Neville paused, unable to tell if this was enough for the bass. 'And that one cannot live one's life through art. Art is a part of life, not vice versa.'

He had spoken but was unsure he understood what he had said, let alone believe it. The bass appeared to be thinking.

'That's not quite what I wanted, but I'll take it.'

There was more applause, and the cellos sounded their own harmonious note of congratulation. Overhead, the violas were beginning to sound a little nervous.

'And finally, with the scores level' — the bass allowed a little pause, to heighten the tension — 'describe the game of "Croak".'

He did not know what he had been expecting, but this final question came as something of a relief. He smiled a little, relaxing as best he could on the small ledge.

'"Croak" does not exist.'

It was the most confident he had sounded about any of his answers. He was convinced that, if he had learned anything, he knew this much. There was a brief pause. Neville waited for the announcement that he had just won the match for the cellos.

'I'm sorry, that is incorrect. The match is tied.'

The bass's words were greeting with a whole cacophony of sound: the viola and the cellos sounding forth, either celebrating that they had not been beaten, or lamenting their failure to win. Applause — mixed with a few quiet boos — echoed around the room again as Neville, trying to remonstrate with the bass, slipped from his perch and fell crashing down onto the prostrate cello whose place he had taken. At that moment, the lights suddenly went out, and all was silent.

Thrown into darkness, Neville lifted himself to his feet. He remembered where the door had been and made his way towards it, his hands out in front of him. A pace or two further on than he'd expected, he found the door. His search for a light switch was unrewarded, and he settled for opening the door.

Instead of finding himself in the ante-room he was in the corridor, and — looking back over his shoulder — saw nothing more exceptional than Colin's empty office. There was no faux street, no murals, and no broken cello.

FORTY ONE

Having regained the corridor and closed Colin's door behind him, Neville was suddenly thirsty. He was tired too, but there was nothing he could do about that: Cliff was due to start his rounds soon and had given him a time limit which Neville was certain this had nearly expired.

He ignored David's door for the moment and walked to the open-plan area at the end of the corridor where the vending machine was located. He selected a coke (the machine was never switched off) and waited as it dropped to the perspex drawer from which it could be retrieved. The can popped open with its customary "hiss" and Neville raised it to his mouth.

After the encounter with Brian, was he surprised that the version of University Challenge in which he had just participated had proven to be so personal? It had been "set-up" for him; he could not believe otherwise. The collapse of the cello, his presence on the set, and those final questions; it was not a situation over which he had any control. All he'd had to do was to walk through the door.

Coming within range of David's office, he wondered if he were about to become tangled in another act of the drama; if, once he had crossed the threshold, roles would be played out as if already scripted. He thought back to his answer for the penultimate question. It might have been any question — there were dozens he had already been unable to answer — and his guess of "London" felt like nothing more than the escape of a random thought. He had no conscious knowledge that Vaughan Williams had written a symphony called "London", so how could it be possible for the scene to have been pre-scripted?

He felt caught somewhere on the spectrum between impotence and complete power. When he walked into David's office — or rather, into whatever lay beyond its door — presumably he could either play along with whatever transpired or try to kick hard against it, determined to buck the system and assert himself. The latter may have been an attractive option, but how could he possibly know if that wasn't precisely what had already been laid out for him?

He drained the last of the coke and walked back to the bin by the vending machine. The can gave out a hollow rattle as it hit the bottom of the empty receptacle, one which sounded like the note of a feeble chime, and he imagined a lone bell ringing in an empty echo chamber. For whom did that particular bell toll?

Despite his uncertainty and this rather romantic sense of foreboding, the one thing Neville was not experiencing was fear. He had come too far for that, and his new attitude — more stoic than any he would have previously adopted — allowed him to contemplate the immediate future with a degree of calm. Thus, when he returned to David's door and pushed it open, he did so with an air of conviction and determination.

Expecting either bright light or darkness, he walked into neither. Anticipating either a conventional office or something that failed to resemble any space which might be recognisable as such, again he was surprised. The room (for it was a conventional room, about the size of David's office as he remembered it) was rather dimly lit from a number of wall lights with, at its centre, a few brighter lights embedded in the ceiling. It appeared to be something of an arena, a fact endorsed by the absence of furniture — and the large chess board laid out in its centre.

The board began about a yard into the room and, with the exception of the little skirt about its edge and in which Neville now stood, completely filled it. The squares — approximately a yard on each side — alternated between a pale yellow and an inoffensive brown.

Neville's arrival — and the closing of the door behind him — triggered activity elsewhere, and from another door in the opposite wall a number of chess pieces made their entrance. He watched them as they walked (in the case of the Kings, Queens, Bishops and Pawns) to their allotted squares, the Knights trotting in behind them. Neville waited for the Rooks but there were none — and then he realised that they were in the middle of a game and were playing from an established position.

His own role was initially unclear. He had begun to reflect on David's character, on the rather scheming intellectual he had often seemed, and realised that the scenario — a chess game — was entirely in keeping with that persona. Of course — and this he realised with something of a shudder — if the theme from Colin's room was to be followed, then this game also had something to do with him.

The Knights were small but intensely realistic horses mounted by well-armoured figures. Consequently, when a white horse appeared from the second door but without its rider, Neville's question as to his function in the pageant was answered. The horse made its way over to him and, breathing a little heavily, came to rest at his side. Without hesitation, he lifted one leg over the horse's back and eased himself into the tiny saddle. Once there, the horse

— with a surprising degree of strength and agility — lifted Neville's feet from the ground, and carried him to a square on the board. They stopped, and as the ceiling lights became a little brighter, a slow solo drum beat began to echo around the room and a thin layer of fog drifted across the board.

From what Neville could see — and he was no expert — the two sides appeared to be even: apart from the Kings, both Queens were on the board, as were a White bishop, another white Knight and three white Pawns. The white pieces were opposed by black's three Pawns, two Bishops and a Knight. It seemed that white had lost his traditional advantage and had been pushed back onto the defensive with the black pieces threatening to overrun their opponents; however all was not lost, and Neville felt his own position — in the centre of the board — could be critical.

On the edge of the board to his right, a black Pawn took a step forwards. Against the backing of the drum beat, Neville tried to get a grip on the position.

'A little tricky, isn't it My Son?'

Neville looked over his shoulder to the source of the voice. The white Bishop — bearing a remarkable resemblance to Samuel — stood just behind him.

'It would appear so, yes.'

'A tactical error in the early part of the middle game, I'm afraid; and now it's touch and go.' The Bishop paused as a white Pawn moved up to block the most recently advanced black piece. Neville was suddenly relieved that he was not expected to make all the moves. The Bishop pushed his mitre forwards in the direction of the black Queen. 'Watch out for her.'

Following the line of the Bishop's gaze, he noticed that the black Queen — Mirelle to a "T" — was bearing down on him. Luckily the Bishop was, at present, offering some protection. The black King moved to a square at the corner of the board, tucking himself away. From his present location, Neville could not make out the face on the black King, but had begun to realise that most of the major pieces seemed to bear a likeness to people he knew.

There was a sudden and familiar shout of "Tally-Ho" from nearby as Neville's compatriot Knight — "Binky" Bingham complete with armoured flying suit — charged at a black Bishop, leaving the latter prone. Two tiny figures suddenly appeared through the far door and scuttled across to the Bishop and dragged it away. Binky's joy was short-lived however, as the exchange was completed by the black Queen simply marching forward and somehow propelling both horse and rider clean from the board. She now stood within three squares of Neville, but — owing to the rules governing his movement — not within his present compass.

'Not expecting to win, are you?' The Queen taunted him in a slow drawl, reminiscent of Mirelle's non-native English accent.

Elsewhere a white piece moved, and this was followed by the black Knight — David of course, lording it as if on home territory — galloping to the Queen's side. Both now threatened Neville.

'Hello, Darling,' the Queen said to the Knight, as the latter pranced alongside her.

'My Queen,' came the reply, and the Knight bowed low.

Neville wondered just how closely this game was meant to be a mirror of his own life; was this a long-suspected infidelity being played out in front of him?

'Better move back,' the white Bishop suggested from behind, 'just by me should be OK.'

With the smallest tug on the reins, Neville's horse responded, immediately travelling to the square in question. As they came to rest, he was still uncertain as to the degree of control he was supposed to have over the game. A whole series of moves was now played out which seemed not to involve him. Two pawns on each side were exchanged — the tiny figures again running onto the board to drag off the stricken — and various positional adjustments were made. From behind him, the white Queen — Neville was confident that this was Mita — made a significant move forwards.

'It won't be long now,' hinted the Bishop.

'Long?'

'Before the decisive stage of the game. Look. The Queens are beginning to eye each other up. I can keep an eye on the Knight — he's all show, that one — but you'll need to get that last pawn.'

Neville looked across to where the remaining black Pawn — a small, faceless piece — stood unguarded. He could not reach it in one move, but could see a way across.

'When should I make my move?'

'Await my signal.'

There was a brief lull before the black Queen moved towards the white camp. Neville could understand the Bishop's logic; things were going to get a little hot. By making the last move, the black Queen had removed some of the pressure on Neville. He wondered if this were to be his cue, but the white Bishop moved a single square behind him. It seemed little had changed.

Gaining in confidence, the black Queen called her Knight forwards. They were now very close to the King, with only the white Queen directly in their way.

'Prepare to meet thy doom, Usurper!' cried the black Queen.

'You are an evil woman,' came the reply, 'and I have Right on my side!'

As the black Queen began to laugh, the Bishop banged his mitre on the board and pointed towards the pawn.

'Now, My Son; now!'

Neville tugged the horse towards the pawn which he immediately threatened. In doing so, he realised that he had allowed a discovered attack by the Bishop on the black Queen.

'Now, Madam,' cried the Bishop, 'as God is my witness, the Righteous shall have the day!'

The black Queen could do nothing in the face of the Bishop's attack; she could only retreat, leaving the Pawn at Neville's mercy. He pulled the lance from his holster on the horse's tack, and levelled it at the Pawn.

'Charge!' shouted the Bishop.

Neville looked back. The black Queen was now threatening the Bishop; surely either it should move, or Neville should try to protect it.

'But...' he began to remonstrate.

'Charge, My Son! Have faith! Charge!'

Levelling his lance, Neville turned to the Pawn again and drove his horse forwards. The lance landed high on the pawn which spun out of its square, and fell to the side of the board. As the retrievers came for the corpse, Neville heard a scream from the centre of the board. The black Queen was bearing down on the Bishop.

'Now I have you! Die!'

And in an instant, the black Queen was in possession of the Bishop's square with no sign of its former occupant. The victor let out a manic laugh. It seemed to Neville that white was about to be overrun, then there came a rallying cry from his Queen.

'Now the black Knight; the Knight!'

Neville turned to see that his opposite number was now within his sights and preparing for an attack. The black Knight raised his lance.

'Try your luck, you imbecile! I've defeated you before, and I can do so again! You used to think that you were so smart, but all the while you were blind; dumb and blind!'

'Not anymore, my friend; not anymore!'

With a dig in his horse's ribs, Neville made for the Knight. There was a clash as lance hit shield, but the black Knight did not fall. Instead he prepared his own assault. This did not appear to be following the strict rules of chess. Neville raised his own shield just in time to deflect the oncoming lance, and though rocked back by the impact, remained steady on his horse.

The black Knight prepared to charge again. Neville dropped his lance and removed his sword from its scabbard, hiding it behind his shield. As the black Knight charged again, Neville was able to deflect the powerful lance upwards with his shield, and then drive his sword beneath it and into the armour of the black Knight. The latter stopped suddenly. There was a scream from the black Queen as her consort felt to the ground.

'You scum! You'll pay for this, like you've never paid before!'

She moved towards Neville, preparing her assault. Neville could see no way out. Then, from behind, he heard the sound of rushing footsteps and turned just in time to see his own Queen flying across the board to his rescue. The black Queen had forsaken all control of the game and was now lost.

The two Queens met head-on in the centre of the board. As they struggled, their robes flying in the fray, coronets and chains were broken and torn from their apparel, and still the drum-beat sounded out its accompaniment. Was this the battle that would decide the result of the contest?

For a moment it seemed as if the white Queen was in the ascendant, then, without warning, she was thrown to the ground where she lay helpless, the black Queen threatening above her. Neville tugged at his horse, but nothing happened; it was not white's move, and the horse would go nowhere. Resolved to do something, he threw his leg over the horse's back and slipped to the ground; then, sword in hand, he made for the black Queen.

She was about to strike when Neville got to her. His approach had been swift but not quite silent. She turned to see him just as he was raising his sword, her face suddenly a mix of fear and bravado. Beginning a wild and loud laugh, she managed but a few sounds before his arm swung and the sword severed her head from her body.

The drum beat stopped. On the board, the face of the black Queen became lost in a newly formed thin layer of fog. Neville could hear the scampering of the two salvagers but could not see them. The white Queen was getting to her feet.

'The King,' she whispered, 'you must get the King!'

Neville looked to the corner of the board where the black King now appeared to be attempting to make his escape. The rules of the game now in tatters, Neville walked to the edge of the board to stand within a yard of the defeated monarch.

'Now,' he said, knowing that the victory was his, 'show yourself!'

The black King stood still, straightened himself and stared at his vanquisher. Neville, still with his sword at his side, stood looking at an image of himself: but it was not the Neville he had now become; this was the Neville he used to be, the one who had lost his wife, his job, his life. Was this what the game had been about all along, the end for which he had been destined? In order to truly find himself did he need to slay himself first?

From behind, the white Queen whispered to him.

'The King; you must slay the King.'

Neville took a step closer. He was expecting a plea, some argument to justify mercy; he was staring at his own death — and his own life. There was nothing. Not a murmur. The drums were silent, and the room echoed to nothing more than the fog. He raised his sword.

'Farewell.'

And with a single movement, Neville plunged the sword into the heart of the black King.

For a moment nothing happened, then the King buckled at the knees and fell to the ground. Neville looked down. All that remained were the robes he had been wearing and a broken crown; the body was gone. And then, in that split second, Neville felt a searing pain in his chest and collapsed.

FORTY TWO

When he regained consciousness, Neville found himself lying prostrate on the floor. A little time had evidently passed, though he had no idea how much. He waited for a few moments, allowing himself the luxury of a little re-orientation, then moved to a more upright position and looked around the room. It was deserted; the fog had gone and, in the dim half-light, the chess board appeared much as when he had first seen it. All was silent.

He was sitting approximately where he had struck out at the black King, though no evidence remained of that or any other encounter. Involuntarily he rubbed his chest remembering the sharp stabbing pain that had rendered him helpless. For a moment he wondered if he might be dead. If this were not the case (and he felt reasonably alive) then the secondary consideration might well be his location as he felt uncertain he was still in David's office.

Pulling himself to his feet, Neville walked to the door nearest to him, the one the chess pieces had used as an entrance. It was locked. Retracing his steps to the other door, he turned the handle. Outside in the corridor, all was silent. He stood there for a moment contemplating the offices and half-wondering if he was now meant to try his ex-Boss's room; yet in his heart he knew that his time in the building was over.

He made his way back towards the lifts. There was a welcoming "ping" as the doors of the lift slid open (evidently it had not moved since he last used it) and the subsequent sensation of descending was strangely comforting. As he walked towards the reception desk he realised he did so empty-handed. Having told Cliff that he was going to collect some things, he patently appeared not to have done so.

Cliff was sitting at the front desk when he reached it.

'Hello, Sir! That didn't take you long. I was going to ring up in a few minutes, just to make sure that you were OK.'

'I'm fine thanks, Cliff.'

'Get what you wanted?' Cliff looked towards Neville's empty hands.

'Yes and no, actually. I found what I was looking for, but then, having found it, discovered I didn't need it anyway. You know how it is with old papers and office mementoes.'

'If you say so, Sir, yes.'

Cliff rose, pulling his keys from the desk.

'I'd better let you out, Sir.'

They walked together towards the door. Cliff unlocked it top and bottom, then pulled it open.

'You look all in, Sir.'

'Do I?'

'Must be the excitement, eh?'

'Excitement?' Neville was a little surprised.

'The Derby and all that.'

'Yes, of course,' Neville had forgotten about the events of the previous day.

Cliff held out his hand.

'Well, at least your friend has waited for you.'

In the car park, the old bus still kept its lone vigil.

'Yes,' said Neville, knowing this had been by no means a certainty. 'Of course.'

'Well, good luck, Sir. And take care.'

'Thanks.'

The two men shook hands. As Neville walked down the steps he heard the sound of the locks turning in the door, then waved back to Cliff. The security man offered a kind of half-salute before he disappeared back into the building.

For a fleeting moment as the lift had descended, Neville had debated whether or not the bus would still be there. After the bizarre events in the office — and the finality associated with their climax — Neville had wondered if he were to be alone once again. He was uncertain how his story would end; when, for example, would he be told of the ultimate decision? If he were heading towards the unwanted outcome attendant on half of option 3, then perhaps at some stage he might feel vaguely suicidal.

Sleep, however, rather than anything more permanent, was really the only thing on his mind as he opened the door of the bus. There was that particular smell to which he had grown accustomed over the previous few days and, along with Samuel's smile, was a good a welcome as he could had wished for.

'There you are, Sir. Are you all right? You look a little bit done in, if I may say so.' Samuel had walked towards him and was standing in Neville's compartment.

'Hello, Samuel,' Neville sat on his bed, 'to tell you the truth, I'm completely knackered.'

'Would you like some tea, Sir?'

'No thanks. I think I'd just like to get some sleep.'

'Very good, Sir.' Samuel seemed on the point of leaving him, but paused. 'Did you find what you were looking for?'

Neville looked up and offered a tired smile.

'I'm not sure, Samuel; perhaps I did. I'll let you know later.'

Samuel nodded. It was a slow, knowing nod; the kind of a gesture that — given his vast repertoire of wise gestures — fitted the moment uncommonly well. As he began to get undressed, Neville wondered whether Samuel was aware of what had recently passed, and — if he'd indeed had one last ace in his hand — whether or not it had just been played.

He was in bed when Samuel returned with a mug of cocoa.

'Just in case, Sir, I made you this.' He set it down on the bedside cupboard.

'Thanks, Samuel.'

'If you don't mind me asking, Sir; but where did you want to go next?'

'Go?' Just at that minute, Neville struggled a little with the concept of "going" anywhere. He remembered his plan. 'Anywhere you like, really. I just want to be at the restaurant in the evening.'

'Very good, Sir. Now you get some rest.'

Samuel's words were already beginning to fade before he got to the end of the sentence, and when Neville awoke some time later he found the cup of cocoa still full by the side of the bed. It was cold.

The bus was moving but the curtains were drawn. It appeared to be light outside, but Neville refrained from opening them. He was not much interested in where they were, only where they were going. Consequently he rolled over, and again offered himself up to the arms of Morpheus.

Drifting in and out of sleep occupied him for the majority of the day. In his waking moments, Neville imagined he was recharging some internal battery that had been run-down to near exhaustion. When asleep, his mind flitted in and out of dreams where his escapades were reordered and recreated, and where the most recurrent image was of Mita saying "Kill the King" and then him being responsible for his own demise.

When he finally managed to fully rouse himself, he drew back the curtains to find that they were in the country, stationary in a lay-by. Samuel, who had evidently heard or sensed Neville's waking, appeared from further up the bus.

'Good day, Sir. I would say "Good Morning", but as it's mid-afternoon, I don't think that would be appropriate.'

Samuel's smile encouraged Neville to feel being relaxed, and he suddenly realised that he was hungry.

'It may not be morning, Samuel, but any chance of a little late breakfast?'

'You don't want to spoil your meal, Sir, but I think I might be able to rustle something up.'

A few minutes later, the two men were installed at the front of the bus, one reading, the other tucking in to a bacon and egg sandwich. Steam rose from mugs of tea, and the sun filtered in through the windows.

Samuel had asked nothing further about the visit to the office, nor had Neville chosen to volunteer anything. He had come to realise — perhaps as a result of his dreams or perhaps because it was the only logical conclusion — that soon he and Samuel would be parting company. Whatever the result of his adventure, such a conclusion to the end-game was inevitable. He had considered divulging the events of the various episodes as he remembered them — especially the game of chess — with a view to obtaining Samuel's gloss on them; but he knew his own interpretation was the one that mattered most and he sensed he had already arrived at that.

They talked for a while, conversations about inconsequential things: the weather, even cricket. It transpired that Samuel had been something of a star bowler when young, but that an injury had forced him to change careers. Neville made some joke about the "magic" spin he could probably impart on a googly, and they laughed together.

Later, when Neville had finished eating and "breakfast" was over, Samuel returned to his seat and turned the key in the ignition. In spite its habitual struggle to rouse itself into life, today Neville sensed a degree of willingness in the old engine — and was then suddenly possessed with the knowledge that he would never again hear that distinctive sound. This wisdom — undeniable as it was — pierced him suddenly. He had not expected it and, to be honest, had not looked for it either. From staring at the floor of the bus (from whence the grinding had emanated) he looked up to his chauffeur.

'Samuel.'

'Sir?'

The old boy turned to look at him, still full of experience and good sense; still kind and unswerving and loyal.

'I'd just like to say "thank you" for helping me through all this.'

Samuel nodded, silently; smiled; then slipped the bus into gear.

By the time they had reached the restaurant, the afternoon was beginning to show signs of giving way to evening. The shadows had lengthened, and the air — which boasted a kind of balmy stillness — carried in it the trace of a fine mist and the aroma of cut grass.

Theirs was the first vehicle in the car park. Neville, leaving the bus to stretch his legs, walked over to the restaurant. It had not yet opened for the evening.

'I'd just relax if I were you, Sir,' Samuel suggested as Neville returned to the bus across the tarmac. 'Perhaps a nice bath.'

Taking a bath seemed to be one of those suggestions from Samuel's armoury — like drinking tea — made in order to ensure that he had the best possible chance to relax. Neville's bath-time experiences had proven enlightening and entertaining, and Samuel's suggestion was again a sound one — if not in this case, wholly necessary.

As he closed the door behind him, Neville hoped to discover the yellow duck bobbing in the water; but he was disappointed. As he lowered himself beneath the bubbles, he realised that this was the second time he had hoped in vain for the duck's company; only when he did not expect it did the duck appear. This seemed a little fable in itself and, as Neville had begun to collect such things — perhaps to collate into some kind of personal philosophy — he added the observation to his growing catalogue.

When he emerged some time later, he did so to discover that evening had descended and the car park was no longer empty. Samuel had laid out some of his casual clothes and, as he began to dress, Neville remembered how on his first visit to the restaurant he had been resplendent in Mister Bossiman's suit. Through the open door of the small wardrobe, he could see the dancing shoes had gone the way of the suit and all that remained was his original and somewhat dull attire.

'I feel a little under-dressed, a little scruffy,' he said to Samuel as he stood at the front of the bus ready to leave.

'You look fine, Sir.'

'But everyone was so smartly dressed last time. They might not let me in.'

'They always welcome old customers, Sir,' and Samuel gave him one of his "don't worry about anything" winks.

Neville paused on the steps of the bus.

'Samuel?'

'Sir?'

'Do you know? Am I going to be disappointed? Is this all just a waste of time?'

Samuel stood just above him and placed a hand on his shoulder.

'How do you feel, Sir?'

'A little nervous. And a lot uncertain.'

The older man smiled.

'But does it feel "right"?'

Neville looked at the building, then back. He nodded.

'Well then; just have faith, Sir. And enjoy yourself.'

Half-way to the restaurant, Neville paused. Samuel, still standing on the steps of the bus, offered him a wave. Neville nodded, then walked on.

On the threshold, the Maitre was manning his bookings podium like a Vicar about to preach a sermon. He smiled when he saw Neville approach and offered his hand.

'Good evening, Sir. And welcome back.'

'You remember me?'

The man gave a professional laugh.

'Of course, Sir! We remember all our old friends.' He turned towards the entrance to the dining room and the waiter loitering there. 'Gustav! You are lucky Sir, we have just the table for you.'

Gustav offered Neville a smart bow.

'Please, follow me Sir.'

They were within two paces of the dining room proper when Neville stopped. He was suddenly scared. He had no desire to walk into the room and be disappointed. In that instant he knew what he wanted to see — and the one thing he would prefer not to know. Samuel's voice "have faith" echoed, and Neville knew that he would never be able to face himself if he did not go on.

Gustav had waited. Neville smiled and walked on.

Turning the corner, Gustav paused to signal to another waiter. Neville scanned the room in an instant, hoping for nothing more nor less than a flash of flamingo pink. There was none. The room was busy with an abundance of colours, but there was no pink. Another waiter joined them.

'Michel will show you to your table, Sir.' Then bowing, Gustav moved from Neville's line of sight.

In the corner of the room, at the same table he had previously occupied and towards which he was once again being led, the smiling face of Mita greeted him.

FORTY THREE

By the time Neville reached the table Mita had risen, tears already brimming in her eyes. They met as friends who were more than that, and their embrace was natural and unconstrained. Several conversations stopped; there was even the muted sound of soft applause from one table.

They stood, hugging, feeling the presence of the other, their physical reality, the certainty of life. Nothing was immediately said, for there was nothing which could be said. Neville, his eyes closed, wondered if this was how it was to end; was his journey now over, or would there be one last step to take?

Mita eased herself away, and kissed him gently.

'Hello,' she said, a coy playfulness in her voice; her eyes sparkling and radiant. 'You made it then?'

He sat beside her.

'Have you been waiting long?'

'Oh, just a couple of days!' She laughed, waving her free hand in the air in a gesture of supreme ease. 'I wasn't sure that you would make it. I mean, make it here. Or how you would know where to meet me.'

'There were messages.'

'Messages?'

'Aren't there always?'

This struck a chord, and she laughed. They were like children who belonged to a private gang: a gang with its own rules and history; a gang with its own secrets too.

'I went to the Derby,' she confirmed.

Neville nodded.

'Busy, wasn't it? I knew that even if you were there, I wouldn't be able to find you.'

Michel brought the menus and Mita asked him to fetch some champagne.

'They've had it ready for me — just in case.'

'I'm pleased not disappoint you then.'

She gave him a soft dig in the ribs.

'Was it at Epsom you got the messages?'

'Partly; but it was there I put them together. The names of the horses, of course.'

'*Restaurant Rendezvous*! Did you back it?' She smiled mischievously, and immediately Neville could tell that she had also done so.

'A little. It was too good to miss, wasn't it?'

They joined hands, still ignoring the menus that lay on the table before them. Michel came over with the champagne, preparing to open it.

'There was another message too...'

'Stop,' she was still smiling, but insistent, 'does it relate to what happened afterwards?'

He nodded.

'Well, there's plenty of time for that; let's not spoil the evening.'

The champagne popped, and Michel filled the waiting glasses. When he had gone, they prepared to toast.

'What do we drink to?' Mita asked, her glass suspended in mid-air.

'How about tomorrow?' Neville suggested.

'How about today and tomorrow?'

There was some satisfaction in the clink of the crystal. It seemed like a contract, a pact almost; Neville — though still harbouring a sense of doubt, a concern that, in the end, there might be some wicked twist in the tail — felt satisfied, more than ever before.

Mita caught a trace of the thought on his face as he sipped the wine.

'You're not sure?'

'Sure?'

'If it's real, all of this. I wondered too; perhaps I still do, just a little. But we're here, and after all we've been through — well, that has to be some kind of miracle.'

Gustav had moved to the table and was waiting for them.

'Would you like to order, Madam, Sir?'

Neville glanced at Mita.

'Whatever we like?'

'Whatever we like!'

'We should have different things, just to prove...'

'And no monkfish!'

Their laughter caused a little concern with Gustav who immediately protested that the monkfish was excellent. Neville assured him that it was a private joke and had nothing to do with the restaurant. He seemed satisfied. Nevertheless, they both avoided the monkfish and, as they had agreed, chose different things from the menu, though what they would eventually eat seemed of little importance.

As Mita handed back her menu, she noticed Neville looking over her shoulder.

'What is it?'

'The fish.'

She turned. The open-mouthed blue fish stared inertly past them and into the room; the eyes remained as Neville remembered them, and he half-expected one of them to suddenly wink.

'Friend of yours?' Mita asked, a wicked inflection in her voice. Neville could not tell if she was asking based on knowledge or guesswork.

'Kind of. That's Bob.'

Mita looked back at the fish.

'Bob, eh? Nice to meet you Bob. Any friend of Neville's is a friend of mine.'

Possibly never having a better invitation to spring into life, Bob remained still and lifeless. Neville was a little disappointed; part of him would have liked to share this return with him, but presumably Bob's day would come again.

They ate between rambling conversations; mouthfuls of salmon and pate, trout and lamb, mixed with a bubbling but understated excitement at what had passed and — although unuttered — what might lay ahead. It took them a long time to get through the first two courses, but time seemed not to be a problem. Gustav asked them if their food was acceptable — it was of course — and Michel kept them topped up with champagne. There was no pressure to move on, and Neville — when the dessert menu appeared — breathed a sigh of relief that here was another sign of normality to which he could cling.

Having placed their orders for dessert, Neville rose and excused himself. At the dining room door he asked Gustav for the direction to the gents toilet.

'Through the archway, Sir, and left at the bottom of the corridor.'

Neville paused, remembering his most recent experience of doors on corridors and, for the briefest moment, considered leaving the building and trying to find a suitable bush around the back of the car park. However, normality — which at last appeared to be on the way back — prevailed, and a few moments later he walked in to the lavatory.

There were no urinals (which immediately struck him as slightly odd) but rather two cubicles facing a wash stand and mirror. Both cubicles were empty. Neville chose one, closed the door behind him, and was soon seated on the mahogany-topped pedestal.

He had been there only a few moments when he heard the other door open and someone enter the second toilet. He waited for the sound of the seat being raised or lowered, or the sound of a trouser fly being unzipped, but there was nothing. It seemed a little odd that there should be such silence. And then he heard Samuel's voice.

'How's it going, Sir?'

'Samuel, is that you?'

'Yes, Sir.'

Neville made preparations to rise, but was immediately halted.

'I'd hang on just a minute if I were you.'

'Hang on?'

'We won't be disturbed, and there are a few things I really think we ought to clear up.'

Neville froze. He felt a sudden chill grip the nape of his neck and then flood down his spine. He shivered, hard. Was this it? Was Samuel's last trick to be the one that sent him into oblivion? If he had been shown just a glimpse of happiness only for it to be snatched away...

'Sir?'

He chose not to reply.

'I know what you're thinking, Sir; but really, you've nothing to worry about.'

'What do you mean?'

'What time is it?'

'Time, Samuel?'

'Please, Sir. What time is it?'

Neville looked at his watch. It was nearly ten o'clock — a little later than he had expected, but time seemed to be passing quickly this evening. And then he realised that the second hand was moving clockwise and that his watch was back to normal.

'It has been like that for a little while now. You are back in the "real world", as it is known.'

'Since when? I mean, when was it all over; when was everything all right?'

'Last night; probably just before you returned to the bus.'

There was a brief silence. Neville thought about the climax to the chess game; his hand went to his chest. He recalled how tired he felt.

'I take it something significant happened, Sir.'

'You might say that, yes,' Neville paused, 'but then presumably you know all about it?'

'A little. Some things I get from you.'

Again there was a short lull, then Neville realised the simple question he had yet to ask.

'Why are you here, Samuel?'

'As I said, Sir, we've got a few things to clear up. Like this, for instance.'

A brown A5 envelope was slid part-way under the door. Neville picked it up and opened it. Inside was all the money he had won at Epsom, including the cheque from the Tote.

'All my winnings?'

'And the little bit you had left over, yes Sir. That — as I suggested at the time — is now yours; please use it wisely.'

Neville laughed a little; his first moment of relaxation since the bizarre interview had begun.

'I think I have learned a little about money recently.'

'And a few other things too, I trust.'

'Indeed Samuel, yes.' Neville waited for something else to be forthcoming. 'You said there were a few things to clear up. What else?'

'Well, nothing terribly tangible, I'm afraid. I've packed your things, and they are in your bags at the entrance to the restaurant.'

'You're going away?'

'Indeed Sir, yes. As soon as I have finished here.'

'But this is absurd, Samuel; we shouldn't part like this! I want to shake your hand; to thank you. Really.'

'Ah, I have thanks enough Sir when I see you and Miss Mita together. Audrey tells me that she had a rather difficult time of it — as you did too, of course. I am pleased she is well; please take care of her.'

Neville was thrown by Samuel's use of the word "well", which seemed strangely out of context. He could not debate it, however.

'You said "my" things. Presumably not the suit or the flying jacket?'

'Indeed not, Sir. I'm afraid certain things were — how shall I put it — repossessed. I hope you understand.'

'I'm not sure I do, Samuel. Indeed, there's much I don't understand.'

'Ah.' There was a brief pause from the other cubicle. 'The only other thing I have to do, is to give you a chance to ask me — well, whatever you like, really.'

'"Have to do", Samuel? It sounds like some kind of rule.'

'Well, in a way it is Sir, yes.'

'And presumably you mean about the last few days, about what happened to me?'

'Indeed; though I must warn you that I may not be in a position to tackle everything.'

Neville considered the whole gamut of his experience and wondered where to begin.

'Do I have a limit?' It was just a hunch, but a constraint was the sort of thing he expected to apply. He was right.

'Yes, Sir; time or the number of questions — I can't say which.'

'OK. Take Pierre, the Pierrot in Paris. Was he on your side?'

'On my side, Sir?'

'Yes; part of the set-up, part of the plan. Was I supposed to find him because that was all in the game? Did everything I experience belong to some prearranged sequence?'

'Sir, there's more than one question there!'

'OK. Take the rescue of Mita on the boat. Was that part of your plan, or was it really me living out a fantasy, just like the Pilgrim advertised?'

'Or was it you living out one of Mita's fantasies, Sir? That could be a possibility.'

'But do you know?'

'Does it matter?'

Neville banged his fist against the cubicle wall.

'Damn it Samuel, yes it does! It matters to me!'

Samuel said nothing. Neville knew he was still there; he could hear his breathing through the thin well — especially as it now sounded a little laboured.

'Does it really matter? *Really*? You know what matters *now*; you have learned what matters — and are still learning. Remember a little while ago you said you had lots of questions to ask, and that I told you that it was a good start to have questions? That is still true. If I told you that it was your fantasy, or Mita's fantasy, would that make any difference? Would it matter if you knew how much of your experience was pre-arranged, or how you managed to find out the winner of the Derby? Does any of that *matter*? Is it truly important to you, Sir, with Mita waiting for you in the dining room? And yes, she will still be there waiting when you get back. Today and tomorrow, Sir; just like you said.'

His voice was beginning to sound a little thick and his breathing even more laboured.

'Are you all right, Samuel?'

'I should be going, Sir.'

'One last question?'

'Quickly then.'

'How much choice did I have in all of this? I mean, when did I actually make a decision that changed things around? Or was it pre-planned — in the smallest of details — and everything I was doing, decisions and all, merely acting out my part like an actor in a play?'

There came a throaty laugh from the other cubicle.

'That old question? Always the same one in the end.'

'So?'

'There are two possibilities: it was all a plan, or you made it happen yourself. Presumably there may be shades in between. But you want to know which is true?'

'Yes.'

'Then again I say, does it really matter? Really? Perhaps it is one, perhaps the other. Perhaps there is a combination of things so complex that one cannot possibly comprehend it. But why should you care if it really doesn't matter? What happened, happened; do you complain at the outcome? People are so lucky, and yet they fret over such impossible things.'

'But people need to believe in things.'

'Indeed. Have faith, yes; but have faith in yourself. Forget those theories, the philosophers' stones. People give names to big things that cannot be explained. If you want to believe in something, then call it "The Big Frog Theory"; it's as good a name as any other — and there might just as well be a frog deciding the outcome of the universe as anything else. But, above all, have faith in yourself.'

The monologue ended in a splutter of coughing and then, for a moment, silence. Neville noticed a strange, but vaguely familiar smell. He rose, half expecting to be told to resume his seat. There was nothing. As he placed his hand on the door latch, he heard a single and distinct sound — a kind of croak — and then nothing.

The second cubicle was empty when he finally managed to get its door open. There was no trace of Samuel, nor of anything else come to that. Neville turned and looked in the mirror. All he could see was himself; but it was the new Neville, not the one he had slain on the chess board. He thought of a quote he had heard a long time ago: "the King is dead; long live the King!" Uncertain as to its origins, just now it seemed remarkably appropriate.

As Samuel had said, his bags were waiting for him to pick them up in the hallway. He checked each in turn. They contained the clothes with which he had begun his adventure — except for the smaller bag where, hidden between two shirts, was concealed his copy of the rules to the game of "Croak".

Walking back to the dining room he thought of Samuel and smiled. There were many pieces to be reassembled before he could understand much more of his own version of the jigsaw, but at least he would not be facing the challenge alone.

EPILOGUE

They approached the town from the hills. The weather had broken during the night and the bright day had given way to heavy summer thunderstorms. By the morning, these had begun to fade and now, in early afternoon, the clouds — white and unthreatening — were in retreat from the bright blue sky.

It had been a long time since Neville had walked the hills; so much so, that his walking boots had at first felt vaguely uncomfortable. There had been no real need for boots — they had hardly strayed from well-trodden paths after all — but even so, first thing in the morning they had stopped in Worcester to buy Mita her own pair.

The remainder of the previous evening and much of the night had been spent in discussion. Neville had said nothing of his final experience with Samuel, but Mita — who was shrewd enough to notice a subtle change in his demeanour — gathered that something had happened.

'The icing on the cake?' she had said, when he returned to their table. He had simply smiled.

It would have been easy for them to launch into vague and outrageous plans for the future, but a walk on the hills the following day — this at Neville's insistence — was as forward-thinking as they managed. As was inevitable, they shared vague references to the recent past, but managed to go no further than allusion or hints. Neville had talked about tangible things — his old job, his previous life with Mirelle (the coincidence of name making Mita laugh), his old Ford Sierra — and Mita, slightly less forthcoming, left hints of her past like a trail she was inviting him to follow.

He had not told her why he had wanted to walk the hills. There had been some excuse; a little romantic embroidery, perhaps. They had eaten their picnic reasonably early (in spite of the meal the previous evening, they were both hungry) and when Neville suggested taking tea in the town, it seemed a logical suggestion.

As they turned the corner into the street on which his tea shop stood, Neville did so without the slightest doubt that it would still be there, that the last thing he would find would be the remnants of the place in diverse piles of rubble across the street. So it proved to be. He had suggested it to Mita as "a little place he knew" which "had fond memories for him". She had shot him a quizzical look wanting a little more — but also aware that more would one day be forthcoming.

He opened the door and the bell gave a ring. Pausing on the threshold, he gave his boots — which, despite their walking route, carried little debris — a vigorous wipe on the doormat. Mita did likewise. His memory of the tea shop was already hazy, but the sight of the counter, the layout of the tables — even the geese on the wall — reinforced all he had retained.

The table near the window — *his* table, and the one he had secretly been hoping for — was occupied, as was the one next to it. Mita, who had overtaken him by now, made for a location at the back of the shop. One of the waitresses, in prim black and white, gave her a brief nod. Neville joined her.

'This is nice,' Mita said, 'quite plain, but perfectly charming.'

Neville was amused by the sense of the place being plain, but felt as yet unready to explain.

They ordered tea and the waitress asked them if they would like anything to eat.

'A little gateau?' Mita suggested.

Neville ordered two scones.

The Proprietress, still as large as — but not larger than — life, emerged from the back of the shop and prepared their tea. As they waited for the waitress to return, Neville relaxed and reacquainted himself with the place. However, he could recall little more than the ducks on the wall — except for the lady who ran the café and who was, by her bulk if nothing else, quite unforgettable. But in truth, as Mita had said, it was indeed quite plain.

They were half way through their scones — and through a discussion about the route they should take to return to Mita's car — when Neville caught a glimpse of an old bus rolling by outside. It was a blue bus and quite dissimilar to Samuel's vehicle, yet its presence — even briefly — was sufficient to unnerve him slightly. He scanned the room again, his mind only half attending to Mita's conversation.

At the table in the window, a solitary man sat staring out into the street. On the table cloth in front of him was a cup of filter coffee. As Neville watched, a waitress took a slice of gateau to the table and left it there. The man appeared not to notice. Voices from the next table — two ladies, one with well coiffured hair — rose and caught his attention. It was not *his* Conservative Lady, but near enough.

And then the blue bus pulled up on the opposite side of the road and the driver stepped out.

Mita had stopped talking, her attention taken by the sudden change in Neville's attitude. She looked where he looked, but without comprehension. She squeezed his arm.

'Are you OK?'

Neville said nothing; his eyes were fixed on the bus driver as he walked towards the the café. He was hoping — and not hoping — that it was Samuel. The door opened and the man, certainly past his prime, entered. He nodded to the man at the window seat, and then to all of them in turn. His eyes rested for a moment on Neville. It was not Samuel, but there was something there…

'I think we should go,' Neville said suddenly.

'I've a little tea left.'

'Mita,' he had turned to her now. She could see he was serious. 'Do you trust me?'

She laughed a little uneasily. There was in his voice and in his eyes, a strange mix of fear and sublime joy; simultaneously, he seemed both possessed yet full of self-awareness.

'Yes.'

'I can now tell you the first part of my story — but not here.' He took her hand and rose. 'Perhaps outside, on the hills.'

As they walked through the shop, Neville nodded at bus driver. By the time they reached the street, he was smiling blissfully to himself. They had walked a little way when Mita stopped and kissed him.

'Is that sufficient for me to get your little story?'

Neville placed his arms around her.

'There's only one place to begin…'